Seek Immediate Shelter

Seek Immediate Shelter

a novel

VINCENT YU

FLATIRON BOOKS
NEW YORK

This is a work of fiction. All the characters, organizations, and events portrayed in this novel are either products of the author's imagination or used fictitiously.

Printed in the United States of America. For information, address Flatiron Books, 120 Broadway, New York, NY 10271. EU Representative: Macmillan Publishers Ireland Ltd., 1st Floor, The Liffey Trust Centre, 117–126 Sheriff Street Upper, Dublin 1, D01 YC43

www.flatironbooks.com

Designed by Leah Carlson-Stanisic

Library of Congress Cataloging-in-Publication Data

Names: Yu, Vincent, author.
Title: Seek immediate shelter : a novel / Vincent Yu.
Description: First edition. | New York : Flatiron Books, 2026.
Identifiers: LCCN 2025035670 | ISBN 9781250410122 (hardcover) |
ISBN 9781250410139 (ebook)
Subjects: LCGFT: Novels | Fiction
Classification: LCC PS3625.U19 S44 2026
LC record available at https://lccn.loc.gov/2025035670

First Edition: 2026

10 9 8 7 6 5 4

For Mom, Dad, and Vivian

Seek Immediate Shelter

PUBLIC RELATIONS

David Li

Beckitt's emergency began on a calm spring morning: an expansive chill in the air; the sun soaring over rangy, adolescent clouds; miles of rolling green mowed into submission, flanked by grand columns of oak and maple, through which the wind shivered.

And a symphony of cell phones throbbing in sudden unison. Terror and confusion jolting through town like an electrical impulse.

David Li, however, had forgotten to charge his phone overnight. All he heard at first was a low diesel rumbling from beyond the window. The hypnotic *beep beep* of a truck's reversal. Twigs scuffing lightly against the gravel.

"Get up! Get up!" his wife, Daphne, was howling. But it was still early. He mumbled something, must have fallen back asleep, because his next sensations were of her swiping a pillow at him. "David. Seriously! Get up!"

And then the rush of sounds, like liquid splashing into a bowl: Daphne's distressed alto, the fussing of their infant, Nathan. The officious shouts of the grounds crew outside their window, everyone bellowing orders. And the abrupt, overwhelming screech of the phone held to his face.

"Look!"

BALLISTIC MISSILE THREAT INBOUND. SEEK IMMEDIATE SHELTER. THIS IS NOT A DRILL.

"Oh shit." David leapt out of bed, feet pattering on the cold wood floor. "Okay, come on."

"Where are we going?"

"The fuck away."

"Are you sure? It said to seek shelter. We should probably stay here. Right?"

But their house, with its ranch styling, felt too spread out, too single-storied. While his parents lived minutes away in a home that had always felt to him like a fortress, with a sizable basement in which he'd spent many carefree hours as a child. And it would be nice, if this truly was the end, to spend his last moments with them.

"Hurry," he said. "Come on, please."

Nathan's screaming. Action, action. Go, go, go.

Daphne was gathering supplies—formula, diapers, water. Ludicrous, to him, when each passing moment seemed drafted from an empty account. When a missile was hurtling toward them, shearing through cloud cover. He was in the car already. He pressed the remote to open the garage door.

Just as there arrived a distant rumbling.

Oh God, something was rumbling. Something enormous and cataclysmic was approaching. *Please.* He didn't want to die.

"Come on!" he screamed. "Let's go!"

Please, please. It was all too sudden; he wasn't ready. How could he come to terms with such hasty, indifferent annihilation? No, please. Not like this, just sitting here. Yielding to it. And where was Daphne? What could *possibly* be taking her so long?

Up the incline of their driveway, past the clattering lift of the garage door, he saw a gathering of legs. As if residents had assembled on the street to welcome an extinction event. Well, he wouldn't be one of them. He'd bowl them over if he had to. He honked the horn. Surely the garage had never been this slow to open?

"Daphne!"

And then came the faint sounds of yelling, as if warning of imminent impact. The unquestionable shadow of something *descending*. The thundering premonition of an explosion. SHIT. FUCK.

He couldn't wait anymore. He could not.

He jammed his foot down on the gas.

* * *

"Well, the motor is pretty weak. Torsion spring is a little warped. And there's a bit more slack in this chain than I'd like, alongside the obvious issue here"—the technician pointed at the base of the garage door—"which is that the bottom bracket's knocked off."

David surveyed the damage, nodding like a foreman. He had the unconstructive habit of noticing faults only when they were identified to him, and being unable, thereafter, to focus on anything else.

"A lot of people don't realize it, but this here is the most dangerous thing in your entire house. The sensor gets messed up, the motor fails, and *wham*." The technician slammed his grease-soiled hands together. "Done for. Accidents like that happen all the time. And you've got a nice family here. I mean, I'd take this as an opportunity to just get the whole thing redone. Fresh start. You get peace of mind for a lot more years."

David turned to Daphne. "What do you think?"

But she'd been quiet ever since he'd charged through the still-rising garage door, scraping the car roof against its bottom, only to find the grounds crew across the street felling a tree, whose branches had ensnared some utility cables.

Ever since he'd stepped out of the car and jogged back toward the garage where she stood, holding Nathan in her arms, and the second message arrived on their phones. FALSE ALARM. Eighteen minutes after the initial alert.

"He makes a good point," he said to her now. "And regardless, we need to get this thing fixed."

Nothing.

"What's up?"

She looked at him. "Seriously?"

"Honestly, this might be a blessing in disguise. We were due to replace it anyway. I can ask for an advance on my bonus to pay for it."

"Fine. Whatever." She turned toward the house.

"Daph?"

She looked back at him, expectation brimming in her eyes, her hopeful face cradled in its nest of thick russet hair. "Yes?"

"So you're good with this?"

And her expression fell into one of despondency, aversion. "Funny that you're thinking of me now."

"It's a big decision. I want you to be a part of it."

The sharp peal of her laughter sent a family of sparrows jetting from a tall birch, their bodies growing smaller and smaller until they were lost to the blue-pink horizon.

While the technician stood there awkwardly. "Maybe I can come back later?"

* * *

"It's weird. It feels like we should be celebrating something *special*," David was saying. "Like we all just got a second chance at life."

They were having dinner at the Anchor with George and Mia Stephan, who'd been together since high school. David raised a glass. "So here's to second chances."

They toasted limply.

"I still can't believe that happened," George said. He had an intelligent face full of sharp angles, a forehead whose ripples resembled a Wi-Fi symbol. "And of all places, *here*. The only newsworthy thing that ever happens here is, like, snow—if we get more or less of it than usual."

David laughed. "It's kind of funny how seriously we all took it. I mean, imagine Russia or China just saying, 'Fuck this one place in particular.'"

"Well, you probably would have survived," Daphne said quietly. "The way you sped out of the house."

"You didn't stay put?" George asked. "You're supposed to shelter in place and stay as close to the middle of the house as possible if something like that actually happens."

"It's literally the only time his Eagle Scout training ever came in handy," Mia said, smirking. She leaned her elbow on George's chair-back and fiddled with the hair at the nape of his neck.

"Oh, no. The second he got the message he was *out of there*," Daphne said with sudden animation. "Which is funny, because I had to wake him up first."

"Well, my folks, you know, they're so close by," David stammered, scratching his delicate beard. (He grew one because most Asian men couldn't.) "And they have a basement. I just figured it was worth the risk, trying to shelter there."

Scattered murmurs of agreement across the table. Daphne's face seemed almost swollen with anticipation, disgust gathering around her mouth.

"So did you make it?" Mia asked. "By the time the all clear arrived?"

David shook his head, paying sudden attention to the lipid nebula dancing on the surface of his chowder—the spirals of butter and cream, the steaming wreckage of whole clams, flecked with garden debris. Never had a bowl of soup been more interesting. He pressed a soft, mealy potato to the roof of his mouth.

"Why don't you tell them how you were," Daphne said.

He blinked slowly, swallowed. "I don't really understand what you mean by that."

"Tell them what you did after you got the alert and unilaterally decided we were going to your parents' house."

"Well, it was all such a blur." And he truly meant it. He did not yet trust his memory as an accurate registry of what had happened or what he'd been thinking. "I mean—I think it'll take a while before we can fully process everything, right?"

"Tell them what you remember," Daphne almost whispered, as Mia and George shifted in their seats.

"Oh, uh . . . well, this is funny—you'll laugh at this," he said, finally grasping a narrative string. "There was this grounds crew working on one of our neighbors' trees just as we got the alert. The tree had got caught in some utility wires or something, and at first they were just going to saw off a few branches, but I guess it was too much hassle, so they cut the whole thing down. So when we heard the boom from that, I mean, that was an extra shock."

Mia and George smiled uncomfortably.

"And do you know what he did?" Daphne said. "When he heard the tree coming down?"

"Well, I was in the car. I was getting it, you know, warmed up."

"Warmed up?"

"Yes. Warming up the engine. It's still pretty chilly this time of year."

"Right. Okay. So then what happened?"

"Well, that's when things become a blur."

"Okay, then I guess I'll pick up the story," Daphne said. "Since I remember how, as soon as the Fast and the Timorous here had the engine properly warmed up—the Fast and the Fucking Gutless—he just gunned it!" She shrieked with such laughter that some of the other diners frowned in their direction. "If he were a cartoon, he would've left a hole the shape of his body in the garage door wall."

"So was the garage door broken? Was it not opening or something?" Mia asked.

"No, it was literally coming up. It needed two more seconds. But I guess he didn't have time to wait for it to fully open."

"Well, you know—that's the survival instinct," George said into his ice water.

"But guess where me and Nathan were?"

"Oh no," Mia whispered.

Daphne nodded vigorously at her. "I was holding Nathan in one arm.

I had my hand on the door. I was about to open it. And my husband, without thinking, decided to step on the gas without checking if his wife and child were safely inside."

Three heads swiveled toward him.

He took another mouthful of hot soup, feeling aswirl in a bolus of sound—conversation and clinking silverware, the simmer and crackle from the kitchen, the chime of the front door opening and closing.

Daphne stared with barbed expectation. "So? What do you have to say?"

"Well"—he cleared his throat, which felt hoarse and somewhat singed—"I don't think there's much of an issue here."

"You don't?" Daphne said. "Seriously?"

"It was a false alarm. There was no actual danger."

"That's not the *point*," she moaned. "Oh, oh, oh."

Mia put a gentle, solicitous hand on her wrist. A hand of feminine understanding and support.

"Look—" George interceded, chewing on an ice cube. "If there were lots of other sounds, like sawing and banging, then maybe it was pure biological reflex. As opposed to a conscious, self-preservation thing."

"Right," David said. "Right. Exactly."

"We can all drive, right?" Daphne asked. "We're all familiar with the amount of pressure that it takes to actually send a car peeling backward?"

Mia nodded solemnly. "It's not something that you can just accidentally push down. Cars are designed to avoid these sorts of things."

"Okay, but take my gun, for instance," George said, carried by his own reasoning. "It has a double trigger. Now, you don't point your weapon at something unless you're prepared to kill it—that's Gun Safety 101—but the manufacturers still account for high-stress, high-intensity situations when your finger slips, or you're uncertain. These are design components specifically included to account for, you know, human error, miswiring in the fight-or-flight response."

"I feel like you're doing less for David's point than you think," Mia mumbled.

"It's all handled by the autonomic nervous system," George kept on. "I teach it to my AP students. You can't control certain reactions any more than you can slow down your digestion or heal a cut quicker. And if you're trying to break down the specific thought process, I mean, consider all the things that go through a person's mind at any given moment. We're constantly managing thousands—hundreds of thousands—of little feelings and ideas. Especially now in the information age."

"Can you honestly say that as you're watching the Red Sox?" Mia said. "Because sometimes you look like you're in a coma."

George ignored her. "All I mean is, there are so many interconnected, codependent events occurring inside us. It's crazy, really—all these reactions we can't consciously account for. But this guy"—he gestured across the table—"I've known him long enough to know he's honorable. He's the kind of person to put his family first."

Daphne glared at David. "Are you going to say anything?"

He wanted to fold into himself, to double up the layers protecting the part of his identity that seemed under attack. "I agree with everything George says."

Daphne cupped her forehead and sighed.

He felt a swift, reflexive flare of rage toward her. "Maybe we should talk about this later."

"If it's not that big of an issue, then we should be able to talk about it here, right? With friends?"

He frowned at his chest. "You're trying to humiliate me."

"I'm not, David. I swear I'm not. I just need you to confront how you were, and I don't know how else to make you do that."

"I just don't remember it the same way as you, I guess."

"How do you remember it?"

"As a blur."

She shook her head. "Do you think that that's any better? Shouldn't you recall a distinct *need* to protect your family?"

"Well, that goes without saying."

"It seemed to need saying, David. You seemed in desperate need of reminding. Otherwise, the roof of our car wouldn't look like a fucking barcode."

Their friends across the table squirmed like live bait; they addressed each other, as if seeking refuge in their own stability. "This food is good with the weather, isn't it?" George said. "Nice and hearty."

"Oh, yeah. Definitely," Mia concurred. "With weather like this, you need something that'll fill you up. Have you guys tried pozole?"

"Stop gaslighting me," David said.

Daphne released another honk of laughter. "Gaslighting you? That's what you think I'm doing?"

"You're making me feel guilty about a scenario I don't even agree with you on. You're imposing a set of events to fit your narrative."

"Why would I possibly want that to be my narrative?" she said. "Why would I try to enforce a reality in which my husband is a coward?"

Stillness descended upon the table. The assertion gathered like a pellet of rain on a window, quivering at critical mass, ready to plunge. The swollen moment heavy on all of them.

"I'm not a coward," he said finally.

"Then just explain yourself. *Please!*"

He cleared his throat. He scraped his voice together. "What you haven't shared with everyone is how long it was taking you," he started. "I don't know what kind of end-of-the-world scenario you were prepping for, but if there really were a missile threat, you'd have been the one that got us killed."

"You weren't even awake when the alert first came!" Daphne banged her fists against the smooth table linen, sending vibrations up the thin necks of their glasses, sending the smaller forks they'd used for their oysters jouncing lightly like a chorus line.

The other diners looked over more seriously now.

"Is everything all right?" their waitress asked.

There was a sudden bout of cheering. A man three tables down was on one knee, rubbing vigorously at something. The engagement ring had been delivered in a slice of chocolate cake, and it was covered in frosting.

They applauded politely.

* * *

David vowed later that evening to come up with a clear, reasonable explanation. Because he knew himself, and he knew what he was capable of doing.

He imagined slitting his own throat if his wife or child needed blood. Holding a defensive position against oncoming hordes in order to buy his family more time to escape. Surely it was in his marrow to behave this way for the people he loved. Surely it was a matter of revisiting the incident and applying a reasonable explanation to the events surrounding it. So many things could *seem* incriminating until the full picture was revealed.

But retrieving the memory from that morning, parsing it into a sequence of events, was far more difficult than he imagined. He could recall the familiar fragrance of the car—its freshly leased upholstery. The rumble of its starting. And his pulse! Like a snare drum, the individual beats coalescing into a low rattle.

And the dread, rising with the sibilant pitch of what he now knew was a buzz saw making its way through all that fleshy bark, the imminent *thud* as the tree plunged toward the asphalt, his heart's jolting, and there—*stop*—that very moment was where his memory split into fractals, the same repeating pattern of terror and panic.

And perhaps because he could go no further down this miserable, suffocating path, perhaps because his mind was in desperate need of an escape hatch, he sought refuge in a happier moment. As if stumbling into a cool air pocket, he recalled the evening he and Daphne had found out she was pregnant with Nathan.

How shocked they were. Thrilled, but shocked. Thankful, certainly. But a bit disappointed. And terrified. Yes, terrified. And stricken. They were newlyweds; they'd been careful. Their plan had always been to travel and vacation while they could still afford it before settling down.

"It's fine," he'd said. "We'll just wait eighteen years. A short, eighteen-year delay."

And she'd smiled at him, through her wet, swollen eyes. "The second he's off to college, I want to go to Hawaii."

"Of course."

"And then Europe."

"Oh, for sure. Every single country."

And never had he felt more assured of himself, more like a *man*, than when he'd held her that evening—her humid sniffles emptying into his shoulder, her body swelling minutely with his child. Rocking back and forth to his own calming incantations. *It's going to be all right.*

* * *

Sunday dinner at his parents' house had the soothing repetitions of a ritual. His mother always ordered a catered meal from the same local Italian place, in vague deference to Daphne's European palate, which meant they were reliably greeted by sturdy log houses of garlic bread and heaping acres of pasta and a token bit of iceberg lettuce and tomato wedges and whole olives that were supposed to count for a salad.

The topics of discussion were as steadfast as the menu—some combination of Nathan's health, his parents' health, and the fiscal health of Li & Peters, the public relations firm that his father founded thirty years ago, where David had spent his entire career. Tonight, though, he feared a serious deviation from the script. He awaited the conversation like a prisoner on death row or a student walking into an exam for which he'd not studied. Both outcomes somehow equally catastrophic.

"Well, that missile alert was really something, wasn't it?" his mother said at the table, spinning its zebrawood lazy Susan like a nervous disc jockey.

"Yeah."

"You know, the state government did a really terrible job with handling the communications effort for that," his father interceded, with practiced authority. "You can't really prevent human error, but you know, if I'm the governor, I take responsibility, I apologize, I promise to completely overhaul the system, fire the people who were in charge, the whole kit and caboodle."

He slurped his pasta as if it were miàn, skimming the red sauce off his lips, letting it fleck his cheeks.

"And I'd say this all during a one-on-one with *The Boston Globe.* I know the political desk chief over there. We just had drinks a few months ago. But I'd go to the *Globe* and the *Globe* only, because in this case the precision of the messaging is paramount. You want to get one clear, concise statement out there," he said, jabbing his index finger at the table for emphasis. "And in this statement, I apologize. There's nothing wrong with a good, earnest apology, especially when you're apologizing for something that wasn't directly under your control. You come across as more human, more accepting, you start to rebuild trust." He turned. "What do you think, son?"

"Well, David drove off without us," Daphne cut in.

Crunch, *crunch*, *slurp*. "Son?"

David was still chewing.

"Say it," Daphne growled.

And it was funny, he thought, how a mouthful of spaghetti might suddenly resemble dangling entrails.

"I won't." He coughed and wiped his chin. "I'm not going to just adopt your narrative like that."

"But you don't have a competing one."

"I don't need a competing narrative in order to disagree with yours."

"Why don't you tell us what you remember?" his mother said calmly to Daphne.

"Well. I had to wake him up, first of all. He was still asleep. And I was so scared. And Nathan was crying, and I was carrying him and trying to find some baby supplies while David went straight for the car. He honked the horn once, he called my name, I told him I was coming, I was moving as fast as I could. But he didn't wait. He drove off. I mean, the garage door wasn't even open. He just drove right through it."

"That's not true." He raked his fingers through his beard; he pinched the short bristles.

"Then say something!" she implored. "Say what you remember! Please."

Nathan began to wriggle and whine in his high chair, the edges of his mouth stained an atomic red. There was much fussing around him.

And how dearly David wished he were at work right now, holding forth over a lacquered mahogany table in one of the spacious fishbowl conference rooms. Or in his office gazing out at the rippling Berkshires, his view only slightly obscured by the ugly DMV building. At work he had something to prove, as a positive case study in nepotism. And so he labored twice as hard as any of the other VPs, he took on twice the number of accounts, all while striving to be a perfectly understanding, firmly paternal leader of his team. At work he could spin narratives as easily and brilliantly as a glassworker.

"I thought you and Nathan were in the car," he managed, although his face grew hot, because it was clear that the table was withholding its inclination to believe. His father's grim aspect felt like a searchlight.

"You did?"

"Yes. And the garage door was opening. It wasn't closed, like you said. It was opening. I thought I had enough clearance to get through. And either way, it's not related to the main issue, which is that I thought you were safe."

Silence.

"How about we all have some dessert?" his mother said. "David, can you grab it from the fridge? Be careful—it's delicate."

And as he stood up, he was accosted by a rapid, disorienting terror. What if he truly was a coward? What if his idea of himself was all wrong?

But this could not be the case. Surely not. Surely he could not be so delusional.

It didn't square with his identity—not that he took himself too seriously. Just months ago, in fact, his team had been hired by a European pharmaceutical company to promote a generic hemorrhoid medication, and he'd been the one to come up with an idea for an awareness festival in Butte, Montana, that had garnered significant, chuckling national news attention.

No, he knew how to joke around. He knew how to read the temperature of a situation and how to behave accordingly.

He brought dessert to the table. Tiramisu. He cut pieces for each of them. And there was something momentarily reassuring about the smooth motion of the knife through each spongy layer. The control and accuracy in his sectioning.

No. You *chose* the type of person you wanted to be. You behaved in a way that conformed with your values. And his values were *right there*, in the steady, confident manner of his distributing dessert to his family. They were as clear and bright as ever, and so he must have been acting in alignment with them, in some way he could not yet apprehend.

He felt a fresh wave of resentment for Daphne. She was making him rush through his coming to terms with the event. She was denying him an opportunity to catch up to his own feelings.

A ponderous silence overcame them while they ate. His mother was making small, mimicable gulping motions as she fed Nathan. And the fireflies were early this year, he noticed. They were coming awake, now, in the rapidly descending darkness, stomachs pulsing with yellow-green light. A squirrel darting up a nearby tree was illuminated in sequence, like a zoetrope.

He and Daphne, as always, offered to do the dishes. His mother demurred, insisting that the dishwasher was right there (she would not use it; she would hand wash them all later, when they'd left). His father flicked on the fence lights and slid open the patio door—a sound reminiscent of childhood summers, of elementary school chalkboards.

A stone pathway cut through the backyard, terminating in a tasteful wooden picnic table shaded by an enormous canvas umbrella. He motioned for David to follow.

"Clare Hilldon just resigned from the firm," he said into the cool night air. "I suspect it's because of her husband's recent passing."

"Oh. Wow," David said distractedly.

"I tried to help her see the bright side. You know, an unexpected death can be great for a legacy. The shock means your loved ones can't fully process it. For a moment, everything is just strangeness, which is inherently threatening. There's comfort in the familiar past, you know? So they go back and grease the story with affection; they burnish the memories. The decedent's reputation almost always gets a bump."

The walkway was too narrow for them to walk side by side. His father reached the table first. "It's a shame, because I was hoping she'd take over for a few years after I retired." He turned to face him, eyes widening. "I guess I'll have to consider other avenues."

David girded himself. The silence was peppered by the rustling of some foraging animal.

"How could you possibly—*possibly*—have thought the alert was real?" his father said finally.

"I don't know."

"But did you not think to conduct a bit of social media monitoring? Or check to see if any government websites were boosting their SEO?" He put a hand on his shoulder and shook it. "I mean, come on. These are fundamental techniques in our field, son. Skills you should have leveraged."

Yes. Right. Unable to brook further rebuke, he made an appeal to his father's authority. "Dad, what do I do?"

His father squared himself. "Well, Daphne seems to be lacking in key indexes of confidence."

"Dad, please."

"I'm serious. Like so much in life, this can be reduced to a matter of branding and reputation management. Basic block-and-tackle PR."

David sighed. He'd heard this precise combination of words many times. "What would *you* do?"

The old professional was silent for a moment. His calm face with its light bronzing, pinched with easy focus. "A good communications manager treats his client like a planet: The same way any large object can sink into space-time and alter fundamental realities around it, so a PR professional arranges reality to best suit his clients' needs."

Right. This, too, he'd heard many, many times.

"Take her on a trip," he said. "Take her mind off it. A person's memories are fickle. Take her somewhere exotic, treat her. Then, when she's relaxed and happy, start to retake the narrative. Tell her that you thought she was in the car when you hit the gas. Remind her over and over and over. Don't even entertain the possibility of an alternative story. That's your enemy. The alternative is the enemy. Get emotional if she doesn't believe you. Take umbrage at what she's implying about you."

He nodded at his presidential father, the jovial authority. The crisis master. He tried to recall the last time he'd heard his parents quarrel and, unable to do so, felt a strange sense of sympathy—almost grief—for his mother. "Did you and Mom ever get in fights?"

"Of course. Which couple doesn't?"

"Did you ever screw up this bad?"

Strobes of bioluminescence captured the old man's face like a series of camera flashes—still images stitched together, giving of otherworldliness. A celestial truth being delivered. "There are a million different ways to screw up. It's how you make up for it that defines you and the strength of your relationship."

David glanced back at the house, his heart still straining with pity. He wondered what his mother was saying to Daphne right now. "Thanks, Dad."

"No problem." His father was radiating self-satisfaction. A master of his craft. A billing rate of $350 per hour. (*That's an hour-long application of my complete concentration, experience, and expertise.*) "You get the family rate."

* * *

It was already past Nathan's bedtime as he pulled the boy out of the tub. He took a towel to his delicate, wispy head, the skin folding over his precious joints. His mouth, with its incipient teeth, like little stylets, like the crystals revealed in a cracked-open geode. Happy burbling. "Da . . . da . . . da."

"Say dad."

"Da . . . da . . . dud."

"No. Dad." He opened his mouth wide, by way of demonstration. "Daaad." Catching his hard palate with the tip of his tongue. "Dad."

"Dud."

It was clearly too advanced of a maneuver for an infant.

He drank a lonely beer in the kitchen, researching the eye-popping ticket prices to Hawaii. The cost of first-class seats, a hotel suite, a series of adrenaline-pumping couples adventures. The costs of rewriting the narrative. Another advance on his bonus.

But his father was right: Staunchness was the only solution. Because the more persistently and aggressively David tried to excavate his memory of that morning, the more damage he seemed to incur upon it. Like using the wrong blunt tools at an archaeological dig site.

He was forced to take comfort in the fact that you never experienced something the way anyone else did. The better, more flattering story line surely existed. A good PR manager changed reality around his client. Why couldn't he do the same for himself now?

Where was the *rock star* who'd gotten ahead of the news of a major security breach at a credit card company? Who'd pinned it on a handful of unscrupulous employees and built the message around their firing and how the new hiring process would incorporate greater diversity and inclusion initiatives?

And who knew if any of it was true? It was reality. Reality had always been enough.

Not anymore. Because the reality was that he was feeling more and more like someone who'd been taken over in those frantic few minutes after the alert. Inhabited by an unauthorized version of himself.

And he worried that this *version* of himself was somehow more authentic, more truthful. As if a life could be reduced to its essence in chaotic moments of high consequence.

He lay in bed, staring at the inert figure of his wife, the russet hair spilling from the back of her head. Moonlight filtered through a tree and passed through the bedroom window, leaving a pattern of bright coins on their bedspread.

"Coward" came her raspy voice.

"Oh, come on."

"That's what you are."

"That's not fair. Please, that is just patently unfair."

"I'm afraid, David. I'm truly, truly afraid."

"Why? In case there's another missile warning?"

"It doesn't need to be that. It can be any sort of emergency. It can be a natural disaster or an—an—an illness or a car accident. It can be, you know, someone just doesn't heed a stop sign, it can be a school shooter, or something on the highway, or, or what if there's a fire—"

"Honey." He put a hand on her shoulder, which she shook off.

"I'm serious. I thought I knew you, but, I mean, how well can any two people really know each other if their lives are just easy and straightforward like ours? If nothing truly serious ever threatens it?"

"I would've thought most people would prefer a life with few, if any, existential threats."

"But then what happens when something comes along? You can't predict those sorts of things. You can't prepare for them. They just *happen*, things just *change*, and then it's too late to find out the real measure of someone."

"I don't know what to tell you," he said, as his eyes adjusted in the dimness. The multistory dresser, the sleek rectangle of the TV sharpening before him. The jewelry box perched on the credenza, with its four feet, its hinged top, the rotating steel teeth in its belly that plucked Mariah Carey's "Hero" when cranked.

"Maybe we should move to some place with a lot of typhoons and hurricanes and stuff, and I can risk my life a bunch of times to make sure you and Nathan are safe—I mean, is that what you need in order to see the real me?"

"It's that I already have," she said. "That's what I'm afraid of."

David sighed at the bottle of Ambien on her nightstand. He was realizing that the garage door was an additional conductor of her memory. How it would need to be replaced while they were traveling. "Well, in a way, it's better that the missile thing happened. It's better because even if—huge *if*—but even if I showed some kind of, you know, cowardice or something—even if I did—I can correct for it now, you know? I know that about myself, and now I can change."

"You are truly so pathetic."

"Look," he said, "I won't let you fuck up this family."

She turned toward him, finally, and began to laugh. A bizarre, joyless cackle that echoed through their little house and that he thought would surely awaken Nathan.

"Daph," he said. "Daphne!" He grabbed her wrist.

She cut it off immediately. She stared with venom. "You're not just a coward; you're delusional."

"No," he said. "No, please don't accuse me of that. Don't try to play that card."

"If you think that you can somehow *communicate* your way out of this, I'm sorry, but you can't."

* * *

David saw her the next day from the bathroom window while she stepped out in her thin dressing gown to retrieve the mail—as wind whipped the silky little thing around her flat belly and rounded chest, the pert outline of her nipples.

She was a slight woman, although she carried herself with quiet authority. And now, as a mother, with an assuredness that resembled grandeur.

Yes, there was something casually stunning about her as she strode across the lawn. He almost nodded in agreement, in sly satisfaction, when he heard the whistle from across the street. Two flourishes—ascending, descending. A wolf whistle. The grounds crew from the other day were working their way down the power line, their bucket truck parked beside another tall tree.

And then he was rushing out the door. "Hey!"

She stared at him, eyes enormous.

"Hey!" he yelled against the wind. "Hey! You fucking animals."

"No," she said. "No, no, no."

For a moment he felt large enough to absorb all their attention. His righteous anger felt strong enough to shame them all.

"You got a problem?" said one of the guys—a burly, mustachioed man in a neon vest and heavy gloves.

"Oh, for fuck's sake—no, David. No, you don't need to do this."

"I saw what you just did. I heard it. You should be fucking ashamed of yourselves."

"Your wife is a very beautiful lady," the man said. "You're very lucky."

"You can't just do that. You *can't*."

"Well, we're awfully sorry if you or the pretty lady are offended." The truck operator was already growing bored. He extended the boom. The worker in its cradle, nearing the offending branches, started a small electric saw.

"For God's sake, David, they have *weapons*."

Although the briefest suggestion of their malice had already melted. They were sneering at him now. Joking. He couldn't take it.

"If you ever even look at my wife again—"

"Can't stop us from looking."

"—I'll call the cops."

"Oh, we get it. So you're a tough guy, fighting your wife's battles. Then putting your dick back in your pants when you realize you're out-pissed."

"Fuck you! Okay? Fuck you!" He took out his phone; he began to record them.

The chief whistler smiled through his mustache. He waved. The others went back to work. David thought about narrating what had just happened, his voice shaking with adrenaline, but Daphne grabbed him sharply by the shoulder. He needed remarkably little urging to retreat.

"What is your fucking problem?" she asked, as he stormed back inside.

"Did you hear them?"

"Yes. And fuck them, but what the hell did you think you were going to do about it?"

"Can't you put some more clothes on if you're going to leave the house? Even if it's to get the mail?"

"I'll wear whatever the fuck I want, whenever the fuck I want." A trail of goose bumps made visible the delicate hairs that ran down her taut, ropy arms. Her nostrils were flaring like jet nozzles. Her sleek jaw, wired shut with distaste.

"So you wear something like that, and those Neanderthals harass you, and you expect me to do nothing? Aren't you mad enough at me?"

"Oh God. Oh, for fuck's sake. Is this you trying to compensate?" Her face wilted. "Wow, you do not get it. You simply do not get it."

Nathan was fussing in his room.

"What don't I get?"

She turned and walked away, holding up her middle finger.

* * *

George Stephan called and asked if he wanted to grab a drink. Did he ever.

They got seats at a young-person spot called the Bellwether, in the adjacent city of Wingham, where the music was so batteringly loud that their beers rippled in their glasses.

"I've never felt so old!" George needed to yell over the noise.

"My chair is all fucking wobbly," David said, shaking the backrest, feeling it lurch. But he was convinced that he needed this. A night out in a cheap, slightly sleazy bar with a buddy. "I need this, dude."

"Yeah." George seemed distracted; the skin around his eyes looked raw. "Same."

They hardly talked at first, electing to enjoy the speechless fraternity of beer-drinking. A game between two last-place teams was being broadcast on a corner TV. An oval analog clock hung above the bar. David sighed—this time from contentment.

"So Mia and I are probably gonna split up," George said, leaning toward him.

"Shit, man." He was caught in a gust of surprise. "What happened?"

"Well, I experienced a pretty serious lapse in judgment." George spoke into his beer, sounding like a crisis counselor. "I guess you could say I was sort of led astray—although, I don't know. I'm not sure what

I'll call it. Plain stupidity, maybe. Or I might just say it's all fake. They need me, after all. Much better to have me as an ally than an enemy."

David waited, expecting more, and was stunned to see his friend shake his head, as if the admissions were over. "So, what did you— Are you gonna be okay?" he tried asking.

George's gaze grew distant. "Do you remember that time we snuck a bottle of your dad's booze into Songline Park and Beckitt's finest showed up?"

"Vaguely," he said.

There came the sudden jangling of the door—a crush of people arriving behind them. Bodies pressed up against their backs. Blustery young men in gingham button-downs with the sleeves rolled up, dangling their credit cards.

"Well, I've been thinking about that! Ever since we had dinner at the Anchor!" George continued to holler in short spurts. "How you kept citing some bullshit law to those cops about illegal Breathalyzer tests! False entrapment of minors! And maybe they believed you because you're Asian! But you bluffed your way out of it! I was so impressed! You've always been able to talk your way through things! That's how I know you and Daph will be fine!"

A young buck abruptly pushed in between them, shouting backward at his female guests and then conveying their orders to the calm bartender. David swiped some other stag's elbow off the back of his wobbling chair. He remembered all of a sudden why he didn't come to these sorts of places more often: the musky, cascading aromas of body odor and cologne; the swift, bilateral assessments between sexes; the easy dismissals; the effortless rending of self-confidence. These exhausting mating rituals.

He felt an insecurity wildly incommensurate to his age. An anxiousness that self-avowals of his own maturity, of being *too old for this*, could no longer dispel. And how desperately he wished to be home with Daphne right now, secure again in her love, instead of here, beside cagey George. He'd never realized the downstream ease with which intimacy could slip into strangeness.

He was mentally planning several exquisite trips—to Hawaii, Paris, London, the Amalfi Coast, strategizing the optimal timing of news delivery—when the crowd at the bar receded, and he found a napkin on his lap. The napkin had a number scrawled on it, along with the name *Cynthia*, with a little heart dotting the *i*.

"Dude, who left that?" George was grinning.

"No idea." He regarded the note with wonder.

Oh, this was exactly what he needed. This was the more compelling story line. He'd tell Daphne about it when he got home, maybe even show her the note—*You'll laugh at this*. And then he wouldn't say any more. Because she already knew the kind of person he was, and the candidness of his love. She just needed to be reminded of his worth, which was contingent on so much more than a single, thoughtless moment—the literal jerk of a muscle, an electrical impulse passing down his nerve stem.

When he looked back up, George's expression had changed. His angular face, shadowed by the dim light, was unfamiliar, almost conspiratorial. "If you do follow up on that," he said, motioning toward the note, "be smart about it."

"What?" David frowned and pocketed the number. "What are you talking about?" But he felt, just then, a hand on his shoulder. A pretty young woman was staring at him—all smooth skin and freckled. Some kind of glitter around her eyes. Lips forming a bashful smile.

She said something. But he could hardly hear her through the thick music. So she leaned forward. She brought her mouth so close that he could feel her warm breath on his ear. He could smell the alcohol in her voice. "I'm so sorry!"

"What?"

"I gave my number to the wrong person. I'm Cynthia." She pressed her fingers and thumbs into a heart shape.

"Oh, it's all right—"

"No, I was— I'm sorry. You look kind of the same as him from the back. But I'm sorry."

The music blaring so loudly, so abrasively.

He held up his hand. "It's fine."

"So can I have it back?"

"What?"

"My number. You just put it in your pocket. Can I have it back?"

He withdrew the napkin, ripping it slightly. He considered crumpling it into a ball before handing it indifferently to her. He threw a careless smirk at George, who reciprocated with raised eyebrows.

He tried to exhibit nonchalance, pushing back against the bar, balancing on the hind legs of his chair, and nearly falling backward when he felt another hand on his opposite shoulder. A stranger's voice. "Dude. What are you doing?"

A grown child was accosting him—an early-twenties punk with archipelagic patches in his beard, a faint pattern of acne scars.

"Excuse me?"

"Don't be a scumbag. Everyone can see your ring. Don't be a tool. Go home to your wife."

"How about you get your fucking hand off me?"

"I'm just saying—be a good guy. It's not that hard to be a good person."

"Look, I'm going to tell you again to get the fuck away." David slid off his chair; he stood up and was confronted by gazes, smirks, unwelcome beacons of attention.

George grabbed his forearm. "Come on," he said with urgency. "This place fucking sucks."

They retreated into the starkly muted parking lot; they caught their breath and shared a nervous laugh. David was still expecting an explanation, some confirmation that his understanding of his friend hadn't been drawn from fabrication, by the time they reached their cars.

"So," George said. "I'll see you."

"Okay."

Driving back home, he could not remember why they'd remained buddies for so long. Whether it had been a mere matter of convenience and proximity all this time.

* * *

Daphne had prepared her bed on the couch.

"Honey," he said, stepping inside.

"What." Her eyes fixed firmly shut.

"Can you just— Can you please?"

"What?"

"Can't you come back to bed?"

She rolled away from him, facing the sofa's back cushions.

"Look, I wasn't going to tell you this, but a woman gave me her number at the bar tonight," he said.

"Oh *wow*." She laughed. "Apropos of nothing, right?"

"Obviously I wouldn't do anything, but."

"No, no, please don't let me stop you. Go sow more oats if you want."

He almost collapsed atop the ottoman. "Are you serious?"

"Well, at least most adulterers still put their real families first. At least when his mistress starts getting antsy, a cheater lets her know his priorities. That's how the story goes, right?"

To think, while walking through the front door, he'd almost hoped she might compliment the trimness of his waist in slim-fit jeans, how well his broad shoulders filled out his blazer.

"Which part of that story do you think applies to our life?"

"The part where you abandoned me and Nathan."

He gritted his teeth. He squeezed his hands. He felt so trapped. He was beaten. He knew it. He couldn't seem to find a better narrative. He couldn't seem to escape this version of himself—a shadow come to life. He thought of George. How suddenly and easily two people might become strangers.

"Okay, I wasn't being entirely truthful just now," David said. "Someone did give me her number, but it was by accident. She asked for it back right away."

Daphne rolled toward him, looking inquisitive. "That is— Wow, that's really embarrassing."

"Yeah, and I guess it made me realize how pitiful I am sometimes," he said. "Like I'm not what anyone wants or needs."

"We needed a different version of you that morning," she said in a softer voice.

Yes. He assented. Yes, he'd been a coward. There was no avoiding it. She'd been right all along. Still, he could not admit it outright! Even so thoroughly vanquished, he could not directly concede. Because to do so, to give her victory, would permanently diminish his status within the family. Would overcome what little inertia still held them all in place. He feared that the tension caused by his recalcitrance was the only reason she hadn't left him altogether.

If only he could somehow surrender without giving in. If he could acknowledge defeat without accepting it.

"I'll do better, I'll be better," he said. "I swear."

"Maybe you can start by not sounding like a fucking press release."

"Okay. I'm sorry."

He could've sobbed for how desperately sorry he was. He wanted to run to Nathan and hug him so fiercely that he might crush his frail bones and burst his little lungs. And he wanted his wife in his arms, too. He wanted to pull them deep, deep into his own orbit, until their combined presence was sufficient to form a workable, agreed-upon reality.

"I'm sorry," he kept saying. "I'm so sorry."

Nathan began to cry from his crib. She got up; the two of them went to him. They calmed him. And when the baby was secure and back asleep, she returned wordlessly to their bed.

* * *

He could still hear the hum and yakking of the grounds crew three days later, from the bedroom. The cautionary beeps, the drone of an electric saw. The *crick-crack* of branches tumbling, paths clearing.

He was booking two tickets to Hawaii. A weeklong trip, full of waiver-signing adventure: windsurfing, zip-lining, perhaps even hang gliding (although she hated heights). Adrenaline-pumping stuff. Plus some romantic winding-down time.

He clicked Buy, watching the wheel spin as the order processed, feeling in cool control of his life. The certainty of these next steps.

Please do not navigate from this page.

He did not.

But after thirty seconds, the wheel was still spinning. And his confidence felt inextricably tied to momentum, like one of those speedy reptiles that could actually *skip* over liquids, the surface tension holding for just long enough for its padded feet to push off. It stalled and sank now, in the absence of digital confirmation. It became something else he'd taken for granted.

The web page said not to navigate. So he refreshed it instead. And it reported back a blank page. A bright white nothing.

"David?" he heard from the living room.

"What's up?"

"I think the internet went out."

He rolled his eyes. "Did you disconnect the router?"

"I don't even know where the router is!"

Where would she be without him? Truly.

The router, when he finally found it at the bottom of a shelf in the kitchen, was afflicted with a static orange light. He unplugged it, counting to himself, reaching thirty or thirty-five, before plugging it back in and waiting, monitoring the light's blinking progress. Seeing, again, the same flatlining orange.

"David?" she called.

"Yeah. The router is busted."

He could hear her footsteps lightly approaching. "So now what do we do?"

How helpless she was without him! How desperately they needed each other.

"I don't know. Get a new one, I guess."

She stepped into the kitchen. "That's annoying."

"It is."

The motorized burble outside was replaced by a prompt, emphatic silence.

"So I was just chatting with Mia," she said. "Apparently she and

George are splitting up. Did he mention anything about that to you when you went out?"

"Oh. No."

"Seems like he messed up big-time." Daphne's hip was pressed against the countertop; her face looked wonderfully ordinary, her voice slightly raised in the delivery of gossip. "I guess it's good to have perspective," she said.

"Do you know what he did?" he asked, just as the doorbell rang.

"She was going to tell me when the internet cut out," she said. "Can you get that?"

And he was walking with such renewed confidence, away from her. With such buoyant belief in his instincts. He was a driver who'd lost momentary control of the wheel and was forced, for an instant, to confront the unthinkable, before wresting it back. Righting himself. *Whew, that could've been bad.*

He was in high spirits, his optimism abounding, when he opened the door and found himself face-to-face with the mustachioed leader of the grounds crew. The wolf whistler in chief. His wide, leering smile.

"So. Whoops," the man said. "We cut a couple of the lines by accident. You folks will be dealing with some outages. Sit tight; it might take a while. A really long while."

APOLOGY

Nina Chang

When they received the news, the first thing Dean Chang did was take out a knife from the cutlery board.

"A knife? What the hell are you going to do with a knife?" his wife, Nina, asked.

"I just wanted to do something."

"Always wanting to do something! Sixty-nine years old and he thinks, what—he'll be able to scare the bomb away? Or stab it to death?"

He laughed, arms hanging loosely at his sides. "Come on, then. Let's go downstairs."

Beneath the sheen of her annoyance, below the constantly shifting crust of her anxiety, Nina experienced a profound, almost reverent thankfulness for everything having turned out the way it had.

An hour ago, lying awake as the sun sheared across her face, she'd been accosted by the perennial sadness of their daughter's departure and felt her disappointment gather like a sponge—swelling into something so threatening and ungainly that she'd needed to get up immediately and hurry to the kitchen to switch on the coffee maker and start her day.

It was happening with greater and greater frequency, this sensation of being beside herself, of overflowing with such feeling that she seemed evicted from her own body.

She missed Cate.

Of course it was natural that children move on, that they seek some distance from their parents. But six months ago, Cate had chosen to fly to the opposite coast, to be as diametrically far away as possible, and something about this had seemed spiteful. Less separation than escape.

Only through the profound exercise of self-control—through tiny, noninvasive questions scattered throughout hours of conversation—did they learn, from the faintest pattern of crumbs, that she'd moved for love.

She'd chased a girl—which was, in and of itself, fine. It was just fine!

Nina was far from old-fashioned. You loved your children no matter what. No matter their phases, their inclinations. But you did not support life-altering decisions based on them. Especially with a child as unfocused and impulsive as Cate, for whom abandonment was so often the solution.

It was the word *phase* that had irked their daughter enough to confirm her motive.

"So you uprooted your life for a phase."

"I'm sorry, but that is just so fucked up, Mom. That is so bigoted and small-minded and old-fashioned."

And she'd had to shake her head and press the phone into Dean's chest, drawing her fingers across her eyes, because sometimes you just could not win.

Parents needed to watch their word choices as carefully as politicians. And if you had a daughter like Cate, who was just waiting to be misunderstood, whose eyes were like portholes, revealing the high watermark of her disgust, your only hope was not to elicit too much backlash.

Well, it didn't matter now.

The basement was little more than a dank, mildewy storage space.

The boiler was edged with rust. The lone lightbulb was accessible by a beaded pull chain that only Dean could reach. It blinked awake, casting the room in stuttering light. There was a set of pink training wheels, old elbow pads, wicker furniture, used computer monitors with the error sign still burned into their globed screens, an ancient cathode-ray television with a cap of silver antennae. Things they should have thrown away or donated long ago. A sense of having been left behind.

Nina took out her phone:

Dad and I just received missile warning. If NEthing happens we luv u.

And then, because she might die, she added:

I guess being selfish was worth it.

* * *

Cate was on West Coast time. Dean's phone did not ring until an hour later. She was wailing on the other end as he comforted her. "Yes, it was a false alarm. I know. I know. Okay, I'll tell her. Yes, I promise. Okay, love you."

Not until she heard him hang up, until she heard his soft, reassuring steps passing through the kitchen, did Nina realize how much of her petulance had been transmuted from pure fear.

Dean looked sadly at her. "Why?"

She was sitting on their bed, arms crossed, staring at the blank television. "Why what?"

"Why would you say that to her?"

"I thought we were going to die."

"And you wanted her to spend the rest of her life feeling guilty?"

"I don't know what I wanted."

"This is the sort of thing, you know— This is why—"

"Why what?"

"Why she pulls away."

She swallowed and looked down at her chest, feeling the loose skin around her neck gathering against her chin.

"If you could just find it in yourself to be kinder to her," Dean said. "To your own daughter."

"Maybe you married a monster."

He shut his eyes, pressed his lips together, as if gathering patience. "I did no such thing."

"And it really is a shame, because if it weren't for me, you and Cate would be getting along famously. Hell, maybe you'd have moved to San whatever to be closer to her and her little girlfriend. You'd grow out your hair like some hippie opium addict and raise their adopted kid while they went about chaining themselves to the fences outside nuclear power plants."

"Good Lord."

"You resent that she bundles the two of us together in her mind. And if you don't, you're a damn fool, because you should."

"I don't resent things I can't change."

"Ha! Ha ha ha."

Dean shuddered and looked away. He was a kind, gentle man with chubby cheeks and a dollop of thick black hair, who'd sat beside her at the Wingham Symphony decades ago and kept turning to smile throughout the performance of Beethoven's *Pastoral* Symphony. He'd found her at the coat check after the concert and immediately asked if she thought the solo clarinet was a bit pitchy during the introduction to the "Shepherd's Hymn," if the strings had perhaps rushed a bit when they were roused to full strength, and if she might want to discuss it all over a drink.

She hadn't been impressed, obviously. A classical concert was an obnoxious place to try to pick someone up. But his optimism was a steady beat, as was his sincerity, along with the fact that she, too, thought the first clarinetist of the Wingham Symphony deserved a swift demotion.

And weeks later, when he shared with her his ambition of creating a local hub for the arts—a music store, perhaps—something in Nina's soul loosened. Opportunity sprawled before her. This chance for a small and gorgeous life. Something she could not have imagined as a child.

Dean's niceness, his sunny nature, was surely a product of the close, emotionally robust, almost *friendly* relationship he'd had with his family, growing up.

Nina's own parents were quiet, conservative folk—first-generation immigrants, whose love was bundled alongside the capacious expectations they had for her, and whose stinginess with outward affection was of a piece with their Confucian values.

"I don't ever want to raise her the way I was raised," she'd told Dean tremblingly.

And he'd nodded and said, "Whatever you want." Because he was just so happy. And because his parents were fully assimilated second gens for whom culture was more hobby than identity.

"You know why all immigrants want their kids to become doctors?" she'd asked once.

"Why?"

"Because you can't make fun of your doctor. At least not when she's elbow-deep in your guts. You can't flip your doctor off and ridicule her eyes or her accent when your life depends on her."

"That makes sense."

"And then you think about why your parents want to protect you from those sorts of things in the first place—the teasing and mistreatment—and the sorts of indignities they had to go through, that they've never told you about."

"My parents never seemed that worried."

"They had a generation's buffer to become American. They didn't even have accents."

And he'd nodded again, because it was best not to contradict her over these things.

* * *

"Did you think it was real? The alert?" Dean asked the next day in the empty shop.

“I don’t know.” Nina emerged from the back office, glowering at him. “Why does it matter?”

He was staring at the row of violins hanging by their tuning pegs, varnished the color of apricot. Beside them was a battery of drum kits and a display shelf strewn with the gilded coils of brass instruments. A phalanx of guitars and upright pianos sat on a raised platform that doubled as a stage for local recitals. “I don’t think you believed it,” he said finally.

“Fine. Okay. So what?”

“So then why did you say those things to her?”

“Why does it matter? I wanted to say them, I found an occasion, so I said them.”

“So, it was just plain meanness.”

Feeling welled in her throat, but she cleared it swiftly. “Well, like I said, I’m sorry. I’m sorry I’m such a horrible, cruel person.”

“I’m not the one you need to apologize to.”

Nina stared with futility at her palms, as if trying to read herself in them. She was relieved when the door chimed and Ruthie Zhang walked in, holding a child’s violin case. Ruthie ran the Beckitt school district’s music program; years ago, she’d struck a deal to rent instruments from their store, Major Third, and host concerts each semester in its little space.

And although Nina loathed the sloppy discordance of novice musicians (while Dean was always first to give an ovation, his face shiny with admiration), she was thankful for the arrangement. How it made their shop into a neighborhood institution.

“I’m afraid you gave us a defective one,” Ruthie said now, opening the case, revealing a standard-issue instrument with cracked enamel varnish and a slanted bridge, thin strips of tape strangling the neck and fingerboard. “You can hear something rolling around inside of it.”

And Nina could not help but retort, “I’m afraid we don’t sell defective products.” She brought the violin up to her face and tilted it, staring through the f-holes into the attic-like interior and spotting the fallen sound post. She shook her head. “This couldn’t have been us.”

"My student said she received it like this."

"I'm sorry, but no way. You only get this kind of damage by messing around and poking something inside the instrument."

Ruthie narrowed her eyes in discernment, as if testing a child for a lie. "I don't have any reason not to trust this student."

"Well, if that's the case," Nina said, as her patience vaporized, "then I have a genuine Stradivarius I can sell to you for a hundred bucks if you come by at midnight."

"Here." Dean stepped in and placed a fresh instrument on the glass counter. "Please take this one. No charge."

The woman nodded. She waited for a moment, as if expecting something more, something Nina patently refused to deliver, before saying, "Thank you," and walking out.

The silence lingered. Now that Ruthie was gone, Nina could remember how much she'd always liked her, had always felt a sense of kinship with her, because customers so often behaved like schoolchildren.

"Fine. I'll apologize to Cate," she said finally. "I have plenty of practice, don't I? I've been apologizing my whole life. What's once more?"

Dean stared at her with his irritating mix of helplessness and pity. He shook his head.

"What? What?"

"It's just that—you wouldn't have to if you hadn't said those things to begin with."

Well, duh. She knew that. Did he think she didn't know that? There was no use explaining it to him if he still didn't understand. If, after so many decades of their being together, he still could not see that she had clouds inside her. That her soul was a sky. And sometimes it was clarion and pristine, and the feelings of happiness and love were as straightforward as the contrail of an aircraft. And sometimes it was so stiflingly overcast that she could hardly breathe, and the only relief was gasps of memory.

"We came to America to give you opportunities."

Memories of her Mandarin-speaking parents, who'd made a fetish out of discipline.

"So why aren't you working harder?"

"Sorry."

"Why aren't you getting better grades?"

"Sorry."

"Why are you such a disappointment?"

They were shrill, extravagant demands, which became far more reasonable if your business was a tiny printing shop with mostly Chinese clientele. If several of your products had already made the rounds on the internet for their *hilarious* mistranslations.

Signs that read NO WATERING PLANTS WITH PISS OF DOG or TODAY IS UNDER CONSTRUCTION.

Restaurant menu items like DEEP FRIED FEMALE or SHRIMP DUMPINGS.

They were expectations that made abundantly more sense if you were continuously forced to mollify angry customers demanding refunds, admissions of error, although you'd only printed what you'd been given. To endure the smugness of Whites, for whom the idea of learning a second language was not just an imposition but an insult, ridiculing your droll incompetence.

She was sorry. She was—she truly was—for not working harder to become a doctor or at least a lawyer or an engineer or someone worthy of a default level of professional *respect*. For falling in love with a third-generation man with frighteningly little ambition. Because there were responsibilities charged to the second generation: root systems to nurture, pride to be recouped. And she'd neglected it all. She was sorry.

And she was sorry, because the least she could be—when she was thirty and they moved to Beckitt—was happy with her life. Was she at least happy? Could she at least give her parents that bit of comfort?

But who could answer such a question? She was happy when she was happy. And other times she was confronted by a storm of such miserable discontent that only her lived experiences—her prior escapes—provided adequate hope in which to shelter.

"We wanted to tell you, we've adjusted our expectations." Her father had called her one afternoon, without warning. *"We're happy for you."*

"What?"

"We're happy that you chose your own path. We respect it."

And when she and Dean finally opened Major Third, right in the center of the Beckitt Shoppes, her parents had been its first, most enthusiastic customers.

She had a hundred such creases in her heart—moments when love had appeared brightly to her and left its indelible mark. Like the memory of her high school graduation, the expensive vinyl banner on which her parents had printed CONGRADULATIONS, NINA. Or the day after she'd finally told them of her pregnancy. The sign that appeared—IT IS A GIRL—on the front door.

She never took for granted that you needed to love someone dearly, almost as much as you valued your own happiness, in order to truly dread her disappointment.

* * *

Nina adored winter. She loved when everything was frozen and halted. When she had time to catch her breath.

Springtime was outright torture by comparison. Things moved too quickly: The temperature ticking upward, day by day, hour by hour, reminding her of the time that was passing. The swift advance of her life. And the dawning realization that Cate was never coming back.

She took up gardening in order to soothe the ache of it.

She planted blue bearded irises that looked like something you might find underwater, like jellyfish mid-contraction. Pink gayfeathers that bloomed in vertical strands. Velvety rosettes of lamb's ears hugging the ground. Violet cranesbills whose flowers were bursts of color in a sea of roiling green, like some inverted fireworks show.

She came to treasure the calm, devoted image of Dean sitting in their kitchen nook, from which bay windows gave onto the prism of their garden. The glasses perched precariously upon his flat, stubby nose. The sunlight settling upon the sheer cliff of his profile. Tiny motes freckling the air around him.

And how she loved to tease him, to feel needed and loved by him.

"Did you see that woman who walked into the store yesterday?" she'd said once. "She was gorgeous, wasn't she?"

Nothing.

"Dean. Did you hear me?"

"She was nothing compared to you," he mumbled, and she could tell that he was being truthful because he hadn't made eye contact when he said it, he hadn't paused to consider whomever she was talking about. Perhaps she'd done it enough times for him to catch on. She didn't care. She chose to believe that you could prance the most beautiful women before him, and those earnest charcoal eyes would never waver from her.

"Oh, darling," she liked to say, "your chinky little eyes."

"The worse to see you with, my dear."

She'd warn the kiddo when they went on road trips. She'd say, "Your father's asleep at the wheel! He's asleep at the wheel!"

And he'd snarl, but you could follow the path of his lips in either direction and see how they curled upward at the very last moment before disappearing into his cheeks.

And how she loved him. She was old enough to know how silly it was to make blanket declarations, and old enough to make them, regardless. This was love: It was saying no over and over again, because when you were a young woman who was uncertain, you were best to round down—and then, finally, *yes*. The ginger surrender, followed by such expansive sweetness.

And the two of them together. The whole-wheat toast with margarine they went through every morning with their coffee, and weekends with rice porridge and pork wool and ash-aged duck eggs whose slices flowered open. And the nights when he'd roll over onto her arm while they were both asleep, and in the morning, how it was a phantom, supplanted by his whole bulk, like they were joined.

And their delirious bouts of sex, and the time he agreed to let her put a finger up his asshole and he'd yelped and farted and she'd laughed so hard she'd pissed herself, and the sheets and the comforter and even the pillowcases had to be washed twice.

And the trips to Maine, to the littoral towns that smelled of brine; the groggy, alcoholic lobstermen who wiped their mouths with their ripped shirtsleeves and looked nothing like the Gorton man; the foam-capped water that bore past the rocks, toward the shore; the coffee they drank at the little seaside inn while the sky achieved every possible shade of gray, and her suggesting that maybe this would be the perfect place to retire to, and his saying that it was exactly like Beckitt except with the ocean. Which was what made it different and perfect, she said. Maybe Cate would like to move here, too.

And the Anchor Grill that everyone in town went to, next door to their little music shop, where his golfing buddies would slap him on the shoulder and insist on buying him a drink, and how his face grew those red, glowing splotches and he became louder and his voice sharper and higher and his hands grabbier, and how she'd always have to drive the both of them home; and he would sulk at her sulkiness and call her a fun killer and the next morning would wear that sly, forgiveness-seeking smile, and what could she do but love him?

And the days when no one—not one single person—stepped into their store, and it was just them and Cate, surrounded by the eerie silence of all those instruments. And the month of his prostate cancer scare, which had so terrified her that she'd obliterated it from her memory—she'd blacked out and only came to when disaster was forestalled by a young doctor whom she was ready to worship if his powers might save her husband.

And the dissonant school concerts in which Cate played violin, then piano, then clarinet, then nothing, and the heartbreak when she left for college and started spending Thanksgivings with her friends and stopped calling even weekly, and how she and Dean had to relearn their old way of being alone together.

All these things were love, and he was love, lit by the dusty basement light, his arm trembling slightly, seeking immediate shelter, and he was the tug and shake that woke her a week later, when she'd found herself on the cold, wet sod of their backyard, crushing the marigolds and foxgloves, his chinky eyes full of adoration and worry and incomprehension—deep, deep incomprehension—when she smiled and looked at him and said, "Dean, I don't feel too great."

* * *

A video call came, finally, from Cate, two weeks after the alert. "Mom, we need to talk."

Mature girl. A mature thing to say. Her stomach hurt today.

Sometimes it felt as if she depended on Cate's wariness—as if it were the only way she could keep the gossamer string of her love attached, because it was the only way they knew how to be together.

"What I texted you, kiddo, it was nothing."

Cate was petite, like her. She had the most beautiful oval brown eyes; full, round lips; an adorable button nose that she'd recently taken to mutilating by piercing a stud in her right nostril; and thick, black hair that she'd cut boyishly short, as if to hide its volume.

"It was clearly not nothing," she said.

No. Nina had broken a cardinal rule. She'd been a selfish, needy parent. She'd put her own feelings first.

Mrs. Chang, there are several options we can pursue here.

"Why did you say it?"

She didn't know. She couldn't explain the smoke and fog that occasionally overtook her. The bleakness of her moods, the inescapable hopelessness, the spite. Only that she did not know how to be any other way.

"It was a passing whim, and I thought we were going to die."

"But that's what makes it worse. I tell my students all the time that you need to consider not just how your words make you feel but how they affect others."

—aggressively treat it, I don't see any reason why you can't enjoy at least—

"So now you think I'm an elementary schooler?"

"Damn it, Mom. Can you just cooperate with me here?"

As if this were a matter of *cooperation*! Oh, she had no idea, Nina thought bitterly. "I just miss you, is all," she said.

"Why do you need me so close by? What do you need from me?"

"We don't need anything from you, sweetheart. We raised you. For the longest time you needed us."

"And now I don't. So, just please let it drop."

"Okay."

We'll schedule some follow-ups—

The gathering silence between them.

"You know, I'm disappointed in you, Mom."

"What?" She might as well have been speaking in a different language. "*You're* disappointed in *me*?"

"Yeah. I just never would've pegged you as a homophobe."

"You think I'm homophobic?"

"I mean, it's pretty clear."

"But you're my daughter. I love you; I raised you. How can I be phobic of any part of you?"

"It's not my responsibility to explain it to you."

But then, whose was it?

She felt a dark mass, a heavy cloud, gather in her chest and rise into her sinuses. And she knew that if Cate heard her crying, she'd roll her eyes and accuse her of something manipulative, and the conversation would end on an even lower note than it was currently on.

She pressed the tablet into Dean's chest and stormed to the living room and wept angrily into a velveteen pillow that Cate had made for her as a Mother's Day gift many, many years ago.

"It's nothing. Mom's a little upset. Yes, it's fine."

A little upset.

* * *

"You didn't tell her," he said.

Nina shrugged. "I didn't really find the right time."

"You need to tell her."

"She hates me right now—let her just feel that. I don't want to overwhelm her."

"You shouldn't have said what you said."

"I know," she snapped. "Do you think I don't know that?"

"She feels pretty misunderstood."

"God, I hate when you're like this. Mr. Fair-Minded, Even-Keeled friend of our daughter. Do you know what it's like having to absorb all her resentment? Even though I know *you* feel the same way?"

"I think I'm better at masking my feelings than you are."

"But we shouldn't *need* to! She's our daughter! We raised her and fed her and loved her and kept her emotionally healthy enough to believe she could love anyone she wanted. We should be able to make our feelings known without being accused of whatever new form of bigotry is in fashion."

"Homophobia has been around for a long, long time," he said quietly.

"I'm not being homophobic," Nina said. "I'm being realistic."

She'd been realistic her whole life, which had meant holding in her disappointment at Cate's lackluster talents, her profound ordinariness, like a swimmer holding her breath—taking tiny, controlled gasps at the very last possible moment.

"Maybe if we were stricter," she'd said once. "If we were a little bit stricter, she could've gone to medical school, she could've met someone more practical, stayed closer."

And Dean had pressed his lips together and shut his eyes. "That is not right. That is not the right mindset at all."

"So what is?"

"Personally, I think she's courageous for uprooting herself like this. For embracing that kind of change."

"You think it's courage?"

"I'm trying to see the upside. I don't have your gift for the sensible."

Asshole, she'd thought. Although she couldn't help smiling. Being realistic meant that she, alone, seemed to remember the six years Cate had spent completing a four-year degree at two colleges; her shuffling between the violin, piano, and clarinet before finally settling on resentment, wailing at and decrying the evil Asian-parent intensity with which they'd tried to imbue her with their love of music; her "emotionally abusive" teachers, who'd "taunted" her with the promise of stickers if she practiced and cruelly "withheld" them if not.

And her insistence on having experienced trauma as a child—trauma! Growing up with parents who'd done nothing but love her.

No, she wasn't upset with Cate for being gay. She was upset at her for using it as an excuse to run away. She was upset at her for leaving, because she missed her. She was a mother who missed her child.

She wished there were some way for her to express this without lighting the wick of her daughter's indignation. She wished it weren't so easy to drive her away.

"I don't want to get into this argument with you," Dean said now.

"And when she gets her heart broken, when that experiment of hers turns to shit, we're going to be the ones comforting her, giving her a place to stay, a landing spot. And knowing this, I should be allowed to say some things."

"Are you scared?" he asked.

"Of course."

"What I mean is, are you scared that she won't care when you tell her?"

Nina hadn't realized how close she still was to tears. How they'd been gathering at the edges of her eyelids, held rapidly back. Unable, now, to be absorbed. "Of course I am," she said toward her chest.

"She's your daughter."

She sniffed. "I used to understand the subtext beneath a phrase like that. I swear I used to. But now, they're just sounds and symbols. It's like I'm relearning English as a second language."

"Your daughter will love you no matter what."

There was a minor cratering in the garden: Their cluster of lamb's ears was curling into itself, thinning, turning the color of sand, in spite of Dean's efforts.

"She has an interesting way of expressing it," she said.

* * *

A few months ago, Cate had let slip that she was seeing a therapist.

It was an innocent-enough mention. "You know, my therapist said the other day . . ." And Dean had continued nodding, unfazed, as if his dumb niceness withstood every attack, every insult, that their unthankful daughter threw at them. And it was up to Nina to pause and ask for clarity.

"You see a shrink?"

"Yeah, Mom." Cate's eyes had steeled, her mouth had pursed on the tablet screen, as if this were precisely the reaction she'd expected, as if that shrink of hers had prepared her for this exact scenario and was ready and on call to hear all the perceived insults, all the meanness, that her mother would have in response.

"Okay. Well. Does your insurance cover it?"

"Most of it," she'd said. "Everyone has one in the Bay."

"Seems like a profoundly unhealthy place to live."

"It's actually the opposite. People are a lot more free, a lot more in tune with their emotions and their childhood traumas."

So my parents got that false missile alert—do you remember that? It was in the news a few weeks ago. My parents were, like, in that area, and when they got it, my mom texted me. She said I'd been selfish. She thought she was dying, and that was the last thing she said to me.

Nina imagined this now and shivered at her own cruelty, at the therapist's cold judgment. The outsider's diagnosis. If a shrink didn't have you blaming your parents for everything that was wrong in your life, was he even worth the money?

Decades ago, her nǎinai had gone to the hospital for an operation, which had encountered a severe complication, the solution to which was for the surgeon to simply lop off her leg, as if it were standard procedure. She'd fallen asleep a fully ambulatory person and awakened in a completely different body.

The shock never properly dispersed.

For months afterward, her nǎinai was struck by phantom pains originating from an extremity that no longer existed. She was made bitter by the unexpectedness of it, the fundamental ways in which she'd been forced to relearn herself, with no preparation.

And since then, nothing had ever seemed more crass, more cruel, to Nina than an able-bodied person recommending that someone lose something as familiar and precious as a limb.

"The thing about shrinks is, it's in their interest that you don't get better, so they can keep getting paid," she said, enduring a ripple of nausea.

Dean was sitting in the kitchen nook. He scratched his cheek and squinted. "As long as she's happy."

"But it has nothing to do with happiness! Her generation has Twitter, Facebook, widget, wodget, whatever. Everyone feels deserving of an audience. People used to think having a voice was enough. You had your voice and you earned your audience. Not now. Now people *have* to listen. And when they don't, because you just don't have anything interesting or important enough to say, you pay someone to do it. It's not happiness, it's vanity."

His face stiffened, as if battling its own extension. He was holding in a yawn.

* * *

"Please just tell her," Dean said after another week.

"When I'm ready to tell her, I'll tell her."

"She has a right to know."

"If she has the right to know, then why don't you spill the beans? What's stopping you? Other than your allergy to being anything other than completely agreeable?"

"I don't know why you're reacting like this."

A stupid thing to say. Why did anyone react like anything? It was like those repetitive questions that children asked: "Why, why, why?" After every explanation you gave. Until you reached the bottommost truth, the axiom. Because it was. She was who she was.

On some days, it was easier to be frightened than to confront herself. Just like it was easier to withhold than to give freely. It was easier to wait and hope that Cate might understand that love was the most basement feeling you had for your children. You loved them, first and foremost. And then you built the rest of your feelings atop it.

Motherhood for Nina might look like a sorry, sad-looking cottage, with cracked paint and peeling tiles, worn away, but the love was there, shining beneath the floorboards.

"What about the money?" he said.

"Probably won't go as far over there. Might cover a few years' worth of rent. Nothing equity-building, that's for sure."

"Still."

She sighed. "Still."

It was their little piece of the American Dream. Her parents, before their passing, had sold their print shop for a surprisingly handsome amount and left her enough money to pay off their house.

And with this cushion they'd been able to live comfortably, to provide Cate with a trauma-free childhood. They'd planned to sell their own store when the real-estate market rebounded, and to put the money away, saving it as a gift for her, for when she'd settle down—hopefully somewhere close.

Why do you need me so close by?

Was there really an explanation needed for wanting to keep a loved one nearby?

She remembered the time Cate had ridden her bike home from school with a friend, who'd crashed into a wooden fence and battered her knee with splinters. How their daughter had insisted on heroically waiting there with her until an ambulance arrived and not once considered contacting her parents to let them know what was wrong.

Nina had nearly vomited at the store, the surge of panic like permanent marker to the dry-erase board of her mind: Everything else was forgettable, forgivable, capable of being brushed aside. But this—please, let this be nothing. Let everything be all right. She cursed herself for not buying Cate a cell phone like she'd asked; for not reminding her to be careful, to look out for strangers, for slow-moving cars; for not imbuing in her a proper terror of the world and its people and their capacity for cruelty.

Dean had been the calm one, urging patience and levelheadedness.

And when Cate's bike finally approached the store, Nina had wanted to smack her and embrace her so thoroughly that she might wrap herself around her silly, theatrical kiddo and keep her permanently thus.

It was she who'd insisted, afterward, on buying her a cell phone, who insisted that she call them on the hour whenever she went out, who raged at her when she failed to meet these directives. And who withstood their daughter's rebellious vitriol, her accusations of smothering and hover parenting.

* * *

Weeks passed. The prognosis worsened. They got a second opinion. A third. She opted for an aggressive course of treatment, which left her weak and feverish and incredulous of a time when she'd ever been healthy enough to spend afternoons with her hands and knees sinking into soil, when her back was sturdy enough to endure the bending over and digging and planting and patting down.

Still, it was difficult to imagine death in a town like Beckitt, where the only change was cyclic—the seasons, the school years. Difficult to imagine something like time ending, when it could hardly be said to exist in the first place.

She tried going back to work at Major Third one empty morning but found it exhausting and surreal just to sit in the back room, scanning inventory and paying bills—her husband, by disposition, was always the greeter and customer service liaison. She felt like the shop's sturdy, familiar presence had grown abstract since her diagnosis. As if every solid object had been replaced by its memory.

She stepped into the showroom and heard Dean's cautious voice. "Nina?"

But the wire baskets beside the cash register were filled with mutes, reed cases, and digital metronomes that reminded her of the young woman who worked at the Anchor, who used to visit the store during her breaks. How she hummed to herself like a maniac while aimlessly browsing, and Nina had grown so very annoyed one afternoon, because they were running a *store*, not a museum, that she'd gone up to her and said, "Miss, is there anything you actually need?"

The woman had started like a baby animal and fled. And Dean had scolded her. "Can't you be a bit more welcoming?"

His worried voice was weaving back into her consciousness. "Nina? Are you okay?"

She nodded at the array of clarinets racked beside the Alfred's method books and recalled the man from Wingham who worked at the urgent care clinic a few stores down, who, many years ago, had brought his young daughter in to choose an instrument. The girl was interested in the clarinet, so Nina had asked Cate to grab hers and quickly demonstrate the "Shepherd's Hymn" from Beethoven's *Pastoral* Symphony. But her ligature was loose and her reed too dry; her fingers were knobby and shaky and incapable of fully covering the tone holes. All she could produce was a series of atonal honks, to Nina's profound shame.

"Nina. What's wrong?" Dean was saying.

She was realizing now that the shame had been directed at herself, at the suspicion that it was she who caused her daughter such anxiety, urging her to play.

"I don't think I can be here anymore," Nina said.

It felt, sometimes, as if she were drowning in apology.

* * *

Spring smoldered and dilated into summer. She awoke one morning to Dean's piteous staring. "I don't think I'll know what to do without you," he whispered.

The day was wet and muggy, the sky stifled by clouds with luminescent bellies, engorged with sunlight.

"Oh, don't say that," she muttered. "Please. Just be a man."

"I—I don't really understand what that means."

"It means that I need you to be the strong one. Please. Because at least you still get to be alive."

"Why haven't you told her yet?"

"I'll tell her when I'm ready to tell her."

Her daughter had a new life. She had plenty of other things to worry about. And Nina didn't want to upset her further. It was as simple as that.

She spent entire afternoons nursing the secret corner of her soul that was relieved that Cate had found a decent therapist. Because she'd felt a vague terror all her life that her daughter might have inherited some of her private storminess. Something of the cloud cover that could smother even the most joyous, persistent sunlight.

And if all it took to cure this was for Nina to become the enemy, then she was relieved. Truly, she was.

She sat for hours in Cate's old room, left precisely intact, recalling her childhood bouts of flu and mumps—and the tender worry, the heart-bruising love she'd felt, feeding spoonfuls of bitter medicine to her kiddo, who'd been so helpless with need. So trusting. She stared at the stack of shiny watercolor picture books she used to read to her at bedtime, until Cate's eyelids had fallen, like two tiny hands pressed together in prayer.

How she would have loved for her daughter to move back and take the house. To keep it in the family. Her mother had told her that, back in China, two or three generations might live in the same apartment, or in apartment buildings only minutes away. This seemed a natural state of affairs. Families were supposed to stay close, not scatter.

"We should sell the shop," she said on a balmy evening. "You can't run it on your own, and the market is only going to get worse. We should sell it now, so Cate can get the money."

"Don't worry about that," he said.

* * *

She spent the majority of the summer bedridden, curiously cold, which she didn't quite mind. It felt like the quickest season of her life.

A moment later, the leaves on the birch and maple and oaks were tumbling asynchronously toward warmer parts of the color spectrum, so that across their backyard, as among the individual trees, the effect was of a controlled series of autumn detonations. The flowers in their garden were receding back into the stiffening loam. Snow was becoming ice, which became a thick, permanent frost.

She hoped, sometimes, that she'd die in the winter. Either this one or—if she really held on—the next. It was easiest to give up your body when you were cold. When you insulated yourself with as many layers as possible, until your own skin was just another coat wicking heat toward some darker, interior essence. She thought that dying might just be an extension of that. A spiky retreat to the basement.

Cate's calls were brief and scrupulously polite. A visit over Christmas might've been an ideal opportunity to break the news to her in a gentle, supportive way. But the invitations were rebuffed.

We wanted to tell you, we've adjusted our expectations.

Nina remembered the abrupt shock of hearing this. And scoffing at her hapless parents, their emotional clumsiness.

Only now did she understand how difficult it was to say certain things—to make yourself so vulnerable to your own child. How you needed occasions for certain revelations.

"What're we listening to today?" Dean asked in the midst of January doldrums, withdrawing the thick, wallet-shaped case that held their Deutsche Grammophon CDs. (She was too infirm, now, to attend full concerts at the symphony.)

Cate had once offered to download all their music into a digital format, to be squeezed into an iPod. And Nina had said, "I prefer listening to the CDs. There's something richer when your music is still physically kept on something."

To which their daughter had rolled her eyes, because she subscribed to the orthodoxy of the MP3, modernity's moral superiority.

Nina requested that old favorite, Beethoven's *Pastoral* Symphony, whose final movement she adored most of all, with its gorgeous, syncopated hymn and dense forest of harmonies—the sylvan cellos plucking on the offbeat, the muscular basses thickening each chord, the bright brass shining through.

She listened and waited for the tempest in her to pass. She might as well have tried to alter the surrounding climate.

"Tell me, are you not even slightly disappointed in her?" she asked Dean.

"Who?"

"Our daughter."

His slightly slowed breaths seemed to draw from a reservoir of patience. "How could I be?"

"Well, you start by expecting that she'll be someone with discipline, someone who achieves a level of distinction, and then you realize that she isn't. She does something until it becomes difficult and then quits."

"She's healthy; she's happy, it seems. She has a stable job and relationship."

"She's a trend follower," Nina said. "She has no convictions of her own besides whatever is popular. She's probably teaching kids how to feel guilty about being American, how to apologize for things that people did hundreds of years ago, how to hate a person merely for what they say, to think that words carry the capacity for violence, to mistake ignorance for ill will."

"It's this," he said, voice trembling. "You're going to have to stop this if you ever want her to stop hating you."

"She's my daughter."

"See? You understand subtext just fine."

She scowled at him.

"You know, Nina, I never pegged you as such a conservative."

"I'm not conservative."

"This stuff you're saying. It's what conservatives say. It's what that celebrity president says."

"Right, and everything that a person says needs to contribute to a label. And everyone needs to be labeled as *something*. Even if the label is a made-up, hateful thing."

"We need classifications in order to make sense of the world," he tried, with his usual circumspection. "We need them to organize the things around us. It's human nature, and I don't think it's fair or realistic to eschew them. It's probably more productive to ask yourself why you've been given certain labels by people whom you love and trust."

"Dear Lord, you are just so amazingly worthy, aren't you?" she snarled. "So fair and balanced. If there were a sword to pull out of a stone, you'd be the one to do it, wouldn't you? Although maybe you should just settle for pulling that stick out of your ass."

"Nina."

"You know I can't stand that buffoon in the White House. I'm not conservative, I'm not liberal. I'm just dying."

* * *

Spring arrived once again. They took walks around the big pond at the center of Songline Park, the ruddy woods and humid air so reminiscent of health, youth, that she was briefly shocked to see her and Dean's hunched reflections in the still water. An old couple negotiating the mossy trails, passing arrows spray-painted on the grass that marked the high school's cross-country routes.

She recalled a long-ago afternoon of comparable weather, when she and Dean walked to the edge of a similar pond in their bare feet (she, barely reaching his shoulder), walked until the water licked their ankles and brushed against the hem of her skirt, the rim of wetness pulling itself upward. The faint, musky sourness of plant life disturbed. The cotton ball sky surging with pink and orange.

And how she'd felt perfectly happy, perfectly safe. Even though mud was squelching between her toes and insects were needling around her ears. She remembered the mosquito that landed on Dean's head, aiming for the warm blood of his scalp, thoroughly stymied by his thick hair.

"I want another baby," he'd said.

Another mosquito landed on his forearm. She flicked it away and looked up at him. "No."

"Any particular reason why not?"

She shook her head almost as a reflex. "I just don't want to."

And the look of disappointment on his face was as heartbreaking as any she'd ever seen. Like the happiness and vitality were being drawn hypodermically out of him.

"I'm sorry," she'd said, to mollify him, to tacitly thank him for accommodating all her refusals.

If only she'd known then that life was recapitulation. That, as you grew older, you revisited the same memories, the same unpredictable loci to which your soul oriented itself. All you came to know about living was born from those handfuls of moments.

And she knew now that she'd been scared. She was scared of herself, of somehow breaking the daughter they already had. Of infecting a new one with the darkness she could not keep quarantined within herself. The fear had only grown stronger since her diagnosis. More capable of sabotage.

* * *

Cate was finally video calling.

"Mom, I think you may have PTSD." She was so beautiful, even when her features were assembled in a look of bleakness.

"What?"

"Like, post-traumatic stress disorder. From the false alert. My therapist was telling me that it's actually a pretty common reaction to something really, well, traumatic like that."

Dean, standing behind the screen, raised his eyebrows in a meaningful way, as if to say, *Just hear her out.*

"Why do you say that?" she said.

While Dean clicked a set of invisible castanets, his hands mimicking two mouths in conversation.

She did a quick tap of the mute button. "What is this, fucking charades?"

"—and Dad says you've been sort of quiet and withdrawn, like there's something you want to say."

She tapped again and said, "Is your shrink speaking from experience?"

"He's *on your side*, Mom. I debated even telling you this, but he told me I should."

"So he gives you instructions?"

"Advice. He gives me advice."

"You know your father and I can offer that for free, right?"

"But it's useful—I mean, not that your advice isn't useful. But it's different. He helps me see things in new ways. He helps me understand things better."

"Sweetheart, have you ever heard of David Koresh?"

In the background, Dean sagged and waved his hand in his capitulating way.

"Look, take it or leave it. But I think if you just opened up to someone, it would help you understand *me* better. It might even help broaden your understanding of other things."

"So if I embraced this person's teachings, you think I might finally be granted the secret knowledge that illuminates how the world is?"

"Look, I don't want to argue."

"You're the one suggesting that I'm crazy."

"For fuck's sake, Mom. Is that what you think of me? Do you think only *crazy* people see therapists?"

"I think that people who can't handle their own lives, who want some semblance of control but don't have the discipline to earn it, I think *those* people rely on shrinks to tell them how great they're doing."

"God, you are such a bitch."

"Oh, nice. I can almost hear the money you're about to spend on this particular conversation of ours. Tell me, does your professional listener charge you by the word?"

"No, Mom, honestly, I have other, more important things to talk to him about. This kind of shit? It's an afterthought. I'm over it. I'm over you."

And again, Nina had handed the tablet to Dean, because she just could not take this, and gone upstairs to shower and, coming back downstairs, refreshed, almost ready to restart the conversation, heard him say:

"People, when they get older, their brains start to sort of, you know, change. The parts that are supposed to show good taste and stuff. They just disappear. It may have been happening for a while now, this thing with your mother."

And never—never in her life—had she ever been more insulted.

She raged toward him after he hung up. "Why don't you just fucking tell her, then?"

He stood pat. "It's not something for me to tell."

"You really are a weasel. You can't bear saying or doing anything that might upset our daughter. You leave it all to me."

"That is deeply unfair."

"You know *perfectly well* how to live without me. You've got the whole Goddamn thing figured out. You have the whole fucking narrative planned out in your head. You're already moving on. Already planning this new and improved relationship with Cate."

His face hardened. "That is completely out of line, Nina. That might be the cruelest thing you've ever said to me."

"It was nothing compared to what you just told our daughter about *me*."

"What choice did you give me?" he screamed. She'd never heard him scream like this. "Do you want her to care that you're dying or not? Do you want her to visit you on your deathbed? At your grave? Do you want her to honor you? Or do you want to keep pushing her away until you're gone?"

For the first time in years, she thought about the generation that gapped them. The additional lifetime Dean's family had spent in this land.

"I gave her her life!" she screamed back, terrified. "I fed her and loved her and worried about her every day. Don't you think that's enough reason for her to honor me?"

He shook his head. His face was closed, the kindness in it stored away. "No. Maybe it was. Not anymore."

* * *

She awoke one afternoon to the sounds of a whispered argument. (The problem with video calling was that you could hear the other side of the conversation just as easily.)

"It's just always something."

"Please," she heard Dean say. "Please just talk to her."

"I just wonder—maybe she's a narcissist or something."

"For God's sake, Cate—just, please."

"Fine, fine."

What had she done to merit such coldness, she thought, as Dean's steps grew louder and heavier; his feet were slapping the floor. "Nina." With both hands, he transferred the tablet to her lap. "Nina, Cate wants us to meet someone."

An unfamiliar face was on the screen, alongside their daughter's. A woman with short hair, a looped piercing through her right nostril.

"Mom, I want to introduce you to Shana."

"Hi, Mrs. Chang."

"Oh."

The woman's eyes were thin and geometric, like sideways diamonds; her hair was shimmery blond, chopped at the shoulders. She was pretty and young, just like Cate. In ninety-nine out of a hundred scenarios, they were just two lovely friends, navigating early adulthood together. Going to parties, flirting with boys, painting each other's nails. Having, in a word, fun!

It didn't compute that the two of them, full of such carefree grace, such feminine beauty, would be involved in something as complex and forlorn as a romantic relationship with each other.

She thought maybe she was a bit homophobic after all.

Shana spoke with the practiced politeness, the mannered graciousness, of having been coached. Nina, for her part, tried to be open-minded and fair enough to ignore how the woman who was sleeping with her daughter chewed her nails—a grotesque habit—and how, beyond the door, she could see the general disorder of their little apartment: the tiny kitchen sink in which plates and pans were piled, the Bob Ross–style painting hung crookedly, the twin yoga mats rolled up and leaning against the door, the framed scrolls with indiscernible Chinese characters (as if Cate had ever shown any interest in her heritage!).

Disapproval accompanied her wherever she looked.

"What do you do?" she heard herself asking.

And when the woman responded with some flimflam about operations for a smartphone application that was supposed to be revolutionizing the way people did an extremely simple thing, she'd carefully suppressed every instinct toward sarcasm.

It was painless enough, she thought. The worst anyone might've thought was that she was *cold*. Well, that was fine with her. She liked the cold.

And still, to see Dean's sad look. His watery, charcoal eyes.

"You could have been warmer."

"For as long as we've been married, have you ever known me to be a particularly *warm* person?"

He shrugged. "I'm just saying. It takes more than a token effort."

"You know we wouldn't have thought anyone was good enough for her," she said. "Man, woman, whatever. I don't see why you're changing your stance now. Like you're seeking her approval, when it should be the other way around, frankly."

He sighed. "She's all we have."

It was true. But that did not entitle her to endless reserves of approval. It never had.

* * *

Nina remembered her own capacious guilt, on the eve of her father's death.

"*I know I wasn't what you—what you expected,*" she'd said in her stumbling Mandarin, as he lay on the hospital bed.

"*Āiyā, don't say that.*"

"*I was selfish.*"

"*Don't think about that.*"

"*I put my own happiness ahead of what you wanted for me.*"

"*Bǎobèi, your happiness was all I ever wanted.*"

"*There was—there was a reason why you came here,*" she remembered saying. "*There was a reason. I could have opened up a store in China. I could have done any stupid thing there that I did here. I didn't help you gain any face.*"

"Please, now. Please. Don't let me die thinking you're so upset."

"I'm not upset—I'm not upset at you. I'm just sorry. I'm very, very sorry."

"Are you happy with your life?"

"I really don't know."

Distress puckered around his mouth, his eyes.

"Sometimes I am, Bàba. Sometimes I'm so happy I think I might burst. And other times, I'm almost the opposite. I don't know why."

"Well, no more being sorry," he said. *"Maybe that will help."*

She nodded.

"Have courage."

"What?"

"Courage, bǎobèi."

She'd never quite understood why he said this. There was so much she still did not understand. Even at her age.

She had all these rangy, spindle-thin notions about the effects of time on families, about what the younger generations owed the elders. What immigrant progress was supposed to look like.

She didn't have the slightest idea about the slightest damn thing.

And she was so frightened by her own cruelty, her capacity for disappointment. So frightened at not being able to properly express how much she loved people. So frightened of spending her life compulsively apologizing. And in each case, her fear had been self-fulfilling.

Courage, he'd said.

* * *

Cate called again the next week. Just her.

"You've lost some weight," she said, a voice behind a black screen. "You look good."

"Thank you."

"Mom, there's something I need to tell you."

Oh, how her heart bundled at hearing that. How the cloud cover shifted inward, cloaking everything. "Same, kiddo."

"Well, do you want to go first?"

Nina shook her head. "No. No, you go."

"Well—" There came the sounds of movement, footsteps. Of fabric passed over the microphone, and then—an infant's soft, wet wail?

The camera turning on, Cate's face suddenly inhabiting the entire frame. "Shana and I, we adopted a kid."

"Oh wow."

"His name's Freddie. He's two."

"Oh wow."

"You're a grandma."

"Wow."

"Mom, you're a grandma."

"Wàipō," she said with an assertiveness that surprised her.

"Oh yeah. Wàipō. Is that what you want to be called?"

She nodded. And now her heart was a hand, clenching and unclenching. Oh, it gathered everything. It mustered every ounce of her into this occasion. "Where did you get him from?" she managed.

"Like, an agency."

"Do you— And you love him?"

"Of course." She could feel her daughter cooling, sharpening, the way water froze into spiky crystals of ice.

"Can I see him? Can I see where he sleeps?"

"Sure."

Cate maneuvered the camera toward a crib of feeble design and cheap material. She pointed it toward a little boy with thick, curly black hair, drooling adorably, kicking his tiny, chunky legs. Nina felt a hasty desire to ask about his race, to make some leading comment, but held it. Courage.

The bed was full of stuffed animals and a heavy blanket, which could be serious impediments to breathing. She wanted to mention this, too.

But it felt like something had gripped the handle of her heart, keeping it open. And love and longing were rushing through her, spraying from the couplings, erupting from fissures everywhere in her unfastening body. She thought she might drown from it all. And what a pleasant thing it would be, she imagined, drowning from this.

"Can you bring him to Massachusetts?" she asked. "To visit?"

"Shana and I would actually love for you to visit us."

How strange, how inconceivable, certain situations might seem, until you were alive in them. Each phase of life was so alienated from the others.

"Oh, okay, well, that might be a bit more difficult."

And her daughter's eyes, gliding in a clockwise arc. "Mom. Come on. Why not?"

She was old and sick, she was drowning with happiness, and still, the petulance that flared in her was enough for her to continue withholding. "It's not what you think."

"Mom, I don't have the energy to deal with this right now."

"Cate."

"Yes. Mom. *What?*"

"Cate, I'm dying."

Her daughter's face froze. "What?"

Dean appeared. Nina spoke a little more. But the words were interchangeable and bled of meaning to her.

"How long?"

It took so long, sometimes, for emotions to catch up. To converge. It could take an entire life to understand who you were and what you feared. There was hardly any time—only a moment, if you were lucky—to gather up your courage.

"It doesn't matter anymore."

"No, I mean, do you know how long you have?"

"I don't know, but I love you very much."

"Mom—"

"I love you so much."

At some point the call ended. At some point she lay down and closed her eyes. Arrangements were made, although she was too tired and happy to consider them. Lightness abounded in her—as if she were finally relieved of worry, of judgment.

And the last thing she remembered thinking before she fell asleep was that she had a grandchild—who was a darling, who would be visiting soon, with her daughter, who was about to learn as effective a lesson as there ever was about being an adult.

CURE

Nick Chen

It was cold. A bracing wind swaying the spring tree branches; the faint ascension of a wind chime—pentatonic, starting on G.

You could tell this was a fancier, more insular neighborhood than the surrounding area. There was a tennis court adjacent to the high school, a languorously rolling golf course, and a music shop, which he'd considered visiting to sell his violin. But he was close enough now for money to make little difference. And anyway, he wanted it with him when he did it.

He stopped at a restaurant called the Anchor to order pancakes, and the rosy waitress addressed him with such sympathy and warmth you'd have thought she knew his plan.

"I hate eating alone," she said, her voice humming. "You know, my shift is over in fifteen minutes. Maybe I can join you?"

His right cheek crumpled, his head bobbed leftward. "I'm fine like this, actually."

"Oh." She frowned and walked away.

He was always making people uncomfortable. His tic emerged like a nervous system response to the presence of anything encouraging.

But he was not used to such blank kindness. He was coming off a month of nondescript highway diners, in which servers with clipped-on name tags and sallow faces treated him as interchangeably as the food they let clatter before him on the counter.

"What's wrong?" his pop might've asked.

Why did something always have to be wrong? He didn't feel like anything was wrong when he was alone, twisting melodies out of his violin, or in his old backyard, staring up at the inkblot patterns of clouds, spinning in place until his eyes felt like windmills and the sky like some swiftly draining liquid that was emptying into him.

People brought out the wrongness in him. And yet, he felt so lonely sometimes he thought he might disintegrate. This was the problem.

When the waitress made another earnest round of her tables, he made sure to note her name tag and smile and say, "Thank you, Janice."

And now he was sitting in his parked car, watching a group of teenagers toss a Frisbee, running and mock tackling each other upon grass so thick it seemed to sink beneath their bodies like one large pillow.

His own gauzy reflection in the windshield revealed a plain, doughy face—each feature scored shallowly, as if to leave enough expressive space for his tics. As if his bizarre impulses were essential to him, scaffolding his earliest memories.

Like the long-ago afternoon as he rode with his pop in the passenger seat of their car. When he became, all at once, entranced by the simplicity of the steering wheel, yawing gently left and right. The vehicle's entire motorized occasion coming to bear upon the smooth, leather-stitched helm.

And how the fascination had persisted, and when his mind was ready to alight upon something else, he found he could not wrench it free, and suddenly he *had* to touch the steering wheel. He had to yank it. Otherwise, he was doomed to reduce every vehicle he'd ever see into an array of circular handles; he was doomed to never learn how to drive. It was as if the very concept of a car were contaminated in his sticky mind.

So what could he do but yank the wheel? And the car, at forty miles an hour down a city block, had swerved and his pop had screamed, "What is wrong with you?"

How could he possibly answer that question?

The more anxious he became of revealing some inner brokenness, the more his mind betrayed him, as if it had a special receptor for self-sabotage. It found new targets of fascination and obsession—things he needed to *touch*, to *experience*, or else risk never having any fresh, undiluted impressions of them ever again.

It settled upon a girl's shiny brown ponytail, dangling like a bell pull on a spring afternoon, and then upon the dark freckle that sat at the center of his dimple, which led to his habit of jamming and twisting his thumb into his right cheek. People began to grimace and recoil when they saw him, like he might lurch at them. Like his tics were contagious.

And how lucky he was to have found the violin, just as he was ready to burst with frustration over his poor grades, his lack of friends. How lucky he was to be able to channel it all into his remarkably nimble fingers, to have an intuition for the way musical phrases needed to be shaped. And how he could rub his hands unapologetically all over a composition. He could leave his thumbprints everywhere.

Most works needed that sort of gropy finessing, anyway. The composer gave you a block of raw material; it was up to you to shape it. And each draw of his bow across the strings became an act of creation.

He became quite good—good enough that it grew into the main component of who he was. Good enough that all his weirdness, all the things that were wrong with him, could be benignly attributed to his violin playing, as if they were the necessary quirks to explain his talent. Good enough, finally, to attend the conservatory in nearby Cleveland.

And then, very suddenly, not good anymore. Mediocre. A minnow in a school churning with more talented, better-adjusted people.

His pop still called him every week. And when he received the first of several care packages in his PO box—an assortment of soaps, candies, socks, and a picture of the two of them at some national park, their arms draped over each other's shoulders—Nick was accosted by a swell of yearning so powerful it spasmed into tears. He missed him.

He took lessons with an elderly instructor who grew thin strands of hair, like cloud residue, in the shell of his ear.

"Could be better," the old man liked to say in his soft tenor voice that harbored a vaguely Balkan accent, sending him home with specific instructions not to practice above a certain bpm on the metronome.

* * *

A crowd of high-school-aged girls was assembling now in the playing field across from the parking lot. The quickest ones jogging over to place stubby neon-orange cones at the edges of the field, demarcating the playing space. Others in yellow pinnies carried mesh bags bulging with soccer balls. The still-rising sun casting such long shadows that it seemed as if their giant counterparts were playing a similar game just beyond them, in the forest.

And the geyser of anxiety. The fear that he might never again be able to enjoy such a calming, heartening sight as a group of teenagers competing in a team sport, unless he somehow made a spectacle of himself. That he was no longer entitled to such moments of peace.

A sparrow perched on a hornbeam outside his car window sang a major third that seemed to vibrate through its slender branch, into the tree's very trunk.

He connected his phone to the car's paltry stereo and put on something soothing—*The Rite of Spring*. He remembered playing this with the main conservatory orchestra, a riot of strangeness and uncertainty to sight-read. Having to memorize the whole piece, basically, while internalizing the cues. The oddly stamping polyrhythms.

He was in the back of the second violins for that concert. His stand partner was a pretty girl from Nebraska named Suzie. They chatted easily during rehearsals, scribbling notes on their sheet music while staring forward at the conductor. He felt like a gentleman, turning the pages for her, although he had the outside seat.

And they bonded over how funny it was, sitting in the harmonic guts of the orchestra. The adjustment, after having been concertmasters their whole lives. How strange it was to cede the melody, which had seemed their birthright.

They went on a date.

And perhaps, because he was drinking, he didn't behave too strangely. He didn't obsess. After dinner, she invited him up to her apartment, which shocked and delighted him. They kissed. It was his first time. When she undressed, he felt like the recipient of an extraordinary, breathtaking privilege. Something he might never experience again.

And the sudden requisite anxiety was so strong, the stress so overwhelming, that he resorted to an old mental compulsion in order to avoid coming entirely apart: He focused on the smooth, taut skin of her forearm. The way it rippled as her fingers danced down his stomach. He felt that if he could keep his conscious mind fixated upon this, he might have enough hydraulic intuition in him to do the other thing.

With his eyes shut, he rubbed his hand in slow circles upon her skin. He let his fingers trawl up and down, from her elbow to her wrist, expanding and contracting, like a steaming basket.

"Dude, what are you doing?" She was staring at him, at her arm, nervousness splashed across her face.

"Oh. I—" His right cheek scrunched, his head jerked as if he were being winched by his hair.

"What's wrong with you?"

"Nothing— Well—"

"Let go of me."

He was trying. He was trying.

"Let. Go."

But if he did . . . if he did, then he might not ever—

"Let go! Let go!" Until finally, he relinquished her, his face crawling with short circuits. "Get out! Get away!"

Word spread. The next rehearsal, she'd been promoted to first violin. She never bothered looking back at him. Nor did anyone else.

He became so lonely that it was almost a relief—a fortifying jolt—when his instructor lightly double-tapped his cheek during a lesson, and then, like someone picking up a small box, readjusted his head to sit more actively on the chin rest.

"What's wrong?" the man asked.

"Nothing," he said.

* * *

Still, there were moments when he played and forgot everything. When he was relieved of his oddness, his stuttering anxiety, and his heart uncoiled. When he was a pane of glass through which sunlight was channeled and music refracted and there was nothing at all wrong with him. Just the effortless way he could pull Beethoven and Brahms and Mozart to life across his bow. Like a gymnast, making sonic ribbons in the air. And his fingers, with their distinct choreographies, like a colony of dancing bees.

There were still moments when he could subsist upon the warmth of his own playing and live inside the melodious reality he summoned with his instrument, when time did not pass so much as pinch off, so that he was in his own private meander, creating music while the world spun on.

Although he was falling behind now. And there was accumulating proof that others were better—unequivocally, in ways he couldn't fully appreciate. No matter how he tried, he failed to distinguish himself. He felt as if his growing technical proficiency, his widening range of expression, only clarified how far he was from greatness. Before long, he'd established himself as a below-average student. And his loneliness, his alienation, added nothing to his playing.

He became certain that no one else—not one single person in this crowded, bustling world, in all its churning history—had ever felt the way he was feeling. No one else had ever experienced the particular blend of anxiety and seclusion and hopelessness that poured through him each morning, that inhabited the hollow, crimped spaces within.

He grew terrified of the obscured faces of the jury sitting in shadowy back rows of the examination hall, grading him harshly for his interpretive choices, his technical lapses.

And then his instructor was staring at him, a tuft of his cotton-candy hair swaying in the light breeze. A muggy afternoon, lethargy hanging like dew upon each note. "Nick," he said softly. "You're failing."

He strode calmly into the Lennon Building, down a hallway of practice rooms. He stepped into one of the soundproof cubes, with its heavy doors, its acoustic foam lining. He was surrounded by the muffled sounds of various instruments, like an orchestra rehearsing nothing in particular. He pressed his forehead against the cold wall.

He screamed.

He didn't care who could hear, or who would think what of him. He screamed and pounded and tore, and when he stopped, the door was open, and a face was poking through the crack.

"You all right?"

Nick nodded. "Sorry."

"Don't apologize. This place will take and take from you." The face was kind, somewhat youthful. The voice, calm and quiet and reassured. The hand was extended warmly. "Darin." It was calloused and firm. Rows of indentations along the fingertips.

"Sorry," he said. "I'll keep it down."

Darin patted the doorjamb. "Actually, how about we get out of here?"

They went to a crowded bar well off campus called Crowe & Ransom that advertised live music. A rowdy guitar duo was on stage, improvising before a lively crowd—the energy so frenetic and consuming that he didn't feel compelled to ruin it. He wasn't even sure how he could.

"So do you teach back there?" Nick asked.

Darin shook his head. He had an easy familiarity with the room and the bartender, a brilliant, understanding smile that reminded him of his pop. Quartz-colored hair gathered at his temples. He bought him a drink. "I was a student, but I left. Couldn't handle it."

"So you sensed a kindred spirit."

"I think I might've screamed my head off in that exact same practice room at one point."

Nick continued drinking—heavily, until the bar's wooden floors slanted, until the cacophony of voices and cheers and dueling guitars deliquesced into something almost lovely: a swaying fullness, an adherence to the one-two beat of his own heart that seemed to encompass everything around him. And his loneliness, kept at a far, hopeful distance.

Darin took him back to his apartment, a block away.

"Convenient spot you have," Nick slurred, stumbling up an endless procession of stairs.

"Did you like what they were playing back there?" Darin asked. "Those two on the guitar?"

He shrugged and swayed.

"I saw you tapping your foot."

"Well, that settles it, then." He grinned.

"You ever play any of that sort of thing, though? Bluegrass?"

Nick heard a squeaky door hinge gliss from E-flat, he felt the sting of an overhead light as he stepped inside. "No."

"I think you might have a real knack for it."

He shook his head in slow figure eights. "I could follow a beat ever since I was a baby. My pop said my first steps were to the second movement of Beethoven's Seventh."

"Jeez."

"I know."

"This school. It doesn't like challenges to its musical orthodoxy," Darin said. "It doesn't like people who don't play a certain way. The instructors provide this incredibly narrow avenue for interpreting a piece, then force your hands all over it, force you to press and mold it into something acceptable for the jury. And sometimes it still doesn't fit their parameters. Sometimes they still don't like it."

Darin was stamping back and forth across the cramped room, skirting its hodgepodge seating—a cream-cushioned dining chair, a ladder-back with spiderwebbed black paint, an angled barstool, and an inviting sofa with pilled gray upholstery, onto which Nick performed a controlled fall. The floorboards were soft with narrow scuffs and the tripod indentations of folding music stands.

"And then once they've gotten it in their head that it's *you*, that *you're* the guy who plays this piece in a certain way, they blacklist your style altogether." He scratched the gray at his temples with his ring and pinky fingers. "Their preconceptions inform everything. They've graded you before you even finish your first bow."

Nick let his head fall forward and back. The room smelled of something cloying, like cheap cleaning solution. Its only other furniture was a plain wooden credenza on which sat pictures of Darin playing with various ensembles, the lone Asian in a carousel of scraggle-haired hipsters.

"Now listen to this." Darin picked up a mandolin and began to pluck. The sound seemed weak and nasal at first. Of a predictable time, forming a melody so loose and languid Nick could hardly hold his hand around it. And then it began to unfold. It evaded the active, searching part of his mind that desired to categorize it, that needed order and precedent.

And how it soothed him! How it luxuriated and spread itself open. While the anxious, thumping parts—the components of himself he'd tried his whole life to suffocate—were instantly placated.

Nick began to tap his foot without realizing it. He kept his eyes closed as he smiled.

* * *

He picked it up fairly quickly on the violin—the sprightly shuffles and major chord progressions. He learned to chop rhythms with the frog of his bow, to let certain notes wobble and slide. He became, in short order, a great improviser. He could keep the pulse going while swinging on the offbeat, while stuffing measures to capacity with virtuosic runs, arpeggiated turns, and heady double-stops.

Darin introduced him to the greats: Scruggs, Flatt, Monroe.

And he thought: Yes, there were passages of classical music that could take his breath away, like gentle blows to the solar plexus. He could still remember the first time he'd ever heard the jubilant final movement of Beethoven's *Pastoral* Symphony, or the scalding intensity of the Paganini Caprices. How witnessing them was like viewing the ocean from the coastline—the interminability of water, its meeting point against the pure blue arc of the horizon, an abstraction rendered visible. A precise expression of the ineffable.

Whereas bluegrass—bluegrass approached from a manageable distance. It beckoned, it flirted, promising a good time, and soon you were stamping your feet and chasing after it. You were panting and breathless with exhilaration.

There were moments in classical music that made him feel overwhelmed, unworthy. Bluegrass made him feel precisely as if he belonged.

"There's so much stagnation and gatekeeping in the industry right now," Darin said, pacing around the chairs after a full day of jamming. "You can't analyze a single piece or performance without discussing where and how it fits in the whole tradition. It's so crowded; there's no more room to do anything new. Don't you think?"

Nick was noticing how all the pictures on the credenza sat in chipped frames, how no two photos included the same band members—which he figured was fairly normal. Meaningful success was so often a matter of experiment and recombination. "Yeah," he said.

They called themselves the Eastern Mountain Boys, which most people found pretty funny, since they were both Asian—perhaps the first Asian bluegrass duo ever. They started playing at some of the local bars, quickly drawing attention. Loud, appreciative listeners. Crowds that whooped and whistled and clapped. An exhilarating new form of approval.

"I think we can do this for real," Darin said back at the apartment one evening, after one of those gigs in which Nick had lost himself in a meander, and his focus had leapt from his own fingers and flown about, settling upon the rafters, viewing himself and Darin from above, enjoying their easy repartee.

"I thought we were already doing this for real."

"I mean full-time. Touring. Getting an agent. Signing a record deal."

"Maybe," he said with hesitation.

Because the notion was terrifying to him. He was a classically trained musician, after all. Bluegrass, for all its *fun*, still lacked sufficient rigor and history—an established framework for judging its merits. It still evoked negative stereotypes of country backwaters, of Appalachia.

And he was beginning to miss the structure of his old routines: the steady cadence of class and rehearsal; the sprawling geometries of campus; the astounding brightness of Mixon Hall, his favorite performing space, whose stage was enclosed by floor-to-ceiling windows, exposing an abundant garden beyond.

"You've got something special," Darin said with gravity.

Nick blushed. It was the first real compliment he'd received since starting school here. At least the first from someone he respected. (His instructor had once frowned and said, "Not bad," after a playthrough of a Beethoven sonata in which he'd only made one mistake.) "I find that difficult to believe."

"I was at your recital, you know," Darin said.

"Oh boy."

He remembered his end-of-semester recital, in which he was accosted by such crumpling anxiety that he'd closed his eyes and basically sprinted through Viotti's Twenty-Third Concerto—swallowing entire bars in the process. Choking on them. His bow breaking its parallel path between bridge and fingerboard, like a speeding car on a wet highway, fishtailing between lanes. He remembered screeching toward the final, inevitable impact—an explosion of rosin powder. His poor accompanist shaking her head.

"You had something special there," Darin said.

"Yeah. A failing grade."

He waved dismissively. "There was something there that no one else could appreciate, but I could hear it. Maybe because we're both outsiders."

Nick swept the thumb of his left hand against the pads of his other fingers. "A sense of abandon, maybe."

"Look, we have a shot at being remembered, here. At leaving a real artistic legacy," Darin said. "I feel like I've been waiting my whole life to play duets with you."

And it was difficult, certainly, reconciling his prejudice with the gratifying warmth of such a statement.

"Now, let's say something catastrophic happens," Darin went on, "like a nuclear winter or something, and ninety percent of the world—people, history, culture—is lost. Wouldn't you want to create something with the greatest chance of making it through? Of surviving that test?"

"How is nuclear winter a qualified arbiter of what's good or bad?"

"What I mean is, don't you want to make something that lasts? Something new and unique and compelling that will move people? Long after you and I are gone?"

"But it's all random. It doesn't matter if it's nuclear war or just a really long period of time. Even the most popular things fade. You can never know what people will remember."

"Yeah, that's the risk," Darin said, his voice trembling slightly. "Plenty of undeserving shit gets recognized—I mean, listen to all the same-sounding robots your conservatory pumps out. But you have to try, don't you?"

He suspected that, for the rest of his life, he'd remember the conviction in Darin's eyes. The intensity of his belief.

"I guess."

* * *

He skipped his semester exams. He made up a sickness so protracted and relentless that his elderly instructor, in concerned emails, urged him to visit the hospital. He transferred his dorm room essentials to Darin's apartment and slept most evenings on the gray, pilling sofa. He received an ominous note one morning from the dean with the subject line "Your Academic Performance" and deleted it, feeling ecstatically free, as if he could finally conduct his own future.

Although there were some days when Darin didn't get up until noon, and Nick, who couldn't practice without waking him, had nothing to do but think of his pop.

Yeah, yeah, you look good. Give me a James Bond. Do a 007 for me.

Dad, that's so lame.

Come on! These are memories! These are for the scrapbook.

Nick was remembering the afternoon of his high school prom. How Isabel Perez had turned him down with a smirk. And no one had invited him to take pictures beforehand, to share a limo. So it had been just his pop, with an old, buzzy digital camera, taking photos of him in the backyard.

Okay, now, just smile. Yeah. Put your arm against the tree trunk and put your other hand in your pocket—yeah. Oh, fancy. Just like that.

His pop, driving him to the Sheraton in the next town over. Radiating such joy.

Have fun, okay?

Some people were strange because their parents were strange—because you never stopped correcting for their mistakes, and because trauma could be inherited as easily as eye color or blood type. But his father was a healthy, reasonable man. All he'd ever wanted was for his son to be happy. If he were ever disappointed, he never showed it.

And this made Nick feel all the guiltier, as he finally called him with news of his dropping out.

"I'm not sure I can support this." His pop's voice was softer, shakier than it had ever been.

"I was failing over there. I like this a lot better."

"Who is this guy? Is he your friend?"

Yes. And his heart split open for the man. For the fact that his pop had spent Nick's entire childhood asking the same question—*Is he your friend?*—full of the same subtext: *Is he being cruel without your knowing?*

"I caution you to take your time with this decision," he said.

"I'm sorry, Pop, but I've made it already. It's done."

An extended pause across the line. The low, tidal swells of his breathing. "Very well."

Darin told him that his pop would understand eventually. "You're too different to play in some big ensemble," he said. "You're too unique."

"I'm just lost."

"The greatest artists have all felt lost in the world," Darin said.

"I'm not a great artist."

"Of course you are. You're just in the wrong medium."

He told his instructor next. The old man nodded, the white hair in his ears recently trimmed. "I saw you at Crowe & Ransom. You and Darin Lee. You were more relaxed than I've ever seen you. It suited your playing."

"You were there?" He remembered, with shame, all the blatant lies in his emails.

"Yes."

"And you know Darin?"

The man's face gathered in a bunch, his eyes seemed reluctant and opaque. "I think he was a student here. Several—many—years ago."

"Did you know him?"

He shook his head. "Best of luck to you, Nicholas."

* * *

They played with exquisite, natural intimacy—they improvised elliptical, upbeat melodies, which they were able to pass to one another with hardly a glance.

"God, I don't know what I'd do without you," Darin liked to say.

"Same."

"It's like we were meant to do this."

On some evenings it felt as if they were skiing down a freshly powdered mountain, borne by an urgency like gravity—the first ones to leave impressions of their wide, sweeping turns, their flumes of melodic flourish.

"You sing at all?" Darin asked once.

"No."

"Same. I have a shit voice."

"Should we find a singer?"

"Nope," he said. "We've got a good thing going. It's the right formula."

They played with preternatural awareness of the other. They internalized each other's preferred licks, preferred tempos. They let classical influences percolate through their sessions, experimenting with counterpoint, modulating unpredictably. They inverted seventh chords and shuttled them back and forth before resolving them. They could improvise for hours, swapping motifs, adding small touches, creating something that was smudged with their shared thumbprints.

And still, they had such capacity to surprise each other. Still, he could be startled by such rapid swells of emotion, such stirring, heart-mangling melodies, that he lost his footing and was dragged from the shore. And out there, unanchored in the cold, bracing surf, pummeled and bearingless, it seemed possible that the feelings passing between them—the shared ambition, the tender understanding, the enthusiasm that kept them performing well into the night—might resolve into something more concrete in the morning. As if the intimacies they nurtured while playing might spread helplessly toward other parts of their lives.

He had it in mind to ask, although he never could muster the nerve.

Until one evening, after a hot, messy performance in which the crowd had howled its approval for hours and hours, rewarding them with ovations, with shots of bourbon. When they were back at the apartment, still breathless with triumph, and Darin had leaned in and gobbled up the words.

Sucked the question right from his lips.

* * *

He was shocked to find his pop one morning, standing outside their apartment door.

He'd always struck Nick as a young-looking man—coasting on a midlife plateau. But he seemed markedly older now: skin pulled taut across his face, his cheeks hollow but pronounced, his hair streaked with startling gray waves.

"Pop. How did you find this place?"

"I can't let this happen." His voice was croaky, tremulous.

"How did you even know I was here?"

"Your teacher told me. Son, I'm worried."

Nick wanted to embrace him; he wanted to weep into his chest. He'd missed him so. And at the same time, he couldn't help but feel as if the party were being busted and the fun about to end. He became deeply and suddenly self-conscious of the mess of chairs throughout the room, its frayed floorboards. From the bathroom came the sounds of Darin showering.

"What are you doing here, Nick?"

"I'm happy."

"You can play bluegrass. You can be in a band. That's not the issue. The issue is him." He regarded the closed bathroom door with trepidation.

"He saved me."

"Saved you? From what?"

"From a shitty experience. From a path I shouldn't have been on. What are you so afraid of?"

"I'm afraid he's using you."

"How can he be using me if he's better? He's the one teaching me stuff. He's the one getting us gigs."

"Call it intuition."

How he hated his father's intuition.

In middle school, he'd asked Ellie Guardado on a date and been so delighted by her demure smile, her shy *yes*, that he'd begged his pop to drive him to the mall to buy a nice shirt and nice pants for the occasion. They made a whole afternoon of it—trying out different clothes, even though there was *something* in the way his pop smiled at each of his outfits, a slight knowing sadness, which billowed and opened fully for him on the afternoon when he sat atop the puffy booth seats at the restaurant and waited an hour for her.

The comfort that was there for him every day after school that week, as news of his being stood up diffused through the hallways.

"Has he tried to be intimate with you?"

"Shit, Pop—"

"Just, please tell me."

"No."

"No, as in you won't tell me? Or no, as in he hasn't tried to do anything?"

"He makes me happy."

"It's not right," he said, voice shaking. "He's much older than you."

"He's a mentor."

"I'm afraid he's manipulating you."

"Manipulating me?"

"Yes. And isolating you."

"From whom? I've never had friends."

Hurt gathered in his pop's eyes, in the wrinkles around his sloping mouth. "When was the last time you responded to one of my letters? When was the last time you answered one of my calls? Other than to tell me you were dropping out?"

Guilt surged through him, but he held steady. Because surely his pop would be more accommodating once he found out that, last month, a photographer for a highly respected music magazine had stopped by their little apartment and taken upwards of fifty shots of them, posed in different positions, and not for a moment had Nick felt self-conscious about the dark freckle on his cheek. Surely he'd think differently if he knew that the profile had included, as its first sentence, "The Eastern Mountain Boys are redefining what bluegrass can be." That they were on the cusp of something huge.

And then came the squeak of water valves shutting, the shower turning off. As the bathroom door opened and Darin stepped toward them, a towel wrapped around his waist.

"Oh. Hello." He extended a wet, pruned hand.

His father took it. "What are you doing with my son?"

"Oh, wow." Darin's face went red as sunset. "Well, it's an honor to meet you. Nick talks so much about you."

"What are you doing with him?"

"Well, it's more like together, he and I are making great music."

"He's vulnerable, you know. He needs proper guidance; he needs an institution, with established mentors."

"I agree that Nick is incredibly gifted, but not in the way that most institutions can recognize."

"But somehow you can?"

There was something sick, almost infantilizing, about this exchange. He felt caught in a custody dispute. And it was clear which side he needed to take—which path led to greater independence, to an audience, fans, to an escape from solitude and strangeness and suggestions of brokenness. Which choice was an exercise in maturity, and which was reversion.

And at the same time, he did hate to let his father down.

He recalled, years ago, misreading his soccer team's schedule and telling his pop it was his turn to provide the snacks for after practice. And he couldn't say why it hurt so deeply, why it made such a sharp impression—the sight of his old man standing beyond the fence at the edge of the field with a bag full of premium snacks while all the other kids scrambled toward the table where they'd already been set up. The sad, stubborn pleat it left upon his memory.

"Why don't you come back home for a while?" his father said now, turning to him.

"Is that what this is really about? You want me to come home to you?"

"I think that if you just step back a little, if you remember the way things were, you might get enough perspective to realize what's going on," he said with calm anguish.

"But I don't *want* to go back to the way things were. They were terrible. Everyone thought there was something wrong with me. You included. You thought it would just *go away*, like eventually I'd fit in somewhere—and the thing is, it actually happened. I've found people. And now you're upset."

"You've found *someone*."

Darin interceded again. "We're making something really new here. We're bringing serious classical form and rigor to the bluegrass tradition. It's fresh, it's compelling. It'll last long after you and I and Nick are gone."

"How old are you?" his pop demanded, and for a moment Darin was unsteadied. His hand leapt defensively toward his ashen temple.

"Old enough to have made mistakes," he said finally. "And to know when I've found something special."

"I am dubious as to your intentions with my son."

"My intention is to make great music."

"Did you purchase alcohol for him?" He gestured toward an empty bottle of Jack Daniel's on the counter. "He's underage, you know. What you're doing is a crime."

"I think you'd be hard-pressed to find anyone who waited until he was twenty-one to start drinking."

"That is despicable. That is a despicable sort of reasoning—"

"What we're doing holds ramifications for the future of music."

"For God's sake! It's not nearly so serious!" His pop's voice, for a moment, rising to its old timbre.

Through the sudden silence came the faint, coin-like drip of the showerhead.

"You're just two people in a bluegrass band. You won't change a damn thing. You'll play at bars for drunks until you become a pair of drunks yourselves!"

And his father, as soon as he said this, made a series of shuddering, grasping motions—as if trying to scrape the words back toward him. An ignominious pot of winnings. Nick noticed, for the first time, the slight shiver in his hands as he did so. The parkinsonian motions. Along with Darin's grim frown.

But it was too late. What was said was said.

"We need to rehearse," Nick muttered. "And you need to leave now."

* * *

They drew larger and larger crowds at Crowe & Ransom, where they had a standing invitation to play, until one evening, when a fire marshal caught word and broke up their gig, to many drunken boos.

They were approached on another night by a local promoter—a slim, middle-aged man with a goatee and long hair that hung past his shoulders—who secured them a gig at an outdoor festival just outside Nashville.

They drank until the morning hours, discussing their influences, their training, their memorable performances. He asked Darin once about his stint at the conservatory.

"It was a surprisingly political place" was all he would say.

And Nick never found the right moment to ask him to elaborate.

Perhaps he didn't want him to. There was something perfect about the vague, surface-level details they had of each other's lives. How the music they made together was the only thing that mattered. And the realization arrived the same way certain melodies did: as a single point, stretchy and dense, which you pulled like a piece of molten glass. Which you drew steadily, tenderly, and let gather a life of its own.

He was in love.

He was in love with the certainty and proficiency with which Darin plucked the banjo and the mandolin. In love with his kindness, his patient guidance when they practiced. And the feeling of being rescued by him, of being granted reprieve from a life of otherness.

He felt comfortable, finally. He felt conscious of his singular talent, which only Darin seemed capable of drawing out. And the difficulty of being himself around other people seemed to vanish, replaced with a longing for crowds, for an audience, admirers. Which meant he must have found a solution to the problem he'd had all his life. A cure.

But they never did kiss sober.

They were welcomed rapturously to Nashville—the only group at the festival to earn curtain calls. And while bowing for the third or fourth time, he stepped in closer, he gingerly grabbed Darin's pinky with his and felt his whole hand engulfed and swept upward above both their heads, as they dipped into a bow.

"People don't need to know about us like that," Darin said backstage.

"Why not?"

"It distracts from the music. People don't need to know about our personal lives."

Which made sense. So much else was happening.

Over the course of several blooming May weeks, as crab apple trees with their pink-cream flowers opened toward the sun and the air heavied with the weight of pollen, they were introduced to Noam Pikelny's agent, they shared the stage at the Brooklyn Bowl with the Punch Brothers, they signed a record deal.

Back in their shared hotel room, after a drunken celebratory dinner, Darin finally hooked a hand around Nick's waist and brought his whole body close. He was surprised at how straightforward it felt, like tumbling downhill. The casual ecstasy when they finally made love.

And when he awoke the next morning, to a headache that felt like a timpani player smashing a cushioned mallet into the soft, swirling matter of his brain, he found Darin already at the breakfast bar, twiddling his pen back and forth like the frantic pendulum of an old metronome.

"What are you writing?"

"Just some ideas."

His toes were perched over the saddle stool's footrest; he wrote in a neat, flourishing cursive.

The birds, serenading
Clouds, parading
Can't hold no candle
To your eyes, blazing
This song, our love's creating

"Lyrics?" He flinched.

"For way, way down the road," Darin said.

They spent several exhausting, disciplined months recording an eponymous album—nine tracks of their shared compositions—which was well received in several trade magazines and a handful of mainstream publications.

The *Courier Journal* ran their pictures on the front page of its Arts section: the two of them at their leisure, their instruments resting against their chair legs. And the headline, THE EASTERN MOUNTAIN BOYS ARE HERE TO CHANGE EVERYTHING.

They became as famous as a bluegrass duo could become. They toured the country. They performed with Béla Fleck and the Seldom Scene and the Greencards. At a gig outside Cleveland, Nick was approached by his old teacher, who grasped both his hands and smiled at him and said, "Good."

He still thought of his pop. Still felt the occasional jab of guilt for not calling him, and the upsurge in anxiety when he recalled his tremors. But the more painful these feelings became, the more justifiable it felt to ignore them in favor of all the readily available euphoria.

"Have you guys considered expanding the roster?" their agent said one evening over dinner. "Maybe throwing in a vocalist?"

"No," he began. "We like what we have."

"Well, actually, I've been thinking . . ." said Darin.

* * *

Sadie Wallace had a honey-smooth voice that could flutter like a hummingbird and resonate as sturdily as a sugar maple tree in the wind.

She was roughly Nick's age—a Nashville native, with blond curls and a smile accentuated by two keen eyeteeth. She and Darin worked remarkably well together. His bright strumming seemed to provide her voice extra lift, carrying it over the other sounds, giving it a natural precedence.

But there was something atonal between her and Nick. Something misaligned—which neither was willing to fix. They missed cues, they came in at the wrong time during each other's solos, their phrasings went in near opposite directions, until the music became almost tempestuous, argumentative.

Darin's productivity, meanwhile, exploded. He became the de facto leader of their little group, renamed the Eastern Mountaineers. He began writing songs that ventured closer to pop than Nick was comfortable with. Against his wishes, they auditioned a drummer and a rhythm guitarist. Their sound grew thinner and shinier without managing to evoke polish. They built three- and four-minute tunes upon single ideas, melodies with hardly any durability. They hewed to the same form: verse, chorus, verse, chorus, bridge, chorus. They made frequent, earnest use of meaningless phrases like *Lose you tonight* and *Everyone, everything*. They drew larger crowds across vaster taste spectrums.

Even live performance lost its electricity. Nick's solos were cut. Improvisations gave way to repetition. He felt like little more than a glorified jukebox, adhering to Darin's printed set lists. And his anxiety blossomed. The rote displays of virtuosity brought old compulsions back. He drank harder, his pop's warning thundering through his ears.

He began taking antacids with his whiskey, just to save time. He grew familiar, then friendly, with the descending steps toward blackout, scraping himself awake the next morning. The crowds grew bigger, although he stopped seeing himself in their applause, their adoration. He became another spectator. It was Darin's band.

"What's going on?" Nick said one evening in an anemic hotel room outside Boulder, while the other band members were out. "What's happening to us?"

"I know." Darin's eyes were brilliantly aglow. "Isn't it incredible? I never thought we'd get this big."

"But look at what it's cost us. Listen to us now."

"What are you talking about?"

"We're completely forgettable. Our stuff isn't even self-aware enough to be ironic."

Darin's narrowing stare, his mouth a thin furrow. "That's not true."

"We're turning into some generic chamber pop band. Any rando can bop to one of our tunes."

"Don't be a snob."

"I'm not being snobbish, I just want to keep our music at a certain standard."

"Then what's this talk about randos? All this gatekeeping?"

"Call it what you want. But there's nothing wrong with requiring that listeners be familiar with a certain framework and tradition in order to fully appreciate what we're doing."

"You're implying that broad popularity somehow lowers the quality of our stuff. You're making it seem as if we've sacrificed something by getting more attention."

"We have!" Nick said, feeling trapped. Feeling the role harden around him. "Look, the mainstream shouldn't be able to access our music so easily. Getting so popular means we're catering to the lowest common denominator. I mean, *listen* to Sadie. She sounds like every generic pop star."

"So Beethoven is a hack because everyone knows his work?"

"Appreciating the full extent of Beethoven's genius and influence requires specialized knowledge, critical analysis. Our songs are three-minute ditties that some GED can get on the first listen."

Darin wore a fresh look of disappointment. "Look, I need you," he said, curling his hand around the back of his neck. "I need you constantly. I can't make music without you. You know that. Please."

And Nick shivered; he felt pressed open. "Okay, then let's ditch all this extra stuff—let's go back to you and me. Let's go back to Cleveland, to trying to make something *new*, something that'll last. Like you said."

"How can we possibly do that," Darin's voice climbing, "without becoming popular enough to be known in the first place?"

"The people at our old bar knew us plenty. Maybe they were enough."

"I just need you right now." Darin shook his head. "I need your talent, I need your love. But I also need your trust."

And Nick was reminded, suddenly, of those last, aching moments in the old apartment, as his pop stammered away. He was accosted by the image of the old man stumbling down a rattling jet bridge, on his solitary way back home.

And he thought, just because someone loved you, just because someone did his best, did not mean he was incapable of hurting you to the point of breaking.

* * *

Backstage one evening before a gig, he noticed their drummer—a man with long hair and a waxed mustache—ingesting some kind of pill.

"What's that?"

The drummer said something; he didn't hear it.

"Give me one."

And at this same performance, during which all five thousand attendees had vacated their seats and were cheering and dancing and whooping, he saw Darin grab Sadie's hand and rub his thumb across her knuckle. He saw the shiny, sweaty brightness of her eyes, her sharp-toothed smile. And his sudden shortness of breath was from disbelief. A patent unwillingness to accept what was before him. A loneliness he thought he'd rid himself of—and which, it turned out, he'd only managed to keep at bay.

The old compulsion visited him—the sense that he would never have the same impressions of losing himself in his own music before a crowd, that something precious had become abruptly unstable, that he would never be allowed to experience it again. Unless.

He lurched toward the microphone, ignoring the piercing feedback. His right cheek buckled, his head snapped left. "Hey, how about another round of applause for Darin Lee and the Eastern Mountaineers?"

The crowd roared.

While he held on to the mic for dear life: gyrating around its stand, thumbing its slick, grated windscreen. "You know, when Darin and I started this group, I was just a mediocre violinist who was failing out of the conservatory that he'd already crashed out of. I mean, we were two hopeless losers, and *no one* thought we were going to achieve anything, especially not our teachers."

The noise gradually settling. A disquiet shuddering through the audience.

"And the thing is, I credit this man—" He stumbled across the stage, swiping at Sadie's mic as he went, the wires following him in a clanking mess. "He fucking saved me. He *saved me* from a life completely lacking in imagination and expression." He threw his arm around Darin's neck, pulled him in, kissed his lean, salty, sweat-slathered cheek. He drew his tongue up against the grain of his stubble, toward his ear.

And the crowd grew hostile. He stepped on an errant pedal, sending a screech of distortion echoing through the hall.

"But more importantly, he saved me from a life of *loneliness*. He saved me from making shit in a vacuum, from never being heard, and now look—look at all you hicks gathering here to listen to us! How'd you like my solo, motherfuckers?" There was a brackish, preemptive gathering of saliva in his mouth, coating his teeth. A fullness in his throat. "Except, I can assure you—I can assure you one hundred percent—that the faculty where we went to school—they've not gained a single additional fuck about us."

The boos were ascendant. An elderly woman in the first row was shoving her middle fingers up in the air in unison, her underarms jiggling. People were streaming out the back.

"They might've—" He threw the rhythm guitarist's hand off his shoulder. He skipped away from the approaching drummer. "A few months ago, we were onto something, and it was pretty fucking exciting, and then we became something closer to this— Well— Oh, actually, this is convenient—" As he vomited all over the stage.

He didn't remember much of the ensuing hours. Just a few sensations—a cold, sandy floor against his cheek. Much agitated murmuring. Being dragged perfunctorily to a hotel bed in which he awoke, hours later, surprisingly refreshed.

"He lives." Darin was sitting at his bedside.

"Hey."

"You feeling okay?"

He massaged the bridge of his nose, humiliated. "I'm sorry."

"You were really fucked up."

"I know. Again, sorry."

"But you're feeling better now?"

"Yeah. Thanks."

"Well then, we need to talk about your future in the band."

"Oh fuck." He sat up sharply, his bare back and shoulders cold against the upholstered headboard. "What the hell does that mean?"

"You have a problem, Nick. You're taking pills."

"Lionel or Keith—or whatever the fuck drummer boy's name is—he takes them, too. He gave me one."

"He showed me the pills he had. They were aspirin."

"You're really going to believe him?"

"You need help, Nick."

He sat up straighter, his skin pushing and peeling against the vinyl backing. "It was one fuckup."

Darin shook his head. "There's the booze, too."

He closed his eyes, dropped his forehead into his hand. "I'll cut it out, I promise, if you agree to start the band over again. If we can go back to the way things were. I won't need it, then."

"I need you to know that I never intended for things to become this way," Darin said, scratching his gray temple. His voice had that old pacing quality, as if rehearsed. "I know that sounds shitty or clichéd, but I really didn't. When I first met you—when we first started playing—I thought I'd found something. I thought you and I had the most special thing in the world."

"And now?"

"People—Nick—people move on."

"I've fucking noticed. But Darin, we sound like *shit* now. You're so obsessed with bucking tradition and not gatekeeping that you've betrayed what it means to be new. You've gone back to being generic."

Darin didn't seem intent on disagreeing. "You and I had something so, so special," he said.

"Don't— Shut the fuck up—"

"And nothing can take that away. I still think, you know, if the nuke were to hit us, it's the early stuff we were doing that would have the best chance of making it through. I'll fucking treasure that, man. I will. I promise."

"You asked me to trust you. Remember?"

He nodded, networks of wrinkles spreading from his eyes toward his temples. "And you didn't."

"Well, fine." Nick was trembling, his head pulsing with dull pain. He became suddenly, uncomfortably aware of their age gap. How many other bands Darin had been a part of. "Okay, I trust you now. I promise."

"Things just—they evolve. Music changes. Our group. It needs a new sound."

The sharp fang of betrayal in his side. "You think that the direction it's going in—this pandering bullshit—you think it's the right one? You actually do?"

"We made the important stuff already. We did it. It's there. It happened." Darin's voice lowered. "It's like when we were together. That first night when we kissed. And then that night when we fucked. That was special, man. Nothing can take that away. It's a memory we should both treasure."

Tears. Humidity welling up in his sinuses. And through the vitreous distortion, he saw with striking clarity how he'd figured—as a stepping stone, a means to a commercial end—in the book of Darin's life. And now, time to step away, to move on.

Although he'd benefited as well. Yes, he possessed all sorts of thrilling memories and unique encounters from their time together. He was a better musician, a household name in some circles. But he'd been, nonetheless, used.

"You have connections; you have a great reputation." Darin sighed, as if it were equally painful for him, saying these things. "You can build your own band. You can follow your own vision. I've been on the other end of this same talk many times, so please believe me when I say this isn't personal."

"But. *Our thing*?"

"It's run its course, Nick. I'm sorry."

* * *

There was little to do now but return home, on a journey that involved a rental car and several sleepless evenings at various rest stops across the Midwest.

A shadow resembling his father was sitting on the porch when he finally arrived. Only as he approached could he be convinced that it was truly him. He was distressingly thin—his eyes were closed, his skin sallow. He had a pair of old headphones with the spongy covers wrapped around his ears. They were plugged into an old CD player.

"Pop."

The moment he woke up, his hands began to tremble. Even as his face came alight with joy. "Oh, son."

"What's going on? What happened to you?"

"Nothing, nothing."

"Pop, come on."

"Well, I'm sick."

The day was strangely warm—a late-winter heat wave was granting hope of an early thaw, although most residents had lived here long enough not to be fooled, to merely enjoy the weather as it came.

The house, as they stepped inside, was exactly as he remembered it. With its richly lived-in smell. Its fibrous, flattened carpet. It was suffused with a quality that was all-encompassing and unlocatable, the fact of its belonging to them—that it had harbored their shared lives.

"What kind of sick?" he asked.

"Oh, well, you know. It's not great."

"God, Pop, why didn't you tell me?"

"Well, things between us haven't been too good lately. And anyway, I didn't want to bother you."

A familiar melody was bleeding through the adjustable plastic headphones. Nick recoiled, the pain delayed but inevitable, like the sudden intimation of heat, surging up through his nerves.

"I really liked your album," his pop said. "Regardless of my misgivings, you two made some phenomenal music."

"Well, I'm done with it now. I don't think I can ever do it again."

"Why's that?"

"You were right about everything."

He nodded, the old sadness in his eyes. He reached forward with his fluttering hand and placed it on Nick's cheek, pressing his thumb against the dark freckle, as if to wipe it away. "I so wish I wasn't."

* * *

They sat together most days on the porch—his father with a blanket drawn up to his chest and the CD player clutched in his shaking hands, a pail of fresh batteries by his side. While Nick tried to embrace the sounds of stillness, to stifle the *boom-chuck* rhythm that still pounded in his ears and through his blood.

"So now what?" his pop asked one afternoon, as a light wind sent pebbles of asphalt clattering down the gutters. As the sun forced some of the snow cover to recede, revealing persistent needles of grass, like reversed crop circles.

Nick shook his head. "I have no idea."

"You can go back to playing, you know. You can start a new band."

He flinched. "Maybe."

His pop gazed somberly at him. A pile of leaves gathered and blew, wavelike, down the street. "The hardest part about being this way is that we're always catching up to our own feelings," he said. "Always looking back in order to catch up, realizing things too late."

It seemed true enough, Nick thought. For how could he have known that those early months playing with Darin, growing close to him, would be the happiest of his life? How could he have known that it was because he'd expected it all to continue? He'd expected it to grow: the steady routine of their being together. And opportunity unfurling in every direction—too bright and endless for him to think of its end. What a shame, he thought, that happiness so often depended on a continuum.

"Although it's not very healthy," his pop added suddenly. "It can get a little obsessive."

Mornings passed, afternoons lengthened. On some days, the gentle heat lingered long enough for them to stay out well past the sun's blushing retreat, to watch the stars pin themselves across the darkening sky.

"I'm sorry I was such a dick," Nick said, one such evening.

"I was selfish, too. I couldn't believe how much I missed you." With shivering hands, his father advanced to the next track on the CD player, its early-millennium *beep* confirming receipt of instructions. "I've always felt lonelier than I could bear. And I feel as if I passed it on to you. This sensitivity to it. I don't know. But I'm sorry."

"Did you ever find a cure for it?"

He closed his eyes, a fragile smile pressed into his face. "Maybe now, maybe this precise moment. The way we understand each other."

He wanted to ask his pop what he meant by this, but his gentle snores were already winding toward the sky. And amid the tinnitic gleam of stars, Nick felt his heart uncoil as it used to. As he recalled how, for the longest time, he'd thought the cure was to be witnessed before a crowd. Or to be remembered. Or to be understood by many. To be loved in spite of his weirdness.

Somehow it all amounted to the same bitter disappointment.

And he'd thought that Darin's gradual pivot toward the mainstream, his abandoning of their musical identity, was what had pierced him. And it had, to a degree. But he'd fooled himself into downplaying the other, truer heartbreak: the grief and jealousy and resentment of knowing someone well, of loving him with love singular and true, and seeing him loved and understood by many others—his heart so easily accessed. Of having to share him and then of having to step aside, to become of little consequence to him—a bauble in his collection of memories. He, who'd needed your love first and most.

His pop smiled one afternoon. "These have been the best few weeks of my life."

They were sitting, as always, on the porch. A snare-drum rain was pattering. Water was gathering in small, pothole-sized puddles. Their divoted surfaces.

"Seriously?"

He brought his chin to his chest. "I could die right now, and I'd be perfectly, perfectly happy."

"That's not funny," Nick said, trembling. "You're not supposed to actually say that when you're sick."

"But it's true." He closed his eyes; he smiled. "Time to stop looking back now. I'm all caught up."

* * *

His father's final afternoon was a warm one. "I would so love to hear you play," he said in a voice like a soft tremolo. Nick assented, although he hadn't touched his instrument since that last disastrous gig; he didn't know if he could ever divorce his playing from the trauma of everything that had happened.

The case had already gathered a fleece of dust. Rosin was stuck like a pelt to the violin's belly; the bow was overtightened, in danger of warping. He wiped the strings with a microfiber cloth; he loosened the bow, fit the rubber feet of the shoulder rest upon the lower bout.

He lifted his right elbow and drew across the lowest, leftmost string. An open G, slightly flat, but warm with familiarity, resonance. He played a steady major scale, three octaves, shifting to third position on the A string and fifth position on the E. Each finger with its own sites of memory, knowing exactly where to fall on the fretless fingerboard. It was all he could manage. When he finished, his father's eyes were closed. They never reopened.

A chill descended once again. The system of warm weather passed over them and on. He took to the road.

* * *

The wind was picking up, sending crumbs of asphalt and pine needles skittering through the parking lot. Across the street, one of the soccer players struck the ball, curving it through the air and out of the opposing goalie's reach, to much jubilation.

It had been while accessing the radio two afternoons ago, flipping acidly through stations, that Nick had heard something he rather liked. It was forgettable and bubblegum-sweet, but with the faintest suggestion of something more interesting. The root of an idea. He waited until the end to hear the song name.

"That was the Mountaineers with their latest single, 'Right Now, Tonight.'"

And then, while at a gas station, as he paid for an energy drink and picked a slimy hot dog off a roller, he saw the cover of *Billboard* along the row of magazines behind the cashier, and a glossy image of Darin and Sadie, arm in arm, in a pose highly suggestive of coupledom.

He wondered what the article would say about them. About him. If he'd be mentioned. If he even wanted to be. If he might ever escape the plaintive misery of existing in the same world at the same time as them, without his pop.

The coast was less than two hours away now. He could be there by mid-afternoon. He imagined the stiff, scud-whipped peaks of waves crashing into him. The foam and the brine barging through his mouth and nostrils, the forced entry. He tried to imagine the spark of wanting to live amid all of this but could not. Good.

And then came a knock at his passenger-side door. The waitress's smiling, squinting face. Her rose-colored cheeks.

"Oh. Janice."

She stuck her hand through as he lowered the window. "Hi. You forgot your change."

"That was all a tip."

She grimaced. "Yeah, I was afraid of that."

"Why?"

"Well." She turned from him to the case laid haphazardly over the back seat. "That's not a gun or anything, is it?"

"It's a violin."

Relief flooded her sweet, round face. Her hair was tied back into a slick cap. "You know there's a music shop right over here."

He looked back. He saw the storefront whose sign was a musical staff, on which the words MAJOR THIRD were wedged between the lines. "Yeah, that's cool."

"Although the owner is kind of a bitch."

"Oh," he said.

"So, do you make a habit of tipping waitresses in one hundred percent multiples?"

He rolled his shoulders. "You seemed nice."

"Well, thanks. But I don't feel quite right taking it. And I actually came into a little money recently, so I don't even strictly need it."

"You can give it to someone else, then," he said, faintly annoyed.

Janice nodded. She seemed to be waiting for an invitation to sit beside him. But he feared that if he extended one, he would lose what little momentum he had to solve his problem. He would lose the impulse to act decisively—even if such an act were destructive. Even if it would be the last real thing he did. Just as long as it would cure him.

"So what are you doing here, really?" she said.

Waiting for you to leave, he thought.

"I'm just asking because your license plate says Ohio. And we don't get a lot of visitors around this time of year, to be honest. Summer, we get people passing through to get to Maine. Then, in autumn we get people who're going north and west to get to the Mohawk Trail or Mount Greylock for the leaves. But not many this time of year. Especially from so far away."

"I'm—" he started. "I am—"

Lacking. Alone. Stricken. Ready.

Each of these were on the edge of his tongue when Janice's phone began to shriek. She withdrew it, frowning. And then her eyes became enormous.

He heard his own shivering phone enter into a morbid duet.

BALLISTIC MISSILE THREAT INBOUND. SEEK IMMEDIATE SHELTER. THIS IS NOT A DRILL.

"Oh my—"

From across the street came the shrill bleating of a whistle. The soccer players gathered briefly around their coach before flocking across the field and draining into a single metal door at the back of their school building.

"Get in," he said.

"What?"

"Let's go."

"Where?"

"I don't know." Although his heart was striding, his mind said, *Forward, forward*, as she tumbled through the door. As they sped out of the lot. "Where's the freeway?"

She guided him down narrow roads, beneath trees just beginning to emerge into spring bloom, stretching their arms across the narrow lanes, meeting each other, forming canopies that would soon be thick enough to block out the sunlight altogether—that, in the fall, would resemble a flaming marquee. "Left here." "Now right." Past redbrick schools and the loping golf course, toward a distant cluster of gray towers. The intimations of a skyline. Blowing through crosswalks and stop signs—the streets empty, the whole town in hiding.

He heard a soft, amorphous melody snaking through the car's interior. Almost harmonizing with the light *vroom* of the engine. Something lovely and spontaneous and reactive.

It was her humming. It was beautiful.

And how strange that being alive could sometimes feel like staying afloat in a narrow, windy inlet, where you could see the waves cresting, you could sense their direction and intuit their distant, buried origins, but you could not predict the angle at which they would crash against the walls, or the rapidity of their succession, or the constructive and destructive interference of their meeting, amid all the foam swells and the churning. You could only react to these bewildering currents.

"See anything?" she sang.

He dipped his neck, scanned the sky through the windshield, and shook his head. All he wanted was to stay alive long enough to play with her.

M.A.D.

Rachel Yen

A short double blast of the whistle. Practice suddenly ends. Coach ushers them back inside.

They march down the dark, narrow hall, into the cement dankness of the locker room, from which emerges a trilling cacophony. Like birdsong for the apocalypse. Each phone in each bag palpitating, as if struggling somehow to come alive.

"Five bucks says it's an active shooter," Rachel says.

"Why would you bet money on that?" says Rianne Montas, her best friend, who volunteers every other week at the Planned Parenthood in Wingham and has endured some fervent protests.

"I mean, what else could it be?"

Whimpers and shrieks break out, like a handful of rocks thrown into water—their scattered impacts.

THIS IS NOT A DRILL.

Rachel slumps against a row of lockers, the slots pressing against her back, her knees against the smooth wooden bench.

Her parents are both at work—one at Lark's Landing, the nursing home, and the other at the urgent care clinic at the far end of the Beckitt Shoppes. They share a car. They'll be worried for her.

"Don't take off your cleats," Coach says, mustache quaking. "We might have to run."

"Does anyone have a signal?" someone asks.

*No*s chirp through the air. The locker rooms are notorious for their bad service. There's a conspiracy theory that Principal Jannick had signal jammers installed in the ceiling tiles to prevent students from sneaking around there and texting during free periods.

"Do you think we're going to die?" Rianne trembles, her long, enviable eyelashes beating like wings.

"Probably not," Rachel says.

Whispers echo through the smelly, mildewy room. Their heartbeats gather around the sonar *ping* of a leaking showerhead.

She has a test next week on the anatomy of the heart. Her head is filled with terminology: *systole* and *diastole*, *aorta* and *vena cava*, *tricuspid* and *mitral*. Her memory is packed with the schema of blood flow: valves pressed open and forced shut; the iamb of heart sounds—*lub-dub.*

"There's rhythm and poetry to it, see?" Dr. Stephan had said, and everyone in class had rolled their eyes, because a test that was 10 percent of their semester grade didn't really lend itself to wonder. Just stress.

But Rachel had seen the pride in her parents' faces as they watched her studying, her brain feeling like a heavy-duty excavator, carrying its payload of knowledge, ready to dump it on the page in one swift, emptying motion. She has to do well. She knows she will (the present moment notwithstanding).

"What if they blow up Harvard?" Gretchen Larks whispers. "Where will I go to college?"

"Yale, I guess," Rianne mutters.

Beyond the high, textured windows is a clear, straightforward sky, a glimmering sun. The sweet, innocent twitter of birdsong rising from sturdy regiments of maple and birch. Westerly breezes. And—can it be—the distant, rumbling suggestion of a lawn mower? Its operator oblivious, perhaps, with big, stifling earmuffs.

Nothing but waiting now. Their hearts galloping nowhere, like a cartoon character whose blurry feet find no purchase past the edge of a cliff.

And for Rachel, the lingering sourness of last week's fight. The approaching possibility that her last extended interaction with her parents will have been that silly, overblown standoff.

How was she supposed to have known?

The girls were having a team dinner at the Anchor, in Beckitt, and Rachel's parents had wanted to drive her there themselves. But the senior midfielder, Charlotte Evans, had secured her mother's Honda minivan, which could fit up to seven passengers. And of the seven invitations she'd doled out, Rachel had been lucky enough to receive one—which had felt pretty cool, pretty gratifying, especially because she lived over in Wingham. But her parents had flatly refused. They'd given her the same spiel about distracted teenage drivers and high mortality rates with which they'd curtailed so many of her other social opportunities.

"And how do you think that'll look?" she nearly screamed. Frustration issuing from her pores. "When everyone else is carpooling with Charlotte?"

"We will take you."

"She offered to pick me up."

"Here?"

"*Yes*. Here. And then we're just going to Beckitt, which is safer, anyway."

"Plenty of car accidents happen in the suburbs. Remember that news anchor who got drunk and killed Candace Chae's son?" her mother said. "Stephen had just graduated from medical school."

"Look. There's no reason why you shouldn't trust me. I do everything you ask. I don't drink or go out past a certain time. I get good grades. I just made first chair. I don't understand why you can't just let me do this *one thing*."

"It is an issue of your safety," her father said. "It has nothing to do with how you behave."

"So you'll just take away my freedom to keep an eye on me all the time? That is such bullshit. I mean, isn't that what you left China for?"

"We left China for you. We left so you could have a better life."

"Right, right." She pressed her palm into her cheek and let it drag. This again.

"Are you ashamed of us?" her mother asked. "Is that it?"

"No!"

She was *embarrassed*, but not ashamed. And because she lacked the vocabulary to explain this nuance in Chinese, Rachel absolved her parents of the need to comprehend it.

"We will pick you up whenever you want."

"It's not just that—you don't understand. When everyone else wants to leave, they'll just get to leave. But I'll have to call you and plan around however long it'll take for you to get there."

"So?"

"It's humiliating. It's overbearing. I'm already, you know, *different*."

"Why? Because you do not live in as nice a town as they do?"

"No, because I'm Asian."

Her mother seemed hurt by this. A ridge formed between her eyes, plunging down her porcelain face, toward her crimped mouth.

"And it's not *bad* different," Rachel floundered. "But—sometimes I just want to be a normal person who does normal things."

"You are not considered normal?"

"I mean—not really, among my friend group."

"So you *are* ashamed of us."

"No. No, not ashamed. Embarrassed, but not ashamed. And not because we're Asian, or, I don't know, not because of that fact alone. It's because of all the—you know—all the *stuff* that comes with it. Like the fact that you're so overprotective!"

Her mother brought a hand to her mouth and burped (a fairly recent habit she'd attributed to heartburn). "Well, this is our final decision."

"Then I don't even want to go!"

"That makes it even easier."

"All that's going to happen is that when I go to college, I'm going to go crazy."

"We will have done everything we can by then," her father said in his calm, dignified way.

And she'd screamed and huffed in a paroxysm of melodrama before retreating to her room, slamming the door shut and planting face-first into her Pima cotton bedsheets, while her parents murmured in Mandarin through the apartment's thin walls at a volume they surely expected her to hear.

"She will understand when she's older."

"She needs to focus on her studies. Her cousin just got a perfect score on his SATs and played piano at Carnegie Hall."

She propped herself on her elbows and texted Rianne.

My parents are so fucking lame

Lol, same. Mine are getting divorced.

Seriously?

They just told me. Dad moving out.

I'm really sorry

"Bǎobèi, we only care about you," her mother said, entering the room.

Rachel pressed her face back into the mask of her pillow.

"Come on." She tapped her lightly on the shoulder. "Talk to me."

"I'll never treat my daughter the way you're treating me," she said damply.

It was a cruel thing to say. But the fight had ignited a rapid blaze, like the magnesium from an old-fashioned camera flash, which had blinded her. And she was unable to see anything beyond its lingering afterglow—her rage at the unfairness, her conviction that her parents were smothering the free spirit out of her.

"Rachel, look at me."

"No."

"Look at me."

She lifted her face, mourning, as ever, the fact that she hadn't inherited her mother's high cheekbones, her sharp nose. How her own countenance seemed so round and plain in comparison.

"You really want your friends to see where we live?" her mother said. "You are not embarrassed by that?"

She shrugged. "I don't care." Although she'd never invited anyone over. Not even Rianne knew what her parents looked like.

"Well, maybe we do. Maybe we are ashamed."

"You shouldn't be," she said, feeling as if she'd already eclipsed her parents' maturity. "It's just a normal apartment."

Her mother smiled. "People change, you know. Their feelings change, their priorities—everything."

"I-know-I-know-I-know."

"We do not expect you to thank us when you get older, but we do expect you to understand."

"I don't understand why you can't just get a life."

"We have one. An okay one. But we hope yours will be even better."

Her phone buzzed. Yeah, it's nbd, they argue all the time anyway

She put her head back into the pillow. Its tearstains had cooled. Already, her anger was receding. "I'm sorry," she mumbled.

"Okay. Go study now."

Her phone shivered once more. Plus, maybe now I can convince one of them to get me a car lol

* * *

There's a calming familiarity to the clammy locker room. Sunlight breaking through the matte window grants the impression of being underwater, of somehow shielding them. And the utter mundanity of this place—its same groaning pipes, its same moldy smell—combined with the unprecedented weirdness of their sheltering, makes Rachel wonder if she's in a dream.

In this dream, she can still remember the cute midi skirt her mother wore to breakfast the morning after denying Rachel her carpool request. She'd never seen her wear it before—a graceful, bright orange thing with a pattern of little white flowers—and was so struck by her mother's quiet beauty that she'd snapped a quick photo of her on her phone.

"That's a nice skirt," Rachel had tried once they were in the car, on the way to school.

"Thanks, bǎobèi."

"Look, Mom, can't you ask Dad if he'd be willing to let me go with my friends this one time?"

"No," she'd said simply. "You know, if you like, I can also get you one of these skirts. We can match. That would be cute, right?"

"—Mom!"

A passing car honked angrily at them. "Mom, that was a stop sign!"

"*Āiyā.*" Her mother brought a hand to her mouth. "Sorry. Sorry. I am a little distracted."

"Isn't that the exact reason why you won't let me get in anyone else's car?"

"There is no problem."

"Look, why can't you just be on my side this one time?"

"I am always on your side. But I agree with your father. And the car will be free, anyway, so it is no trouble for me."

Rachel had crossed her arms and sunk liquidly into the passenger seat. She should have known better than to try pitting her parents against each other. They were a united front, always walking in lockstep when it came to her.

Although the hushed conversations weaving throughout the locker room suddenly remind her of a spate of evenings, weeks ago, when her parents were not so aligned. When her mother and father had argued in such thin, desperate whispers that the winding threads of Mandarin barely reached her through the wall.

"You're sure?"

"Yes."

"How could we let this happen? What do we do?"

"I don't know. Damn you, I don't know."

She remembers her father's tremulous anguish and her mother's steady remorse, their voices kept so low they blurred into androgyny, while she held her ear against the wall. "*Quiet. Don't wake Rachel. Her sleep is important.*"

And how her parents had somehow managed to retain their composure in her presence, to sink their roiling upheaval beneath miles of calm water, only allowing it to surface in the late evening.

"Isn't this why we came to America?"

"We already have our reason for coming. We already spent all our money, our time, on her."

"And what if I leave you?"

"You would do that to us?"

"It's no worse than what you want."

It had felt like a profound violation, like walking in on their making love. The raw, bleeding hurt.

And hearing the same set of questions, night after night: "*How can we do this? What will happen to us?*" Until she realized they were not rhetorical—or at some point had ceased being so. They were straightforward and logistical.

How would they do this? When? Who would they tell? And the slow transition of their discussions to the topic that was perennially at hand.

"We need to keep all our focus on Rachel."

"What if it distracts her from school? What if she hates us?"

"You can't tell her. Promise you won't. We'll both promise."

And then one evening the conversations simply ceased. It astonished her. And her parents emerged from their room the next day and each following morning with the same tired, determined looks on their faces. They continued to go to work and pick her up and ferry her to her practices and rehearsals and club meetings. They'd formed some kind of an agreement out of untenable circumstances. A fresh equilibrium.

She felt equal parts guilt and awe.

* * *

"It's been ten minutes," Rianne says.

In ten minutes, a ballistic missile slicing through the air might cover twenty-five hundred miles.

"Do you think we, like, stopped it?"

Rachel doesn't think it very likely that a hostile nation would send a single missile toward their minor, mountain-padded sector of America. Even if it were a nuclear one—or whatever. No, there were countless even more powerful warheads stored throughout the country, ready to be deployed in an instant. And to have tried to disable even a fraction of those would have led to swift and devastating retaliation.

She remembers learning about it in history class. Mutually assured destruction. Clark Cowell had phrased it as "Basically, fuck around and find out" to some amused laughter. And their teacher had said, "Yes, but consider also how conflict can lead to cooperation. We obey laws, for example, because we operate under the assumption that everyone else will obey them, too. The stakes are shared."

And this reminds her again of her parents.

"Are you happy with everything? Like, with your life?" she'd asked her mother one morning, during the time of hushed arguments. She was in the back seat with her clarinet case and folding music stand, being chauffeured to another extracurricular. And the wind was slapping the side mirrors, the air so cold that she could hold her palm an inch away from the window and still leave the foggy premonition of a handprint on the glass.

"Of course."

"Have you always been?"

Her mother knew immediately what they were talking about. *"I thought—"* She quavered and burped. It was Rachel's first time witnessing it.

"Are you okay?" she said, worried.

Her mother made a brushing motion with her hand. *"Sorry, I'm having some heartburn."* She breathed in and began again: *"I used to think that I could start certain things over, that I could complete them with the same energy I had when I was younger. But I was wrong."*

"I don't think you're wrong."

And her mother's eyes now took up the entirety of the mirror; they were directed at her. "*You're only entitled to the outcomes of a very, very small number of decisions in your life. You know that, right? And you can try to delay some of those big choices, but when you do, your options change, too. You can't expect the world to stay still for you.*"

"Ó. Hǎo de." Comprehension was slow to dawn. Sadness welled in its absence. "I just think that you shouldn't have to stay in a life that makes you miserable," Rachel tried again. And in her broadness, she felt as if she were performing a battery of allergy tests along the tranquil surface of her parents' life—searching for a reaction, some diagnostic clarity.

"*Who says I'm miserable?*"

"I just mean, if there's something you want to do, or an aspect of life you want to radically change, I can manage. Dad could manage, too. I could help him."

"*Bǎobèi.*"

"I'm serious, Mom. You deserve happiness."

"*I don't want to talk about this anymore. I don't want you to ever bring it up again.*"

And so Rachel focused instead on the spitting and popping of gravel beneath the wheels, the street's minor imperfections amplified by their passage.

"*Everything is fine,*" her mother said, bringing her hand to her mouth, gulping. "*There was something—an opportunity, you could maybe call it. But it's been resolved.*"

"What about Dad?"

"*Your father agrees now.*"

"Why won't you just tell me what's going on?"

"*Because it's none of your business, bǎobèi. We need you to focus on your own future.*"

Frustration began to throttle her other feelings. "You know, if you treated me like an adult, for once, I might surprise you. I might even be able to give you some advice."

And Rachel thought she saw her mother sneer in the mirror: a slight, contemptuous rise of her lip. "*Just know that you might spend your entire life convinced of who you are, only to encounter something that makes you entirely foreign to yourself.*

"Hǎo de."

Cars were whipping past them in the opposing lane. Heavy-framed projectiles aimed to miss by inches.

"We ask a lot of you, I know. But we depend on you, too. Once you've endured something, you want to be able to pass on what you've learned." Her mother sighed. *"But maybe not every experience is useful. Maybe nothing prepares you for life better than living through it."*

And as Rachel nodded (in placation, rather than understanding), she thought of the incident from her freshman year on the soccer team: how she'd pulled her back during an unsuccessful slide-tackle attempt and been unable to walk for weeks without terrible pain. How she'd never been as aware of her body as when it was in distress. And how she was never more thankful for the functions that kept it balanced—the million interconnected actions, the metabolic symphony, that allowed her to walk simply, without pain or encumbrance.

"Please try not to think about this anymore," her mother said. *"At least not until you're much older."*

* * *

Chatter begins to rise.

"I don't want to die," Sophie Selman says in low sobs that echo across the cavernous space.

"We're not going to die," Coach mutters with uncertainty. And Rachel wonders if anyone else feels the weirdness of a man's presence in the girls' locker room. Neither threat nor reassurance.

Coach had tried to demonstrate a curved shot last week and missed the ball completely, landing on his ass. He'd spent the rest of practice with grass stains on the back of his track pants, to their giggling delight.

"Stupid fucking phones," Desiree Johnson says. "If we survive this, I will . . . I will . . ."

And Rachel thinks, *Yes*, this is the time to make those sorts of promises. When life's capacity for sudden, irrevocable change materializes like a wall against your back.

Or, perhaps, like a dinner knife upon your plate—a shoring instrument, for whatever you're trying to gather.

I want to be able to travel the world, she thinks. *I want to be in love. I want a family.*

And isn't it all so wild to imagine? How things so far out at sea that they're almost incoherent before the horizon can be borne implacably toward you. A birthright for those who stay fixed upon the shore.

"I want someone to depend on me," she says without thinking.

"Don't your parents already sort of do that?" Rianne says. "No offense."

They do.

"Well, then I want a lot of people depending on me," she says. "And I want a dog. I want to get drunk. I want to have sex."

Someone snorts at this. She doesn't care. She feels greedy, greedy. She feels like someone parched before a puddle. Falling to her knees, angling her head, her cheek pressed against the muddy ground, slurping what little there is to offer. Those first few drops. The unfolding promise of more.

"What if I never lose my virginity?" Rianne whispers. "I knew I should've agreed to fuck Brian, or I could've at least given Ronnie Kelleher a shot at that party."

Rachel sighs. "Maybe it's better to die a virgin than as someone whose only sexual experience has come at the end of Ronnie Kelleher's penis."

"Girls, please—"

They stare blankly at Coach, whose chest empties. His shoulders sag. He shakes his head and walks past the showers, toward a cluster of seniors.

"Ronnie's not bad," Rianne continues. "He just gets breakouts."

"I keep imagining, like, his acne pus dripping down while he's on top of you."

Rianne shoves her. "That is so fucking gross."

She laughs. It seems almost obscene to do so while everyone around her is stricken with grief and terror. But it feels good to laugh a little.

"You should've at least kissed Clark Cowell," Rianne says.

Rachel drags her cheek down with her palm. Clark Cowell is an undeveloped, overcompensating little nerd who unironically refers to the world as full of "alphas" and "betas" (he, always a model of the former) and carries scoliotic copies of Nietzsche and Plato under his arm, as if to hammer home the point. His father is managing director of Lark's Landing, the nursing home where her mother also works.

And she resents the way the other juniors, in their eagerness to pair people together, whisper on occasion that they'd make a cute couple. It makes her cringe—as if her insides need to be wrung of any suggestion of it.

But she did notice him staring at her the other afternoon during precalc, while they were supposed to be silently solving systems of equations, and was the tiniest bit flattered by how thoroughly she could hold someone else's attention. What it suggested of her future.

And she'd sensed him gathering the confidence to approach her as they both waited after school for their parents to pick them up. So unalpha-like of him, with his balled fists, his pits dark with sweat. (She was glad when his father arrived in a silver Toyota, and Clark pretended once again to sink his nose into his little show-copy of the *Republic*, before getting up to leave.)

She is barely seventeen, facing obliteration. And she can't help but desire real romance. To be seen and swept away.

* * *

There comes a sharp cry from the benches beyond the showers.

"Are you serious?" Gemma Wise, the senior captain and goalie, says. "With Dr. Stephan?"

Rachel sees Charlotte Evans nodding, ponytail swaying.

The voices lower, like the hiss of hot water from the sink.

"You need to tell someone."

"I can't. He'll get in trouble."

Rachel catches Charlotte's eye. She frowns and turns away.

Dr. Stephan is reedy and dorkish and dresses like a college professor—his wardrobe is all tweed and khakis and sweater vests. He's rumored to have worked at the CDC or NIH before experiencing a mental breakdown and returning to his hometown, accepting a lowly gig teaching AP Biology to high schoolers.

His enthusiasm for the subject, however, is still intact and oddly charming.

"It's crazy, isn't it?" he likes to say. "It's crazy, all that complexity inside you, keeping you alive in ways you're not even aware of. There are chemical reactions and electrical impulses and a million other things we've yet to understand or discover, and somehow it all adds up to *you*. A conscious being who can form patterns and create a personality, who can learn things and apply them, who can understand concepts like cause and effect, actions and consequences."

Love, too, she wants to add.

The instinct for it. How it can arrive as a realization, a discovery: the conscious mind catching up to the heart's intuition. And what a contradiction it is, to long for this—as if to prepare for a surprise. Yet she does. She thinks, at this moment, that she might never grow tired of chasing it.

Well, unless she dies. *Dies*. The idea hiccups within her. The prospect of such a thing. Her existence narrowing to such an absolute point. And then gone. How utterly inconceivable it had seemed, minutes ago, when she was just a girl running around a soccer pitch, cradled in the familiar.

She tries to recall smaller details, parcels of life she will take less for granted. The crispy chewy nián gāo that her father makes: sautéed in syrupy oyster sauce, flanked by tendrils of tender pork. And her favorite, the delicate xiǎo lóng bāo whose nibbled-out interiors exude steam like the spout of a teakettle. And the lavish admiration she elicits when she plays her solos with the Wingham Youth Orchestra or charges the ball toward the opposing team's goal or meets Clark Cowell's timid gaze. And the monthly trips she and her parents take to the nearest Asian supermarket, thirty minutes away in Hartford. Its backlit signage whose bulbs are always partially or entirely burnt out (once, NO. 1 GROCERY became NO. C RY). Its crates of produce, the bok choy in perspiring bags, the pears and persimmons sunk into cartons, with their individually wrapped foam netting.

"My parents are so dumb," Rianne is saying. "They've been arguing nonstop. I'm sort of glad they're finally pulling the plug on their whole thing."

"Maybe this will bring them back together."

"Maybe," she says. "Although, from the things they've said to each other—some of those things you don't really come back from."

"I'm sorry."

The grainy scratch and shuffle of their cleats against the locker room floor. The thin *clang* of locks rattling against metal hooks.

"It's just that their whole lives, they've been so lovey-dovey. And now they can't stand each other. And it's scary—like they're making up for twenty years of not bickering, like they're discovering these entirely new aspects to themselves and these pockets of resentment that they're letting burn." Rianne's eyes are shiny, the skin around them reddening. "I guess you never really realize how much of yourself you give up when you decide to love someone. Even my thing with Brian. It felt like we had parts of ourselves that were only for each other."

You can spend so much time thinking you know exactly what you want, exactly who you are.

"Is that what it's supposed to feel like, though?" Rachel says.

And her friend shrugs. "I guess."

"Like, you have something of the other person that no one else has. And you hold it selfishly, right? No one else can have it?"

"I did more than just hold it."

Snickering.

Coach is talking to Gemma and Charlotte.

"Because he *told* me" comes one of their voices, muddled with tears.

Others have begun to cry, as if taking their cue.

But Rachel feels no such dread. Only a dull, throbbing disappointment. She wonders if there's something wrong with her. Or if the realization has yet to arrive, if it's still too abstract and far away. A person's emotions can lag hours, sometimes days, behind the reality of a situation, or a decision made on impulse. She wonders how much of a person's life could be spent waiting for her feelings to catch up.

She remembers a strange moment from several weeks ago: how her mother had abruptly craved peaches, and her father had offered to drive to the local grocery store. How he'd returned with a bag of bright oranges that he'd dropped, pointedly, in her lap.

"I should have stayed with Brian," Rianne says bitterly. "We were perfect for each other. God, I'm so stupid."

And Rachel recalls how she'd hoped that Brian Viola might ask *her* to junior prom. How she'd swallowed all her hope and longing and disappointment when he'd asked Rianne instead. She hadn't told anyone, had hardly acknowledged it herself, for fear of getting too upset.

And how she did not realize until they broke up that she'd been possessed by a silent sense of betrayal each time she saw her best friend with him.

She suspects it's the same for others, too—these asynchronous realizations. The way life can grant such fresh, baffling perspectives. Because when news came from China that her wàipō had died, her mother had received the information with startling stoicism, had hardly given away any feeling, until a month later while they were performing their monthly grocery shopping binge. Her mother had passed by the open tubs of silken tofu and begun to weep so ferociously that they'd had to escort her out of the store, let her catch her breath in the car.

She misses her parents. She wants to be with them. She surprises herself by casually considering how feeble the rules are that govern the road. The mutual trust that exists between you and every person behind the wheel of every car. How such a fragile, unmappable skein of understanding keeps you (or someone you love beyond your own capability to understand) from complete annihilation.

* * *

Moments stretch and contract like the caterpillar she notices crawling up the window jamb—the way it gathers itself in a loop and lunges forward. Boredom begins to cluster within her. The prospect of death still feels hypothetical, as if she's being stingy with reality, unwilling to grant it to something she hasn't fully considered and accepted.

She looks through pictures on her phone, which are almost exclusively of her and Rianne: fooling around on the soccer field, doing the sorority squat with their palms covering their rounded mouths.

"Those are hot," Rianne says. "Send those to me."

"Once we get a fucking signal."

"Yeah."

"And also, so long as we don't get blown up."

She finds a burst of photos from a week ago. She remembers the moment with tremendous clarity—the startling bite to the air, the wind steady and powerful enough to send the trees swaying, and her parents late to pick her up. Clark Cowell, too, was sitting on one of the benches outside the building, peering over his Nietzsche.

"Just talk to him," Rianne had said.

"Absolutely not."

She'd called home instead. And her father had answered, his voice murky and choked. "*Āiyā*, sorry, sorry. I forgot."

"Dad? Is something wrong?"

"No, nothing."

"I can just ask Rianne to give me a ride home. I swear."

And her scrupulous father had paused—incredibly enough. He'd shown a moment of hesitation, before clearing his throat harshly and insisting that this was not a tenable solution—not this time, not ever—and telling her to wait a few more minutes for him.

Now she swipes right and notices a familiar pattern: white flowers against a bright orange backdrop. The candid morning photo she'd taken of her lovely mother, sitting at their three-person dining table, her hand over her mouth.

But there's something distressed in her pose that Rachel hadn't noticed prior—the way her shoulders are hunched, her eyebrows gathered in a corrugated ridge. As if mid-retch.

"Is that your mom?" Rianne says, leaning over.

"Yeah."

"Huh. Weird. I think I saw her at the clinic."

"What clinic?"

"Planned Parenthood."

The first ounce of realization is like a droplet of ink in a glass of water, surging toward the edges.

There was something—an opportunity, you could maybe call it. But it's been resolved.

The nausea and heartburn, the covert mourning.

Rianne fans two fingers over the screen; she zooms in on the skirt until it loses its capacity to render, bouncing back in a heavy-pixel blur. "Yeah, I recognize the skirt. It's cute."

"When did you see her?"

"Like a week ago," she says. "Probably nothing, though. We do a ton of general wellness stuff."

Rachel's heart is thudding in great, heavy whacks against her ribs. The resonance traveling through her bones.

She's shocked at how much has escaped her notice, how selfish she's been. Because amid all her gripes over personal freedom, beneath the hissing pressures of having to remit her immigrant debt, she's always relied on constancy from her parents. A mutual effort built around their dedication to her.

She imagines herself, for a moment, as the warhead that may or may not be skidding toward them. And at the same time, she is the ground and the country. The incipient stalk with its head of roots. The destroyer and destroyed.

Rianne is flipping through her own photos now. Weeping quietly. "If this is how we die—if my parents die hating each other—God, that'll be so stupid. So, so, stupid."

"They'll both still love you," Rachel says offhandedly.

"Yeah, and it wasn't enough to keep them together. Maybe that's a shitty way to think of it, maybe it's self-centered, but they couldn't even stay together for my sake."

Rachel opens her messages. She writes to both parents: Did Mom get an abortion? But doesn't yet send.

How little she really knows about living, about the muscles in a heart, or the systems of equilibrium that govern a person's life—some of them better calibrated than others. Some of such delicate balance that the slightest unexpected variable might be enough to collapse the entire apparatus. How foolish she's been not to realize the full scale of what could happen. At any time, extinction. Instant and irrevocable.

She feels a rapid shortness of breath, each moment passing before she can properly perceive it, before she can appreciate having survived it, and prepare herself for the next.

Isn't this why we came to America?

Perhaps it had been her mother's idea at first, and her father had been staunchly against it. Perhaps they'd swapped positions and vacillated until they'd grown sick with argument, reckless with emotion. Until the exigencies of money, time, energy had forced them back to the only consideration that really mattered. Their shared stakes. At some point, conflict became cooperation.

We already have our reason for coming.

She wants to scream. She understands, oh, she understands now, why her parents kept it from her. How the impact of such a disclosure, its searing implications, could warp the topographies of her soul. How its towering fallout could generate such confusion and guilt, such resentment and secondhand trauma—the half-lives of which might linger in her heart for years. This ghost of a sibling.

We already spent all our money, our time, on her.

Her sense of normal has been permanently blighted. She doesn't know how she'll ever find it again. She feels far less independent, less capable of *going crazy* in college, than she did a minute ago. How long has it even been now? And the room is contracting swiftly. The air filling with crisis, the growing untenability of her staying here. Because something is arriving.

She returns to her messages. She adds bc of me? Then taps the arrow icon. She sees the blue line steadily advance.

And with it comes a distant, rising commotion. The swift, echoing patter of footsteps from the school's back entrance, down the narrow hall; voices gathering in dismay. Rumbling. Rianne gripping her arm so tightly that her nails pierce the mesh jersey. Gasps and screams from her teammates, something building, building. Faster, nearer. Hearts thumping.

The blue progress bar, like a missile's steady contrail, paused at 99 percent. As the door to the locker room crashes open.

* * *

For a moment, Rachel's parents are a cartoonish tangle of limbs, pushing through the narrow entrance: Mom's elbow pressed up against the jamb, Dad's nose somehow in her armpit.

"What are you doing here?" she says.

They uncouple and stand there, heaving. Systole, diastole. *Lub-dub.*

"Here. For. You."

What else could they have done?

Mom had probably driven straight to the urgent care clinic—ignoring every warning, every traffic law, calling Dad on the way. Telling him to meet her at the front entrance. And because they knew her schedule and her whereabouts minutely, they'd screeched right into the parking lot and run into the school, prepared to shield her with their bodies, to provide their own blood for hasty transfusion, if only to provide her a fraction of a chance of surviving.

Breathe. She realizes, for some reason, that her parents had grown up riding their bikes everywhere. Back in China, bikes had outnumbered cars hundreds to one.

Breathe. She feels so inundated by love. And how she wishes that emotions could form their own closed circuits, that a person could bear and resolve her own feelings by straightforward reflex, without having to take a real look at them.

A message flashes on all their phones, eliciting a few screams of surprise, and then laughter. A joyful collective exhale.

FALSE ALARM.

She runs forward, embraces them. "*Bǎobèi, bǎobèi.*" But as they steer her out of the locker room, she feels a renewed apprehension. A sense of being evicted. She longs for the brief life, the amniotic seclusion, of twenty minutes ago. Her state of unknowing. She has the sense that once she leaves this place, it will be impossible to revert to that earlier version of herself. She'll need to adjust quickly. And there's danger in this sharp, stinging new reality she's poised to enter.

Still, they push her past the door. She has no real say in the matter. They squeeze her through the tight, humid hall, into the startlingly bright and cold morning. Her teammates all around her. Coach with his arm around Charlotte Evans's shoulder as they veer right, toward the administrative office.

And as they step out, she hears two *ping*s in succession from her parents' phones.

EVOLUTION PRESSURE

Clare Hilldon

Clare Hilldon was enjoying a coffee across from Jacob, her husband of seven years, when their phones began to seize.

"Huh," she said, staring over her paper at the screen's gleaming warning. It certainly *seemed* legitimate, but she was perpetually wary of unscrupulous people—hackers and scammers and such that she'd read about in the news—who could hijack mobile devices, who might try to take advantage of her. And so she was inclined toward skepticism, to find the alert vaguely amusing, until she glanced up at Jacob. His panic-streaked face.

"Oh no," he said. "No, no, no."

"Relax, there's no way this is real."

His height was still startling, as were his heavy, ursine shoulders as he stood up, knocking back his chair. "I have to, to—"

"To what?"

But his expression tightened into a grimace. He stared down at his feet, gripping his chest with both hands, his right wrist over his left.

"Jacob. Honey—"

He staggered backward, gasping. "I have—" And for a moment his eyes went wide with something fearful and resolute and despairing, as he swooned and crashed.

The next voice was that of the operator, over the more trustworthy landline.

"Ma'am, we're aware of the current threat, and we recommend you seek some kind of shelter—"

"No! It's my husband! It's my husband!"

"Your husband? What's wrong with your husband?"

"I think he had a heart attack."

And the operator's voice, melting with futile sympathy. "Oh, I'm sorry, ma'am, but I'm not authorized to dispatch any emergency services to your address at the moment. Not until we get the all clear."

"Please, just, please, as soon as you can. Please."

She rolled him onto his back and slapped him hard on each cheek. She shouted in his face. She tried a violent set of chest compressions, bringing all her weight down on his sternum—practically leaping upon him—until she felt a hideous crack and fell backward, screaming.

And then the agonizing stillness. Beyond the kitchen's ample French windows, cars remained in driveways, homes un-evacuated, Beckitt unmoved. And the magnitude of her sudden isolation became so severe, so oppressive, that all she could do to stop from vanishing completely was focus her attention on the apocalyptic pas de deux of their phones. How their rhythmic palpitations made the glass table hum.

She made a final attempt at mouth-to-mouth but wound up just kissing him.

* * *

There were few people to notify. Just the other partners at his firm, who immediately placed her in a conference call with their legal counsel; then her older sister, Jorie, who seemed too distracted to say anything but "Oh, honey."

And because she didn't want to seem like one of those pathetic types whose only refuge after personal upheaval was work, she resigned from her own firm—which she immediately regretted for the fresh dimensions of solitude it introduced. How it left her idle before death's formal traumas.

"Did your husband mention any recent discomfort?" asked the pathologist, who seemed fused to his office chair. "Anything that might've been triggered or agitated by the alert?"

"Maybe." She thought of Jacob's dark brown eyes, his pewter-gray hair and eyebrows. His bearish presence. "I think he'd been having some chest pain."

"Right." The doctor briefly tucked his lips between his teeth. "Well, high-stress events have been known to induce cardiac arrest, especially if there are underlying conditions like elevated cholesterol, obesity, even chronic anxiety." And as he slid and skittered on his chair toward the mobile computer station, she thought he resembled nothing so much as an octopus juggling multiple tasks. "Anything else you might have missed?"

"How does this help again?" she snapped.

"You're right. It doesn't, really." And with a flippant, final jam of the Enter key, said, "What's done is done."

"Wait—what is that supposed to mean? *What's done is done*?"

Everyone had been so quick to call it a false alarm and move on. Haggard officials on the news were already apologizing, promising accountability and improvements. She, alone, seemed to have suffered a real, thundering impact.

"Nothing," the octopus doctor said. "It doesn't mean anything."

* * *

The chill of winter dawdled, even on perfectly sunny days, as pale lilies of the valley and violet geraniums shot color into the backyard. It became essential that she not mourn excessively, that she avoid thinking of Jacob's steadfastness—how he made her coffee from a French press every morning, how he constantly texted her the names of new restaurants he thought they should try—because too much anguish was unproductive. It diluted her sense of self.

She began to loathe being alone in their big, empty house. She raged at the injustice—how, just as she was finally getting used to being a wife, life had made her a widow. She'd wanted, above all, to evolve on her own terms.

And so she was surprised but thankful when Jorie arrived, unannounced, to keep her company.

Her big sister was a divorcée with a government pension, two daughters from her first marriage, and a son from her second, all three of whom she liked to say had "scattered to the wind." Her life since retiring from the New Jersey Department of Environmental Protection seemed dedicated to finding novel ways to amuse herself—making extended visits to old sorority sisters, reading romance books with scintillating covers, spending several invigorating and later heartbreaking months volunteering for the latest Democratic presidential candidate, and, most recently, bird-watching.

"I need a change of scenery, and you need someone to be vulnerable with," she said, dragging a suitcase through the front door. Whistling, as she always did, at the bright, echoing grandness of the atrium, with its crystal chandelier. "It's perfect."

They regarded each other in silence.

"And anyway, I've missed you."

"Yeah," Clare said. "Yeah. You, too."

She counted three years since they'd last seen each other in person. At a holiday dinner marked by an awkward fight between Jorie and her son over the former's unsolicited financial advice, during which Clare and Jacob had cringed with silent relief at their neater lives, their superior choices.

Since then, there'd been perfunctory birthday calls, spammy emails jammed with pictures of new friends and unremarkable birds, updates on poor boyfriend choices, and, once, a loan request, which Jorie had paid back with surprising swiftness.

They settled just as swiftly now into a routine—gathering for coffee in the morning (at the same table beside which Jacob had died), dipping carelessly in and out of daytime soaps, ordering takeout. The house was big enough for them to be roommates. And Clare was thankful for her big sister's presence, even on days when Jorie spent hours reading her romance novels or standing in the backyard, gazing at the conical spruce trees. Her closeness provided insulation; it saved her from having to think about her future.

"I thought there'd be more birds to see around here," Jorie said one evening. "It's goldfinch season, you know."

"Sorry to disappoint you."

"Not your fault," she responded with perfect seriousness. "Are you hungry?"

Clare shook her head.

"Well, I am. So if you don't mind, I'm going to use your marvelous Martha Stewart kitchen to make some dinner."

"When did you buy groceries?"

"This afternoon; you were sleeping."

And as Clare let herself be lulled by the rhythmic *swoosh-clank* of drawers sliding open, the *click*, *click*, *whoosh* of the stove's arousing, she began to think of Jacob. His weekly purchasing of her favorite brand of coffee; his tendency, whenever he mowed the lawn, to wash her car for her as well. How she'd grown dependent enough on his constancy to coast a little through her own life, to embrace the uncertainty of whatever was to come.

At some point she began to sniffle. And there was Jorie's attentive, motherly understanding.

"You've been through a traumatic experience," she said, ripping a paper towel from its holder and offering it.

"I'm too old for that sort of thing—for trauma."

"What are you talking about?" Jorie moved back to the stove, cracked a bale of spaghetti in two, and dropped it into a pot of boiling water. "No one is too old for that."

"I'm too old for it to matter."

"God, you sound self-pitying." She stirred the stiff pasta until it formed a collar along the edge of the pot, until each strand capitulated beneath the surface, cycling through the water's salty turbulence.

"I'm trying to be the opposite, actually," Clare said.

Jorie was remarkably deft with a knife. She diced tomatoes and peppers and onions with ease, sweeping them into a sleek, oiled pan, in which they crackled merrily. While Clare stood there, awash in strangeness; enveloped by a fresh, unfamiliar bouquet of sensations—the kitchen coming alive with smell and sound—because she and Jacob had never actually bothered to cook. The powerful stove and gleaming countertops had all been for show.

To feel foreign in her own home. At her age. And she wondered, briefly, how many other such ordinary experiences, how many fresh ways to come alive in daily rituals, had she and Jacob missed during their stint as a married couple?

Her guard had been up when they first met—back when he was a partner at a private equity group that specialized in buying up nursing homes, and she an executive VP at a PR firm. His company had hired hers to assist in the rebranding of a newly acquired place called Sunnyvale. And he'd been, of course, handsome and intelligent, but also self-deprecating and funny and deeply curious about everything, even the minutiae of a standard awareness campaign.

She was wary when he first asked her out, even more so when he queried her about exclusivity. But there'd been something flattering and irresistible about his confidence, his romantic convictions. She remembered their first dinner at the Anchor (a bit casual for a date), and his humblebrag about having studied a "scientific mystery" in college—one that engaged his interest in physics *and* poetry.

"It's called quantum entanglement," he'd said (without asking, first, if she were familiar). "Two particles can be light-years away. They can have no relation, no discernible connection, no history, and yet, they can be entangled."

"And what does that mean? Entangled?" (She decided to indulge him.)

"They behave the same way and experience the same things, even though they're not communicating." The flicker of the votive candle at the table's center gave his face a portentous glow. "It's as if they share something essential."

"How do you know they're not communicating?"

"Because the shared behavior is instantaneous," he said. "If they were communicating, there'd still have to be a delay, because nothing travels faster than the speed of light. I mean, technically everything you see is delayed, because it still takes a discrete amount of time for light to bounce off an object and into your eye to be processed as an image."

"Right." She was feeling slightly talked down to; tired, frankly, of his yapping.

But then he'd smiled and said, "That's us."

"Us?"

"We're entangled particles. We're connected in mysterious, inexplicable ways."

Well, she'd laughed at that. Laughed so hard that the candle's flame danced and nearly blew out. But his stare was serious, as if he'd handed her a thesis, a proof that they belonged together.

And as the dates continued, as his persistence grew from amusing to endearing, she gave herself gradual permission to feel incomplete, like half a system. To encounter spontaneous tides of feeling when they were apart—unprovoked stabs of sadness, giddy moments of possibility—as if her emotions were meshed with his.

And when he proposed that she sell her luxurious apartment and move into a nice, suburban home with him in Beckitt, she allowed herself, finally, to submit to his schmaltz, to concede that their souls were perhaps entangled. Because there was a degree of relinquishing and adaptation, after all, when it came to love.

And now that he was gone, what of her remained? What had she left to feel?

"You know you could've called," Jorie said suddenly, over the din of the range hood.

"Didn't I?"

"No, about the missile thing. I was worried about you."

"It didn't even make the news until later," she said. "Everyone knew it was a false alarm by then."

"Yeah, but I had a feeling."

"A feeling."

Her big sister nodded with utter seriousness. "I've always known when you needed me."

* * *

"Do you remember Kevin Rostam?" Jorie asked one night, striking a match, throwing it atop a Duraflame log they'd hauled into the fireplace.

"Of course. God, I was so into him."

The humid *thunk* as they extracted the cork from a fresh bottle of wine. The melodious pouring, before they settled on opposite sides of the couch.

"I knew." Jorie's voice was muffled as she sipped. "I said I didn't, but I did."

Clare snorted into her glass. "You sneaky bitch."

"I'm sorry!" She sat straight up. "But he was a piece of shit."

"So you slept with him to prove that?"

"I knew he was trouble, and the only way you'd stay away was if I ruined him for you."

"That is remarkably selfish and self-righteous of you."

Jorie smiled innocuously. "Sometimes I think my job in life was to step on the mines before you could."

"By that logic, I should be a lot more successful than I actually am."

The fire burned fiercely. Jorie gazed at the shadows dancing across the walls of the living room, lengthening upon the ceiling molding. "You don't consider all this"—she made a vague, sloshing gesture—"you don't consider this a mark of your success?"

"All I know is that I'm old and alone."

"Do you regret not having children?"

"A little," Clare said. "More so since Jacob died. Which makes me think I probably wouldn't have been a very good mother. Too cold, and then suddenly too needy."

Her sips were growing less and less restrained. Her cheeks were loosening like sails.

"They're overrated," Jorie mumbled. "Offspring, I mean. There are better ways of avoiding loneliness than pushing screaming, watermelon-sized little demons out of your vagina and worrying about them for the rest of your life." She yawned. "Not to mention nine months of absolute misery. By the third trimester, you're in constant pain, and you can feel it floundering inside you—like you're just a fleshy vessel, like you're a prop from an alien movie. Maybe that's why men are the way they are: They never get humbled like that. They're never forced to understand how much of life is just meat."

"I've been this way for so long," Clare said, only half listening. "And I don't think I can keep being like it much longer."

"Admittedly, a squad of well-adjusted, conscientious adult children ready to descend upon you might've been exactly what you needed," Jorie went on. "Unfortunately, you'll have to settle with this pile of used parts."

"You're not a pile of . . . whatever the hell you just called yourself."

Her sister giggled. "You're drunk."

"So are you."

"Indeed."

"But seriously, you really do look great," Clare murmured. "Like, if someone told me your actual age, I'd never believe it."

"I'm a lizard and you know it."

"No. No, you are not."

Her sister was long-legged, shiny-haired, although her skin had a yellow sallowness that affected smokers (she'd quit years ago, but the damage was done), and her hair color was clearly from a bottle now. But her eyes were still shining marbles of mischief, her lips voluptuous and peach-ripe. She still projected that lively, effortless warmth that Clare had tried and repeatedly failed to replicate. Because there was a flintiness to her own eyes and mouth, a wariness she'd never been able to smudge away.

"Kevin Rostam was a fucking grenade," Jorie mumbled. "I had to jump on him for you."

Clare didn't remember falling asleep. Only shuddering awake, once, in the middle of the night, and seeing the glowing red bar of the Duraflame log persisting beneath a coat of gray ash.

* * *

She was awoken the next morning by a miserable throbbing whose source she could not immediately locate. Not until consciousness fully ambushed her did Clare realize the percussion was emanating from her own head. It was her heart, pounding in her brain.

She could hardly focus on the handwritten letter that had been slipped through the mail slot, addressed to her.

Dear Mrs. Hilldon,

I want to send my deepest condolences to you over the death of your husband. I know this will come as a shock to you, but, a while ago, him and I had an affair and conceived a child. Jacob was paying a monthly stipend that provided for our son's basic needs. I'd have never bothered you, but his passing has created immense financial difficulties for us. I would be profoundly grateful if we might meet to discuss a potential resolution to our situation.

With sincerest sympathy,

Emma Chou

She handed it to Jorie, who prodded her gums with her tongue as she scanned, her eyes scudding across the page and darting instantly back, like a procession of combers sweeping toward the shore. Finally, she looked up. "Well, that's pretty fucked," she said.

"Seems scammy."

"It doesn't read like your typical scam."

"It might not be," Clare said. "A typical one, that is."

"Well, she knows where you live, at the very least."

She reread the letter. Its swell of implications reminded her unpleasantly of a recently published exposé on Lark's Landing (formerly

Sunnyvale). Something about minuscule budgets and rampant misuse of opioids. The overwhelming surge of unease as she'd skimmed it.

"Does it seem possible?" Jorie asked. "What this chick is saying?"

She shrugged. Because it seemed deadly to speak, to even think coherently, at this very moment. Her heart was simply not up to the task.

"You gonna meet with her?"

She shrugged again.

"Maybe you should. Just in case."

She shut her eyes and took a deep breath, and Jorie seemed to understand.

"Let me know what you decide."

Clare spent the afternoon nursing a bottle of water, ingesting an irresponsible number of aspirin, in an effort to steady her feelings. To wonder why she was inclined to believe the note and its author, in spite of having seen Jacob's straightforward will. In spite of the still-vivid memories of his love.

She felt like someone dropped over an island without a parachute. Falling. And past the sheer canopy of her doubt, through the jagged lashes of her husband's betrayal, beyond the piercing heat of all that intrusion was the hard, unyielding shame of not having known. Of having transformed against her will once more.

She remembered the confrontation that preceded their engagement—Jacob standing in the bedroom in only his boxer shorts, his broad torso tufted with white hair, gut sagging slightly like a knapsack. As if offering himself for inspection mid-time-lapse.

"So I was wondering," he'd said. "Since neither of us found the right person, you know, early on. But now. And we're not *that* old, and there are plenty of procedures, even adoption . . ."

She'd prepared for this conversation, obviously. Still, she felt so vulnerable and anxious before his hopeful inquiring. Indignant, too, at the attendant guilt. As if she were somehow letting him down with her decisiveness.

"No," she'd said. "Never wanted them."

And when he asked her why, she said it was because some people wanted certain things while others didn't—it was really that simple—and she didn't have any sort of in-depth psychological explanation for a straightforward yes-no decision she'd made many years ago, nor was he entitled to one, and if this was a deal-breaker, then so be it, and he'd laughed and sheathed her in his arms. He'd called her his entangled particle and asked her to marry him, regardless.

Oh, the relief she'd felt! The heat of his whole flank against her that night. His chin on her shoulder, arms draped around her waist. How her heart had softened like warm putty.

The announcement was printed in *The New York Times*; they'd saved it somewhere.

"Can I ask you something that you might be offended by?" Jorie said later that afternoon.

"Sure."

"Why did it take you so long to find someone and settle down?"

"No one seemed right."

"You know, not everything in life can be perfect."

"Thanks, Jore. That's really helpful."

"But look"—Jorie hooked her forefingers together like a link of chain—"was it that you were so focused on your career, or on finding the perfect guy, or both, that you just ran out of time? You know, to have a kid?"

"Please stop," she said. "I'm not a character from one of your smutty books."

But Jorie persisted. "Or could you, like"—she lowered her voice—"could you not have them or something? Was it a fertility issue?"

"Look, can you just fuck off?" Clare found herself nearly shouting, because there was something inescapably condescending about a person's pity. Jorie's especially. "I don't need my decisions questioned. I'm entitled to make them and move on. That's it."

Jorie winced. "I guess I'm just old-fashioned."

"You are."

"And, I mean, it's not like my kids add all this richness to my life, you know, when I hardly even see them."

"They don't."

"That being said—"

"Yeah. I know, I know."

She called the woman. She didn't give her a chance to speak. "There's a restaurant beside the music store."

And Emma Chou, who sounded all of seventeen, said, "Yeah, the Anchor. I'm an assistant manager there."

* * *

She dressed up on the morning she was to meet her. She wasn't sure why, but she did, to the very hilt—in her black suede flats and wool skirt, her white tie-neck blouse, gold bracelets, gold necklace, her wedding ring prominent, her hair tied back. Her arms were still sleek and toned; there was a faint constellation of freckles on each of her shoulders.

"Whoa," Jorie said. "Hubba-hubba."

She realized, stepping into the Range Rover, that she hadn't left the house since Jorie arrived three weeks ago.

But a place like Beckitt was too pruned and picturesque to inspire change. It was all sloping fields and well-kept zoysia, wind-bent birches swaying gently at the alighting of local finches. Maple seeds whirling toward the ground. She imagined a snow globe sometimes. You shook it, things rattled, and there was an occasional burst of activity. A weather-related phenomenon. Or a false missile alert. But things invariably returned to equilibrium.

She wanted to make the woman wait, so she arrived purposely late. She parked at the far end of the lot, strolling past the urgent care clinic and the row of Beckitt Shoppes. When she walked by Major Third, Clare waved through the window at the solitary old man at the counter from whom she'd purchased a guitar, months ago, for Jacob's birthday. She remembered her giddy excitement at the idea, her intention to buy the most expensive model she could find, because Jacob had lately become obsessed with this bluegrass violin-and-guitar duo called the Eastern Mountain Boys. He'd even mentioned learning some of their songs when he retired.

And the pleasant, unassuming shop owner had been so enthusiastic on her behalf, so full of consultative questions: "How much time does he have to practice?" "What are his favorite songs?" "Does he know the basic chords?"

Until his wife, who seemed the savvier businessperson, butted in and said, "Dean, you're talking her ear off. Can't you see she already knows what she wants?"

He threw her a weary smile now. A look of kindred melancholy that fortified her as she stepped into the restaurant.

Emma Chou was waiting at a table by the bar. She seemed half Clare's age. Her baggy slacks and restaurant-branded polo were remarkably dowdy. Mom-like. A light, peachy fuzz drew a path from her cheeks to her chin. She was not unpretty.

"My husband—Jacob—was a very careful and thorough man," Clare started. "He left the proper documents in the event of his passing. Nowhere do they mention anything about you or a child."

"Well, I was working on him." Emma Chou's voice was just as juvenile in person as it was over the phone.

"What does that mean, you were working on him?"

"I was trying to get him to alter it. He said he needed to be careful, because he didn't want to hurt you."

"Well. How thoughtful of my doting husband."

And Clare remembered, suddenly, how she and Jorie used to host fake weddings when they were children. Switching turns for whoever got to be the bride. Lining their stuffed animals up in a procession. Making gowns out of toilet paper, asking their mother to buy them pears of a certain brand in order to scavenge the net-shaped foam sleeves of their packaging to use for veils.

And how Jorie's ceremonies were full of pomp and celebration. There were speeches and toasts and dresses with long trains that she'd managed to stitch out of tissues and paper towels. While Clare's were simple and short—only her favorite toys in the wedding party. Her dress took half a roll, at most.

She and Jacob had gotten married at a courthouse on a Friday afternoon, in front of a justice of the peace, with their secretaries as witnesses.

"How did you two meet?" she asked the girl now.

"Well, he came here pretty often."

"Of course."

She thought of the myriad evenings in which he'd returned late. Her pride in not caring, because she spent plenty of late nights in the office herself. They were partners, after all. And how she'd long ago dismissed that pastoral notion held by certain helpless breeds of people, wherein states of poverty and need somehow led to a more acute, genuine form of romance. No. Wealth had no such bearing on love.

"And did you know he was married? Did he tell you?"

The girl flushed brilliantly, averting her eyes. "It was sort of unspoken at first. And then—I guess, well, obviously it became spoken. And then I was pregnant. And it stopped after that. Like, that *part* of the affair." She forced herself to look back up. "I'm sorry. Truly. I would never do something like that now."

Clare resisted the urge to ask how long the physical thing had lasted, exactly. "Look," she said. "Can you get me something to drink? A glass of wine? Something white and expensive."

The girl acknowledged and got up, leaving her to stew in lonely acrimony, to take brief inventory of her hurt, which was like grabbing a hot pan bare-handed. She was almost grateful when Emma returned with a streaked glass, which she swirled but did not drink from.

"Okay, can I see a picture or something? Of the two of you together?"

Emma's face clouded. "He never wanted to take any pictures of us."

"Right. Well, what about your son?"

To this she pulled out her phone, scrolled, and settled on a photo. She held the screen up to Clare's face. Just a kid—six or seven—in a soccer jersey, standing on the verdant pitch. His dark hair slicked with sweat upon his forehead, his cheeks ruddy and radiating good health. Yes, the resemblance was there. The same heavy eyebrows, the same heart-shaped lips.

"And this is a recent picture?" Clare asked.

"It's from last week."

At this, Clare pressed her mouth into a grim seal; she grasped her wrists to prevent their shaking (although her bracelets still tinged against the table). Because she'd made such an effort to evade the violent sense of erosion, but now she was cornered—forced to acknowledge that she and Jacob had been practically newlyweds when he'd done it. That he'd lured her in with all that nonsense about physics and poetry and, in the same breath, betrayed her. "Unfortunately, we'll never be able to know your little one's paternity for certain," Clare managed. "Jacob is gone. He's kaput. In the ground."

"But don't you believe me?"

She was startled by this. "I'm afraid proof is more compelling than whom or what I'm inclined to believe."

"But then I'd need, what, like a DNA sample?"

"And that presents certain logistical hurdles, doesn't it."

"Or, are his parents still alive?"

"They're not," Clare said. "He had a little old aunt down in Florida, but I'm afraid she's not blood related."

"Does he have any siblings?"

"He was an only child."

"Well, I have records of the deposits. You'll see that they're pretty regular."

"He could've been paying you to clean his office."

"I have emails."

This wounded her. She wavered for a moment, before regaining her composure. "Do send them."

"And I guess there's exhumation," the girl said, with surprising frankness.

"*Exhumation?*" Clare could hardly keep her voice from shaking.

"That seems like the only option that'll satisfy you."

"Well, there is another," she said quietly. "Which is that you leave a grieving woman alone. You give me back my privacy."

"I really am sorry about this."

"I'm sure you are."

"But—I think it's fair."

"Fair?"

"To us. To me and Kevin."

Kevin. She turned her head and blinked pointedly, as if water had been thrown at her face. And there was the young boy bearing Jacob's features, projected on the insides of her eyelids. "Sweetheart"—she felt she could call her sweetheart—"I think it's time for you to go back to work."

"Oh. But—"

Clare stood up and strode out of the restaurant, feeling cold, triumphant. She felt like the rich, barren matron who was the villain in most stories—her flats clipping the pavement, her necklace jangling to the beat of her heart, her bag tucked securely beneath her arm. And a tongue of hate licking her insides.

Nestled back in the Range Rover, she looked up the DNA-retrieval process on her phone. She'd only scrolled halfway down the page before she felt a rising sourness in her throat, a gulping inevitability, and vomited in the parking lot.

* * *

"How was it?" Jorie asked when she arrived home.

"I don't buy it."

"She didn't have any sort of proof?"

"She wanted—" Clare's throat cinched; she swallowed and tried again. "She wanted to exhume him."

"That's fucking grim."

"Apparently hair can be unreliable. You have to scrape a sample off the bone to be sure."

"I bet you're regretting splashing out on a burial, huh? If he'd been cremated, you could've scooped some of him up and shipped him to a lab."

"Will you shut the fuck up?" Clare blazed with anger. "Can you just show some fucking respect?"

"Sorry, sorry. I just think—I mean, as soon as you got that letter, I stopped feeling bad for the guy."

"I'm not convinced it's real."

"You're not?"

"No," she said, ignoring the smirk painted on Jorie's lovely face. The irresistible mischief in her eyes. How it must have driven men crazy.

"Wow, I didn't know you took a trip to Egypt recently," Jorie said.

"Shut up."

"Seriously, how was it? Especially, you know, traveling down that big river that goes right through it? What's it called again?"

"I'm serious. Shut up."

"Because it seems to me you might still be slightly in a state of—"

"Shut. Up!"

Jorie prepared dinner that evening as a peace offering. She made a luxurious squash ravioli with brown butter and sage; a hectic salade Niçoise with smoked oysters; a pan of roasted figs, sliced in half to reveal their bloody, marrow-like centers.

And as Clare wolfed down seconds (because *fuck* her weight, *fuck* her figure), she allowed herself an ugly thought—that, if it had ever agreed with her, she'd have made a far better mother than Jorie. She was better than her at everything.

They washed the dishes side by side, just as they'd done as kids at their chores.

"It's a big opportunity, if you think about it," Jorie said. "You can completely redefine yourself."

"I never asked for anything like that."

"Who cares? Most people would kill for it. Especially without the burden of kids. Why not travel? You could go anywhere you wanted, and then you could blog about it."

"I never saw myself as much of a traveler."

"So how did you see yourself, moneybags? After you were done working?"

Clare considered the vacant clade that had been her and Jacob's postretirement. She wondered why they'd never spoken about it at length. And perhaps this was another reason for his, his . . .

"That missile thing might've been nice for me," Jorie said, as they retired to their sides of the living room couch, opposite the fireplace. "I've always been so afraid of missing out on things—not trying enough, not being enough. Knowing it was all going to end like that might've been a relief. In a way."

"Lucky for Jacob, then."

"Were you sad when you got the alert?" Jorie asked. "Like, was there anything you were bummed you'd never get the chance to do?"

"I had other things to worry about," she said. "And I was never convinced it was real."

"Not even for a moment?" Jorie's eyebrows leapt like ballet dancers. "You can produce a lot of thoughts, experience a lot of feelings, in eighteen minutes."

And Clare made an earnest effort to consider this, but when she tried to cast her attention backward to that horrible morning, she was reminded of the powerful scanning microscope she'd been trained to use as a research student—how it sent a beam of electrons at its subject intense enough to irradiate and kill any living tissue. How every sample was of some already dead thing.

It was the same way with memory, she thought. Each purposeful recollection was its own form of interference—even violence. Retrieving it from wherever it lay. It was like rewinding and rewatching a bit of old VHS, wearing upon the tape itself.

"Not really," she said.

And so much had happened in those thick moments after the all clear, so many memories charred by the detonation, raining down like ash, landing in her palms—only to disappear.

She wished the missile were real, too. How much neater it would have been! To have missed all this ravaged aftermath. To have had the simple privilege of knowing exactly who she was while facing the end.

"You know what really got me hooked on bird-watching?" Jorie said now.

Clare produced an ambivalent groan.

"It was this realization that each distinct species represents a successful attempt at survival. Each unique trait—the color and pattern of plumage, the shape of the beak, the rhythm and pitch of a call—is a random adaptation in response to change."

"I know how evolution fucking works," she said.

"Well then, I hope you know you're not starting from nothing."

A notification tinged on Jorie's phone, an ascending pair of triplets. She stared at it wryly, then stood up. "Calling it a night," she said, climbing the stairs.

And as the filigree of evening sounds poured into the living room, as darkness stripped her surroundings of context, Clare began to recall the hours she'd spent with her older sister in their cramped childhood backyard. How they'd made a game out of collecting different kinds of rocks, storing them in individual pails. And how Jorie had always been better at finding the good ones, specimens of all sorts of arresting shapes and colors, stippled with fascinating patterns.

Until one afternoon, when Clare located a surefire winner—a marvelously smooth pebble the color of deep lilac—which she'd shown proudly to Jorie, supremely confident in her triumph, only to notice three of the same sample in her sister's collection. How she'd nearly screamed with frustration.

And Jorie had laughed—her lovely, careless laugh. She'd said, "Relax, silly. It's not a competition." Before upending both pails on a patch of sedge, mixing the specimens together. As Clare sizzled with envy and gratitude.

* * *

Emma Chou forwarded her a series of emails the next day.

Jacob was, as Clare had expected, cautious and restrained in them. He responded to her more sexy messages—See you tonight big boy; You are SUCH an animal—and other salacious notes with a simple ok, or sometimes nothing at all. But her heart began to take on water when she reached the emails about the child.

Kevin needs formula

Kevin's sick

And his more elaborate responses.

I'll get him whatever he needs

His occasional questions.

How is he doing? How are his grades?

The timestamps on the emails matching receipts for bank transfers, the entire correspondence somehow inviting the same insecurity Clare had experienced as a child, growing up beside her more beautiful, popular sister. The sense that she was helpless and uninteresting in comparison.

It felt, suddenly, as if all her maturing since then had been a matter of constructing attractive identities and layering them upon that same little girl. A little girl on whom this injustice had now fallen.

She spent the afternoon performing the sort of home maintenance Jacob would've normally done. She found a bag of asphalt patch in the garage and used it to fill the cracks in the driveway, in which rivulets of grass had begun to sprout. She climbed a precarious step ladder that seemed to grow wobblier the higher she ascended and, with gloved hands, scraped leaves and particulate from the gutters. She yanked the start cord of the lawn mower over and over, like a deranged person sawing a plank of wood, before it finally belched awake.

And as she nudged it in a stuttering back-and-forth across the yard, she could not help but fixate over *what* Jacob had found so lacking in her from the beginning. And she knew such obsessions were unworthy of her time, they were blind alleys of misery, but it was a fundamental prerequisite of marriage, wasn't it? You wanted to be enough for the person you loved. And he'd seemed so certain about her.

Clare's hands were vibrating when she came inside. Jorie greeted her in an apron; she'd set the table with leftovers and a flight of colorful minicocktails whose ingredients were likely borrowed from her dead husband's liquor cabinet. They performed a convincing domesticity, sitting down to dinner.

"Have you considered a dog?" Jorie asked. "Like, something you can take care of and be responsible for?"

"Please, Jore. Just take the day off."

"I just want to help you move on."

"How about you cast that generous, maternal gaze back at yourself for once? What's *your* next step? More trips? More flings?"

Jorie sliced through a roasted fig, considering its seed-strewn flesh. "I guess I've always felt this population inside me," she said finally. "This aversion to being any single thing. I think it's because I just thought I had more time; I felt like I was still growing. Even now. I'm still scared of committing to a single future."

A fist-sized bird landed on a bough just outside the window. It was brown-headed, with a brilliant splash of yellow above its eye and muddy-gold plumage throughout. Its black wings were punctuated by broad white bars.

Jorie noticed her staring at it. "Evening grosbeak," she said.

* * *

Summer arrived in its quavering New England way: a series of false starts and hasty retreats, before a steady quilt of heat finally settled. And with it, the rising chorus of suburban yard maintenance. The droning slap of Weedwackers, the rhythmic *fut fut* of sprinklers.

"They keep scaring all the fucking birds away," she heard Jorie say to herself.

She awoke with a shiver one morning. In a ghostly act of muscle memory, she'd swung her arm over the empty side of the bed.

She immediately sat up and called Emma Chou.

"Hello?"

Questions spewed from her: "Why don't you have a real job? Why can't you afford to take care of your own son? Why do you need this money so badly?"

"I do have a real job."

"Okay, then my second and third questions stand."

"I *can* afford to take care of him. Mostly."

"One more."

"I'm entitled to that money. We're entitled to it."

"There we go."

"Yes. That's the truth. It's rightfully mine—mine and my son's."

"And yet, you can't prove it. I've neither seen nor heard anything so far that isn't circumstantial."

"Well, you're blocking the only sure way. You're being unreasonable about it."

"Unreasonable?"

"Yes. I'm sorry, but if you could just see it from my point of view. I think any objective third party would agree."

"Well then, take me to court."

"You know I don't have the money for that."

And how she enjoyed sneering at this binding paradox. The hint of moisture in her adversary's voice.

"Look—" The girl's tone grew pleading, childlike. "Could you at least lend me something?"

Clare snapped her hand to her waist. "You want me to lend you the money to sue me?"

"You know, he always spoke about what a good person you are. Your ambition, how insanely hard you work. Your kindness."

"Did he ever mention anything to you about entangled particles?" she surprised herself by asking.

"What particles?"

She pressed her eyes shut and let her nostrils flare, ashamed of her momentary relief. "Nothing."

"I just— It was clear to both of us that you were the one he really loved. He and I were just diversions for each other. He loved you—and Kevin, too. But the idea of leaving you wasn't even a consideration."

"Young lady"—she felt she could refer to her this way—"I don't know what you want me to say to this, I really don't. Other than that you are out of your fucking mind if you think you can somehow appeal to a part of me that you and Jacob killed. Goodbye."

Her decision was unimpeachable. She was completely within her rights, regardless of what this silly girl thought. And it was a thrill to be this callous, this cruel. To punish someone for wronging her. She wondered if she weren't a little glad, even, for Jacob's infidelity. How much easier it was, now, to wash down his passing.

"You're not gonna help her?" came her sister's voice from the hallway.

"Of course not."

Jorie pushed open the bedroom door but remained where she was. "Sorry, but, why not?"

"Because she fucked my husband."

"I thought you said you weren't sure."

"Well then, because she's a stranger trying to scam me."

"But you have plenty of money," Jorie said, her index fingers grasped together.

"I do."

"So—I just don't see why—if you really want to part with his memory, and if you have enough resources of your own, I don't understand."

"Jore, there are a lot of things you probably can't see or understand."

"It's just that—you've changed," her sister said softly. "Sometimes I hardly recognize you."

Well, of course she'd changed since that morning. Layers of identity were singed off, her memories smoke damaged. How could she remain as she was?

"But this isn't you, Clare."

Stupid, she thought. Such a stupid thing for Jorie to say. As if a person were elemental, instead of amalgam. As if growing older were not a matter of being replaced, part by part, over time. She thought about the central row of shops here in Beckitt. How she'd seen them all steadily bought out and swapped, like one of those word games in which *wretch* became *fetch* and then *finch*, until the sequence of storefronts spelled something entirely new. You realized these things if you paid attention.

"Don't, please," Clare said. "Don't act like you have this private connection to me. Like we're anything but acquaintances at this point."

"Okay, then let's get to know each other better," Jorie tried. "Let's go somewhere, see the world or something. We could visit the Galápagos and go bird-watching together."

She felt a prick of annoyance that Jorie would suggest such an expensive trip without being able to afford her share of it. "I told you, I've never been the *Eat Pray Love* type."

"No offense, but it seems to me like you have no idea the type of person you are, or the type you want to become."

"So you say, from your fucking lazy river of a life."

Jorie ignored this. "You never told me how old the kid is."

"It doesn't matter," she lied. "He's, like, six, I think."

"So Jacob—he might've been using the girl, too."

Clare drew a long breath. She pulled at the string of her patience and found that she'd reached its frayed, spindle end. "Remember how you asked me the other day why it took me so long to settle down?"

"Yeah."

"It was because of you."

Jorie looked at her, injury welling in her lovely eyes.

"It was because I wanted to be as different from you as possible. I saw how reckless, how unserious you were about things, and I just couldn't imagine being the same way."

"Be careful now, ClareBear, or you might hurt my fucking feelings."

"So if you were going to get knocked up and marry some worthless piece of shit, then I definitely wasn't going to fuck a guy just because I felt bound to some societal timeline. I was going to wait until someone worthwhile came around, and well, look what the fuck happened. Ha!" Her vision was blurring, her throat thickening. "Aren't I a fucking sap?"

"Clare—" Jorie rushed over and planted herself so swiftly on the bed that the mattress jumped. She swung a restless arm across her shoulders. "None of this is your fault. You know that, right?"

She did and she didn't care. She was suddenly so sick of her life in this little snow globe town. Its watery suspension. She hated how Jacob had stranded her here, plundered her future and bequeathed her such miserable considerations. She hated that she might possibly empathize with his motivations—the instinct to put your name to something, the fear of disappearing through time.

And she hated the part of herself that was still too pained to imagine digging him up and unsealing the casket, removing him from the handsome suit in which he'd been buried, scraping DNA from his decayed femur. Because as swiftly and brutally as things might shatter, you couldn't simply abandon your feelings. They waned and atrophied like muscle.

"Just tell me this," her sister said. "Did you really love him?"

She bristled. "Of course. We were *married*."

"Oh right." Jorie slapped her thigh. "I totally forgot that's how all marriages work, right? It's a truth universally acknowledged that two people in possession of separate fortunes are in want of shacking up at a relatively late age."

"I may not have been as *traditional* as you when it came to finding partners," Clare said unkindly.

Jorie paid this no mind. She switched to full motherly mode, adopting a look of heartfelt urgency that Clare found insufferable. "It's just that you seem a lot more upset about the fact that he betrayed you, and that you managed to be betrayed, than the fact that you've lost him."

She recoiled. "Stop-stop-stop. You do not get to make those sorts of pronouncements. My life isn't another one of your little distractions that you can dive in and out of."

"Look, I know how angry you are," Jorie continued in a low voice. "I won't try to imagine how much pain you're in. But it might help to be generous. Not just to the girl. To yourself, too. It might help you move on."

"Move on from what?" Clare screamed. And again, quieter, "From *what?*"

Because it was so terrible and destabilizing to realize that her most cherished memories were subject to interpretation, even after she'd made herself from them. That, in her careful pursuit of what was enduring and worthwhile, she'd managed only to deceive herself.

She thought of her precious job—the disappointment she'd masked during the partners meeting when David Li Sr. informed her that her last name would never be incorporated into the firm's title.

And Jacob's injunction on the evening they'd closed the Sunnyvale account: "Don't ever put me in there," he'd said. "Seriously. Just shoot me instead. I give you my full consent." Which she'd not acknowledged, because he could be so melodramatic, and which only now struck her as something more sinister.

Well, she was glad he'd done the job for her. Glad he was fucking dead, that she no longer needed to waste her time with him. Her time. What was left of it.

"You know—" Jorie adopted a new expression, one of stern solicitude. "It's kind of crazy that you can't see how much I admire you."

Clare blew out a jet of air. Her sister was relentless, in a way. Always finding the right things to say in the right circumstances. She was a chameleon of selfless belonging.

"I'm serious," Jorie carried on. "It's not because you're a badass, or a boss bitch, or whatever. It's because you're decisive. You're not afraid of big choices, because they just give you more of an opportunity to create yourself on your own terms."

"Thanks, I guess?"

"I never had that kind of courage," she said. "I've always depended on things happening to me in order to figure out how I want to live. It's like I've had to triangulate my own understanding of myself. And now I've retired—I was made redundant, actually—and I want to be there for my kids, but they don't seem too eager for my help. So I try to distract myself, but it's a weird feeling, let me tell you, no longer being useful."

And here Clare was accosted by another faint gust of memory. A distant afternoon when their mother had taken the two of them to a water park. How they'd shared one of those figure-eight-shaped tubes and torn down a slide so quickly her eyes had blurred with chlorine and tears, and a wet rope of Jorie's hair had slapped her clean across the cheek. And how they'd emptied into a surging basin that was just a touch too deep, how the force had knocked the wind out of her lungs.

She remembered all the cloudy, ammoniated water, the slow-motion sensation of being suspended in it, and seeing a rogue Band-Aid slithering between various sets of legs. A clump of hair like tumbleweed. How, even on her tiptoes, the thin film of it separated her nostrils from the open air.

And the swelling panic—the terror—as her lungs spasmed with need, as shadows encroached and narrowed upon her field of vision.

Until Jorie had found her flailing hand and taken it, tugged her lightly forward. Just enough for her feet to find purchase, for her to surface and cough and take deep, reviving lungfuls of air.

"Come on!" Jorie had said, laughing. Unaware. "Let's go, let's go!"

And Clare remembered the old combination of gratitude and envy in equal measure, crystallizing as her vision returned, as her coughing ceased. Seeing her taller, sleeker, cooler sister. Able to so effortlessly save her life.

* * *

A letter arrived the next day, addressed to Jorie. Clare found her standing in the kitchen, hunched over her phone, elbows resting on the island counter. Her head was at a playful tilt as she made swiping motions with her index finger. Her foot rocked left and right on the fulcrum of her big toe.

"Did you set up a forwarding address?" Clare asked.

Jorie looked up, her eyes informing on her. She shook her head.

"Then what's this?" She brandished the letter before her. The word URGENT slashed in red across the front. The return address said *Monetorium Inc.*

"Damn. How did they find me?"

"What is it?"

"A bill of sorts." She linked her forefingers together again. "For overdue payments and such."

"You're trying to outrun debt collectors?"

"Not strictly outrun so much as gain a little breathing room." Jorie bent her head in a half nod. "But that's not the main reason why I came."

"What was the main reason, then?"

"Because I'm your big sister, and you needed me."

"Well, wasn't it convenient for you, for my husband to have died when he did."

"From what I've heard, he should've died much sooner," she said, activating the dancing suggestion in her eyes. The effort to downplay the seriousness of things, an entreaty to forgive. "Look, I never asked you for anything," she added.

"You asked tacitly," Clare spat. "You asked for free lodging and a place to hide. You asked for heat, electricity, water, furnishings."

"For fuck's sake—how many rooms does your house even have?"

"It doesn't matter. Fuck! And all that talk of *generosity*. You're no different. You are truly no different than her."

Clare grabbed her head with both hands. She'd been betrayed again; careless, again. All around her, people were on a mission to help themselves to her things. People who had no excuse for their own relative lack of them. She and Jorie had grown up in the same household, under the same economic conditions. She'd worked hard; Jorie hadn't. Nor had Emma Chou. Now they had their hands out.

"I cooked, too, you know," Jorie said. "I cleaned, I took out the trash, I was your Goddamn maid."

"Fine." Clare snatched her pocketbook off the end table; she withdrew a bundle of twenties and slapped them on the counter between them. "There."

Jorie didn't move. "I wasn't going to ask for anything."

"Who was going to help you when they caught up to you and repossessed your house?"

"I would have figured it out."

"You would have figured it out. Like you figured out marriage and parenting?"

"You know, you are the loneliest person I've ever met," Jorie said. "You've spent your whole life convincing yourself it was independence or cautiousness, but it was just a fear of winding up exactly how you are now."

"Maybe I can take after you and try to fuck the loneliness away."

And it was suddenly, vitally important that Jorie understand how she suffered, that she witness the vileness that had arisen from her pain. Careless Jorie, who collected hobbies and flings, who framed her lack of discipline, her endless sampling, as some insatiable hunger for experience.

"You think you can scoot into my life," Clare said. "You think you're entitled to my things, my attention, my confidence without realizing how fundamentally selfish it is."

"Selfish? Are you serious?"

"You've been intruding. You've been a leech. You claim that all you want to do is *help*, because there's no other way for you to feel relevant. You're no kind of individual, you can't do anything meaningful. You hardly even exist."

And yes, *yes*, she knew the arithmetic was all wrong. That her anger was disproportionate and misdirected, but since when did the rage that spilled from heartbreak ever abide by logic?

"So wanting to support you, wanting to be here for you after your roaming-dick husband died, that's selfish and meaningless?"

"It is when you use it as justification for your own neediness."

"I didn't want anything from you!" Her voice grew pleading. "I fucking swear, okay? I didn't expect you to help me. I didn't want it. I wasn't going to tell you."

But Clare had been fooled already by simple steadfastness—by heartfelt avowals whose repetition somehow lent themselves to truth. She felt cursed to be forever looking back, addressing old memories in new lights. To have nothing stable on which to build a future.

"And if you want to talk about selfishness, what about you?" Jorie kept on. "Sitting on all that gold? You could set that girl up for the rest of her life, pay for her kid's college."

"I would literally rather burn it."

Jorie's face grew ugly, constricted with disgust. "Or maybe you're just terrified of not having anything else to show for all your intelligence. All that focus and sacrifice. What did your firm give you when you left? A pizza party?"

"Yeah, that doesn't make you sound resentful at all. Sorry I was always the smart one."

"We made the same mistakes," Jorie said faintly. "You can't be that much smarter than me if you fucked up the same way I did."

"And that was how?"

"Trusting a man who betrayed you."

Her breath hitched—like a tiny hiccup, caught upon the edge of her old self. Anxious, compensatory, vigilant. The needy younger sister.

"Clare?"

She steadied. "Well, the difference between you and me is that I never make the same mistake twice. No one who betrays my trust gets to stay in my life."

She marched upstairs; she stepped into the guest room and began tossing her sister's belongings into her suitcase. Jorie appeared behind her and grabbed her wrist. "I'll do it myself."

And Clare couldn't pinpoint *why* this thought occurred to her, as Jorie packed away her life, but it did: that she would not be the least bit surprised—not the least—if she found out that Jorie had seduced him at some point. Jacob. The two of them, sneaking surreptitiously from a particularly boisterous Thanksgiving conversation, or during the doldrums of a Christmas afternoon.

It would not surprise her if her sister had seen that loathsomeness in him the same way she'd seen it in Kevin Rostam all those years ago, and pounced on it. The motivations would be the same as they'd been back then—when it was never about being a protective big sister. It was because Jorie was a shitty, selfish person. She was a collector.

"Did you ever fuck him?" she asked. "My husband?"

Jorie's marvelous eyes widened, then fell into an expression of genuine hurt. "I don't even know how to begin justifying that with an answer."

"So you did?"

"No! Of course I didn't. And truly, fuck you for considering it." She zipped up her suitcase and carried it swayingly down the steps.

But nothing was beyond consideration now.

You hardly knew yourself; how could you possibly know another person? You thought you recognized her outline—the least and most likely things she might do at any given moment. And you performed the internal calculus based on data you collected, you made an educated guess. But it was approximation, through and through.

"I'm sorry I didn't keep in better touch," Jorie said, standing before the front door. "Good luck."

* * *

The debt-collection letters ceased. As did the emails, the calls from Emma Chou.

"You could be like his godmother," she'd said in her last plea. "Or his grandmother. You could be in his life. I think he'd like to meet you, actually."

"Wow, you sure know how to finesse a deal," Clare drawled.

"Will you stop being so fucking sarcastic with me? Will you please just speak to me on my level?"

"The woman who fucked my husband and is now begging for money from me demands respect! Dignity! Ha! Fuck you. Go seduce someone healthier. Let this sad widow be."

She withstood the shrill silence, the vacuum contentiousness of a long, hot, empty summer. She passed the Beckitt Shoppes one afternoon and noticed, with a pang, a GOING OUT OF BUSINESS sign posted on the window of Major Third. She stepped in, dismayed at how much emptier it looked—the instruments sparse, the raised performance stage stripped of carpet. The solemn man at the register looked up but didn't bother smiling.

"Why are you closing?" she said with no preface.

His cheeks were daubed with uneven stubble, his hair thick but laced with gray. "My wife is dying."

"Oh. I'm so sorry."

"Let me know if you need any help finding anything."

"I recently lost my husband," she said. "It was unexpected."

Tenderness beaded in his eyes. "Well, my condolences, too." His jaw trembled. "How are you handling it?"

"Poorly." She laughed a little. "On pretty much all fronts."

The man smiled. "Same. God, I'm so scared. And I feel so guilty for it, because my wife—she's the one who's actually suffering. My problem is just trying to conceive of life without her. To keep up some working version of myself."

"That's the tougher task in my case," she said. "My husband got off pretty easy."

He placed both palms on the glass counter. "Tell me this: How can a person be almost seventy and still have no idea how to live? What have I been doing all this time?"

"It's not like you've wasted it."

"No, of course not," he said soberly. "I guess you find ways to adapt. I just hope I have enough time for all the trial and error, you know?"

Futility broke over her. All at once, her refusals seemed inextricably linked to control, to maintaining some reliable form of existence. "Yeah."

Clare awoke a week later to a voicemail:

"Hi, this message is for Mrs. Clare Lang—oh, Hilldon. Anyway, I'm calling from Wallace Hill Memorials to inform you of an act of vandalism committed upon your late husband's grave site. As you, uh, may know, these sites, after they're dug out and the departed is placed within, the earth that we use to cover can take a while to settle and reintegrate into the local ecosystem. So, whoever had the intention of disturbing Mr. Lang's grave was able to reach the actual, uh, funerary apparatus. Although, thankfully, this person was not able to open it in order to access the, uh, the remains. Obviously, we'll replace the site and we've contacted the police, and if you'd like, we'd also be happy to offer you a complimentary reburial—"

She put the phone down, astonished by the sudden scale of her desertions.

She realized, *I have no one to love.*

And she began to cry. She could not remember ever crying harder, or longer, or for a less-discernible reason. She wore her hand like a mask and released a gale of grief and anger and shame and betrayal and regret and relief.

I have no one left to love.

All of which threatened to carry her off and deposit her on the sunken margins of her next life, with no foothold, her nostrils just barely kissing the surface, once again.

And her sister standing there, with her fingers hooked together.

* * *

She was finally cleaning out the guest room, sweeping the blond strands of hair from the pillow, when she noticed a book tucked beneath the sheets. Left there haphazardly, it seemed, during Jorie's quick evacuation.

It was a stubby, travel-sized atlas of South America. Its corner folded to a page on the Galápagos Islands. And a picture of a dainty bird, beneath which the text was underlined:

The Galápagos finches. Charles Darwin famously noted their varying beak sizes, which ultimately contributed to his theory of evolution. He hypothesized that all finches had a common ancestor that, when brought into new environments, developed traits that allowed it to better adapt to its surroundings. The Galápagos, comprising numerous islands of varying sizes and ecosystems, were key in allowing for rapid and robust differentiation, creating a classic example of adaptive radiation.

In the margins was a note, in Jorie's handwriting: *Tell her she isn't starting from nothing.*

Clare closed her eyes and heard a sharp, unfamiliar sound, a mewl of pain—looked around and realized it had come from her. She smiled at the splayed-open book in her hands. "You sneaky bitch," she hiccupped. Weeks had passed since she'd last heard from Jorie, from Emma. She had no firmer grip on her past, no clearer an idea of her future. She had only the sudden enormity of her intact, inalienable self. And what an alarming privilege it was to feel so unmapped, to find such occasion for courage and exploration, to accept that life could change irreversibly, without warning. And to know that she would survive, regardless.

Her old life was gone. But here—*right here*—was a gorgeous new one. New surroundings. Fresh DNA. Such myriad ways to adapt, to say *yes*, to change and fail, to say *yes* again. She'd thought that all she knew about herself came from memory, from the past, but how could that be when so much had yet to be experienced? Perhaps you were expansive in all sorts of cramped, interior ways: a parachute stuffed in a backpack. And you never realized the extent of your capacity to become until you were given the space and opportunity to billow.

She stood up, feeling featherlight.

Jacob's ill-begotten money could pay for Kevin's college and scoop Jorie out of debt, and still, there was enough of her own with which to throw a dart blindly at a map and run away, to evolve. To learn an appreciation for birds from her big sister, her entangled particle.

She called Jorie. The line rang twice before she was sent to voicemail. She tried again—the same thing. So she found her most recent address and put it in her phone. She got in the Range Rover and texted her:

So how many kinds of finches are there?

She drove off.

BIRCHES

Chase Sun

The regional headquarters for the Massachusetts Emergency Management Agency were located on the top floor of the Wingham DMV building—a beige block structure designed, Chase thought, to evoke vague existential terror. Eternity's unadorned doorstep.

The handoff was supposed to happen at 8:00 AM sharp. But it was beautiful outside. The wind possessed a faintly humid chill—the crumbled remnants of a brittle winter. The sun was bright and complex, and the office high enough to supply a generous view of the rolling, freshly verdant Berkshires.

"You're late," Dan Hinge said.

Chase nodded. "Sorry, sorry."

He was one of three contracted employees who handled the morning shifts—alongside Felicity, who took smoke breaks every half hour and could go through nearly a pack a day, and Trent, who was ancient and only occasionally sociable.

"If you're lucky, you'll never need to perform your responsibilities ever," Dan had said with a chuckle when he'd first interviewed. "It's a quiet part of a quiet state."

But test calls still came in every once in a while. Drills run by officious supervisors at random times, mostly for weather-related phenomena: flash floods, tornadoes, hurricanes. Once, a test had arrived in the form of a "catastrophic biological contamination event," which had given them all a good kick.

Chase did not think he'd find such a drill very interesting right now. He'd not slept much the past few nights. A brief, unexpected quarrel with Mick had spilled over into the next day and the day after that. He was rattled and exhausted.

"You look like ass," Felicity said in her husky voice as he slouched toward their shared desk.

"Maybe I should take to smoking."

"Ha. Ha."

He collapsed into his chair, thumping his thermos on the desk. Behind the adjacent cubicle wall, Trent jumped.

"Hey," Felicity warned. "Wanna share what's on your mind before you give the old man a heart attack?"

He unscrewed the lid, coffee greeting him with a plume of steam. "What would you do if you learned your partner was kind of an ass online?" he said.

"Hmm." She tapped her mouth with her fingers, a compulsion that usually preceded a cigarette break. "Only online? Not in person?"

"No. At least, I don't think so."

"What kind of an ass are we talking about, here?"

"A troll, I guess. Someone who insults another person and tells him to kill himself."

She raised her shoulders toward her cheeks. "Well, I'd have a conversation about it, but unless it were part of some larger, real-world pattern, I think I would just tell him to knock it off and move on."

"Really?"

"I mean, it's just a different reality—the lives people have online versus in the real world. It's like video games. Just 'cause a guy wants to shoot up an intersection in a game doesn't mean he has any sort of inclination to do that in real life."

Chase closed his eyes and nodded, as if coaxing this bit of reasoning down his throat—and as soon as he did so, he felt the warm ministrations of sleep begin to carry him off.

"Hey—wake up." Felicity flicked his temple. "Dan's in a mood today."

His weariness reminded him, chillingly, of a dinner he and Mick had once had with two friends on the verge of a breakup. How the hungry exhaustion in their faces suggested evenings full of conflict punctuated by fucking, and the thickening air of capitulation was just another thing to argue over.

He snapped to attention once again as a call blared.

Felicity picked it up and put it on speaker. "—threat inbound. Seek immediate shelter. This is not a drill. Estestest."

"All right, go time," she said, marvelously calm.

She initiated the countdown clock, she recorded the estimated time to impact. She clicked the notice that would activate alarm sirens and interrupt news broadcasts across Hampden County. She tapped with a focus and precision that he could not possibly emulate.

"Chase—come on."

Yes, right. He had a job to do. A straightforward job. Although—had he heard the instructions correctly? Because the test script was off. Key phrases seemed missing. Others, unfamiliar, had been added in. *This is not a drill.* Well, it had to be; the alternative was implausible in a million different ways.

But Chase was delirious with exhaustion, in no condition to interpret orders. Only to follow them. And to know that the script was sacred; it was the partition through which the hypothetical became reality. Each word was meaningful. *This is not a drill.*

* * *

He and Mick had met at one of their friend Ollie's "legendary" board game nights, both of them first-timers. Strangers to everyone but the host.

"I guess most are taken already." Ollie had frowned, gesturing at a shelf. "I had Boggle, the Game of Life, Operation, Jenga, Catan, Ticket to Ride."

"No Monopoly?" Chase said.

"Absolutely not. Friends don't let friends play Monopoly."

"What about Twister?"

"Of course. How do you think we move to the orgy part of the night?"

They settled for the only remaining thing they both knew how to play: Snakes and Ladders. They brought the faded game board out onto the patio, feeling like kids, grinning in mutual embarrassment.

"Isn't it chutes?" Chase asked. "Chutes and ladders?"

"The game as it originated in India always involved snakes," Ollie said solemnly. "Colonialism brought it here and capitalism replaced the snakes with chutes, but this is the more authentic version."

"And where are the super-traditional, culturally significant game pieces?" Mick said.

"Lost them a long time ago. Just use whatever."

Chase had some loose change in his pocket. He gave himself a penny. Mick smiled wryly—his sleek hair like the flourish of an ink pen, a tiny chip in his front tooth—and picked up a dime.

Roll, three, forward. A ladder right there. Up.

"So what do you do for a living?" Mick asked first.

"I work at the state warning point for emergency communications."

Another lucky roll, narrowly avoiding a snake's goofy cartoon jaws.

"What sorts of emergencies?"

"Anything, really. Terrorist threats, attacks by foreign governments, environmental disasters." (He was inflating his importance, here; they'd only ever conducted tests of these sorts of things.) "Most of it is weather related, though."

"Well, thank you for the snow days."

"Those were probably school district decisions."

Another ladder. The penny was halfway up the board already.

"You?"

Mick rubbed his handsome jaw; he massaged the palm of his left hand with his right thumb. "I work at the nursing home, Lark's Landing."

"Oh," he said. "That's nice."

"But only part-time."

A tough roll sent his penny tumbling. "Down the digestive tract I go."

"My main source of income is actually betting."

"Ah." And Chase's heart sank a little, because there was always *something*, wasn't there? "So do you go to Vegas a lot?" he asked, rolling another four, sending him down a farther procession of snake guts, to be shit back out at the start.

"No."

"Oh God, Reno? Atlantic City?"

"No, no. It's all online. And it's mostly esports. Video games."

Well, this seemed a bit better, Chase thought. Profoundly nerdy, but a bit more civilized. A bit less potentially deviant. He miscounted his next roll; Mick didn't seem to notice.

Or perhaps he was kidding himself.

The stone patio provided a gorgeous view of Ollie's sprawling backyard—empty, now, in the falling evening; hemmed by a color guard of maple, pine, elm. All the other guys eventually went back inside, where lights blazed from the kitchen and living room. Only the two of them remained, sitting, talking.

Chase told him about his favorite hiking spots up and down Mount Greylock, how his younger sister, Janice, was a waitress who wanted to be a singer.

Mick told him about his medically diagnosable sweaty hands, of which he was so self-conscious that he made biyearly trips to a plastic surgeon in order to have grids of Botox injected into the pores of his palms.

"Seems a little extreme, don't you think?" Chase had said.

"It's very low-risk."

"What if they swell up and you look like Mickey Mouse for a month?"

"Speech to text, I guess."

They left together before the end of the night, Ollie smiling. "Perfect record."

It was all aggressively casual at first. There followed a few more meetups, a couple more hangouts, hosted at their respective places. All of it low-key. Chase organized a weekend trip of hiking and camping on Mount Greylock, which Mick staggered and wheezed through as if on a death march. Mick insisted on a *Star Wars* marathon, which felt to Chase like some kind of cultish indoctrination. Chase admitted nervously that this was the first time he'd dated someone of his own race—not that he'd ever been against it or anything. It was just funny, is all.

Mick nodded sedately. "It is kind of rare, isn't it."

"We're like the final level of 'siblings or dating.'" Chase cackled, although he took genuine pleasure in the shared squareness of their faces, their same mounded noses and combined voluminousness of black hair. It felt like a privilege to see himself in the appearance of someone he cared for.

And he found a novel comfort in their shared experiences—the Sunday-morning Chinese school; the receipt of gold dollar coins in red envelopes each Lunar New Year; the lingering injury from middle and high school classmates, addicted to provocation, who'd mocked them with grotesque, squawking accents.

Progress between them went from adventitious to inevitable. There was meeting Janice, who smiled with deep compassion when Mick revealed to both of them how his mother had been infirm for a long time, how he worked at Lark's Landing in the hopes of moving her higher up on its resident waiting list.

And growing accustomed to each other's habits, embracing each other's passions. (Chase learned how to play *League of Legends*; Mick learned to identify different tree species based on their leaf shape and bark pattern.) Their lives grafting.

And then a funny thing happened—for Chase, at least—which was that sex began to seem less than fully satisfactory. It was still great, it was fantastic—the best he'd ever had. But like moving up a tax bracket, it only gave him a wider-lens view of everything else he could be enjoying, this prompt abundance of feeling. A grumbling hunger for more.

Which he wanted to bring up with Mick. But the impulse to do so was like inviting your coworkers to compare salaries: You needed 100 percent buy-in. And still, it might make people uncomfortable. It might not be worth the risk. The chance of nonreciprocation, the painful recollections incurred by prior acts of emotional vulnerability, scared the ever-loving shit out of him.

"It's like I'm losing myself more and more to you," Mick said on his own, one evening. "And I want it back, but I want to take you with it. With me. Does that make sense?"

"Not in the slightest."

Mick rubbed his palm with his thumb. "It's that I can't fully be *me* without you in my life."

Chase smiled. "I think you're trying to say that you love me."

"And what if I did?"

"Well, I'd say that I love your ass, too."

"Mick and Chase. We sound like a bad sitcom."

* * *

THREE DAYS BEFORE MISSILE ALERT

Mick had three glowing HD screens set up on his desk, arranged in a slight curve, from which he liked to play video games and engage in his gambling habit. He had an ergonomic chair that looked like a spaceman's; a mouse whose glowing, oblong complexity resembled something otherworldly.

There were shower sounds coming from the bathroom when Chase arrived home, carrying some Chinese. And as he navigated toward the kitchen table to unload, he bumped into the desk on which sat mission control, which must have knocked it out of sleep mode. The computer purred awake. Its screen was a beacon.

He stared. There was some kind of online profile for a professional video game player, and a freshly typed comment beneath it, from Mick's account:

Why don't you kill yourself you bullshit fucking chink.

And then came the vocal *pip* of the shower stopping. The metallic sweep of the curtain being drawn. Mick wouldn't towel off properly. He never did. He left the bathroom floor puddled with water after his showers. The door creaked open.

"Hey." A playful smile breaking over his damp face, the chip of his front tooth.

"Did you write this?" Chase pointed.

And the look was expunged, like a squeegee pulled across his features. Blankness. "What?"

"On the screen. Here."

He pattered toward him, squinting. Face full of guilt. "Oh yeah. It's nothing. It was a throwaway thing."

"You suggested someone kill himself as a throwaway?"

"It's just a figure of speech, not like an actual directive. It's just how we talk."

"And you're aware that you and I have both been called that same word?"

"Well, if anything, that gives me more right to say it, doesn't it? It's like I'm retaking the word."

"Not if you're still using it *as a slur*. And if the other guy doesn't even know your race."

"Okay, you're right," he said, with soggy conviction. "I'm sorry."

"Don't apologize to me."

"I'll delete the comment."

"That's a start."

"What would the next step be, then?"

And how this annoyed him! How Mick needed everything to be constantly *fine*, how he was so desperate, sometimes, to clear the air around them that he didn't bother waiting until his feelings coalesced, until he understood what the issue was to begin with.

"I really don't know," Chase said. "But I could use some space."

"Space." He grunted. "Okay, fine. Fine, whatever."

* * *

As a child, Chase could consummate an entire day of fun with a single young birch tree—first carving words and shapes into its remarkably supple trunk, revealing its pink salmon flesh as easily as you might swipe chalk upon a slate tablet; peeling off entire sheets of its papery bark, like tearing layers of old flyers from telephone poles.

And then climbing slowly upward, toward the junction. And finding the sturdiest, outermost branch and gradually tipping his weight upon it—letting the whole thing bend slowly toward the earth, until he imagined he could plant his feet on the ground and push off, holding on with all the strength in his mittened hands, as if to swing himself back up.

Although it never worked. Most trees never bowed more than a few degrees. His feet only once ever grazed the stiff, frostbitten dirt.

"What made you think it would?" Mick had asked, when he recounted it to him.

"Some poem they made us read in school, I think."

"Weird."

"Weird" was perhaps all a person could say about something like this.

Still, the memories were vivid. He recalled the exposure of being so far up, the tree's spindle-thin branches poking through his coat, flicking his eyelashes. The vast curve of the sky, with its iron clouds. And the terror—for he'd always had a fear of heights—of the entire endeavor collapsing, bringing him crashing toward the cold, hard earth.

Although this trepidation disappeared the more attempts he made, the longer he stayed up among the branches, and transformed, gradually, into a comforting solitude. The smoke of his breath rising higher than it had ever risen, the distant kinship with white-throated sparrows and butter-yellow finches who'd stayed put and braved the winter.

To this day, he could imagine no better a life than one spent amid all that open space, disappearing into the natural world.

* * *

The more he thought about Mick's comment, the more disgusted he became.

Eating dinner alone in the den—hunched over a mishmash plate of takeout balanced on the ottoman—he considered the gall it took to write something like that to a stranger, which could not be excused as callowness. At their age, it was cruelty. A host of unwelcome stereotypes flooded from the periphery: basement dwellers, racists, alcoholics, still living with their mothers, none of which he could reconcile with his understanding of the man he loved.

He knew this for certain: He was discerning enough not to fall for someone so capable of hating others and himself. He'd thought he was.

"Look, you're overreacting," Mick said, stepping into the room.

"I'm eating."

"Come on. Just sit at the table with me."

"No."

"You're being crazy. You're being so deeply and fundamentally unreasonable."

"Maybe you should tell me to kill myself."

"It was in the heat of the moment, okay? I wasn't even thinking."

"Are you telling me that if you don't consider a thing before you do it, then you don't hold any moral responsibility for it?"

"Yeah, sort of. I mean, there are exceptions, obviously, for physical acts that you actually *perform*. But this was just an internet comment. I made a mistake, but it was harmless."

"Why do you think it's okay to treat a person like that?"

"I mean, I lost a ton of money on him. I was upset."

"That doesn't make it any fucking better."

"It was like yelling at someone in traffic. I was frustrated."

Chase shook his head, recognizing the familiar motions and rhythms of their fights.

"Look," Mick said. "If you want to be like this, then fine. But I fucking wash my hands of it. I explained myself, I apologized. This is now officially *you* being unreasonable."

They didn't fight often. Their last had been at a hotel in Atlantic City, where the room was not ready when they arrived, despite Mick's early check-in note and his high loyalty status with the hotel group.

And how he'd made such an embarrassing fuss about it! How he'd asked to speak to the manager on duty, how he'd threatened to reach out to his "Platinum Elite contacts," taking up time and attention until, finally, housekeeping was finished—the woman with her heaping trolley of towels and soaps, rocking down the hall, toward the next room.

"You treat service workers like they're trash," Chase had said to him, as they unpacked.

"That is such bullshit."

"It's not bullshit. You act so snobby. You think somehow your *status* grants you time-travel benefits."

"Oh, fuck this."

And Mick had stormed into the bathroom, from which there came the angry churn of piss, and the sink running, the toilet flushing. The low-decibel reverb of a wobbling glass shower door. The steady *rat-a-tat* of water smacking the tub.

Minutes passing. Before the door finally opened again. "The soap is nice," Mick said, his hair wet. "It has those rough, gritty parts for exfoliating."

"Like pumice?"

"Yeah, exactly. Feel my hands."

And the argument was over. They were built upon sturdy bedrock. But this one felt different. For Chase, at least.

Perhaps it was merely an issue of timing. How, months ago, his boss at MEMA had told him about a National Park Service opening in Yosemite.

"It's basically like hiking for a living," Dan Hinge had said. "The job is yours if you want it."

The offer had been thrilling and terrifying in equal measure, then swiftly untenable.

Because the very next evening, while at dinner at the Anchor, Mick had asked, "Do you maybe want to take the next step?"

And he'd said, "What does that even mean?"

To which Mick, blushing, mumbled, "I was just thinking that maybe we could get a place together."

"Ah." As red plastic lobsters gleamed from their hanging spots on the walls.

"No pressure."

"You'd want to stay around here, right?"

"Well, yeah. Because of my mom."

And Chase had answered, "Okay. Yes."

"Are you sure?"

"Yes."

Yes. While relief surged so strongly through him that his heart felt like its own autonomous creature. Like something muscular, with wings, capable of taking off inside of him. How he loved this man. How he valued his initiative, his boldness. His fearless certainty when it came to their being together.

And he believed firmly that when you found a love like this, you took it. You chose it over anything else. Because life was baffling, and its capacity for loneliness terrifying. He thought of his parents: their seamless intimacy, their self-containment. How each moment in his relationship with Mick seemed superimposed over the example they'd set.

"Are you still upset with me?" Mick asked now, as they lay awake in bed. Like checking the temperature gauge on a machine to see if it was safe to touch.

His head was a rolling pin, flattening the pillow. "No. Not really."

"You still seem upset."

"Yes, but not at you, necessarily."

"Then at what? Or who—whom?"

"Just upset at how some of the things in my life turned out."

"God, you are so dramatic sometimes."

"What if that person wound up hurting himself?" he said to the dark ceiling. The moon obscured by thick, glowing clouds.

"He didn't."

"How do you know?"

"He's playing again tonight."

"Fine."

"Please, Chase, I'm sorry. I took down the comment; I apologized to the guy. I'm sorry."

"Good."

"Good, as in are we good? Are you going to stop acting weird?"

He snarled into his pillow. "No. Good, as in, at least now you should be able to sleep easier and not bother me."

* * *

TWO DAYS BEFORE MISSILE ALERT

It was a vibrant spring day beyond the window. There were bright yellow daffodils planted in the Anchor's window box, their trumpets pointing westward in unison. Lush maples limned the parking lot.

He and his sister were having their yearly lunch on the anniversary of their mother's passing, which had so shattered their father that it might as well have been his, too.

"Cheers to Mom and Dad," Janice said, holding her wineglass aloft.

"Cheers."

Their parents had been high school sweethearts—the sort whose acne-ridden prom pictures were still framed along the staircase that led up to the bedroom—who'd loved each other simply and straightforwardly their entire lives, living completely up to each other's expectations. And who'd made him feel, sometimes, as if the past truly were a gateway to a simpler, happier time—when feelings were more accessible, when people were forthright about who they were and what they wanted.

He told her about the thing Mick had written.

"I don't think it's a big deal," she said, humming lightly between little forkfuls of salad.

"It just makes me wonder what else there is about him. Like suddenly there's this completely different aspect of his personality that I wasn't aware of."

"I think he deserves to be taken at face value."

Janice was lovely and innocent and infinitely trusting. She liked to believe people, to infer their gentler nature. And all he did was worry about her for it.

Years ago, while a senior at Beckitt High, she'd gotten pregnant by some worthless fellow whose parents had paid to send him to Stanford (Yale had been his first choice, but alas, she'd ruined that for him by being so close) and offered to have the fetus taken care of. Since then, her lack of dates; her persistent, cheery satisfaction as a waitress at the Anchor; her tendency to hum to herself, as if keeping loneliness or panic at bay, all seemed a vague sort of penance for having carried the child to term and put him up for adoption, instead.

An inability to move on.

"You know, I'm officially the age Mom was when she had you," she said. "Although by now, she and Dad had been married for years already."

"It was smart of them to wait."

"Yeah, I guess."

She navigated her salad, which was artfully plated with frisée lettuce that looked like branching pieces of coral; slices of tight-leafed brussels sprouts vaguely reminiscent of matryoshka dolls; taut, lipstick-red tomatoes that regularly escaped her fork's lunges.

"It's weird," she said, looking up at him. "For the longest time I was fine with this life—you know, with working here, staying in town. But recently it's felt like I'm waking up. It's like I have this sudden urgency to do all this stuff, to live in all these different ways, and I'm just so scared of being clueless about it all. I feel so old."

"You're twenty-seven; that's very young."

She smiled. "I know that's a default thing to say, and I appreciate your saying it, like how 'it's never too late for this or that'—but, Chase, I feel so behind. I feel so behind that I don't know if it's even worth starting. I don't even know what that would mean. I don't know what the first step would be."

She began to hum. A slight, inoffensive sound, like that of a violin's tuning. Or perhaps a set of chimes, brushed by the wind.

"I don't think there's anything useful in comparing yourself to milestones set by Mom and Dad."

"Is that what I've been doing?"

"I think so."

"But I have a kid somewhere."

He nodded.

"And he turns eight next month." She closed her eyes. She mouthed the word. *Eight*. "You're supposed to get better accustomed to things as time passes, right?" Her eyes were still closed. "You get better used to their existence. But I swear, it's different when the thing itself is changing, too. It becomes this mental object that you can never fit yourself around."

Chase remembered attending the high school pops concert the winter before Janice got pregnant, hearing her perform a marvelous solo with her a cappella group. *Run away, run away. Let's run away together.* Such conviction in her voice. Such desire.

"Do you remember that crazy thing you used to do? With the trees?" she said.

"Hanging off them?"

"Yeah. Like in that poem."

"Uh-huh."

"Did you ever get low enough to try and launch yourself? Probably not, seeing as you're still alive."

But he had, once. On a cool afternoon, when none of his friends were around, he'd found a supple-enough tree, with few branches and a slim yet sturdy trunk. He'd climbed up until his weight overcame its center of gravity, until he felt it sinking toward the ground. The bending and splintering of the wood was like the sound of a sticker being slowly peeled. And he remembered the thrill of his feet meeting the hard earth, dipping low enough to bend his knees, and feeling the desire to kick off, to fly over the fence, into his neighbor's backyard, which had a trampoline. He felt intuitively capable of doing such a thing. He felt certain of the birch's springiness, its angle, the timing of his release.

But his daring abandoned him at the very last moment, as he crouched, as the spark of action jolted down his body—he let go of the tree. And still, the force of its swaying sent brittle air whipping at his face. A branch lashed his cheek; he bruised his ass on an exposed root.

"Mom saw the whole thing," he said, nodding. "She was so mad at me."

Janice regarded him with sudden conviction. With a fierceness he'd never seen in her. "Mom was the one who wanted me to give him up, you know—the baby."

"Seriously?"

"It was one of the last things she told me before she got really, really bad. That she thought I should."

"Why are you telling me this now?"

Her voice drained abruptly of melody. "Apparently, she—well, they, Mom and Dad—left me money. You too, presumably."

She handed him a plain, ripped-open envelope. In it was a note from the family attorney, stating that, according to their late parents' wishes, there was, enclosed, a check for ten thousand dollars, to be paid out on the eighth anniversary of their mother's death.

He looked up. "Why did they wait so long?"

"I have a theory, but it's just a theory."

"Which is?"

Janice chewed carefully. "They didn't want me blowing it right away on a kid I'd decided to raise. At least Mom felt that I shouldn't, and I think Dad just went along, because of everything that was happening."

"Weren't you always going to give him up for adoption?"

She shook her head. "Not at first. I only decided after Mom died, and Dad told me there was no money."

Chase felt a quake move through him. Something tectonic had shifted in his understanding of his parents. Something he could not yet fully survey.

"I guess the plan worked," Janice said.

"Weird to think Dad was in on this, too."

"I don't think he had the heart or the energy to go against Mom when she was like that."

They were silent for a moment, carried off in separate reveries. He thought of Mick, whose comments were presumably dwarfed by this new information. Although Chase's unease lingered—like a persistent vertigo. The sense that the old state of things was permanently gone, that he needed to understand his family, his partner, all over again.

A woman roughly Janice's age, with downy fuzz that ran down her cheeks and an ASSISTANT MANAGER name tag pinned to her shirt, set an empty check holder before them. She smiled, double-tapped the edge of the table, and said, "On the house."

"You're the best." Janice stood up and gave her a hug. Chase thanked her, too; he remembered hearing from his sister about a coworker who was also a young mother, single, who never took from the tip pool and paid a generous rate for babysitting.

They kept quiet until the woman was back at the greeting station. "So she and I were closing one night and decided to borrow a bottle of gin from the bar," Janice said at last. "And when I told her about my adoption thing, she confessed to me how her own kid is the result of an affair with a married guy. His wife still doesn't know."

"Sounds, uh, precarious," Chase murmured.

"And she kept saying how weird it was, having all this guilt attached to a child she was constantly falling in love with. Weird that her biggest mistake, the shittiest thing she'd ever done, turned her into a more considerate, loving person. Someone who never would've done it to begin with."

Janice began humming something wild and loopy—something evasive, as if giving herself wider berth to think. "Do you think there's really such a thing as making a wrong choice?" she said.

"Of course."

"But there are so many factors to consider, aren't there? All the other things you can be at any given moment, which you aren't aware of. And all the different interactions between what you've done and who you are that are impossible to fully trace. And the fact that you can't predict your own future."

"I guess," he said.

"It's just— How is anyone supposed to know? How long is a person supposed to live before he figures out which choices were the right ones?"

"Why are you thinking about this sort of stuff?"

"How can you not?"

"Maybe some choices are better than others," he said. "But they lead to others that may be worse. They branch out. It's like a tree—a decision tree. That's a thing, right?"

"So how can you actually link certain choices to specific outcomes in your life?"

He had no idea. Who did?

She looked straight at him. "Did you know they give you the option of an open or closed adoption? And if it's open, you can keep in touch with the kid, with the new parents. But I chose closed, because I was afraid of how guilty I might feel. I was afraid I wouldn't be able to move on, with the constant reminders of how I'd abandoned him"—she raised her hand before he could intercede—"and for the longest time I wasn't sure if it was the right choice, you know? Well, it's been eight years now, and I'm starting to think it really wasn't. Because this feeling I've been carrying for so long, I'm pretty sure it's more than just guilt; it's regret."

* * *

ONE DAY BEFORE MISSILE ALERT

He wondered how much of his life resembled his parents' by coincidence—memories sprouting at convenient times—and how much was purposeful: those scenes, moments, he recapitulated and hardly understood.

Their last anniversary had been their thirtieth. Mom had passed first, swiftly, of cancer. And their father, who was still healthy when it happened, simply could not be convinced to rejoin the world of the living. He died shortly afterward of multiple organ failure, to a whiff of relief.

"No point," he'd said in those last months. "Better not to start anything new."

It was equal parts sweet and tragic. Although Chase had always thought there was something profoundly *wasteful* and *selfish* about an able-bodied person not using his last years to the fullest. Willing himself to die, instead. There were always other opportunities, other ways to impose yourself upon the world of existing things.

His father's determined surrender had always felt attached to something else—some further consideration that was of a piece with his parents' closeness, the casual fierceness with which they guarded their privacy.

And an alarming lightheadedness emerged when he thought of his folks now—holding their inheritance hostage. A rapid hypoxia, as if normal breaths no longer delivered the same payload of oxygen. As if he needed more and more simply to retain the same idea he had of them, and to remain familiar to himself.

He remembered what Mick had written.

And you forgave a lot in love. You reacted, you made room. You made excuses, exceptions. This was reality. You adjusted your expectations. But that comment! Why couldn't Chase let it go? Perhaps, yes, because it implied an entirely separate existence—a cruel, dissociative identity. Perhaps because it defied emotional logic—that someone could so heedlessly perpetuate the same hurt of which he'd been a victim.

Perhaps Chase was just unhappy, estranged from his own life.

He thought: Sometimes things could progress with such galloping hurry, such heedlessness of waypoints, that when you finally paused—or crashed—you lacked the benefit of a *before* picture, or even a set of blueprints. Sometimes it came down to what you left for the recovery crews.

He wondered if they'd reached this point.

And the usual steps toward resolution weren't working. The tepid, slinking smiles; the abashed "Hi"s. The slow forays they made toward each other, like grappling hooks flung between two old wooden ships for the purpose of boarding.

"Please don't tell me this is some sort of deal-breaker," Mick confronted him that evening, back in the den.

No. It probably wasn't. But it drew his attention relentlessly, like an irregularity amid a vast, blank sameness.

"I swear, I don't— Well, I didn't do it often."

"What does that mean? Quantify it for me."

Mick's forehead was shining. "Do you want to see my chat logs?"

"No. Just tell me."

"Tell you what?"

"Tell me how frequently you encourage people to kill themselves on the internet." Chase placed his dinner plate on the floor, let his head sink back into the couch's velvet throw. "Tell me how frequently you engage in cyberbullying, cyber-racism, whatever."

"Like, a handful of times, maybe."

"You've told a handful of people to kill themselves."

"Look, it's not me. The person who does that, it's *not me.*"

"Then who is it?"

"It's, like— It's my id. It's a part of myself that I save for these sorts of situations. Just to blow off steam. It's like when you play a video game and you shoot civilians. It's not real."

"Those were real people you were insulting."

"But they understand it, too, is what I'm saying."

"How do you know?"

"It's just tacit. I mean, imagine how pathetic you'd have to be to kill yourself just because someone online said so."

No. No, this was not the right response. This was only making things worse. And what Chase had thought were advantageous traits in the man he loved—his initiative, his staunchness and candor—took on a more troubling luster now. They made him seem controlling. They suggested possessiveness. A firm, unilateral grasp of the narrative.

"They're just words." Mick stooped awkwardly over the ottoman, bringing their faces level. "Please."

"It's not about the words themselves," Chase mumbled, feeling suddenly fussy, childish. "I fucking swear. It's not. It's that I misjudged you. I misjudged everything. I thought I had this idea of what I wanted my life to be like, and I thought I was happy, but I think I got it completely wrong. I think I chose wrong."

"Chose wrong? With what? With me?"

"I don't know." He shook his head; he spoke toward his feet. "At some point, I chose something wrong. Because I'm not—I'm just not—" He stopped, because going on would make him sob, would make him feel like someone in need of precarious rescue. "I'm just not happy right now."

"What can I do?" Mick asked with utmost seriousness.

Well, what could he do? What could Chase ask for?

In the absence of a forward path, he turned back. He returned to their first meeting, that evening at Ollie's. The toggled decision to go back to Mick's place, to fuck. And the similar branching-off point of deciding the next morning not to leave, to stay for breakfast. To answer the polite, calibrated text messages.

And to overlook their early fights. To remain in love. The selections he'd made at various checkpoints. At the Yosemite marker. To stay. To move in. To arrive home with Chinese, which lengthened his commute by twenty minutes. To see the message. To realize, as he was realizing now, that he was not happy. That there was no path that might bring happiness—not unless he could somehow go back two or three steps, unless he could unfork the branches that had split from his decision, months ago.

That he should have held on and let the tree throw him.

"By the way," Mick said, straightening and handing him a letter. "You got this in the mail."

He opened it. A check for ten thousand dollars. Along with a handwritten note. His mother's neat, compact cursive heaving him into the past: *I'm sorry for the wait.*

"What is it?"

He shook his head. He needed to get out of here. He drove to the Anchor.

* * *

"Your sister's next door," the assistant manager said, before adding, "Is she all right?"

"She's just—evaluating," he said.

The woman grew solemn, her face compressed by unease. "Sometimes I wonder if there's any real benefit to knowing the truth, if all it does is remind you of a past you can't change."

Chase didn't respond.

A concert was ending just as he stepped into Major Third. Elementary schoolers were putting their instruments back into hard plastic cases, posing for photos taken by eager parents. Janice, in the back row, noticed him and cocked her head toward the empty folding chair beside her.

"Did you get the check?" she said as he sat down.

"Still not sure how to feel about it."

"You know, Mom told me something else." She scratched at her name tag, voice braided into a frenetic melody. "Before she died. And I'm sorry I didn't tell you—I just thought it wasn't something you would appreciate knowing. And you have to know that the only reason she told me was because she was so upset with me, and the decision I was making—"

"*What?*" he said.

The humming stopped. Her cheeks were even warmer and pinker than usual. "She said she was going to leave at one point."

"Leave what? Who?"

"Us." Her voice became a staccato chirp. "She said she felt like she was going to die unless she could somehow escape."

Escape?

"Why didn't she tell me?" he said.

"Probably because you weren't on the verge of a major decision after having been knocked up."

"Did Dad know?"

"I don't think so."

"Did she ever try it? Running away? Or"—his voice undulating—"suicide?"

"I don't know."

"But I don't understand. Did she regret it? Us? Did she hate us?"

Janice let her head wobble. "She just said that, at some point, everything became sort of hopeless. She couldn't quite explain it. I guess it just felt like she had nothing of her own—not even her individual life, or her future."

"And she got over it. Right?"

Janice stared at him with vague disappointment. "How could anyone expect to know that about someone else?"

Chase made a visor with his hand, pressing both temples. He was astonished by the expanding universe of things he did not know—what few certainties he possessed, condensed into the size of an atom. He thought his heart might collapse from the weight of everything new to consider.

And he felt saddest, for some reason, when he considered his father: his limping resignation at the end, his need for a partner to keep him moored to the living. It felt so much more distressing now. So much more of a shame.

Why don't you kill yourself you bullshit fucking chink.

* * *

THE MORNING OF THE ALERT

"—threat inbound. Seek immediate shelter. This is not a drill. Estest-est."

"Chase—come on."

There was protocol for these things. The script was supposed to begin with *Exercise exercise exercise*, but he'd not heard anything until Felicity put the call on speaker, and the voice had said, *This is not a drill*...

There was a chain of command. A hierarchy of approvals sought and granted. Orders passed down. Like the stacking and unstacking of cups.

But it was an individual who always performed the command. And the command had corresponded with the protocol for emergency notification of an inbound ballistic missile threat.

He clicked through various screens; he made his stepwise way through the warning system. Pausing at each node. Guided to the next. He reached the drop-down menu.

TEST Missile Alert
Missile Alert

He clicked.

The computer asked, Are you sure? And he clicked Yes, because why wouldn't he be? He knew the script; he knew what he'd heard. And he knew the process. He'd rehearsed many, many times.

He'd done so much rehearsing that he wasn't even thinking as he made his way through the remaining alarm schema. He wasn't really internalizing the instructions, the contents of the dialogue boxes, as he considered the developments of the past few days. He was following the animal commands of memory, the screen's prompting, following the decision tree's branches. Confirm. Yes. Send.

"—Chase. CHASE."

He looked up. Felicity's face, lit with fear. Dan Hinge staring at him with fury. "Did you just click the alert template?"

A message on his phone from Mick: The fuck?

* * *

The conference room in which he was being dressed down contained a single wide window that gave onto a boundless expanse of undulating greenery. He tried not to stare too longingly through it.

"What were you thinking?" Dan said, sweat gathering in dark pools around his armpits, in a Rorschach pattern down his back.

He shrugged. "I thought it was an active alert."

"You thought that it was an *active missile alert*?"

"That's what I said, yes."

"Did you hear the 'test' note at the beginning?"

"Felicity put the call on speaker after it started, and I was listening for the word *exercise*, which is part of the established test script. All I heard was the message and the fact that it wasn't a drill. Which is not a part of the script."

"So you really thought that there was a ballistic missile coming toward us? Here?"

Chase shrugged again. "I thought that there was an active alert, and my job was to get that alert out to everyone."

"But did you even stop for a second to consider the plausibility of it? Of a missile being sent *here?* And what that would mean? Like, geopolitically? And how people might react to a thing like that on their phones?"

"With respect, that's not my job, is it?"

"It's your job to practice common sense, for fuck's sake."

Once the alert was out, there was no way to retract it. (He could only cancel it, which prevented any phones that had just been switched on from receiving it afresh.) Nor was there any protocol for sending out a new message to negate the first. They needed to re-create the entire alert process; they needed to push a bespoke all clear through a system of such bureaucratically inept design that no single person had any idea of what the whole process looked like. No one knew any more than his or her own role.

And phones were ringing endlessly. And Dan Hinge, in his office, was saying, "Yes, sir, yes. Yes, sir. Absolutely."

While Chase sat in a stew of dread, numbness across his skin; although his insides felt as if they were *buzzing*. As if a light shock were being delivered to his blood, his viscera.

"What I think we'll do is put you on unpaid leave for now," Dan said, sometime later.

He nodded.

"We'll put you on unpaid leave and try to mop up the mess to the best of our ability, but in the meantime, I'm going to insist that you don't talk to the press, you don't divulge any more information. You just sit on your fucking hands for a while."

Felicity approached him tepidly on her way out for another smoke break. "Think of it this way," she said. "At least now you can figure out your thing with Mick."

* * *

He arrived home still in shock.

Mick ran up to him and embraced him. "Holy shit. Holy shit. I was so fucking worried." He stepped back. "Are you okay?"

"I fucked up. I really, really fucked up."

"It was you?"

He nodded, briefly grateful for the refuge of Mick's company and understanding.

"Was there not any indication that it was a test?"

"I didn't hear it."

"The system has waypoints, right?"

"Yeah."

"Like, places where it let you know that the next choice you made couldn't be reversed? That all other options were no longer possible?"

"I said yes."

"So now what?"

He didn't know. He was still stranded in a haze—stuck somewhere well outside reality. How desperately he wished to will himself out of this existence. Like a bad dream whose falseness he was convinced of, that he somehow still could not escape.

If only he could go back a moment. Just a moment! To click a different icon. (And perhaps, also, to avoid the desk as he walked toward the kitchen with his bag of takeout. To tamp down his curiosity, to avert his eyes from the computer screen.)

How deeply unfair it was that something so trivial, so eminently conceivable, was so impossible.

* * *

A span of time passed. Mick left and came back.

"I got you your favorite." He laid a wax paper bag on the kitchen table.

In the bag were all sorts of sweet bǐng from the Asian supermarket thirty minutes away in Hartford: custardy, singe-dotted dàntǎ and creamy pineapple cake, velvety red bean buns glazed in a sugary egg wash and topped with toasted sesame seeds.

"That's really sweet of you," he said, although he wasn't hungry. He let them sit on the table. "Why weren't you at work?"

"I took some time off," Mick said. "I thought maybe we could go camping or something. Have a restart."

Well, he was about to have plenty of time for that.

The press offensive had begun. MEMA administrators, EOPSS officials, members of the National Guard, all of them covering their asses.

The employee who triggered the alarm had a history of poor performance and a difficult time separating harmless practice from the real world.

Well, he bristled at this. That was neither fair nor accurate.

The employee's colleagues had noted several instances in which his behavior seemed distracted or erratic.

The employee was on a performance-improvement plan when this latest incident occurred. Since his hiring, our vetting process has undergone significant updates.

"They're hanging you out to dry," Mick said, standing beside him and reading along. Occasionally releasing little huffs of indignation.

"I know."

"They're scapegoating you."

"I said I know."

"What are you going to do?"

"I don't know yet," he said.

"Why can't you tell me what you're thinking? Why can't we be a team about this?"

He looked up sadly at him. He was imagining the damage an actual missile would have visited upon the gorgeous Berkshires. "I don't think there's any use."

Mick made a strange, guttural noise. A combination of scream and sob. "I am so tired of this," he said. "I'm really fucking tired of the guilt you're forcing on me for *one* thing I said. It was a mistake, and I apologized. But it wasn't real, it didn't matter, *especially* considering the shit you're in now."

"You don't need to apologize anymore."

"Then be mine again, okay? Please, I want to help you figure this out." His handsome face, mangled with yearning. That face in which, for so long, Chase had seen himself and felt contentment, security. And now, restlessness. "Stop pretending as if you don't need me," Mick went on. "Stop acting as if you can internalize all this shit you're going through. Talk to me, for fuck's sake."

"What is there to talk about?"

"Well, to begin, there's the fact that you sort of fucked up monumentally at work, enough to make national news. No offense, I'm not judging you, but what you did is about ten thousand times fucking worse than any throwaway comment I made on the internet."

"I should have just waited."

"Did it ask if you were sure?"

To have been asked again if he was sure. To have paused and gathered and then said, simply, *No*.

He was shocked to consider how certain junctions were of such gravity that the decision to do nothing, to remain the same, was as drastic as transforming wholesale.

If only the world presented real checkpoints. If only there were genuine chances to re-create your life at a certain moment, to reconstruct how it was before the big thing that changed everything had occurred.

He remembered those winters with the birch tree. His feet grazing, then settling, on the frozen ground. His knees bending.

* * *

Word got out. It always did. People found his name, then his email address, his Facebook account.

> Do you understand how scared I was? You stupid fuck. Your just a pussy lib trying to undermine the president's foreign policy. You hate how successful he's been.

> I hope you die a horrible, terrifying death, like the one you put us through.

> Why don't you fucking kill yourself you dumb chink.

He stared at Mick, who hung his head.

Someone from CNN wrote to him: We'd love to hear your side of the story.

But he had no side. His story was just a smaller story inside a larger one—the facts were all there. He *had* been distracted. He *had* fucked up.

He drove to Songline Park, which was lovely but altogether too cramped and pruned, too lacking in biodiversity, to have ever been a proper refuge. Still, he was comforted by the sight of puffball wrens and theatrical waxwings teetering on dowel-thin branches. He envied their purely physical selfhood, their ability to fly without feeling overwhelmed by wonder.

He strolled around the central pond, shoes sinking in the fresh mud. He took some solace in the mucky duckweed, the unwinding cattails like corn kernels mid-pop, but not enough.

Had familiarity always felt so smothering?

* * *

TWO DAYS AFTER MISSILE ALERT

He felt like a leper, a disgrace, when Dan Hinge called him back into the office. The horrible, dank building. Felicity's lack of eye contact. Her swift, grim nod.

"So, obviously we're going to have to let you go," Dan said.

Chase sniffed and blinked. "Do you know if anyone got hurt? Because of it? Me?"

Dan shook his head. "Nothing that can be directly drawn to the alert."

"What about indirectly?"

"How is anyone supposed to know?"

Chase's head sagged. Mick had told him about several employees at the nursing home who'd overdosed on painkillers during the period between the alert and the all clear. How they'd been found in the abandoned rooms of residents, who'd been wheeled into the basement by a single, heroic orderly. Surely that could not have been a coincidence?

How can you actually link certain choices to specific outcomes in your life?

"Look. I feel bad about this whole thing," Dan Hinge said. "I do. I swear. I know it's a shitty system. Everyone up the hierarchy knows, too. That's why they're doing this to you. They need to cover their asses."

Well, this meant something, at least.

"Strictly speaking, you helped to expose a critical flaw. You did everyone a favor in the long run. Things could have been far worse."

"Glad I only paid for it with my dignity and my career."

"Look, Chase, I reached out to some folks. Remember that job in Yosemite? It's yours, still, if you want it."

Something in his soul shivered and leapt. "Seriously?"

"Yes. But the caveat is, you can't go to the press. You haven't gone already, have you?"

He shook his head.

"Well, then—yeah. You can still take it. And again, I'm sorry."

* * *

He was thinking of his family. He was thinking of love's point of no return. What to do, where to go, when your heart demanded so much out of life.

"What's up?" Mick said.

"I want to leave."

Yes. Saying it was like a spell, ushering in the feeling, that poured over and splashed and colored everything.

"What do you mean?"

"California. Yosemite."

"But we just moved in together."

You tried to space all the big decisions evenly throughout your life. As if their timing were somehow related to their consequence.

But months ago he'd been given a choice, and the choice had been clear-cut, like a drop-down menu, and he'd selected what he thought was the right answer. But it wasn't. He could see this now, in the clarity of retrospection. In the aftermath of everything. Certainty snaked through him.

I was just thinking that maybe we could get a place together.

Are you sure you want to send this alert?

And he was lucky—so lucky to have this. A checkpoint to return to.

"Okay." Mick nodded. "Okay, that's fine. I can make California work." He said this with quick, poignant resolve.

"What about your mom?"

"Well, when do you need to actually make a decision? How long can you push it off?"

And the split-second suggestion made a painful, shuddering wound. "No."

"What?"

"I need to do it alone."

"Alone." His continued nodding gave the impression of someone trying desperately to keep a ball in the air for as long as possible. "Okay, and I'm assuming you've thought about— Have you thought about doing long distance?"

"No."

"How about we open it up? An open relationship?"

"Come on. Honey."

"I'm trying"—Mick's fists were clenched, his face pointing at his toes—"I'm trying to come up with a way to stay in your life."

"Mick."

"We can be poly. That's a thing, right? You want to be polyamorous, or whatever?"

"You know that neither of us is programmed for that kind of thing."

"I have no idea what the fuck I'm programmed for. Neither do you, frankly." Blood was rushing through his face, his chipped tooth gnashing against his lip. "Please don't do this."

"Mick."

"Please. I'll do whatever you want me to do." He worked his right thumb deeply, twistingly, into his left palm. "I'll be whoever you need me to be. That thing I said, it was a one-off, I swear. I fucking swear to you it was. I've never said anything remotely similar to that. You can check my chat logs. It's not who I am. And you know that. You *know* that."

"I do know that." Chase spoke slowly, with gathering conviction. "This has nothing to do with you or what you wrote. My life was moving this way—it's been moving away for a while. I just didn't realize it until recently. Until a few things happened."

Mick collapsed on the ottoman. He pressed his fingers, hard, into his eye sockets. "Do you have enough money saved up?"

And Chase could not tell if this was a challenge or a genuine point of concern. "I do," he said. "From some recent stuff."

"Was it that letter? You were being so cagey about that."

He nodded.

"Please. Take a moment, rethink this."

"It's not fair of you to make this so difficult."

"It's not fair of *me*?" Mick said.

"It's better—"

"Not for both of us. Definitely not for me. For you—*maybe. Maybe* you'll manage to convince yourself in a few years that it was the right decision. But it's because you'll be scared. You'll be too scared to admit that maybe it was the wrong one. You'll be too afraid to have tossed an entirely good life aside. Our life."

"Maybe."

"How can you possibly be okay with that? I mean, I thought *I* was the gambler."

"I don't know."

"But you're sure?"

He thought of the alert. How his willingness to believe the implausible had already made a brief reality of it. More, now. Further. Toward a richness of possibility as vast and diverse as a park biome. "Yes."

And he would need to store away happiness; he would need to guard his memories; he would need to make a thousand fresh, vital decisions, each with a thousand separate, unknown outcomes. He knew this.

There came a quick shudder—the prolonged chirp of his phone in his pocket. It was a call from Janice.

"You'll never guess where I am," she said.

"Where?"

"I ran away! Chase, I ran away!"

"What does that mean?"

"I'm in Nashville. I'm singing!"

"What? How did you even get there?"

"I met this guy—a violinist named Nick! He's so talented. And when the missile alert happened, it was like this jolt—we just started driving until we got here. We play together now." She was breathless. She was as excited as he'd ever heard her.

"I wish I could see you right now," he said.

"Come to Nashville!"

"No," he said, "I mean, I wish I could see you as you are. Right now. You sound so happy."

"I love you," she said.

He thought about new people. New land. A fresh sun, a fresh day. How old was he? He didn't know. He didn't care. He wondered how lonely it might get. As Mick swung away.

But you took these opportunities. You had to. And regret felt like a quaint certainty—like a distant, convergent wave, which he knew he could bear. Which he knew he could outlast, with the same intuition he'd once had for the springiness of birch.

To be amid sprawling forests and meadows, to stand before enormous granite peaks daggering toward the sky, was reminiscent of his early solitude, among the snarled network of branches. He'd relied back then on the certainty that the tree could always lower him back to Earth. Always, he could return.

Not anymore.

He imagined the calm, delicious solidity of the ground, and using it as ballast for his feet to push off.

A SECOND CHANCE

Russell Zhang

I.

He would never forget how utterly spontaneous it was. The abrupt, shattering disturbance. And the urgent rumble of Ruthie's footsteps, her skidding into the living room. "Oh my— Oh *shit*. Russ? Russ, where are you?"

"Bathroom!"

"Since when do you not bring your—"

"Dad! Dad! Your phoooone, your phone!" Miles, their son, came tumbling downstairs with surprising effusiveness and slid Russ's phone beneath the door, where it was promptly wedged.

"Damn it—"

The device made a series of violent, insectoid chirps—vibrating against the ceramic tiles, the screen flashing with alarm—before Russell got down on his knees and feverishly coaxed it in his direction.

"Holy shit." He stepped into the hallway, looking up at his family. "Is this for real?"

"It explicitly says *not a drill*," Ruthie said, trembling.

"But it could be for somewhere else. It could mean nothing for us."

"Then they wouldn't have sent it to our phones, right? It's all geolocated." Ruthie's eyes were round, wide basins of shock. "What even is a ballistic missile? Is that the same thing as a nuke?"

"Probably," he said. "If we're getting bombed, they'll want to take us out right away."

"Oh God."

They tapped shakily at their phones while Miles swung silently between their waists, yanking at each of them for information.

"See anything anywhere?"

"Nothing."

"Well, it's only been, like, thirty seconds."

"But if it was serious, it would've been sent everywhere, right?"

"I don't know. Isn't there an air force base nearby? Westover or something?"

"Come here, sweetheart," Ruthie said, gathering Miles.

There were no cars in the streets. No sirens wailing from any direction. Quiet morning, quiet town. Adrenaline drove them forward in a series of controlled, engine-like bursts.

"Where do we even go?" she asked.

"Bathtub, right? And let's get the mattress."

"Why the mattress?"

"To, like, put over it."

"Is that a thing? Should we check?"

But there was no time. No time. Any moment. *SEEK IMMEDIATE SHELTER.*

Their home had two bathrooms: one on the first floor, one on the second, only the latter of which was outfitted with a bathtub.

"Obviously you and Miles get in the tub," he said.

"Promise me you'll find somewhere to hide, too."

He nodded, clichés running through his head. He imagined their neat, blocky neighborhood cast beneath a heavy shadow, the devil-red mushroom cloud rising in the distance. And all of it so strange, so dreamlike, because his only reference points were movies.

THIS IS NOT A DRILL.

The surrealness persisted as he approached their bed—its blankets unmade, its sheets creased in random diagonals from heat and sweat and pressure. Like a piece of modern art. He dragged the mattress across the hall.

They lowered Miles into the tub on his back, just as they'd done when he was a baby. Ruthie got on all fours, on top of him.

"Shh, shh." She thumbed his hair across his forehead while he sniffled.

Covering them with the mattress, Russ felt as if he were plugging a well, sliding a stone over its wide, yawning mouth.

"Find somewhere safe," Ruthie said, looking backward and up at him, the light thinning to a splinter across her face.

And then he was alone.

He wondered, briefly, if the securest place in the house was actually somewhere on the ground floor (the advice was always to "get low," wasn't it?), although this directly contradicted the only other thing he knew about disaster preparedness—the sacred importance of "getting in the bathtub."

Find somewhere safe.

But the prospect of being somewhere safer than where his wife and child currently lay—the prospect of surviving an inbound missile attack while they perished—was so abhorrent to him, so unthinkable, that he didn't move. He could not.

So he lay down beside the tub. Upon the cool, cream-colored tiles. The lattice of grout needed to be cleaned, he noticed. The shower curtain was developing a faint grist of mildew along its inward edge. Outside, a crooked branch rose and fell, scratching lightly against the window like a reminder.

And it struck him that these observations could be his last, that any moment might arrive and blow him and his family out of existence.

He heard his son whimpering. His wife's calming hush. "Shh, it's going to be okay. We're going to be okay. Daddy's going to be okay."

And two *ping*s in quick succession.

The first, from an unfamiliar number: I've never stopped thinking about you.

And the second: FALSE ALARM. PLEASE DISREGARD. ALL CLEAR.

The mattress flopped off. Ruthie stood up, her face wet and red. Her eyes swollen. "I thought you were going to hide," she said.

He sniffed hard, grabbing her hand so she could step out with Miles. "I couldn't leave you."

* * *

Only hours later, after the news had made NBC and CNN and *The New York Times*—SMALL MASSACHUSETTS COUNTY RECEIVES BALLISTIC MISSILE ALERT IN ERROR—after it had wound its circuit around social media and evoked its requisite cycle of outrage, jokes, and memes; after interest seemed to wane and settle, like a feeding frenzy in which only bones remained, did Russ finally let his shoulders slump, did he finally cry a little.

What now?

He recalled the text message.

Who is this? he wrote, staring at the bathroom mirror.

Russ Zhang was profoundly unremarkable. Of middling height (tall for an Asian man), average build and looks. Never romantically in demand. His only feature of note was a slight crookedness of jaw, so that he spoke more from the left half of his mouth than his right.

And he loathed how this observation always brought to mind his father, who'd been the same—his lips arranged in a thin line that dragged suddenly downward, as if the page of his face had been yanked away at the last moment. And who'd deserted them, inexplicably, on a cold morning many years ago.

He remembered his mother after his father left—a quiet, lovely woman, who grew bitter and cruel in her bafflement. And how his wàipō had descended from China to care for them in his wake, to absorb their emotional blows.

His phone double-spasmed with a reply. Milly

And a thud of disappointment. He did not remember meeting anyone named Milly. I think you might have the wrong number.

No response. Thin, feathery clouds were pressed into the pink evening sky.

He judged the day's events as extenuating enough to merit a trip to the bottle shop, where he bought a six-pack and a few travel-sized vodkas—the illicitness, the anticipation of Ruthie's disapproval almost heightening his excitement.

Russell was not a mean drunk. Nor was he a stumbling-dumb one. He was, if anything, kind and contemplative, better humored, when he drank. And a bit whinier, a bit more emotional. But he liked the feeling, as if each beer were a balloon tied to the dreary realities weighing on his mind—lighter, lighter, until he'd had enough to cease thinking altogether.

He'd learned, through casual perusal of the textbooks he sold, that the precise feeling of happiness was produced by specific chemicals in the brain, which the friendly presence of alcohol helped boost. And so a pleasant airiness suffused him as he drank, like a familiar embrace, or a conversation picked back up.

He was swaying and gliding through the rooms of his home, enjoying the lightness of feeling, when a fresh message arrived on his phone:

You're Russell Zhang. We met in Wingham. I was at the bar.

And the recollection was like the spark that emerged from plugging a charger into an outlet. How he'd been to Wingham months ago for a company conference—one of those sales-strategy meetings that devolved invariably into bacchanalia—and spoken to her. He could vaguely recall her short hair and narrow face. Her glassy oval eyes. And the quick, forgettable conversation that he was certain (yes, certain) was all that had transpired between them.

I know it sounds crazy, but I felt like we had a connection. Like we could figure things out together. Haha anyway. It's probably also bc I thought a missile was coming.

A stampede of questions gathered at his fingertips. But the day was already so jarring, so teeming with strangeness. And old obsessions had begun welling inside him—memories of his father, full of longing and sticky-sad residue, which threatened to clog up the efficient machinery of his life.

So he sat alone in the dark, the empty craft beer cans stacked into a neat little pyramid. He could have had more, but he didn't. He felt secure in his self-control. He sat and watched the shadows of the trees sharpen, the moonlight percolating through the dappled leaf cover. He did not remember falling asleep.

* * *

Ruthie accosted him the next morning.

"You left your phone in the sink last night." She handed it to him.

He nodded, gulping down water, squinting at the sharp light.

"I thought we had a deal about your drinking."

"Nothing happened."

"It resets your count back down to zero."

He stared at her, nonplussed. "This isn't AA."

"It's just that I thought you weren't going to touch it anymore, outside of social events and your conferences and stuff."

This felt like something of an imposition. Drinking alone was, if anything, more responsible. But Ruthie had grown up beneath the shadow of a father who'd drank himself to death, and Russell, who knew all about absentee parents, had always tried to accommodate her.

He'd not touched the stuff in the early days of their relationship for fear of driving her away. He'd been so breathlessly in love with her height and elegance, the thick brown hair that descended in liquid waves down her shoulders, that he was willing to contort himself into all sorts of different shapes to meet her standards.

And then one evening, in an excess of terror and self-sabotage, he'd gotten so wildly, irresponsibly drunk that Ruthie had needed to care for him as she would a child, mopping up his vomit, wiping away his maudlin tears, keeping him on his side so that he might not aspirate on his own stupidity.

He'd never forget the next morning, amid the barrage of shame and the grim certainty that he'd driven her away, finding her asleep beside him, bathed in golden 8:00-AM light. Her face so lovely and placid.

You did such stupid things out of fear, he'd realized. You pushed people away. You conflated courage and control.

"Hey, what would you do if you woke up and you were twenty again?" he asked now.

"I don't really like those kinds of questions," she said. "They're unrealistic. They just bring up hurtful things."

"Hurtful?"

"All I mean is that I'm perfectly happy with everything in my life—speaking of which, some of my kids have a recital over at Major Third tonight, so just make some pasta for Miles, please."

"Sure, sure," he said, following her to the kitchen. "But you would have tried something different, right? If you had the time back?"

"Of course."

"Of course?"

"No one doesn't make mistakes."

"So. Like what?"

Ruthie's eyes widened, her face steeped in exasperation. "I'd have switched my major in college. I'd have gotten my master's in business instead of education."

"Seriously?"

"Yes. I'd be a management consultant."

"Really? That's it?"

"You asked me what I'd do. That's my answer."

"Well, it's not too late," he said. "If you want to switch careers."

"Yes, it is, Russ. I know when a ship has sailed." She narrowed her eyes and widened them again.

"You know," he said quietly, "when it was happening—when we thought it was happening—I didn't think about him at all. I was only thinking about you two."

"Who, your father?"

He managed to grunt in the affirmative.

"Well, I'm proud of you," she said.

"But now I can't stop."

"What—thinking about him?"

"Yeah."

She sighed. "Well, don't forget, you already have a pretty good thing going on right now, family-wise."

He kissed her cheek. "Of course."

Six months into their dating, after having been introduced to Ruthie's gentle-mannered mother and haughty older brother, after learning about the many rounds of therapy from which she'd emerged with a clean bill of mental health, Russell was finally compelled to share how his own father had abandoned him.

"How old were you?" she'd asked.

"Six."

"That's horrible."

He'd shrugged. "It happened."

That there'd been no indication of the man's unhappiness; that he was quiet and patient, with good stature in the community; that Russ could still occasionally summon his oaky presence in the living room sofa's upholstery, could still remember calling him Bàba, only sharpened his confoundment when his father left.

"But you have to hand it to him," Russ had added. "He never looked back. He never tried to reconnect or make amends."

"You're impressed by that?"

"There's an integrity to it. A dedication to change."

"Or maybe he just sectioned himself off and amputated the part he couldn't stand. He tossed it away."

"Amputation is still a form of change."

"Well, that's very magnanimous of you."

"It's more of a self-preservation thing. It's so I can move on."

"Right," she'd said.

Pragmatism was key to self-preservation. It was why Russ had grown up cataloging the possible banalities that had driven his father away: how the rattling of the tin cup that held his toothbrush, or the shard of light that broke through the window at the same angle every morning, or even the vaguely distorted mirror of his young son's face—the crookedness of mouth that confirmed their kinship—one or all of those things had probably become too much to bear.

He imagined that sometimes it came to that.

And other times a ballistic missile warning made in error might so thoroughly shift the axis of your thinking that you were induced to consider all the other ways you could have lived—all the opportunities for transformation that you were squandering.

* * *

Back when Miles was a baby, Russ had enjoyed finding increasingly elaborate ways to play peekaboo with him—sometimes standing at a distance and waving, holding a blanket before him and then vanishing into another room as it fell.

He remembered doing this once, standing out of sight behind the door, waiting to hear his son's whimpers, his panic, and hearing, instead, his giggling. The sounds of life moving on. He'd stood there, slightly aggrieved, then embarrassed. A grown man, still obsessed with object permanence.

And he'd managed to keep such obsessions in check for most of his adult life. But there'd been moments since the birth of his child (and especially if he'd had something to drink) when Russell had fallen into a loop of anger and compulsion, and tried to look up his father.

There were more than a few Zhangs out there, more than a few of whom were pharmacists, like his father had been. Nothing conclusive ever came of his Google searches. Nor did his memory help very much. All he could conjure was a quiet man with a crooked smile and a coiffed wave of black hair. Someone who'd once gently cupped the side of his neck, breathed in the smell of his scalp, and called him érzǐ.

And how relieved Russ had been at the ease with which he was able to love his own quiet son. How delighted, when Baby Miles began sucking on his middle and ring fingers instead of his thumb—pinky and forefinger perched on each cheek—which Ruthie had said resembled the sign for *I love you* in ASL, and which they soon adopted as a broad family gesture, like the sign-off at the end of a phone call.

But his boy was almost six now—the same age Russ had been when he was abandoned. And while Miles had never been an especially verbal child, he'd developed a reticence lately that seemed stubborn, almost withholding. Like a preemptive distancing.

Ruthie said it was anxiety related. Russ, for his part, could not understand what might make a kindergartner anxious. Nor could he explain why it revived his own shameful fear of somehow inheriting his father's instinct for desertion—as if his dedication to his family might suddenly seem contrived, and the family gesture, *I love you*, might become a reminder as much as an affirmation.

The worry only intensified when he recalled certain occasions, growing up, when he'd unironically admired his father's resolve. When he'd imagined heeding that same call-of-the-void temptation, the thrill of all that woundedness left behind.

Or those moments that had cut through his glowing hatred, that subsumed the near-sexual fantasy of approaching his father and throwing his fist in retribution, when he'd thought he might like to get to know the man, too.

These desires were like itchy scabs—they had their own irresistible topologies; they were growths that had risen from the wound and developed a scaly, fascinating pattern. And yes, you were supposed to leave them alone. Let them dry out and gradually fall away. But if you'd never had one before, how would you know to do this?

And why hadn't his father left a note? Anything? Even a brusque *I'm sorry*? The difference such a tiny, effortless gesture would have made. The frail peace they could've spun from it. *He was suffering from something. It was inevitable.*

Instead of evenings that withered with grief and recrimination. His mother shouting at his wàipō in Mandarin: "*If you hadn't made me marry him, none of this would have happened. None of this. I didn't even like him!*"

And his wàipō, nodding at the ground, her hands grasped behind her back. "*I did what I thought was right. I did what every mother was doing for every daughter. I'm so sorry.*"

"How could he do this? Why weren't we good enough for him?"

"Sometimes the only thing you know about a person is what he says."

"But he was so quiet."

"Yes."

And moments, eventually, that came to resemble happiness, or at least contentment.

As on those short winter days when the sun began to set at three or four in the afternoon, when the three of them stumbled through the backyard, collecting fallen boughs and clusters of pine cones and scrolls of birch bark in plastic grocery bags, so that when evening arrived, they could start a fire whose flickering enchantments portended a better future.

Or the afternoon when his hapless mother had tried to teach him how to drive their emphysemic little shitwagon, with Wàipō in the back seat screaming to avoid trees and other cars that were many *feet* away, and how, in a climax of confusion, he'd actually rear-ended a police cruiser—the officer stepping out of his vehicle and raising his arms and shouting, "Are you kidding me?"

The lunacy of it. His mother laughing so hard that tears gathered at the edges of her eyes.

As he grew older, he thought: a family was of modular design. You could swap out the broken, truant pieces for new ones. You could regain the old functionality. It was resilient in that way. There was no tragedy, no wound, that might destroy it.

Except, perhaps, wholesale annihilation.

* * *

And then it was Monday, and during his call with the other regional salespeople, someone brought up the errant missile alert as if it were a joke.

"If it happens for real, is it cool if I get your accounts?"

"I'm surprised you didn't send a final eff-you email to Vicki."

And Russ laughed relievedly along with them, because their flippancy allowed some welcome space between himself and the haunting recollection of believing he was going to die. Of lying beside his family and still feeling hopelessly separated by inches of porcelain and steel springs.

Most of all, it helped to dispel the nagging sensation that he was squandering some sort of opportunity for rediscovery: a second chance brought about by a somewhat-near-death experience.

"We're running low on milk," Ruthie said when he greeted her. "The eggs lack *fluffiness*."

He kissed her. He was going on the road that evening, his trunk loaded up with textbooks. And their tradition each time he went on these trips was for him to return with a carton of milk, as if he'd only been gone for a few minutes.

He liked this part of his job. The time away from his wife and child made him realize how much he needed them. There were moments when he was lying on the scratchy, dry sheets of some Courtyard by Marriott or Days Inn, when he imagined his family like perfectly idealized avatars of happiness. Like golden sprites, kept safe in a separate life.

It almost made him happier to have them at a distance, to be certain in his memories of them and his sensations of being with them. As if his own presence were an intrusion that might break the spell of their being together.

He liked visiting colleges, too. He liked how each campus seemed its own miniature civilization, with its own distinct culture, all pomp and privilege. He admired the hardy potential of the students: lusty, emotional, confused, risk ready. All around him, the sense of continuity and renewal.

There was also a new edition of a chemistry textbook he'd leisurely perused, recalling with pleasure certain familiar topics, which he needed to convince professors to adopt for their courses. And as he waited one late afternoon for an appointment with a department chair, Russ noticed a familiar-looking face.

A young man, Asian, with the same curvature of the mouth as his father, as himself—subtler, nearer the very edge of his lips. But regardless, there. He listened in on the conversation.

"My dad is a pharmacist, and he basically confirmed that sildenafil citrate is also correct in this situation."

"Leo, I'm sorry, but the reaction mechanism isn't the same," the department chair was saying. "It's not the answer I was looking for."

A pause, in which even the indignation felt vaguely familiar. The sense of being entitled to something and having it snatched away for no particular reason.

He waited in the hallway for the kid to emerge, the fluorescent lights reflecting in bursts off the skid-streaked linoleum, until finally, he saw him exit toward the main double doors. He ditched his own meeting, following the kid out onto the quad's latticed walkway.

They were of similar height, their strides of similar length. His entire existence seemed focused to a pin. It was vanishingly unlikely. And yet, hadn't he been ready to believe, mere days ago, that a ballistic missile was cruising toward his home?

He caught up and put a hand on his shoulder. "Hey, you said your dad is a pharmacist, right?"

The kid turned swiftly, alarm painted on his face. "What? Who are you?"

Yes, the similarities were striking. The timbre of their voices, the angle of their noses, the slight skew of their mouths. It was like staring at an alternate version of himself.

"How old is he, roughly?"

"Hey, man, I don't know you."

"And your name is Leo? What's your last name?"

"Dude, back the fuck off."

"I'm not trying to fuck with you. Okay? Please, just, can you just show me a picture of him? I'm sure you have one on your phone."

The kid was backing slowly toward one of the blue campus security boxes.

"Wait." Russ put his hands up. "Let me buy you a beer. How about that? Please."

And this seemed to ever so slightly lower his inhibitions. He paused before a lamppost. "Who are you?"

"I'm a textbook rep. But I think I might know your dad."

"What does that even mean? Haven't you heard of Google?"

"Well, I need to know his name. What's your dad's name?"

"Francis Song."

His heart scudding. "Okay, well, my dad—he could've switched his name or changed his identity or something. Come on, let's get a drink."

"Dude, no. Get the fuck away." Leo reached the security box. He placed his palm over the gleaming red call button. "Go. Get out of here. I'm serious."

"Fine. Fine."

Russ returned to his hotel room with fresh urgency and few sales leads. He was fraught with a heightened desire for explanation, for closure. And as he stared at the unsold chemistry textbook, he was reminded of a familiar concept he'd encountered in its pages: the uncertainty principle. How every act of perception—sight, smell, touch—amounted to an inference drawn from the way tiny particles reacted when unsettled. How this meant you could never measure anything at the atomic scale with complete certainty, because the mere act of observation was itself a form of disruption.

He'd felt a shiver of recognition, reading this. A sense of neediness and looming isolation that returned to him now and drove him toward his phone, to the chain of messages he'd exchanged days ago with a near stranger named Milly. To respond to the latest one with Hey.

He recalled the details of his meeting her with growing confidence. A slick, brass bar; ebullient vodka sodas. The lights low and swaying. Her cherry lips slightly parted, as if his words were the bubbles spritzing high above their drink glasses and she was catching them with her mouth.

Hey, she wrote back.

He didn't know why he asked if, maybe, she wanted to catch up? There was a casual place in Wingham, the Bellwether, did she know that one? Yes, she was familiar.

Perhaps the missile had left a very real impact in his mind: It had collapsed a false floor, revealing a room full of old memories, old regrets.

Did she want to meet there?

Yes. When?

He would let her know.

*   *   *

Russ thought he found him once—his father.

He'd been a prospective student, visiting campus, when he noticed an older man of roughly his own height and build, with the same asymmetry to his lips and a scholarly crest of black hair, striding across the acorn-skittered lawn.

Their glances intersected for the briefest moment—just long enough for him to note the man's surprise and, possibly, panic. His drooping mouth. But by the time Russ collected his own courage and willed himself to follow, he'd already lost track of him in a weather system of tour groups.

"Did you ever hear anything else about him?" he'd asked his mother later.

She was remarried by then to a kind fellow named Robert—a white man with a limp from a work accident, who lived comfortably off the settlement money and moved them into his home.

Wàipō had stayed alive just long enough to attend the backyard wedding, blazing with happiness. And Russell, who'd been accepted to nearly every Ivy League college, was experiencing the compulsive thrill of being sought after. They were a living rebuke to absentee fathers.

"*No*," she'd said, as they sat together in Robert's spacious dining room. "*I'd like to think he just started over.*"

"With a new family?"

"I don't know."

"Or maybe he just wanted to be alone forever."

"Please, bǎobèi. I learned a long time ago that this isn't the right way to think about things."

"Would you give him a second chance? If he came back?"

"Definitely not."

"What if he'd come back after a year?"

She let the question linger while tapping a march on the table. *"Not with what I know now."*

"What do you know now?"

"Just how happy I am with you and Robert."

"What if you didn't feel that way?"

Her expression muddied. *"Then yes, probably."*

He didn't know why he was asking or what to do with the information. Or how to reconcile the fact that he'd never stopped seeing apparitions of his father in every Asian man he encountered. How his first instinct was always to glance at their mouths.

"Would you forgive him? If he came back today?"

"Āiyā, I don't know."

"You really don't?"

A cool, dry gust disturbed the dining room curtains. *"Things can change like you wouldn't believe,"* his mother said through a sigh. *"The world is too huge, and life too tiny, for you to ever stop making mistakes. I don't want to get any bigger than I am right now. My life is just the right size, I have just enough beautiful things. So don't ask me that other stuff anymore, please."*

He'd assented. There was a wiseness to her that squared imperfectly with her youth, as if the grief and disorientation of the past decade or so had imparted a lifetime of thoughtfulness upon her—an openness to life's mysteries, an almost yearning for its heartbreak.

She was still impossibly beautiful and elegant when she had her first stroke, and Robert—who really was a good man—asked Russ's permission to move her into an assisted-living facility.

* * *

"You forgot the milk," Ruthie said, frowning, when he got home.

"Oh shit," he said. "Sorry."

"Ironically, this time we actually do need it."

"I can go get it."

"It's fine."

The days were growing incrementally warmer, the sun winking through trees whose branches were brimming with leaves like full heads of hair. And soon would arrive the lazy sibilation of insect life, the local school district's weeklong fanfare of graduation and matriculation.

These were soothing rhythms; they did an anxious heart good.

"If the missile thing were real and I died from it, what would you put in my obituary?" he asked her.

"What kind of question is that?"

"Just humor me. Please."

"I'd say Russell Zhang, a good father, a good husband, with slightly obsessive tendencies."

She made a cuckoo sign with her finger around her ear, and Miles giggled (he had Ruthie's straightforward mouth). She drew her fingertips over the boy's forehead, brushing a forelock of curly brown hair out of his eyes, just as the checkered outline of the kitchen window shadowed them both. A mother and child, separate from him. As if he were staring in on their lives.

"No, not my headstone. I mean my actual obituary."

Her seeking eyes were like camera lenses, trying to read him at various depths, to understand what was going on and bring it into focus. *Good luck*, he thought.

"Sweetheart, go watch some TV," she said to Miles instead. She waited for the volume to rise before looking back at him.

"I need you to stop acting weird for a moment so we can talk. I want Miles to see a specialist. His teachers say he still doesn't speak enough, and he doesn't seem to be making friends."

"So he's shy," Russell said, feeling crushed by sudden futility.

"I'm worried it's something else."

"So you want him slapped with a diagnosis and put on some sort of medication for the rest of his life? At his age?"

"We can have that conversation when it comes up."

"I don't want this messing with him, with his confidence."

"I— *We* won't let it."

And the abrupt, unbidden thought: How it sometimes felt as if the only way to reconcile his feelings of abandonment, his desire to be deeply wanted, was to abandon his own family in turn. To transfer the hurt down another generation.

He shook the idea out of his head.

Ruthie was scrutinizing him. "They fired Mrs. Coombs, by the way."

Days ago, Miles's teacher, Mrs. Coombs, had asked them to draw their feelings about the false missile alert, and Miles had returned home with three ghoulish skeletons sketched in black crayon, standing before a soot-colored house bathed in spiky red flames.

Russ had flinched. "Fucking yikes."

"What the hell did she expect?" Ruthie had said.

They learned later that the little assignment had produced such an outpouring of disturbing art—humanoid figures dashed with bright red X-shaped eyeballs, family dogs with limbs torn asunder—that the district had shelled out money for a child therapist to visit each classroom.

"Maybe you want to see one, too?" Ruthie said to him now. "Like, a therapist?"

"I am completely fine."

Her eyes widened. "You're sure? You have nothing to unburden yourself of?"

He wondered, for an alarming moment, if she'd peeked in his phone and seen the messages from Milly. "So is this your cure-all now? Just send everyone to the doctor?"

"Well, yes. I'm of the opinion that a person with a clinical issue should, generally speaking, avail himself of professional support if it's available."

"And what is my issue, exactly?"

"Grief," she said matter-of-factly.

"You have to lose something, presumably, in order to grieve."

"You have. You lost your dad, didn't you?"

Yes. Decades ago. A full lifetime, basically. And he had so little in common with the hurt, angry boy from back then. He'd made such a conscious effort to abandon him.

Although a resonant truth struck him now: how a traumatic event might very well reactivate old feelings. And no matter the time that had passed, no matter the maturity incurred, a person who'd been running from something for as long as he could remember, who was far enough away to have lost track of it altogether, had still oriented his life around its occurrence.

"You know I hate it when you do this," Russell said softly. "When you use what happened with my father as a way to undermine my opinions."

Ruthie shook her head in resignation. "That's not what I'm trying to do at all."

"I'm fine," he said. "And so is Miles. Neither of us is going to see anyone, because we're both fine."

Ruthie kept her expression neutral, although he noticed the same twitch at her temple, the same subtle ripple of her jaw, that emerged when she spoke about her childhood. "Can't you see, though, how you might not be the best judge of that?"

"Of what?"

"Of whether your son needs help? I mean, what if there's something inherited that you wouldn't know about?"

"Anyone can get diagnosed with something if they're looking for it," he said heatedly. "I know a guy who was so anxious his doctor wouldn't prescribe him Xanax that he got prescribed Xanax for it."

"Russell—"

"Look, I thought you said you were happy. Remember when I asked you? You said you were perfectly happy with everything in your life."

"That doesn't mean—"

"So you were lying."

"Russell, let me—"

"Tell me, yes or no: Were you lying?"

He was hardly aware of raising his voice until he heard his son's from the kitchen entryway. The boy's precious, withholding squeak. "Stop yelling, please."

"Oh, buddy." A fierce regret doused everything Russell had been feeling a moment prior, leaving only shame. "I'm so sorry."

"Stop yelling, please," Miles said again, his expression eerily calm, open in a way that suggested receptivity, absorption.

"Your mom and I— Sorry." He held up his hand; he made the pronged *I love you* sign. Although it felt vague and insufficient now. Diluted with too much historical meaning.

His boy returned to the living room without acknowledging. While Ruthie threw him a beseeching look, an implicit appeal to *snap out of it*, before following Miles.

II.

The sound was like that of an insect colliding rhythmically, repeatedly, against a window. The reverberant *pitter-patter*. His phone buzzing upon the countertop.

"Dad! Dad!" came Miles's voice from the living room. "Your phooone!"

"Thank you, Miles. I can hear it." (And he hoped Ruthie could hear it, too—their perfectly verbal child.)

The screen read ROBERT, his stepfather.

"First of all, your mother's okay," he said when Russ answered.

"Robert? What's going on?"

"She's going to be just fine, but she'll need more specialized care. I'm thinking of moving her back into the house. Maybe hire a nurse or a physical therapist to live here part-time, too."

"What happened?"

"She had another stroke," he said. "It's bullshit, what was going on at that nursing home. I'm going to sue it out of existence."

Russell pressed his forehead against the cool window, re-creating his hairline in fog against the glass. He squeezed the bridge of his nose until his nails pierced the skin. "But it's not bad?"

"Like I said, nothing to worry about right now. She's resting at the hospital."

He felt an enormous swell of appreciation for his stepfather. "Thank you. Truly."

"But Russ, she's having some trouble communicating. The doctor says she may have developed some kind of condition. Aphasia or something. Like, all her words are scrambled. Her speech doesn't make any sense."

"What? That can happen?"

"Apparently. And I think she wants to see you. I think she might want to tell you something. I got that impression, at least. So, come soon, if you can."

He rushed out without telling Ruthie and found his mother at the hospital, fastened with a serene smile. She was a bit grayer and thinner than before, but her eyes were full of awareness as she grasped his hands with hers.

She opened her mouth, swallowed. She said, "It left after, I try plan to . . . to seek it."

"Mom. Sorry. What? Do you want to try Chinese?"

Her face contorted with effort as she nodded. Her breaths grew raspy. "*A pair of paper*"—swallowing—"*A strand of message.*" She shook her head and squinted, as if language were fleeing from her. As if she had to chase down and fully ingest each word in order to relearn its shape, to match signifier and signified, and teach her tongue and throat to form the proper sounds.

It hurt him so deeply to see her like this.

"Fah-ther," she said finally.

"My father?"

Robert shifted on the lumpy chair beside the door. It gave a faint squeak.

Her head pitched in strenuous confirmation.

"What about him?"

She motioned to Robert, who faltered over, disposed toward his intact foot, and handed him a sheet of paper, folded sharply twice to fit inside an envelope. There was a faint yellowing along its pristine edges. It crinkled as he opened it.

A handwritten note:

Please don't contact me again.

And when he looked up, her eyes were glassy, the skin around them red and swollen. Her jaw rippled fiercely.

"What is this? What happened?"

She opened her mouth again, but all he could hear was a dry clicking. A helpless frustration emitting from her throat.

He turned to Robert, who shrugged. "I think it's from your dad. I don't really know anything more. She kept bringing it up on her way here. How she needed to have it and, I guess, give it to you."

"Why are you showing me this now?" he asked her.

"I have a chance, but I what also not learn of."

"Is there something you want me to do with this? What are you trying to tell me?"

"Face not to rise."

"Mom. Please. What's going on?"

"I am in debt to you a sorry," she said in Mandarin.

Robert turned toward the window that overlooked the parking lot. He put his hands on his crooked hips; he let his shoulders shake.

* * *

Russell spent hours after he left the hospital driving aimlessly around town, trying to distill what he knew:

That his mother had searched for and found his father, although he had no idea how recently it had happened. And he could only hazard the vaguest idea of what it had been like: The two of them standing before each other. The questions posed and answered. The occasion fraught with such awkwardness and hostility.

And even these dubious imaginings caused him exquisite pain.

Perhaps she'd seen his gorgeous new home, his attractive new family. Or perhaps he lived in a bachelor's sad, empty apartment. Perhaps she'd smacked him or screamed at him or made a big scene or begged him, piteously, to come back. Perhaps the two of them had reconciled, followed by his change of heart. Perhaps he'd revealed whatever it was about Russell that had been worth abandoning.

Please don't contact me again.

And how pathetic Russ felt! As he recalled those treasured moments with his own family—at the vinegar-scented orchard, picking apples at sunset; at the windy beach, watching Miles race his shadow to sea. And how he'd been invaded in each instance by a rogue desire: that his father might be there to witness all he'd made without him.

Although he knew now that the man would not have been moved. He'd been given a kind of second chance and hadn't taken it. He'd been offered redemption on a platter and waved it away. And how could Russell possibly understand someone like this?

At some point he texted Milly. He asked if she was free to meet at the place they'd discussed. The Bellwether, right? She said yes.

* * *

"Gosh, I'm so embarrassed!" she shouted, eyes zigzagging across the cramped, divey interior. It seemed fairly empty for a Friday night, although the music was so loud and percussive Russ could feel the tiny bones in his ears rattling.

He scooted his wobbly chair closer to the edge of their table and angled forward. "There's no reason to be," he said. "We thought we were going to die."

"I was so scared."

"We all were."

She was as he remembered her: wide-faced, long-haired, roughly his age, with twin divots in her cheeks that resembled the sandy top half of an hourglass—its cavitation as time passed.

"I think I was most scared of not having done anything or left anything behind," she said. "Which is so silly, when you think about it. Because, I mean, who knew what was really going to happen? Maybe the entire world was going to end. Maybe it was the start of a serious nuclear war. And then, why would it even matter who I'd been? Or what I'd left behind?"

Her nervousness, her want of affirmation, reminded him of an arctic animal navigating springtime—trembling as the ice cracked and began drifting in sheets, forced in a moment to decide which piece to stake her future upon.

"Were you not convinced?" she said.

"I never thought it was nothing. But I guess I was skeptical."

And the way her mouth fell slightly open confirmed that this was an impressively nonchalant, masculine view to take. She seemed eager to keep talking. "So, do you still like your job?"

He nodded and put back his drink. He asked a passing waitress for another; he spoke more expansively. "Well, the thing is, I always had these high expectations for myself in Hanover—maybe it was because of all the stuff they gave you to read, all these great thinkers, these incredible ideas that have shaped the world. So when it was time to get practical, I didn't want to give myself to any old company. You only get one wild and precious life, you know?"

He was vaguely aware of having repeated this speech several times throughout his life; it was designed to elicit admiration.

"I wanted to do something where I could keep learning," he went on easily. "So when I graduated and left Hanover, I thought, okay, well, why not work in books? Why not work at the nexus of knowledge creation, basically? Know what I mean?"

Milly nodded lightly, but she wasn't hanging on to his words like he would've hoped. She hadn't even given him an opening to say that he'd gone to Dartmouth, which he always liked to mention in an abashed way.

"But then again, I was limited by the nature of editorial gigs, because editors can only focus on one book at a time, and they have to develop a niche, you know? So I was just lucky that this position opened up as a salesperson, and that getting to know our list and how to sell it involved learning the material, mastering the pedagogy, in order to make a convincing argument to university professors that our books teach their students better than others. They say that the most effective way to prove your mastery of a subject is to be able to teach it, after all."

"Right." And now her body language was pure indifference: her slender fingers tapping some coded distress message on the table, her big eyes wandering across the room, settling on the clock hanging above the bar. She regarded him with coldness. "I'm not interested in an affair, okay?" There was a vague note of injury in her voice.

"Oh, no, no." He shook his head. "Neither am I." Although hope seemed to leak from a hidden puncture, which was quickly infected by shame. The fact that he hadn't thought of Ruthie until now.

"So then, why did you want to meet if nothing has changed?"

He didn't realize how drunk he was until he motioned for another drink and clipped the edge of a nearby plate, sending it wobbling noisily along its rounded axis, while she cringed. "I guess because it was new to me," he said. "Getting a note like that."

Because he'd never been on the other side of such an incommensurate impression. And because he'd hoped she might reveal a more compelling, interesting version of him to himself.

"I have to admit," he added, "I don't really remember what we talked about that evening."

"Well, it started with this exact thing with your job. Then I told you how I was a music therapist who worked with incarcerated people, although I was on a leave of absence because someone had recently broken into my house."

"That's incredibly brave and noble of you."

"Yeah, you said that, too."

Russell was curious about the rest of their conversation but too ashamed by what he might've uttered about his family, and too alarmed by what truth there might've been to things said and done on impulse, while free of inhibition.

He grimaced. "Sorry, I can really drone on."

"It's okay," she said. "It was stupid of me to text you."

"This whole thing was maybe not the best idea."

She looked up at him, her eyes shining with urgency. "The thing is, I thought I was going to die. And I was *so* not ready. I was so disappointed, suddenly, with the way my life was. And then when you started writing back, I don't know, I thought maybe you'd have some kind of solution, or maybe you somehow were a solution. I don't know why I hoped that. I think I was just desperate."

"A solution to what?"

"To this hunger I have sometimes," she said. "This feeling that I'm entitled to more—I don't know—a longer future, a wider life."

A tremor passed through him. He noticed how thin her wrists were. How childlike. "You know, my dad abandoned me when I was a kid," he said.

And her head canted, her look sharpened. "That must have been difficult."

"It was."

"Do you think about it a lot?"

"I used to, but not as much now," he lied. "I actually learned to sort of respect him for it, because he never tried to reconnect or make amends. There's a certain integrity to that."

She inhaled sharply. "Do you think it's actually possible?"

"What?"

"For a person to make that kind of a decision and not be a monster? To accept it, like it's a part of her, and then to put it away?"

"I thought so." A drink was placed gently before him.

"I was engaged for a while," she said.

"Oh?"

"To a really nice man. I mean, just the kindest, most thoughtful person. And at some point, I guess, I realized I didn't love him. Or if I did, it wasn't enough. I was constantly weighing him against my own future. Which is funny, because I didn't have any idea what my future was supposed to look like, or what I even wanted. But when you're having those kinds of thoughts—well, it means something, doesn't it?"

He had no idea. The din of the bar was like a trellis, carrying her voice toward him.

"I remember waking up before he did one day, staring at him, and feeling as if I were looking at this—this rack of features. Like, everything about him was so peaceful and straightforward. And for some reason, I blew on his nose to disturb him a bit, and when he blinked awake, it was like when you break in a game of pool—his entire face opened and there was this moment of confusion and doubt before he realized it was me, and he smiled like everything had come to rest exactly as expected."

She took a large gulp of wine. Through the distortion of the glass, her face seemed magnified, abstracted. She left a faint spore of fog from her exhale.

"And I couldn't stand it," she went on. "I couldn't stand the way he relied on me. I couldn't stand being *seen* that way—the look in his eyes, my reflection in them. I couldn't stand the idea of coming to life through someone else." Milly gazed at him with entreaty. "And isn't that terrible? Don't you deserve every kind of loneliness if you refuse to give yourself to someone who will see you in the most favorable way? Someone you know will always love you, no matter what?"

"Yes."

"But there were plenty of other mornings," she said, signaling for another drink. "So many ordinary, beautiful mornings. I remember when he and I were staying at this cabin on Mount Greylock, and the light was shining through the pine trees. It was early; I was outside. And the air was sharp and cold, and my feet were sinking in this bed of dead leaves and pine needles, and I remember feeling so lucky, so happy, knowing he was there with me—but *inside the cabin*. And I thought, if only I could expect mornings like this to keep arriving—these opportunities to just *watch*— then I might be fine with all the other uncertainties, the exhaustion."

Russell imagined himself staring into a translucent globe in which his family was safely stored. And a larger one nested around him, through which his father gazed. Generations with their noses pressed against one-way glass. Estrangement as inheritance.

"Sometimes I'm shocked by how tiny the world is," she said. "How it can't possibly hold all the lives I want to live inside of it." And his phone's abrupt jittering reminded him, again, of Ruthie: her self-assuredness, her precisely bounded identity. How she deserved someone similar. He ignored the call.

"The idea of a missile attack probably shrank it even more," he said.

"Oh yeah." Her fingers made slight, feathering contact with his shirtsleeve.

"Do you regret it at all?" he said. "Leaving him?"

"Most of the time I don't—not the decision itself—but I keep wondering what my choices say about me. I keep imagining him looking me up, finding out I'm with someone, or finding out I'm not—and just—what it would seem like to him. I feel like I need to be living in a way that justifies what I did. And I have no idea what that looks like." She swayed slightly on her chair, eyes closed, as if mid-fall. "You can try to escape certain people, try to let them go, but you just become beholden to them in different ways."

Yes. A shudder of recognition passed through him. He thought of his family, his father. He thought of those moments when he was accosted by Miles and could not help but lean in to breathe his sweet, innocent smell, to kiss his forehead. Those spasms of love—yes, *love*. He was certain of it.

Certain?

Or perhaps there was a degree of performance at the core of his life, as if each paternal act were colored by filial memory. Perhaps it was somehow Russell's fault his son was so quiet.

"But we'll move on, right?" he said in hardly a whisper.

She tilted her head at him. "I think I need to at least see the different possibilities—you know, the different ways I can be alive. Not necessarily live them. Just an impression should be fine. Maybe a sampling. Enough for me to imagine myself in them."

"Is that enough?"

"I think so. It is for some people. God, I hope I'm not wrong about myself." And now her lips were rounded in anticipation. "I'm sorry I texted you," she said. "It was stupid. I was being stupid."

"I'm glad you did."

He wanted to kiss her, to embrace her. He thought that if he went no further than this, if he stayed assiduously within those bounds, he might be able to reconcile this behavior with his conviction that he was still a good man. He might be able to couch it as a natural response to the overwhelming fear that he'd sleepwalked thus far through this life.

He might even understand his father a bit better.

So he leaned in further. And her face grew big, her eyes expanded, as she pushed herself back.

"Oh. No, no. I'm sorry. I can't."

"It's fine," he said thickly. "I need this."

"No, it's not that."

"Oh." He sat back. "What is it?"

"It's just that—this whole thing was a bad idea. I was being stupid. And you were the only one who texted me back."

* * *

Russell drove home in a haze of needling guilt, interrupted by a momentary panic when he noticed a police car following close behind. But when he maneuvered onto his street, it turned on its lights and blazed past him.

He felt like someone for whom object permanence did not apply. He was there until he wasn't. How stupid to have thought he'd left a lingering impression on someone—a fascination powerful enough to surface in her final, panicking moments.

He was standing abruptly before Ruthie, his hand on her shoulder, shaking her awake.

"Russ? What is it? Where the hell have you been?"

"You don't regret marrying me, right?"

"You fucking reek."

"Or the life we have, right? And whatever's going on with Miles, it's just a phase. Right?"

"What?" Annoyance pooled in her glare. "I'm not talking to you when you're like this."

And through his wavy drunk logic, Russell perceived insult and unfairness, a profound lack of warmth. But most of all, frustration. Because no one—not one single person—seemed capable of straightforward communication. Of granting him the certainty he craved, of easing his turbulent anxiety. And because he was beginning to feel as if disrupting his own life and observing the subsequent response was the only way to truly know if he was going about it correctly at all.

"If I want to drink, I should be able to drink," he said. "Ninety-nine percent of the time it doesn't even affect you. I keep to myself ninety-nine percent of the fucking time."

She gathered the blanket and rolled away from him. "Sofa for you tonight" came her distant voice.

"Look—" he sputtered, then steadied himself. He was feeling equal parts desperate and resigned, his heart growling for self-destruction. "Did you go through my phone?"

"What?" She rolled back.

"Did you?"

"How could you accuse me of that?"

"That's not an answer."

"Should I have?"

"Still not an answer."

"I'm not talking to you in this state," she said, her composure only intensifying his recklessness.

"Look, this is such bullshit. Just because, you know, your dad was a bum doesn't mean I automatically become one by having a few drinks."

She sat up, locked her elbows behind her. "Get. Out."

"No, what I mean is—"

"Get out, Russell." Her voice was still low and controlled, but her face was closed to him. Her look was granite. "Get out. Right now."

And then it was the next morning, reality assaulting him with particular callousness as he awoke on the living room couch. And his concussive hangover was of a piece with the anxiety pounding through his body. The leaky, plunging feeling.

He rubbed his eyes. Blurs of color, smudges of light, coalesced into Ruthie and Miles, standing before the front door. "So, I think we should take a break," Ruthie announced firmly.

"A break?"

Miles's face was a palette of fear and mourning, although he stood straight-backed beside his mother, as if already prying himself of his need for two parents.

Ruthie's expression was frighteningly impassive. She was a model of competent adulthood. "Just a break from being a family."

"You're kidding."

"No."

"Come on. Please."

"You need to figure your shit out, Russell." She chopped the air, as if lecturing a student. "All of it."

"And that's a great reason to leave me, is it?"

"Do you even remember what you insinuated last night?"

"That was nothing."

"Do you really feel stable enough to raise a child? To make important decisions about his future?"

His breath faltered—another swoop of dread. And he felt the same helplessness, the same inability to persuade now as he had when Leo was backing away from him, toward the campus security box.

"You've been unbalanced ever since the missile thing," she said. "And I don't think you'll recover until you confront whatever it brought up. And I love you—I love you so much. Miles, too. But I work with enough kids, and I will not be your mother, too."

"There's nothing to confront," he said immediately.

A bleakness settled on her face. "I don't exist just to soothe every irrational fear you have, like some screwed-up game of Whac-A-Mole, because you feel some new emotional kinship with your father. So now you have your second chance. We're giving it to you. Use it well."

Russell stared at his son. "Miles," he said. "Say something."

The boy looked back at him, a mute face scalloped with unease.

"Did you hear me? Say something, please."

"Goodbye, Russ," Ruthie said.

"Miles!" Russell held up his hand and made the pronged family gesture, though it felt fully inadequate. He was so hopelessly far from language, from anything that might address or ameliorate the situation.

He was more like his mother than he thought.

* * *

He sat alone while the evening descended. Until the sun's brilliance was smothered altogether. His dim emotions, like the contours of the darkened room, were hardly distinguishable.

He recalled that concept he'd encountered in the chemistry text—the one about uncertainty and the contradictions of measurement. The necessity of disturbance. Well, he'd done a fine job of that, hadn't he? He felt the temptations of a shame-erasing drink.

Instead, he got in his car. He drove through the night.

The receptionist at the Courtyard by Marriott recognized him. "No reservation, Mr. Zhang?"

"No, unfortunately."

"Well, we can find a room for you, I'm certain. One moment."

The weekend campus was like an entirely different country: Jouncy music echoing from across the quad. The streets and walkways twice as populated. Room lights left blazingly on.

It was far simpler than Russell expected, finding Leo again, as he made his way from his dorm building. The kid's eyes were hazy with drunkenness, his face loose and relaxed. His mouth, as ever, crooked.

He smiled and said, "Fine. I'll take that drink now."

They sat down at a campus bar, on opposite sides of a sticky wooden table from whose surface rose the chlorinous smell of disinfectant and light beer dissolved equally into a solvent, spread by a mildewed rag.

The drinks arrived in plastic cups before them.

"I really can only stay for one," Leo said. "I have a party later." And he added, "Sorry, no randos allowed."

"No problem." Russ was thankful for how weak the drink was—diluted to an extent that could only fool undergraduates. It made him less tempted to want another. "So, I think I may be your brother," he said. "Well, half brother."

The boy nodded. "You know, I thought you were maybe hinting at that when you were stalking me. But I'm pretty sure my dad doesn't have a past life or a hidden family somewhere."

"My dad left me and my mom when I was just a kid. He was a pharmacist, too. And look, we have the same mouth." He pointed at the corner of his lip; he dragged it down for effect.

Leo laughed. "Well, okay, here." He swiped through his phone and found a satisfactory picture. He held it up before him. Russell squinted. A happy family. Father, mother, and son, standing at a mountain's scenic lookout. The man did not look familiar. There was no particular jaggedness anywhere on his face, no profound similarity in his gaze. Although perhaps some people changed more severely than others. Perhaps age lent a certain genericity that erased the other features.

"So, is that your long-lost pops?" Leo said, his arm still extended.

"It could be. Show me some more."

He handed him the phone from across the table. "Don't scroll past the photos from that hiking trip, unless you want to see dick."

Russell frowned up at him in a big-brotherly sort of way. "Who keeps his own dick pics?"

"They're not all mine."

"Oh. Okay." It took a moment to register the implication. "So does that mean you're—"

"Yep."

A minor surprise. And as he tested it out—*My little brother is gay*—the prospect filled him with a curious pleasure. A quaint, unexpected warmth, as if the narrative were no longer entirely of his own making. As if there were now something he could react to, with love.

He flipped through the photos. A happy family, standing before miles of brilliant, sweeping seascape. If anything, Leo's mother resembled his own to a far uncannier degree. They had the same lovely smile—dimples so low they nearly dotted their chins. The same high forehead.

"Where is this?" he asked. "Maine?"

Leo nodded. "Acadia. My folks are big on national parks for vacation. At first I thought they were cheap, but after living in these crowded-ass dorms for two years, I kind of get it. All the open air, the open space."

He himself had never been on any vacations until Ruthie took him, one sunny weekend, to the Cape. He gave the phone back.

"So," Leo said with a tinge of fear and expectation. "Is it him? Will I have to hold an intervention or something with my dad?"

"I can't really tell."

"Ah, well, I'm not giving you a DNA sample."

"That's fine." He motioned for the check. "You had a good childhood, right? All things considered?"

Leo shrugged. "I guess. I mean, you probably know about the whole demanding-Asian-parent thing—or, actually, maybe not—"

"I do," he lied.

"Well then, yeah. I mean, it could be annoying at times, but yeah. I did; I'm grateful for them. Sorry, no offense."

And the ache in his chest, at this very moment—was it from disappointment or relief? He didn't know. He could take stock a hundred more times and never quite know. "Thank you for this. For talking with me."

"I hope you figure this shit out, man. Seriously. I hope you get some peace."

The evening's impressions were softening, the moments of consequence committed to memory. Russ wondered briefly what kind of certainty he'd truly been seeking since the missile alert. Perhaps whether he was disposed toward a more detached form of love—to being a watcher rather than a participant, which might stave off the inevitable mistakes he'd make as a father and husband.

And perhaps the uncertainty had been the basis of anxiety, too. A mistrust in his present happiness, a fear of its ending. As if there was something slightly more tolerable about a heartbreak of his own making.

He stood up. They shook hands, the boy's firm grip lingering over his own. "Take care of yourself, man."

And for a moment, Russell thought he'd have loved to switch lives with the child now leaving the bar. A sophomore in college with nothing to worry about save grades and getting laid. A relationship with his parents that comprised neither guilt nor rebuke. A healthy, straightforward accord between past and future. Yes, these were things that had been denied him, to which he was reasonably entitled.

But a more sober, mature part of him thought that this should be the end of it—the end of all his wishful thinking, his obsessions. It was one of those things he knew but hadn't truly accepted until now—that growing older was the methodical destruction of possibilities. Like a network of tributaries, filtering into the main trunk of who you were. And, perhaps, who you were always going to become.

He would carry this moment with him—the clearest glimpse he had into the life of his remodeling. He would turn to it during spells of excessive need or introspection or both. And the inky dark purple descending as he stepped outside; the lingering scent of stale hops, evicted by nighttime's damp bloom; the squalls of insects frantically orbiting lamp-post bulbs. The start of something new, and a past he still needed to remedy.

He'd been thinking of them, only them, when the alert came.

SAID AND DONE

Dean Chang

The support group meets in the basement room of the Beckitt Presbyterian Church every Saturday. The room is drafty and dimly lit, with a single window that opens at ground level and gives onto a patch of crabgrass and dandelions. The chairs are arranged in a horseshoe, which, on busier weeks, nearly closes into a full circle.

And Dean Chang is the new presence that eventually settles into the steady rotation of members. The sequence of faces reminds him of the beds of peonies and carnations that Nina liked to plant, that would flower each year and promptly die—the ranks changing, although the garden itself never did.

The group leader is a brisk, assertive woman in her fifties named Nadine Chard, who lost her mother two years ago after an extended stay at the nearby nursing home. She also runs the most successful Mary Kay unit in western Massachusetts.

"One thing everyone needs to realize is that the Kübler-Ross model—denial, anger, bargaining, depression, acceptance—it's all crap," she says. "That's not to say you won't go through certain similar stages, but it's pop psychology. It's not how the mind works."

A thin woman in sneakers and a terry cloth robe honks her nose into a tissue.

"Everyone heals at their own rate," Nadine continues. "Some of you might feel like you're getting better, and *wham*, the grief hits you while you're driving or doing your laundry or at spin class, and that's okay. It's *okay*."

Dean goes for the same reason he suspects they all do—because he is lonely. Because grief erects a private room around its sufferer. And while there's no reliable way to escape, no way to predict when the door will unlock, you can at least pass the time with neighbors.

"Anyway, I'll see you all next week," Nadine says. "Remember to stay positive. And if anyone is interested in any Volu-Firm Lifting Serum, please also see me at the snack table."

He stands up and grabs his jacket, the static clicking as he draws it from the chairback, and feels a tap on his arm. An unfamiliar woman.

"Were you recruited for this?" she asks.

"Pardon?"

"Are you actually grieving? Or are you a plant?"

"My wife died three months ago," he says. "What in the world are you talking about?"

The woman is tall and elegant, her eyes an oceanic blue. Her hair is clipped short, her mouth pressed into a tight thicket of wrinkles. She smells vaguely floral—like lavender. "Sorry. My mistake."

Although her apology seems evasive, almost mischievous. Her face seems only a few taut muscles from falling into a grin. It reminds him, with a pang, of Nina. Her giggling moods.

"Nadine has fake mourners attend these things?" he whispers.

"Well, I've heard she scouts the obituaries. Then she goes on Facebook to find the next of kin, to try to get them to join her group instead of Delilah Fister's."

From across the room, at the spindly snack table, Nadine casts a glowering look at the both of them.

He thinks of the neat, handwritten card he received from her after

Nina's passing. The polite response he'd sent back. Her remarkably sincere lines of questioning. Her casual mention of a low-commitment grief group, in which he could heal on his own terms, in his own time, if he was interested.

"Don't worry, the ugly look is for me," the woman says. "She hates when I'm here."

He's about to ask why, when futility swells in him. A hopelessness so shattering he wants to roll into himself, to guard the trembling soft tissue, the raw woundedness of his heart. Before it shrivels like the rest of him.

He nods and walks back to his car.

* * *

Cate calls him every other day for a perfunctory check-in (they'd ditched the tablet after Nina's passing—too awkward to cry over video call), although her own melancholy seems to have been subsumed by busyness, her Bay Area employer progressive in every aspect save paid family leave.

"Shana and I are getting worked to the bone. We had to hire an au pair for Freddie, but we're afraid it'll mess him up, like, he'll think he's being given away again."

He can't remember ever hiring a babysitter for Cate. In the early days, he and Nina had taken shifts, one of them working the store while the other took care of the fussy child. As she grew older, she became a capable salesperson—her facility with multiple instruments helped convince several hesitant parents to purchase them for their own children.

In fact, Tom Yen, who worked at the urgent care clinic and used to stop by the store to boast of his own daughter's growing achievements, never failed to mention how Rachel had been inspired to pick up the clarinet by Cate's demonstration all those years ago. Dean realizes suddenly that he hasn't seen his old friend since Nina's diagnosis. And his store is just an empty lot now.

"Dad?"

Sometimes it takes his breath away—the blossoming sadness. Like missing a stair.

"Dad, are you there?"

"Yeah, it's nothing." His voice is muddy.

"Dad, sorry, but time for some tough love, here. I know Mom was a great woman, but she was also abusive. She could be so cruel. And everyone had to abide by her moods. I personally never felt safe to express myself."

"Stop that," he says sharply. "Stop it right now."

"I'm sorry, but she was!"

"Cate, you have no idea what it's like—what it means—to sustain a decades-long marriage."

Her hurt carries silently across the line. "Fine."

"And you will one day, I'm sure. But until then— It's not— Your mother wasn't perfect, I know. But you learn to love that about people."

"I get it. I'm sorry."

He wonders if he's picked up some of Nina's old spikiness as a way of coping with her absence. If this is why he's also been feeling bitter about her long-ago refusal to have another baby. Because he knows how lonely it can be as an only child, faced with the intensity of your parents' need. And how Cate had always felt particularly responsible for the happiness of those around her, which was perhaps why she took Nina's moods as such personal failings. He understands why she had to flee.

* * *

The woman is there again the next week. She sits next to him, her floral scent like a rising tide, mixed with the slight, sour funk of mildew. "I'm sorry about your wife," she whispers.

He nods. "Thank you."

The meeting is a pageant of sadness. Tears, tears. A box of Kleenex for every two seats. No trash can, so they're left clinging to the damp, clammy things. Stuffing them in pockets. Letting them pill into lint.

"Quinn, do you have anything to share?" Nadine says tightly, like a schoolteacher.

The woman shakes her head. "No."

They meet in the same corner across from the snack table when it's over. It seems like the beginning of a soothing routine, Nadine's scowls notwithstanding.

He battles his shyness; finally, he manages to speak. "So, uh, do you come here often?"

And she laughs. A high, thrilling shriek.

"Sorry, bad joke."

She sets her luminous eyes upon him. "My son is in prison," she says.

"Oh."

"He drove drunk one evening and collided into another person."

"That's— I'm sorry" is all he can muster.

She shrugs. "It lacks a certain neatness. It's not a very straightforward tragedy, in my case. That's why Nadine thinks I'm crashing her group. It's not so clear-cut with me."

But it is interesting, he thinks. And he is in desperate need of ways in which the world may remain interesting. "I think guilt can be a form of grief," he says. "Not that that's what you feel, but all the big emotions can be filtered into smaller, finer ones, I think."

"Survivor's guilt?"

"Maybe."

"What about guilt over lack of guilt?"

He frowns. "I suppose."

"The thing is, it's been seven years. You'd think that seven years would be enough to figure it out, but it's honestly not even close. There are some days when I think he was treated totally unfairly by the courts. Maybe you think I'm a monster for that, because it's so easy to pass straightforward judgment on cases like these. And sometimes I feel the same way—trust me. Sometimes I find him and what he did to be utterly contemptible.

"But on other days, I feel like intention matters as much as the result. I think about all the alternate realities where nothing happened. And all the ones where he got his license revoked and that was enough of a wake-up call, and I feel horribly shortchanged."

"Do you believe in that?" he asks.

"In what?"

"Alternative realities."

"Oh, no. Too heartbreaking. Because I can't think of a worse outcome than the one I'm living in. I'd be the most unlucky version of myself."

"Well, what if he had died?" Dean blurts stupidly.

She looks at him, her eyes like telescopes. Her gaze narrows and lengthens into a pierce. "I should go."

"Oh, I'm sorry."

"No, no, it's fine. But I should go. If Nadine stares any harder, she'll burn a hole through my shirt."

"Maybe I'll see you—"

But the words are caught in the sweep and flutter of her jacket. The vacuuming thud of the door.

* * *

She's not there at the next meeting. And the shock of his missing her, the surprise exposure of his expectation, sends his heart freshly off-balance.

He calls Cate.

"Hey, Dad, what's up?"

"I was wondering, you mentioned getting an au pair for Freddie, and you know, what's a grandparent for if not to provide some free babysitting?"

He can already hear, from the tightening silence on the other end, that the idea is a dud.

"Dad, you know I love you, and Shana and I would so, so love to have you visit. But the thing is, it's already pretty crowded around here and, you know, hectic. And I just think maybe you need some more time to heal after Mom—and, you know, just get used to a new form of life before you try to make another wholesale change."

You're a burden.

He understands. He should've known better, honestly, than to try to invite himself into his daughter's life. To have suggested it so open-endedly, without even mentioning a length of stay. It strikes him suddenly how pathetic he's become. Nina would've said so. She would've warned him before he committed such an impulsive, embarrassing act.

Although there were times, as well, when she'd abided by a strict economy of speech—like that month when his prostate began acting up, and her worry was a heavy, soundless presence throughout the house. How, among her acts of silent caretaking, she'd clipped simple bouquets of carnations and lamb's ears and replaced them nightly on his bedside table, in a vase embossed with a lobster that they'd purchased as a joke from a Maine gift shop.

"Why are you doing that?" he'd asked finally.

"Doing what?"

"Tossing them when they're still fine."

"I didn't want you to just watch them die."

* * *

He almost doesn't go to group the following week. He lies in bed in a quantum state of action and inaction, wondering if his hesitation has anything to do with how desultory and unhelpful the sessions have become.

Or if they've lost their luster, now that Nadine's motives have been laid so bare?

Or if he's afraid of the disappointment of not seeing Quinn (*ding ding ding*)?

He calls Cate but gets her voicemail and then a text. Sorry, at work, can't talk. All okay? He wonders what kind of work a teacher is doing on a Saturday morning. And before he knows it, he's getting dressed and climbing into the car.

It's a rush of cool air to see her. The capacious blue eyes. Her mouth easing into a smile. He realizes he's happy merely to be in the same room as her, to be sharing the same space. And to be reminded of what it's like as a teenager, sneaking glances at her when he thinks she might not be looking and noticing something new and beautiful about her each time—the smooth skin of her forearms, the freckled delta of her eyes and nose.

He hardly follows the discussions. He nods serenely and doesn't offer anything when asked to speak.

Nadine corners him afterward at the snack table, accompanied by a thunderhead of perfume. "Dean, I've noticed you seem a bit, you know, a bit *quiet*."

"Haven't had much to say."

"It's just that moving on from grief requires a bit of active participation."

"I seem to remember your saying something about taking my time." He's nibbling at a Hydrox cookie, sipping at lemonade so sour-sweet it stings his gums.

"Look, are you thinking of joining Delilah Fister's group?" she asks, as the fluorescent light gleams off her lipstick, as it catches the sparkly grist of her foundation.

"What?"

"Are you thinking of joining her support group? Because she serves edibles at them?"

"I had no idea about that."

"Okay, good." Nadine is breathless. "Because I hate to tell you, but someone may have already anonymously tipped off the police about that. It's still illegal over here, you know. At least to distribute."

Quinn hooks his gaze while standing in their usual corner. Her lovely mouth breaks into a smile—a snicker. He catches it and can't help smiling, too. Approaching her.

"Would you like to go to lunch?" he asks.

Her blinking eyes are like camera shutters. "Okay."

"Have you been to the Anchor? It's along that row of shops, next to my—the old music store."

"Not in a while."

"It's pretty standard stuff. I mean, we're as far from the coast as parts of Vermont, but they still insist on serving seafood there. You can tell the oysters are from a can. They just pluck them out and put them on used shells." (He doesn't recall ever feeling so critical of the place; he can only remember the many satisfying evenings spent there with Nina and Cate.)

"Oh stop, stop," she says. "You've struck oil already."

It's a slow afternoon. The walls are lined, as ever, with booths beneath shell-shaped pendant lights; the central bar remains standing like an island in the center of the room, with its row of branded tap handles; seaside kitsch is still strung from the ceiling molding—foam anchors, grids of worn rope. A familiar-looking server gawks at them, whether in confusion or disapproval. *Well, it's not like this is a date*, he thinks.

"I'm sorry about what I said two weeks ago."

"What did you say?" Her expression is clear, receptive.

"Oh, just, about your son."

"I've heard enough ugly things said about my son to develop a pretty good filter. If I've forgotten about it, then it must not have been so bad."

He orders a beer.

"Water," she says firmly. And he realizes his gaffe.

"I gave up everything—coffee, booze—after what happened with Alexander," she says. "That's his name, by the way."

He can't think of anything besides "I'm sorry."

"No, don't worry. I don't judge or anything. I'm not even sure why I deny myself. Just an overarching sense of penance, I guess. But it's my thing, not yours."

"Why did you ask if I was a plant at the first meeting?"

She raises her shoulders noncommittally. "You didn't seem very visibly upset."

"Neither did you, if I recall."

"Well then, let's say I sensed a similar-mindedness."

"But I was upset. I still am."

"So am I."

At some point the food arrives. A crab cake of largely mayonnaise and breadcrumbs. Clam chowder from a Progresso can. He's nervous and overcritical, even though this is decidedly not a date.

"Do you find it difficult sometimes?" she says. "Finding reasons to stay alive?"

"All the time."

"I do it for my kid. I think."

"My daughter and her partner just adopted a baby."

"Congratulations." She eats steadily, methodically. Almost rhythmically, he notices. Bite, bite, sip of water. "I only visited him once in prison," she says. "It was such a terrible place. Guards standing there, making sure you couldn't get too close to each other. He was wearing this orange jumpsuit. He hardly said a thing. Only that it was constantly noisy, and the food was terrible. No salt. People sold packets of those ten-cent ramen squares to each other and hoarded the seasoning pouches."

"How long is his sentence?"

"Twelve years. But he's up for parole in eight."

"How many has he served?"

"Seven," she says. "And it'll be such a different world for him when he gets out. I mean, can you believe we elected that celebrity moron to be president? When that missile alert first came I was sure it was because of some dumb shit he pulled. You didn't vote for him, did you?"

"No, no," he says vigorously.

She nods. "I think, sometimes, that if Alex gets out and he doesn't need me, I'll be, like, nothing. No one to anyone."

He makes a vague, assenting grunt, which becomes a throat-clearing sound. "My wife—you know—she said I was too much of a pushover with our daughter. She said all sorts of kooky stuff near the end, but one of the things that really stuck with me was, she said that she and Cate—that's my daughter's name—she and Cate might've had a better relationship if I weren't so busy trying to be the good cop."

"Does Cate still talk to you?"

"Only out of charity, she's got her own life out west."

"Better than my son."

"Does he— Are you two not in touch? There are phones in prison, aren't there?"

All tact thrown to the wind. And now an extended silence, his gut churning mightily in its attempts to digest the crab cake. He's not eaten anything so rich since Nina's death.

"We're not in touch, no. We were. But not anymore."

If this were a date, he thinks, there'd be no hope for a second one. And he remembers the high threshold he used to have for letting new people into his life. How, if he and Quinn weren't so desperately lonely, if they weren't each so uniquely bereaved, the strangeness of their meeting would've repelled him.

But you have to change as you grow older. As people peel off and fall away like petals before whatever dried-out filaments of yourself remain.

"I've been trying to do some renovations on my house, but it's a nightmare," she goes on. "I was hoping Alexander might help with that when he gets out."

"What sorts of renovations?"

"I'll show you." She lets her spoon clang on the plate. She chucks a scatter of bills on the table and says, "Follow my car."

He does so without a word.

Her home is a stout one-story property on the edge of town. A layer of cerulean paint peels off in flecks at the edges of the bottommost clapboards. The gutters are home to numerous bird families; a crooked downspout is aimed with missile-lock accuracy at a bed of diseased marigolds.

"There's a lot of work to be done."

He nods. Although he's mostly shocked by his anxiousness, his reawakening hunger.

He can still remember the last time he and Nina made love. It was three years ago, on the morning of his birthday. How their yielding, infirm bodies had seemed to suddenly reinflate with purpose. As if pneumatic instinct and memory had brought them back to an earlier, more productive stage in their lives. And then the urge had drained out of him. It never returned. Another thing he thought he'd lost with age.

But as he follows Quinn through the little house, his various observations—its scoured, empty neatness, its lack of mementos and heirlooms—give way to the raw anticipation of wanting to do it again.

He expects the bedroom to be similarly sparse. Instead, it's packed with knit clothes. Woolly gray sweaters, painting smocks with the initials AM embroidered into the chest. Gloves, scarves, hats. Yarn filaments like lazy worms, floating in the air. The overpowering scent of lavender detergent.

"They're for my son," she says. "Well, they were. It was a compulsion, I think, to keep myself busy, because I kept thinking about how miserable he must've been."

Dean takes in his unfortunate reflection before the dresser mirror, rubs his gaunt eyes and makes helpless note of his ebbing hairline; the ungainly flab beneath his shirt resembles a bag of potting soil.

While she sits miraculously at the edge of the bed, patting the space beside her. "So."

* * *

"So I've been sort of talking to someone," he says to Cate.

"Like, in a therapist way? Or a romantic way?"

"Not sure. Maybe like something in between."

"Uh-oh, Dad. That's really not a good idea. It's a huge conflict of interest. Shana had a therapist who she realized was sort of hitting on her, and she reported him and got his license revoked."

"No, she's not an actual therapist. I met her at the grief group."

"Oh—" And her voice immediately changes its timbre. It becomes brighter, more cheerful. "Then that's great, Dad."

"It's just—I never thought I'd feel lucky compared to someone else. But I feel lucky compared to her. And I feel sort of horrible for feeling that way."

"Why? What happened to her?"

"A lot. Just—a lot."

"Oh." She doesn't push. She knows better. "Well, I just hope you don't let guilt get in the way of your other feelings."

"What other feelings?"

"You know . . . love, right?"

"No, no, that's entirely premature. Stop that."

"You brought it up!"

"I brought up romance. Not love."

"Oh right. Then I stand marginally corrected."

"I'm serious, Cate. Stop that."

"You know, I like to tell my kids, 'Don't be afraid to express yourselves. Don't try to push down feelings, even the ones you think are ugly or embarrassing. It'll help in the long run.'"

"So now you're giving me advice you usually reserve for elementary schoolers?"

"God, you're sounding a lot like Mom right now."

"Is that supposed to be an insult? Your mother and I were a lot more alike than you think. That's how we stayed married for so long."

"Dad, all I'm saying is that you shouldn't be afraid to embrace certain feelings, especially if they're healthy, and especially if the only thing preventing you from embracing them is the shadow that Mom has cast over your life."

He wonders when, exactly, Cate began to think of her own parents as children. Whether it's a reaction to whatever hurt they imparted to her. Or a defense against what trauma they still could.

He misses Nina.

* * *

They're in bed the next week, on the day of support group. The gentle morning sun seems woven into the fabric of the comforter, into their skin.

"We're supposed to stop going eventually, right?" she says. "It's like a dating app; the goal is to delete it from your phone."

He shrugs. "Nadine probably wouldn't like it."

"Nadine can go and piss rocks."

He feels a bit shy now, in the frankness of dawn. In the evenings, when they grapple in bed, all timidity is eclipsed by the strength of their attraction. Consent is a matter of physical durability. (He's noted, with discomfort, how she's a foot taller than Nina, and how this occasions certain new and astonishing impressions.) But now, he feels a sudden desire to flee, as if from an ill-considered hookup. And he's shocked at how vividly he can experience this—not a memory, but a real live sensation—at such an age.

He looks around for a distraction and settles upon a pale gold ring on the nightstand. "What happened to Alex's father?"

"Divorced," she says. "After the accident."

"Oh."

"We said some horrible, horrible things to each other. Un-take-backable things."

He nods solemnly, stupidly, because there's nothing else for it.

"Did you and your wife fight?" she says.

Of course, he thinks. What couple doesn't fight? "We did. Mostly about our daughter."

She smiles. "Kids are the fucking worst, aren't they?"

"It's odd—I can remember the bickering. Hours and hours of it, probably. And I remember it being about our daughter, even before she moved away. But I can't for the life of me remember which things we actually said to each other."

"Maybe you don't want to."

Doesn't he?

She turns to him before he can consider love's hidden agendas. The austerity measures it implements upon memory. "With my ex-husband, a lot of the terrible things . . . a lot of them were just lying there, waiting for an occasion to be said. And if the thought already exists, if it just needs to be brought out into the open, isn't the marriage, the relationship, whatever, isn't it fucked, regardless?"

He shrugs. Maybe. Although there are plenty of things that, when articulated, gain an entirely new and burnished existence. There are things, still, that he is afraid to say.

"Dean?"

"I think the life you have with other people—it can bend. It can bend quite a bit without breaking."

"Well, mine was wicked brittle," she says. "Mine broke right away."

His alarm chirps awake; he swipes it off. And they seem to agree tacitly that group isn't happening today.

"Your son. He must have seriously hurt the other person, right? For the prison sentence to have been so severe?"

He's surprised at his bluntness, which feels almost self-sabotaging. But she nods. "He put the other guy in a coma."

"Oh."

Cars zip noiselessly down the street, flinging their brief, angular reflections upon the drawn curtains.

"Did you ever talk to the person's family?"

"Oh yeah," she says, gripping her hands together and twisting. "It was terrible. They were these really spiritual Buddhists, and they forgave Alex right away. Like he was some sort of situation that they needed to navigate around. Like he was a manifestation of how shitty the world can be to some people, and they needed to accept it quickly."

Something about this makes Dean deeply uncomfortable.

"At the same time, you know, they wouldn't take their guy off life support. Even after the doctor told them there was no hope. You'd think, with that sort of mindset, you'd be more open to abandoning the corporeal body, or whatever. But who fucking knows?"

She lets go of her hands; she holds out her index and middle fingers and walks them, like a pair of legs, across his chest. She gives them various routines—as a Rockette, kicking in rhythm; a cabaret dancer, sultry and lurching; and then a stiff compass, staggering forward in measurement.

"I used to think—about life, about marriage—that the longer you lived a certain way, the sturdier everything became. Obviously, that's wrong. It's like flipping a coin and getting heads five times in a row. You think somehow that the odds are tipped in that direction. You never realize how swiftly everything can change." She clears her throat and rests her cheek on his diaphragm. "Still, back when Alex made that stupid decision and wound up colliding with the other guy, it just didn't seem possible. It didn't seem like my life could be so—so suddenly *fucked* like that. And obviously, my husband and I had no idea how to be with each other afterward. It was like this shared layer of intimacy that we'd been building around our lives was ripped off. Everything hurt. Even the wind."

She climbs out of bed and capers lightly toward the dresser. She stands there, her graceful back facing him, flipping through the sweaters, the shirts, the smocks. Like a decorator examining swatches, gently dispersing their lavender scent.

"These clothes. I used to imagine sending them to him in prison. And each time I was about to do it, I lost my nerve. I put them in the wash and then let them sit there. I don't know why. I think he'd like them. He always wore the things I made for him, although maybe he only wore them to see me. He was so thoughtful."

She turns toward him. She looks tiny, diminished by the rosy light, the blankness of the walls around her. This exhibit of her life. And he can't help but notice the rippling forehead lines she shares with Nina, the similarity of their button noses. He shivers at an intrusive thought: that he might find Quinn more straightforward and predictable, perhaps easier to be with.

"You know, I taught nearly three decades at the high school here," she says. "And roughly a year and a half ago, right around the time of the missile alert, these accusations came up that one of the teachers had an affair with a student—at the very least, he behaved inappropriately. It was this big scandal, because the district had tried to sweep the whole thing under. They wanted to keep him because he had a PhD, which made the school look better. Isn't that ridiculous? Anyway, the asshole just kept denying it, and in the end, the student wound up changing her story. It's why I finally decided to retire. Because the entire time it was happening, all I could think was, How is it fair that a person with so much intent to cause harm isn't punished, but Alex is?"

Dean shakes his head.

She sighs. "And then I would remember that he *killed* someone. I keep trying not to say that, as if that somehow changes reality. But he took someone off this earth without a motive, out of pure carelessness. How do you forgive that?"

"I think maybe the justice system— Maybe that's the reason, you know—"

"Where were you when that missile thing happened?" Her voice carries a fresh intensity.

He frowns. "My house, I think."

"You *think*?"

"No, I'm sure," he says, recalling Nina on her phone. The triumph and distress on her face. "I was in my house."

"Where? In your basement?"

"Yeah."

"What did you do?"

"I just stayed there," he says. "My memories are sort of vague."

"Seriously?" Her eyes dilate into saucers, pierced with skylight. "Didn't you think it was real?"

"For a moment, maybe."

"Did you think you were going to die?"

"Maybe."

"Maybe? How can you not remember?"

"I guess once I realized it was a false alarm, I forgot about it."

"But wasn't your wife still alive?" she says. "And your daughter? Don't you at least remember the terror of losing them?"

"So many things happened in the year afterward—real things."

"The missile warning was real."

"It just didn't feel that way to me."

"It may not have led to anything—but for eighteen minutes, it was a real thing. It was *there*. It was *happening*."

"What's going on? Am I saying something wrong?"

"Sorry." She shakes her head. "Sometimes I just wonder if I even know how to react to things in a genuine way anymore. Or if I'm just following a set of expectations."

He shrugs again. He feels the same way at this very moment.

* * *

"How's it going with your gal pal?" Cate says.

He hears a toddler's wails in the background, Shana's hopeless shushing, and he reminds himself not to comment, lest he seem too pathetic. "She's not my gal pal."

"Then what is she?" The sounds grow distant, a door groans shut.

"She's nothing. We're just keeping it casual."

"Exactly. That's a gal pal."

"Okay."

"I'm proud of you, Dad."

"There's nothing to feel proud of me for."

"It's just— It takes a lot of courage to move on."

"I haven't *moved on*," he says, twisting with guilt. Embarrassment, too. "I don't even know what that phrase means. You don't just *move on* when you're my age. Everything accumulates and stays with you."

"Okay, okay."

"It's just a casual thing."

"I said okay, Dad."

Casual.

Although he finds himself awake in Quinn's bed, morning after morning. The awkwardness swiftly receding, the comfort and familiarity like a childhood blanket.

"I slept with this guy, once," Quinn says. "Totally normal outside the bedroom. But he went on one of those fetish sites and ordered a kit and made a silicone cast of his own penis. And he asked me to use it once, which was, like, okay, fine—a little weird, but sex positivity, right? So I get it, and as I walk back into the bedroom, he's on all fours on the bed!"

"So, like . . . ?"

"Yeah, cheeks spread, ready for me to go in." Her spirited laugh. "The best part was, well, we broke up, obviously. It was this whole argument. And the last thing I told him was to go fuck himself—literally. And his face! When I said that!"

Dean is in tears, laughing harder than he has in months—years. And he only stops when he tries to think of anything Nina said that had ever made him laugh so uproariously as he is now.

"What's wrong?"

Nothing. Nothing is wrong.

They grow entitled to handfuls of each other, to every prepositional connection. And he recognizes a feeling from long ago—something he never expected to experience again. The early spring of love. He feels it, even though the fallen leaves give off a mineral luster beneath layers of ice. Even though a deep, halting freeze has descended upon Beckitt.

His blooming heart.

Even the coldest mornings hold a promising gleam. Daily routines take on a buttressing quality, as if he's building credit, grinding into reality a life that he's too afraid to hope for.

He remembers—he can't help also remembering—afternoons when he and Nina achieved a perfect happiness in their routines: the opening of the shop, the checking of inventory, their staggered lunch hour, and then the quiet closing, returning home. How he'd been petty and privileged enough at times to find those days boring! What a shame that you could bring previous perspectives to bear upon the present, but never the opposite. If only you could do the opposite.

He and Quinn take strolls through Songline Park, bundled so tightly they resemble toddlers, wobbling forward. The frozen pond like a cataract at the center of the forested eye.

"Early on," she says, snatching at his arm, "back when I was in the denial phase, I kept thinking that if a single thing had changed—just one tiny aspect of the situation—my life never would have ended. I mean, there are so many things interacting at any given moment. If Alex had taken an extra second at a stop sign, if the car he crashed into—if the driver had only been a little bit more, you know, *alert*." She sighs. "Maybe I've just never made it out of that stage."

"Those are bogus stages."

"And yet, waypoints can be helpful."

"What about your husband? Didn't you say you two were unhappy?"

"We were." Her breath curls upward and falls, like a cat stretching. "But I'd have stayed in a bad marriage for another fifty years if it meant

Alex might've avoided the accident. Sorry—that's bargaining. That's another stage, isn't it? God, I just wish I could move on."

And now a swift chill penetrates his jacket. It noses through his shirt, lands somewhere in his chest.

You have the whole fucking narrative planned out in your head. You're already moving on.

"Do you ever wonder how he turned out the way he did?" Dean asks. His tone is suddenly unfamiliar, almost cawing.

"What do you mean?"

"Like, how he became someone who killed someone else."

She stops. "I told you, it was an accident."

"Was it, though? Completely?"

"Alex is not a monster." Her arm flexes around his. "He made one careless mistake."

"So what he did is not a judgment on his character?" Dean says, recalling his own brief, monstrous hope, as Nina was still dying, that once she passed, perhaps Cate might finally move back home.

"It wasn't on purpose."

"Of course it was on purpose. Not the killing, but the decision to drive drunk. You have to take moral responsibility for all the possible outcomes, all the ramifications, of the things you do."

"What I mean—" And as she turns toward him, her eyes seem to transform into a light, steel gray. "What I mean is that being irresponsible is not equivalent to being vicious."

"Maybe if he was brought up thinking that sort of thing, you know, focusing on intent instead of consequence—"

"Actually, I have to get home," she says, wrenching her arm free. "I have this headache."

"Do you need me to get you anything?"

"You should probably go back to your place, too."

Something is freshly broken between them. Probably irrevocably. He's crossed a line. And yet, he thinks, it's better now than later, when his feelings are too inextricably tied up in hers. When confronting the issue would have been staggeringly more painful.

And if the thought already exists, if it just needs to be brought out into the open, isn't the marriage, the relationship, whatever—isn't it fucked, regardless?

He'd always valued Nina's frankness. The need for clarity between them. *Noxious air gives you lung cancer*, she used to say when he was silent and angry at her.

And so they'd confronted all sorts of issues throughout their marriage: his ugly feet, her snoring, his embarrassing predilection for crying at the ends of sports movies, her sharpness with certain customers at the store. His feeble parenting. Her repeating her own parents' mistakes with their child.

Although he can remember, too, driving through Maine one summer afternoon: the sun breaking in ecstasy over the endless ocean, a rusted lighthouse holding its charming vigil over foaming current, how Nina had begun to laugh—a snicker at first, which gathered enough momentum to become her full-throated howl, like blasts from a trombone.

And how he'd caught Cate's smile in the rearview—the silent understanding passing between them that a person like Nina, so blustery with love, could experience bouts of frantic joy, could feel it keenly enough that it needed to be rapidly expressed, and then perhaps jettisoned, in order to keep the more vital parts of her intact.

She'd been afraid to hurt them, too. Afraid of being unworthy of their love. He knew this. Had he told her?

"It sounds to me like you're getting serious," Cate says when he mentions the fight. (Was it even a fight? A lovers' quarrel?)

"Serious?"

"You pushed Quinn away because it's starting to feel real, and it's scaring you."

"That's just a cliché, kiddo."

"Right. So?"

"Clichés so rarely reflect the complexity of what's actually going on."

"So maybe you're two late-blooming fuck buddies who are slowly losing interest in each other."

"For God's sake."

He hears Freddie's chronic wail again, Cate's name being shouted, the door slamming. "One or the other, Dad," she says distractedly. "You have to be *something*."

No, no. He shakes his head. How unfair.

Because it's too soon. It's all happening too soon. You needed time for your denial, your anger, your bargaining, your whatever to distill into something cohesive. To become something else from which you could move on.

He remembers saying *I love you* for the first time to Nina—back when they were still kids, basically. How it had arrived as a reflex, because the words had seemed right, as they lay beneath the covers in his apartment. And how he'd felt such instant regret for it—for the falseness it left on his lips. Because saying something did not make it real by necessity.

She'd smiled and shaken her head. She'd understood. She was always smarter than him.

And all those decades later, when she was thin and pallid, her eyes glittering with pain and terminal lucidity: the faint, shivering smile as she said goodbye. *Goodbye.* What a joke. The vastness of their shared life rolled into a two-syllable salute and cast off.

"I'm sorry, but you don't have the luxury of good timing anymore," his daughter says, as if reading his mind. "It's reality, isn't it? When you're young, you can afford to be choosy and whatnot, but then you reach a certain point, and you stop noticing red flags and start looking for deal-breakers."

"So if I'd met her at your mother's funeral?"

"But you didn't. You met her at a gathering for like-minded people."

"You're making it seem as if we were at speed dating. It was a grief group."

"I thought you said it was just a front for some woman to sell you Mary Kay products."

Yes, he'd said that. He'd said all sorts of things. He'd said things too early, in advance of his feeling them. Too late. Words and thoughts are not automatically fungible, he thinks. Or they shouldn't be. So rarely do they arrive at an understanding together. And so aimlessly could certain remarks float through your mind without binding to any single concept. So often did you say what you did not mean. The opposite, too.

"She's messy," he tells Cate.

"No offense, Dad, but someone your age doesn't really get to escape that sort of messiness. You can't enter the dating market with your sort of baggage and not expect everyone else to carry a significant amount of their own."

"Sweetheart, I don't think you really know what you're talking about here."

"I'm just saying, you're not exactly young anymore. People your age can't be so stubborn and inflexible. You have to accept new ways to be happy. You have to accept change."

"Her son drove drunk and put a guy in a coma."

"Oh. Okay, wow."

"Yeah. So. A bit more complex."

"Sure, but I still don't strictly see the issue—like, how this would affect your relationship with her."

"There's a lot of emotion that she hasn't really worked through yet."

"Maybe you can help her."

"For God's sake, Cate."

"Dad—"

"Why are you so eager to see me move on?" he says suddenly, angrily. "Did you really hate your mother so much?"

An instant regret zips through him. And yet he cannot immediately apologize. He waits for the silence to subside, for her quickening breaths, her bruised recrimination. But the waxing and waning of respiration that he hears is his own, and his phone, when he looks at it, has defaulted to its home screen.

"Cate?"

She's hung up on him.

* * *

He and Quinn meet a week later at the Anchor.

It's busier this time, and everything is painfully formal again. As if they've regressed to an older, sadder way of knowing each other. The same server smiles at them and says, "It's good to see you both again." They ignore her.

"I should apologize," he starts. "For what I said to you. It was uncalled for. I don't really know how to be a person in one of these—one of these things."

She shakes her head. "It's fine."

"And our—whatever you want to call it—it was always just casual, right? A fling? If you want to call it that?" Although he feels far too old and too tired to be dealing with relationship semantics.

She doesn't acknowledge the question, anyway. "You know, the man who Alex killed—his mother is in a nursing home now. I check in on her every once in a while. She's got Alzheimer's. Which I know is terrible and unfair. But if your life has been defined by tragedy, if you've been forced to live in its shadow, a disease like that can seem just a little bit merciful, can't it?"

"I suppose."

"Ask me anything you want," she says. "I don't care."

"What?"

"Ask me any question. Get it out in the open. I want to know what you're thinking."

"*I* don't even know what I'm thinking."

"Ask me whatever you want."

"Fine," he says. "What did he do? Alex. What was his occupation?"

"He was a news anchor. For a local station, actually. You might've seen him. He did early-morning stuff mostly, but he was in line for a spot at six PM."

"Do you think he deserves parole?"

"Yes," she says with startling force. "Of course."

"Do you blame yourself for what he did?"

"Yes," she says a bit more quietly.

"Do you resent him?"

"No."

He thinks: *Self-delusion is a critical survival mechanism.* He says, "Do you hate me?"

"No."

"Are you angry at me? For the things I've said?"

"No."

"Do you think I was unfair?"

"Yes."

"Do you love me?"

She looks up. She clears her throat. "It's that you don't remember the missile threat," she says. "That's what I can't get over." Her soft, white eyebrows like clouds over cobalt irises.

"What's wrong about that again?"

"I can't really explain. But you must have thought about your life ending. Your family's lives ending."

"Probably, yes."

"How can you not have a vivid, coherent memory of it?"

He shrugs. "Something much more traumatic happened afterward. An actual ordeal."

"Are you suicidal?" she asks. "I was suicidal for a while. I think I still am."

He nods. "The thing is, I don't want to burden anyone with any sort of aftermath."

"You could jump into a volcano."

His lips twitch. His heart stumbles open. "I went to the basement," he says. "With my wife. When it happened. And she was texting our daughter. She said something very unfair to her. She said something that was really, really ugly in what might have been her last moment."

"Do you resent your wife?"

"She's dead."

"That's not an answer."

"I do." He breathes. "I think I'd be much closer with my daughter if it weren't for her." And a rapid bitterness coats his insides. A Nina-like disappointment in himself, in his family, for the ways in which they'd alienated each other, when understanding was a mere matter of perspective shift. They should have all tried harder.

Quinn closes her eyes. "When the missile alert came, for a moment, I was *relieved*," she says. "I thought, *Finally*."

He thinks of Nina, tapping spitefully at her phone.

"I mean, I was having a hard enough time choosing to live each morning, before the threat of a nuclear war."

He nods.

"But a part of me thought—a part of me also thought, *I hope it gets the prison*."

Oh.

"I tried to brush it away. I tried to convince myself it was a passing thought. An intrusive one, or whatever. But he used to always call me, and as soon as I picked up the phone and heard the automated voice—you know, the one that says that it's coming from the Department of Corrections, do you want to accept?—I would hang up. I would avoid his calls until he learned to stop." She stares ahead, her eyes fixed upon some point within him. "It's crazy. This is the first time I'm saying any of this out loud."

She swallows and coughs. As if trying to extract another thought from her throat.

"I abandoned my son," she says. "You were right to bring it up the other day. I *did* wonder how he turned out the way he did. I spent years wondering, until I was so angry and tired and sad that I stopped wanting to have anything to do with him. I wanted to move on. I tried to think of only myself—and guess what? I found out I was nothing without him. Nothing anchored me to the world. I considered running away, starting fresh in San Francisco or something, but in the end, I couldn't even abandon him properly. I stayed put; I still made all those fucking clothes."

"My daughter lives in that area," he says without thinking. "The San Francisco Bay."

"Do you want to be out there with her?"

"Yes."

"Would your wife have agreed to move? If your daughter asked?"

"I think so."

"Even though she sent those messages to her? When she thought she was dying?"

"She still loved her very much," he says stiffly.

And she shudders. "What happens when you can't forgive the one person whom you're supposed to forgive without question?"

"You're supposed to love him without question. Forgiveness is something different."

"Is it really?"

"And so is moving on. It's all different." He stares at the soft, wooden table, tracing the intersecting pattern of rings left by countless carelessly placed mugs.

"It all means the same to me, insofar as it all means nothing," she says. "These words. These concepts. They're so far from anything I can really understand or act upon." She takes his hand and flips it over; she spreads her fingers over his palm. "And part of me thinks—thought—that if you weren't really that scared of losing your family, then we had the same thing wrong with us. And I wanted that, you know? I thought it would make us great for each other. We could start over the same way. And then another part of me was disgusted, because it was almost like you were taking your family for granted, like you didn't care about losing them, even though I know that's a crazy thing to think. It's a crazy thing to say. Because what does that make me?"

He shakes his head. He feels so old, so tired before the swaying anchor of her need. He imagines her shattered heart, smudged with fingerprints from her countless attempts to fit its jagged pieces back together. He imagines the endless fatigue of someone for whom staying alive is such a constant act of reassembly. A person got so tired from carrying his own unwieldy grief.

"I felt so guilty when I met you," she says. "So guilty for how happy you made me. Like, I hadn't yet atoned for everything that happened with Alex. Like he and I were finally ready to move on, even though neither of us deserved to."

"For what it's worth, it doesn't seem like you've moved on *too* much."

She looks up at him, voltage at the edges of her lips, jerking upward. "And I was afraid of not deserving all that happiness, I was afraid of forgetting what I thought about on the morning of the missile alert. Forgiving myself. Although how could I forgive myself before I forgave him? I'm sorry, I know this sounds like such a mess."

And if the thought already exists, what does it take to bring it out into the open?

He thinks, *The threat of drastic change.*

"I was falling in love with you," she continues. "Which, why would I do that? And I think it's because I was rushing toward certain feelings, because something momentous was—is—about to happen. I can see an end to this way I've been. Even though I don't know if I've reached the stage of wanting it yet."

"All stages are bullshit."

She draws a deep, shuddering breath. She opens her lips. She mouths the words *I do love you.* Although no sound emerges. Only the vague form of it, drawn with her teeth, her tongue. The piercing blue of her eyes—as clear and bright as he's ever seen.

"I don't know if I can," he murmurs.

And she nods, almost relieved. "A few months ago, I found out my son's parole hearing was pushed up. Something about exceptional progress and model rehabilitation. Apparently, some therapist even taught him to play an instrument. I was about to go to group when I heard. Wound up staying home that week."

Oh.

"It's in fourteen days."

"I see."

"And I'm allowed to go," she says. "To make my own small case."

"Will you?"

"I don't know."

What if I went with you?

He struggles to look at her. Words that had tumbled so easily, so thoughtlessly in the past are dammed up in his throat. Although he knows that if he could only break through a tiny bit, they might rush through and tip over the thing that is already brimming.

Cate had been right: He'd tried to evacuate it all. He'd tried to empty himself of feeling and love, and all he'd managed to do was distract himself while it accumulated, until it was impossible to overlook.

"I should get home," he says.

"Okay."

"If you end up going to the hearing—" he starts, but doesn't know how to complete the thought. He doesn't know what the next words should be. "If you end up going, let me know."

And she lifts her hand, she opens it, as if dropping some invisible parcel into his palm. She curls his fingers over it; she squeezes his fist shut.

* * *

Out in the cold, wet parking lot, with the wind slapping his skin and his back pointedly facing the shops, he feels like one of those ancient prospectors—stupid with hope, dipping his pan in a fast-moving stream of sediment and parsing with clumsy fingers through the grain, everything glimmering. Searching for the speck that outshines the rest, that is *there*—he knows it is *there*—but in what quantity and what form? In what degree of accessibility?

He's old, he thinks. He's been an old man for so long now. And life has made such a fool of him.

He remembers visiting his doctor once in his early thirties for knee pain. And the woman's commiserative nod as she maneuvered the cap beneath his skin.

"This is just a part of aging, I'm afraid."

"So there's nothing I can do?"

"Just try to manage it. You can take some Aleve."

And for years, each time it throbbed in the middle of a jog or as he stood beside some customer at the shop, he was reminded of that realization at the doctor's office: that the body's chief function was no longer growth but maintenance. And eventually—perhaps even soon—those faculties would be unable to keep up with the rate of diminishment.

He turns around now and walks up to their old store. The sign is removed, but the words MAJOR THIRD remain stenciled cleanly against the yellowed stucco facade. He gazes through the window of his former life. An empty, rectangular room. Carpet and fixtures gone, lights shut off, the raised platform just a wide step. Ceiling to floor, saturated with memory.

A warm rhombus of sunlight presses against his cheek. Funny how he'd always appreciated Beckitt's stillness. Although he knows now that it's an illusion. Families cycled in and out of homes, storefronts shifted, generations were processed and graduated by its schools, so many lives transpiring beneath the carapace of sameness.

And he thinks: Surely someone cruel and simple, someone *young*, like Cate, had created the fiction that people like him (of *his* age) were somehow recalcitrant, somehow purposefully less flexible to change—that the physical brittling was mirrored in the emotional.

False.

No one spoke of how much maintenance went into merely existing, remaining yourself as you grew older. And how difficult and terrifying it was when your friable heart was faced with newness. How similar change could feel to violence.

And how you embraced it, regardless, if only to avoid the alternative: living in the world of things you missed.

He presses his head against the locked door and weeps. How he misses their fights, although he cannot remember their contents. Only her paroxysms of anger, his indignation. And her smell, her feel. Her silent partnership. Their shared youth. His own.

There is such beauty in this world, such hideousness. Too much of either to bear in one single life. He misses Nina. He misses his old existence, its old landmarks, their comfortable equilibrium. He always will.

He always will.

* * *

He counts down the days until Alex's parole hearing.

Cate calls him three days before it's to happen.

"Shana and I almost broke up, you know." Her voice is low, sober. "About halfway through the adoption process. We got so scared."

"Oh, kiddo. Do you want to talk about it?"

"No, we're fine now, I think. But it would be great if you came to visit," she says. No hint of forcedness or recrimination. "Shana and I realized we could really use your help. And it could take your mind off things—you know, seeing your grandson."

How long he's waited to hear this! Like a fresh log tossed into a dying fire. A forceful bellow of life, to feel needed. "Do you mean it?"

"Yes, Dad." Her voice is soft, drained, familiar.

"Well, okay. How long should I stay?"

"As long as you want. We could really, really use the help."

"Really? You're not just saying that?"

"Yes, Dad. Yes. As long as you can. We need you."

They need him. His daughter, his grandson. And the parole hearing is in three days. And his heart somehow reconstructs itself—sturdy and new. He laughs, as he imagines Nina might laugh (perhaps she had, with irony), in realizing that life's end is precisely what grants him freedom. These opportunities for radical change.

Yes. Oh, you said yes. Even when you were uncertain, and the complexities were so myriad and profound they took your breath away. Yes.

"When?"

"Whenever."

"But specifically."

"As soon as possible, Dad."

An entire constellation of people who need him now, a fresh system of responsibilities. He feels giddy. Young again. So full of love.

"Okay," he says. "I need at least three days."

REPOSITORY

Grant Gao

At one point, the Sunnyvale Retirement and Rehabilitation Center in Beckitt held exactly eighty-eight patients in thirty-nine rooms with two beds each, and ten additional "suites" of precisely the same dimension and amenity, but with one bed. It was a somber facility of bright fluorescent lighting and clean halls, led by an exacting group of administrators, in which Grant had begun his career as an orderly.

His plan had been to get some authentic healthcare experience before applying to medical school, to see what he could handle, and Sunnyvale had obliged with a constant flow of crisis and drama. There were patients who, through clerical errors, went days without baths. Patients who slipped and shattered what limited mobility remained in their bones, who were left alone for hours in the bathroom by harried staff whose avalanching tasks kept them running from wing to wing.

And at first, each such blunder, each shoe-gazing apology to an upset adult child, tore his heart asunder. The bleak helplessness of old age wiped away all sense of himself. There were days when he forgot to eat or use the restroom, when only the distant pounding of a headache reminded him to drink water.

Grant made the grave mistake, in his early career, of befriending some of the residents—of respecting their privacy and considering them as people with futures, who hadn't just reached the final station of their lives. And so, when they passed without fanfare, with nothing more than a rattle and a gasp, faces taut with pain, he realized he needed to grow more accustomed to death, to the idea of it.

Which meant becoming coarse, because this was the only way to withstand the heartbreak—by preemptively killing the more sensitive parts of himself.

Roughly a year into his career, a star system was introduced through Medicare in an attempt to standardize nursing home quality across the country, at which point the family owners of Sunnyvale sold the place to a private equity firm in Wingham.

Within a week of the sale, a fresh group of admins held a workshop with new protocols for reporting incidents among residents and an internal auditing system that oversaw everyone's reported hours and patient records.

The place was renamed Lark's Landing; a logo was commissioned of a delicate bird that seemed to be either alighting upon or taking off from a faint cupola. A few months later, it was slapped with a five-star rating by the government. Fees went up, as did demand. The new resident waiting list grew steadily and without interruption.

It was as an employee of Lark's Landing that Grant was party to even more thunderous falls, to the catastrophic mishandling of medications, and patients even more severely unattended to. He witnessed various staff breakdowns, resignations tendered en masse. He was there when they found a nurse in the supply closet with her eyes rolled back into her head, an adhesive fentanyl patch stuck to her tongue. He noted this in his reports. He lived in constant apprehension of a descending press corps, a bombshell exposé, some reckoning. And the longer it took for these things to arrive, the more responsibility he felt toward his residents. The more acutely he sensed their dependence. Until the act of quitting felt like abandonment.

It was in his eighth year, at a Q3 general staff meeting, that the managing director of the place, Bob Cowell, announced that the ownership group was *twisting the spigot*, so to speak. He told them that the staff was expected to *leverage existing assets* and *expand their collective bandwidth* in order to *synergize* more effectively with the rest of their parent company's portfolio.

"What the hell does that actually mean?" said Dana Yen, who was the de facto staff leader and the only person who spoke sharply enough to Bob to cut through his jargon.

Well, it meant that there would be a hiring freeze (although they were already down four nurses) and some overbooking of residents (although they were already six beyond capacity). And if they could all just understand this and realize their shared, family-like commitment to quality elder care and rehabilitation, they would weather the storm together. If they could just keep up morale, they would emerge stronger. They'd be taken care of.

But the timing was dangerous.

And Grant could remember with extraordinary clarity the drab autumn morning, most residents having finally fallen asleep, when Olive Bowden, a nurse, took his wrist and led him down the hall.

"Jim O'Hearn in 33A died. Can you come witness with me?"

Olive was a single mother, five years his senior, with a stripe of bright gray through her hair and a jolly rapport with the patients. She had a ferociously cheerful laugh that pinballed down hallways, a vivacity that made her popular among residents and staff.

So he'd followed her into Jim O'Hearn's newly emptied room—still warm and sebaceous smelling, his belongings wedged in a cardboard box perched upon the stripped bed—where she handed him a small circular white pill.

"What's this?"

"You swear that you've seen me carefully dispose of controlled substances that were originally prescribed for a patient who has since vacated the facility and been relinquished from our care?"

He nodded.

"Well then, fucking cheers."

"But wait—*wait*. What is this?"

"Oxy," she said. "You can sell yours, but, I mean, it's a pain in the ass. And if they catch you, it'll suck a lot worse."

And on any other day, Grant thought, he would not have taken it. He'd have thrown it in the garbage and given Olive the sternest possible look he could give. But Milly had called that morning. (Her name on his phone still felt like a bag of ice emptied down his stomach.) She'd told him that she didn't have time for another visit to pick up the remainder of her things, that he could just toss them or pawn them off if he wanted.

And he'd not anticipated his rage and dejection at hearing this.

Their separation, which had been rigorously polite and agreeable thus far, belied a furious struggle for moral edge. Milly, however, had family money—enough to keep her afloat as she restarted her life, enough to wound him with her niceness, her lack of pettiness, her agreeable self-denials. Some of her things, like the barely used high-performance skis and the Fujifilm camera full of pictures from their last trip to the cabin on Mount Greylock, could be resold for considerable amounts.

Olive was staring at him. "Just take it."

So he did. Because fuck it.

And *the feeling*—the feeling it produced was astonishing in its comprehensive pleasure. The liquid warmth sliding through him, a smooth velvet impulse sweeping down each nerve simultaneously. Like a mother's cool hand upon a sickly forehead. Like Milly's soft voice in the morning: *Babe, time to get up.*

He spent the rest of the day in a tender, lapping haze, chatting idly with the residents, smiling, being agreeable, as the warmth gathered in a sort of gentle euphoria at the pit of his stomach—a radiating guarantee of contentment.

"You seem happier today," Dana Yen said. He beamed and remembered that she had a high-school-aged daughter named Rachel, whom she was crazy about. And so he asked how Rachel was, to Dana's delight, and was startled by how interesting it all sounded, with the Oxy coursing through him—the soccer team on which she excelled, the biology tests she was acing, how she'd be all of their bosses one day.

And the thought of Milly, which, for weeks now, had been a reliable source of cloud cover, which could suck the energy from his chest like a pin-sized hole in a pressurized container, did not seem remotely as depressing as it normally did. Like an old message written in water. And Grant thought, this stuff might be a very real solution to his heartbreak. So long as he was responsible and smart about it, so long as his self-control was intact: Bring it on. More, more!

The first problem:

Awaking in his dark apartment, his phone reading 8:00 PM, with no recollection of having arrived. Although, from his lack of angry text messages and his car parked pristinely in its usual space, surely he must have clocked out at the right time and driven accurately home, guided by some unconscious instinct, the neural certainties of muscle memory.

And the second:

How quickly the craving for more tore through him.

* * *

Lark's Landing was transformed the very next day. It became a maze of opportunity.

"This is fucked," he said to Olive.

"I know," she said.

"I need more of it."

She nodded. "But we have to be careful."

And how lucky, how thankful they were that Gwendolyn Chard had just passed, that she'd been a bit *dramatic* and especially vocal in her end-of-life pain, so that the doctors who saw her wrote generous, generous scripts, which he and Olive pocketed and wasted together.

"I'm kind of scared that this is the best I'll ever feel," he drawled, wafting in the glow of his high, as if the distinction between himself and everything around him were arbitrary. As if he'd been spilled and blended into an emulsion of Gwendolyn's room and its formerly discrete contents.

"It'll be fine," Olive said, her pupils needle thin. Her stare pinning him in place.

"Will it?"

She nodded. "You just have to ask yourself, 'Where do I want to be in five years?'"

"Oh, I hate that question. Everyone hates that question."

"Indulge me."

He had the sensation that he was producing an uncontrollable amount of saliva—that it was gathering in the corner of his mouth faster than he was able to slurp it back up. "What was the question again?"

"Where do you want to be in five years—ten years?"

"I don't know. Why are you asking?"

She looked at him with impatience. "It helps put the drugs in context. It helps when you have a concrete idea of what you want your future to look like."

His future? The purpose of getting high was to obliterate such considerations, because his past ached and throbbed so much as to intrude upon each approaching moment. The point was to be yanked out of the present, to step out of time altogether.

Milly had shown up outside his room on the morning they were to be wed with deep-blue pouches beneath her eyes.

"Let's just take a step back," she'd said. "It's not that I don't want to get married."

"Okay."

"It's just that I'm not ready yet."

"Okay."

"Can you say something other than just 'Okay'?"

And he'd swallowed. He'd measured out the next words as precisely as he could because he loved her so much, and he could not think of anything worse than losing her. He'd said, "I will be whatever you want me to be." And realized, in an instant, that he'd chosen incorrectly.

How her eyes fell with such pity and disinterest, her pursed frown camouflaging her dimples. "Well then, let's be each other's backups."

"Backups?"

"I just think we rushed too quickly into this thing. I mean, I couldn't believe you were asking me. And I want you to know . . . I was so honored and so flattered, but I could never quite believe it was real. And I guess last night it finally caught up with me. I thought, How could he be so sure?"

"Love, I guess."

"Well, see? I don't understand how you can be sure about something like that without getting a larger sample size—without living more. What if there are other people out there who will see us in different ways? Help surprise us with who we can become?"

A larger sample size.

"So there's someone else."

"No, no, there's not."

He thought he heard a faint hiss, as if the space between them were expanding, rupturing. The sound of their private, shared life escaping.

"But I don't do it for you."

"I don't even know what *it* is, Grant. It's like I only know what I don't want. Like I'm steering through a fog, and there are these hazards that only appear at the last moment, and all I know is that I have to try to avoid them."

And how his chest collapsed, hearing this. How his shoulders sagged. What rotten fortune. "I can start applying for med school, you know. If that's what's giving you pause."

"No." Shaking her head.

"I can get a new job. A better one."

"No, it's not that. I swear." She kept shaking her head, her hair forming its own disclike torque. "I'm sorry. I'm so sorry, okay?"

"How many times have you quit these?" he asked Olive now. His cheek on her collarbone, saliva dripping down the chest of her scrubs.

His head lurched to the motion of her shoulders. "Half dozen," she said.

"Fuck."

"Doesn't help that this job is always cracking you open and dumping out whatever humanity you once had."

"How did you get started on it?"

"Back surgery."

* * *

He began feeling fortunate again. Fortunate that Lark's Landing, by dint of its star rating, was allowed to play fast and loose with its orders of various physician-prescribed painkillers, antipsychotics, and beta-blockers, which meant plenty of stock kept in a storage closet at the end of B-wing, to which they had access.

Fortunate, as well, that the nurses who checked each other's tallies and witnessed each other's waste and ministered to their own patients were too overwhelmed to pay more than superficial mind to potential diversions, and were perhaps diverting themselves.

Still, his policy was to take only from those who'd passed. It was safer that way, and harmless enough, because the place really was a revolving door of residents. And a dead person, by definition, was no longer any sort of individual.

So someone would kick the oxygen habit, and he and Olive would check the active prescriptions and see that end-of-life pain management had been assigned, and they would take it and waste it together.

It worked extraordinarily well. It helped him suffer through the day's desultory burdens—the disposal of sharps, the refilling of PPE. It helped expunge the embarrassment incumbent upon more intimate tasks—the administering of baths, the changing of certain horribly smelly dressings, the emptying and swapping of Henry Lacoste's ostomy pouch. No more secrets here. No set of privacy laws could save you from the sprawling indignities of having a body.

"You seem different," Dana Yen accosted him one afternoon.

"Do I?"

"Yes. Are you feeling all right?"

"Oh yes," he said. "Yes, yes, better than ever."

"Well, I am glad to hear."

He made a mighty effort to pull himself back to the ground. "And what about Raquel? How's she doing?"

She frowned. "Rachel."

"Oh, sorry. Rachel."

"She is great. She has a soccer tournament coming up. She wakes up at seven AM every Saturday, practicing with the team. And we only have one car, so taking her there and picking her up has been difficult for my schedule."

"Maybe she can get a ride with someone else."

"Oh no, not necessary. I spoke with Bob and moved some shifts around."

* * *

"You hear about the Eastern Mountain Boys?" a resident named Mitch Morehardt asked him one morning.

"No," he said, high as fucking tits. "Are they any good?"

"Well, you like bluegrass?"

"Not really."

"My kid's in Nashville. He saw them play, got me the CD, and helped me put it in the computer. I swear, they are something special. Here. Listen."

He removed a plastic set of airline headphones from around his neck and handed them to Grant; from his shirt pocket he withdrew a boxy iPod whose make and model dated from sometime in the early aughts. With a palsied forefinger, he drew a clockwise pattern along its wheel, the highlight bar advancing and settling upon a track titled "Nick's Song."

A warm, loving sound seemed to pour from the foam earpieces. A violin, sweeping like a cool wind over a banjo whose plucking was like drops of water in an enormous lake, rippling outward until the sonic wash of the melody overcame him. He was enveloped by nostalgia's half reality. A blooming wonder at the old, unexamined parts of his life—how they'd managed to fade so thoroughly into the periphery, although they'd once been as real and urgent as anything now. A vague heartbreak for the past.

What was happening to him?

* * *

He made it home after every shift. He found ways to eat, to sleep. To get up in the morning. To go back to work.

"You piece of shit," a resident named Norma Lozano spat at him. "I hope one day your kid puts you somewhere like this; I hope your kid abandons you and you have to deal with people fucking with you every hour of every fucking day. Torturing you."

He stared at her.

"What?" she snarled at him. "What the cunting fuck are you gonna do?"

"I've already been abandoned."

"What? What the fuck does that fucking mean?" The plastic cup she threw at him bounced off his chest, spilling water down his front.

He picked it up and refilled it from the tap. "Someone left me here, too."

"Good," she barked. "Good."

"I've never felt so alone in my life."

"You deserve it."

"I don't think I'll ever find a way to be happy again."

He knew it was silly to make such declarations at this point in his life, but anyone who believed in the absolute rightness of two people together had to acknowledge the wrongness of every other pairing. That so many people in the world found love was a statistical anomaly. A triumph of romance over rationality.

Or a failure, in his particular case. One of several, parading before him: alongside his lack of advanced skills or training, his financial precariousness, his profound sense of unbelonging. And the enduring suspicion that she'd never taken him seriously—not since their first meeting at Lark's Landing, when he'd shown her the way to her ailing grandfather's room. That their relationship, for her, had been nothing more than performance.

"You need to take your medication now," he said to Norma.

"Or else what, chinky? What are you gonna do?"

He looked through her chart. There. He rifled through the little paper soufflé cup, like a clumsy claw machine, until he found the one he wanted.

"Hey—"

He popped the entire thing in his mouth; he waited. Until he felt his pupils constrict—twin dead ends retreating down the lengthening tunnel of his irises. And the warmth plunging through him. Although it was more of an echo, now, of how wonderful it had been those first few times.

Which was fine—fine! It would do.

True, that memories lacked the force of the present, but what else did a person have with which to create a cohesive version of himself? And why else did the afterimage of Milly standing at the door, the stunted echo of her voice, her dwindling scent, still make him want to die?

"Look, I'm sorry, okay?" Norma said hoarsely. "I'm really, really sorry."

He smiled. He left the room.

* * *

"—money last night. I knew that guy wouldn't be able to cover the spread."

His consciousness flickered like a lightbulb. He was sitting in the dining area, across from his orderly friend Mick Luong.

"Huh?"

"And the thing is"—Mick lowered his voice and leaned forward—"I was going to use the money for a ring. Maybe put some of it down for a venue."

"That's—really great," he said.

"Although, knowing Chase, he'll probably just want to have it in some shitty forest campsite."

He was glad he hadn't told Mick or Olive about his own situation. He didn't need their helpless pity, their indignation on his behalf. He was already sick of his own constant reassessments: how he'd felt like an impostor, sometimes, when he was with her—too underprivileged, too unrefined. Immigrant boy. And his suspicion that this was precisely what she'd found appealing about him, as if their relationship were an entry point into a more authentic, interesting kind of life. Well, until it wasn't. Reality had intervened, and all reality was material.

Worse was that Grant couldn't say he hadn't felt the same transactional way about her, to an extent. Mercenary, striving. He couldn't deny the exhilaration of being with someone so settled, so indifferent to money.

It was funny, he thought: You weren't supposed to take for granted those things you could not afford to lose. But how did a person manage to avoid the constant anxiety, otherwise?

In the end, the only person he wound up spilling to was the woman at Major Third, who'd addressed him with a wariness bordering on hostility as he attempted to return an electric keyboard he'd purchased for Milly. Her pretty face was scrunched into knots. So imperious, though she couldn't have been taller than five feet.

"What's wrong with it?"

"Nothing. It was a gift. For my fiancée, actually. But she doesn't love me anymore. She doesn't want to be with me. Her parents have a Steinway at home, anyway."

And how the hardness in her face seemed to melt. Sympathy flooded her wrinkles. He felt like he could've been her child.

"You poor thing," she'd said. "Have courage."

He didn't know what she meant by this.

* * *

And then a spoon was in his hand, which was lunging forward, toward a yawning open mouth. His eyes adjusting, wheeling like gears finding their setting. The mouth belonged to Candace Chae. The spoon held applesauce. He was fucking hungry.

"You're a good boy," she said.

He formed a tight smile. "Thank you. Open wide, now."

"Is Stephen coming?"

Stephen? Right. Her son, Stephen, had died in a car accident several years prior. Something about a drunk driver. Somewhat high-profile. Perhaps a local news anchor?

"Yes, he should be here any day now."

"Oh, that is so good. Oh, I'm so happy."

"Well, I'm happy that you're happy."

"Stephen, Stephen, Stephen."

He checked her chart: She had no serious physical ailments; she was not dying anytime soon. And so she would need to extend her delusion for months—*years*, perhaps. He wondered how a person managed it.

And then he thought of himself.

* * *

Soon the patients, the other nurses, the orderlies became hiccups—extraneous fragments hovering in the background of his need. The occasional shard striking but never piercing his ballooning desire.

As when Mick walked in on him as he poked through the drawers of an empty room, and he'd had to provide some bullshit about looking for sharps after a recent incident in which they'd been improperly disposed of.

"Oh, okay."

Or when Jane Lemming asked him to witness with her, and his hope had been like the contents of the syringe, filling, filling, as she withdrew the precious Oxy from its vial—and suddenly evacuating, as the plunger expelled its payload down the trash.

"Wait!"

The look she'd given him when he half lunged, as if to stop her and catch it, was all hostile sympathy. "Stay away from that shit, Grant."

He reduced and reduced and reduced. Until he came to define people based on their proximity to pain medication and their capacity to help him achieve it.

Olive, who was already his friend, became a key ally. Others, like Dana Yen, became low-level hazards. Dana was someone to avoid because he knew her as a rule follower. And she was closer to Bob Cowell than any of the other staff.

* * *

Tina Zhang was recovering from a stroke.

"*Do you speak Mandarin?*" she asked as he attended to her medication.

Grant jerked his shoulders. "*A little.*"

"*That's good. My son was never very good at Chinese. He never studied. Did your parents make you study Chinese?*"

"*I just grew up speaking it.*"

She nodded. "*Good, good. And you still talk to them, right? Your parents? If you don't talk to them enough, they will get worried. Parents always worry. I still worry about my son, even though I'm the one here.*"

"*My parents died a long time ago.*"

"*Āiyā. Sorry.*"

He scanned her chart. "*Are you still feeling numbness in your hand?*"

But she wasn't listening. "*Do you want to hear a secret?*"

He sighed. She was on beta-blockers, but nothing stronger. "Hǎo de," he said, and sat down beside her.

"*When I was still young, my husband left me. He abandoned me and my son. It was terrible. I was so angry and sad. I wanted to kill him and beg him to come back all at the same time. And then one day a friend told me she saw him. He was close to Boston, working at a CVS pharmacy there. Āiyā, I'm so ashamed to say this, but I found him. He hadn't remarried. He didn't have any children. Just the same face, the same crooked mouth. And everything I was going to do—all the things I was going to say to him—I forgot it all, because he seemed like such a stranger. I realized he always had been. And I was so lonely. And he seemed lonely, too.*"

Grant nodded.

"*Well, we spent the afternoon and the evening together after I found him. We made love, we hardly spoke. And the next morning I tried to ask him what this was all about—what it meant, you know? But he just shook his head. I tried to ask him why he left in the first place, and he said nothing. I asked him if he even loved me, if he loved our son. Still nothing. Then he asked me to leave. And what could I do? I could have still screamed at him, but it would have seemed in response to another rejection, and I couldn't accept that. I couldn't accept feeling that pathetic. There was a note in my mailbox a few days later, asking me to not contact him anymore. So I guess I'll die never understanding."*

Grant listened with the headlong intent of someone who was teetering out of orbit, who needed the story to root himself in something lifelike.

"*But do you know what?*" she said.

"Shénme?"

"*I got pregnant again. From that visit. I got pregnant, and I thought that maybe if he knew this, he'd come back. It's pitiful, I know, but I was so scared. And my heart hurt so much for him—even though he was a stranger. Even though he'd been so cruel to me. Sometimes your heart is like a child—it misbehaves, it doesn't listen.*" She frowned with concentration at her left hand, as if trying to transmute clarity into pure will. As if undoing the effects of the stroke. She tried to flex her shaking fingers. "*I was going to tell him that a person can't be so selfish, you know? You need to take responsibility. You need to understand how your choices destabilize the people in your life—even if they're choices regarding your privacy.*"

"*What happened?*"

She let her hand fall to her hip. She sighed. "*I miscarried.*"

"Ó."

"*I thought that I would understand by now—about myself. I thought living a full life would be enough for me to find some peace. But you never run out of decisions to make. Not until your very last moment.*" Her fingers began to tap seemingly without her noticing. "*I can tell it still bothers my son—about his father—even though he has his own life now. And I wonder, sometimes—would sharing the note help him?*" She shook her head. "*You know, his mouth is a little bit crooked like his father's. And it hurts me, every now and then, just to look at him and remember.*"

* * *

Management eventually caught wind.

People began noticing discrepancies in stock—Percocet and fentanyl and Oxy were disappearing at rates far quicker than what the doctors were prescribing.

Around Christmastime, as his and Olive's hunger reached new peaks, Bob Cowell announced that access to the stockroom at the end of B-wing would be permanently limited, and that the doctors had been put on alert. A facility-wide drug holiday was put in effect.

"Well, that's bullshit," she said to him. "It's not us. We only take from the dead ones." She gave him a hard look. "You've only been taking from the dead ones, right?"

He nodded, dreading his upcoming swing of night shifts.

"Well then, some other greedy fucks are doing it. This place is so fucked. I swear, it is so, so fucked."

Evening at Lark's Landing was already a particularly treacherous time. Sundown syndrome was like a contagion, pressing against walls, slipping through doors, infecting minds. The most docile residents—the ones with dementia or Alzheimer's—were often the most vicious and cruel sundowners, thrown into a constant state of fight-or-flight. Candace Chae was infamous for biting orderlies so hard she broke the skin. Gwendolyn Chard had once thrown a loaded diaper that exploded right on Dana Yen's chest.

Moans shook the unlit hallways. Shrieks of babbled nonsense. Childlike sobbing. The cruel reversions of life. Hysteria was ascendant.

And as Grant made his rounds, armed with tranquilizers, as he led various residents through their messy, chaotic ablutions, as he endured the vitriol of the more vicious ones, he took special care to check their active prescriptions. To note with horror the stingy quantities they'd been allotted for pain relief: just enough to lock up, to spend their final days and hours in fogged agony, to faint deathward. While he, like a vulture, skulked the edges of their last moments, to find naught.

There was nothing he could do, nothing left here. And how his hunger roared. How his need incinerated what little self-control remained. How it left the charred outline of an identity he had to squint in order to recognize.

Olive stared at him with shining, sweaty desperation. Moonlight was glancing off her forehead, her silver band of hair. "We need this. I need this. You need it too, right?"

"No shit."

"Then think. Help. Think."

* * *

He knew where her family lived, the big, blazing house in Beckitt. The door that led from the back patio to the garage, and then the basement. The spare key they kept beneath the geranium pot. He knew that her parents often fell asleep in twin chairs before the television and that Milly spent evenings out with her friends or on dates, now that she was finally free of him.

The bathroom was down the hall from the living room. He would check there first. Doctors tended to write more generous scripts for rich folks. But the medicine cabinet held only a rattling case of multivitamins, some generic Prozac, a few expired Advil. He slipped back down the hall, up the stairs.

Milly's parents kept her room in the same suspended state it had been in since she was a teenager. Stuffed animals were gathered in excruciatingly organized rows in one corner. In the other were track-and-field ribbons, a collage of photographs pinned to corkboard, framed diplomas, a desk lamp shaped like a paper clip.

He stood there for a few moments, awash in the old sadness, the tender recollections: How she'd become convinced one afternoon that there was an intruder in their rent-controlled Wingham apartment. (They'd politely refused her parents' offer to cosign for a gated condo in Beckitt.) How she'd called him, whimpering, from the closet, and he'd sped home, only to find a stray cat, pawing at the laundry. And how they'd fallen in love with the little guy: its padded-paw fleetness, its recalcitrant sense of need, despite the HAVE YOU SEEN ME? notices that began to appear throughout the dimly lit complex. How they'd argued the dubious ethics of keeping him, of teaching his former owner a lesson, before deciding, finally, to return him. How heartbroken they'd been.

"We would make good parents," she'd said.

"Cat parents or human parents?"

She hadn't responded.

He was summoned back to the present by a ripple of movement from the bed. A sheet peeling off. Milly's head, backlit by the moon.

"What the fuck?" she said.

He was wearing a ski mask. He'd remembered to put on a ski mask. He checked his hands. Blue nitrile gloves, too.

She screamed.

"What is it? What is it?" came her father, from downstairs.

"Oh my God! Help! Help!"

"No—wait," he said, hand outstretched.

"Grant?"

No. He had the presence of mind, at least, to shut the fuck up. He tore back down the stairs, tripping, sliding, toward the front door, straight into her father, knocking him over.

Grant was sprawled, for a brief moment, on the old man's chest, before scrambling back up. Holding out his hands, gesturing in vague supplication. *Sorry. Sorry.*

"Sidney!" her mother shrieked.

He found the front door, he wrenched it open. He staggered out into the cold evening. He tried to regain his footing. And when he looked back, he saw—could it be? Her mother, with an ancient-looking shotgun clutched against her shoulder.

And then a thundering *pop*, like fireworks set off inside a shallow pot. A simultaneous scream. He felt something sharp hit him. Like a flying piece of gravel. Embedding itself in the meat of his calf. Just a pinch. And the warm, sticky wetness that pulled down his leg and soaked into his shoe.

He ran and ran.

* * *

"The irony is that right now, you really could use some Oxy," Olive said, observing him.

He flinched. "Can you just take it out, please?" He lay prone on her couch, his leg propped awkwardly on the ottoman. Blood blooming into a towel. He had no idea how he'd gotten here.

"Okay, but my son, Jesse, is asleep, and I don't want you to wake him." She handed him a wooden stirring spoon. "Bite down."

He gave a croak of assent as she peeled the wet, sticky, bloody layers of towel off the wound.

Heat was radiating from the entry site. Throbbing. His sense of it was enormous—like a tumor, or another leg—growing heftier, exposing more of him with each pulse. Merely grazing it threatened excruciating pain. To stick something sharp into the exquisitely tender, fleshy center seemed unfathomable.

He would do anything—*anything*—to avoid these next few moments. He couldn't help but whimper when he saw the glint of the metal tweezers. He bucked and moaned and punched the carpet when they dove into him.

"There. It's done, okay? It's done."

He let out another hoarse groan, his teeth aching against the splintery wood.

"Oh, for fuck's sake." Olive got up, returning with a pill and a hammer. There came a muted pounding, as she crushed the tablet into a grub of powder, and then the delicate rasp of paper being torn, a slice of it brought to his face. He snorted blindly. The effects were instant.

Gratitude swept through him. The warmth, the miraculous cessation of the pain. And the staunching of embarrassment, too. Relief from the shame of what he'd just done. Oh, it all felt better. So, so much better.

"I'm sorry," she said. "I'm really sorry."

"It's fine," he said, shifting onto his back. "I wasn't being careful."

"No, it's that I wasn't really thinking straight when I first brought you to Jim O'Hearn's room—well, I was fucked up—and I wasn't sure—but then you just took it. I'm sorry. I had a little crush on you, to be honest."

"It would've happened anyway," he said, forearm pressed against his eyes. Lulled by the comforts of his high, and free to think tragically, Grant suddenly remembered learning of telomeres: bits of repeating code at the ends of each chromosome that were like protective caps, necessary because each act of replication imparted damage upon an organism's genes. The same way that merely existing—simply crawling through time—could feel abrasive and unfamiliar.

"Maybe we can try to wean ourselves off," Olive said.

Eventually the telomeres wore down completely. The cell could no longer replicate itself, and died.

"Maybe you can meet Jesse. Not like this, obviously. In a different context." She was looking at him, the love in her eyes as plain and unadorned as the thermal curtains that covered the window of each room at Lark's Landing. Her silver strip of hair gathering an almost pearly sheen.

"Okay. Yeah."

And then she led him, limping, to the bedroom. "We have to be quiet."

* * *

The Oxy wore off. The rekindled agony in his leg added an entirely new dimension to his cravings. An inevitability that wiped away past scruples, old standards.

He hadn't realized until now how much pain was another, more severe form of need. You mapped your life around it. You traveled along its jagged shape, hemming closely to its border, for fear of being destroyed by it. He'd been hampered his whole life, it seemed, by errors of dimension. How minor the old things seemed now, what little they amounted to, beside the planetary considerations of pain and the gravity of its exigencies.

On his rounds, he found patients forced to seek comfort in empty vials and used gel packets. Prescription orders that would keep them just barely outside of pain, skirting its razored edges. He felt for them, certainly. But he felt sorrier for himself.

"Please," Mitch Morehardt was saying.

"No." Grant shook his head. "No, I'm sorry. It's against the law."

"Grant. It's the right thing to do. It's the merciful thing."

"I can't."

"Oh, damn you."

He was so sorry. "I'm so sorry."

"Then please—call the doctor. Call someone. Please."

"The doctor can't do anything more."

"Just—PLEASE! *Do something*."

His lips and cheeks trembled with tears, but Grant shook his head. And Mitch's eyes widened, as if flooding with the truth of his last moments. "This can't be."

"Hold my hand. I'm here."

"There must—there must be something else. Something better than this."

He died that evening, in a shivering, shuddering mess. Paroxysms whipping through him. Eyelids flayed open. His motions growing more desperate, more fitful—stretching, pushing, as if trying to escape his own skin. His own body.

"I'm sorry," Grant kept saying, because there was nothing else.

And no one else was around. No one else to witness. He let go of the man's hand. He slid onto the foam-cushioned seat beside the bed and gazed blankly at the linoleum. And he palmed the crinkly gel packets in his pocket—the remnants of Mitch Morehardt's prescription. He feathered his fingers over the slender bulge, outlined against his scrubs . . .

"Grant."

He blinked. Olive's face before him.

"Grant. What the fuck?"

It took a moment, as he wiped the drool from his mouth, as consciousness seeped into the empty bowl of his mind. A foul, sour smell had soaked through the room. And there was Mitch Morehardt's body.

Olive, frantically flipping through his chart. "Did you tell anyone? Did you mark the time of death?"

He shook his head.

"Fuck."

And then the slow dawning. The mushrooming hunger in her eyes. She pointed at the patch on his forearm. "Is there anything left?"

He unlatched his mouth, but the ability to speak, to reason, to convince was like a vague memory. Each distinct thought was like a film frame that he needed to pause, observe, and interpret, at which point the picture had moved on. There was an entirely new layer of reality with which to familiarize himself.

"Earth to Grant. Hello? This is not cool, okay? Not cool."

He felt a spike of anger. She was ruining his trip. "W-whaddayou want?" he slurred and struggled.

"Is. There. Any. Left?"

"None. Okay?"

"You're a fucking liar. Get over here. Give it."

"Hey—hey!"

It was like trying to yell in a dream; his lungs were at 5 percent capacity. As she reached for his thighs, patting them, her fingers trawling around his crotch. As her hand slipped with astonishing dexterity into the thin pocket of his scrubs—an intruder, rooting around, grasping. Bits of himself poked and prodded and grazed.

He did not like this. He was so deeply unhappy about this. But there was no force in any of his limbs. No capacity for action.

As she finally withdrew from him, snarling. The other gel pack clutched between her middle and ring fingers. "Don't try to pull this shit again."

* * *

Winter persisted. A blanket of silence, an insulating chill, seemed to wrap around his life.

Rumor spread that Edie Spelman was selling access to the closet at the end of B-wing for $1,000 per vial—far above street value.

"Fucking bitch," Olive muttered.

The carousel effect grew stronger. The new residents were interchangeable strangers, all of them arriving at their last stop.

Time wrapped around itself. It became a cycle of terrible need. And its obligations met just enough to maintain another agonizing loop. A narrowing of everything else. He was losing entire chunks of his recollection. He was moving in a daze, fulfilling the bare minimum of his responsibilities, inhabiting the bare minimum version of himself. He was an endless well of craving.

And each unfamiliar name, each bleary resident, became someone to whom he was comfortable administering a partial dose of a prescribed painkiller, before pocketing or outright ingesting the rest.

It was abominable. He knew it. Olive would hate him if she knew. Well, he hated her, too.

He heard the moans, the confused notations from the other orderlies. "I'm sorry but I can't give you any more. The doctor only prescribed this much."

He felt guilty in the abstract way of someone who worked for a big, ugly corporation. He was able to section it off, to address it in a separate, less urgent part of his mind.

"What's the point of being alive?" he asked one evening.

Olive shrugged. "I have no idea. Do you?"

"Nope."

Although he could remember a time when he believed there was something sacred and private, something worth guarding (and equally worth sharing), at the center of each person. Something intrinsic to being an individual, which ceased to exist when you did.

"I think the point is just to stay alive," he said now. "So we're basically set up to fail."

They locked the door and sat upon the cold, hard linoleum, backs against the plastered wall.

"I have Jesse," she said. "Jesse is the object of my life."

"Jesse will wind up just like this guy over here—" He pointed to the corpse lying in the bed across from them.

"We all wind up like that. Like him."

"So I ask again, what's the point?"

"To overcome something," she said forcefully. "To quit this shit."

He didn't bother with an acknowledgment.

"I don't want it in my life anymore," she said. "I don't. I don't."

"Ironic that you introduced it into mine."

"I know." There was sorrow in her eyes and a vague expression of self-pity, reminiscent of Milly. "And I really can't tell you how sorry I am. But together, we can try to beat it. Together. Imagine if we could do that. We could do fucking anything."

"Or we could accept that this is what kills us."

She shook her head. "I have a kid, remember?"

Footsteps scampered down the hall, obscuring the bar of yellow fluorescence that passed beneath the door. Everyone was sneaking around. Everything was done in darkness.

"Let's say we beat it," he said, his head resting on her chest. "What is there to do once you achieve that thing you've always wanted to achieve? What's left?"

"Time to enjoy having done it."

"How about a reward?"

"Sure."

He nodded into her collarbone. He breathed her sweet, soft, milky smell. "What if there's no better reward than the indulgence of the very addiction you've been trying to overcome?"

"How do you know that?"

"Know what?"

"How do you know that there's nothing better?"

He considered the nonentity lying in the bed before them. The self-digestion, the active cell death. The body was a dying ecosystem. What stories—what books—had this man let expire with him? Entire volumes of feelings and memories. Cascading events stamped in time. Obstacles overcome. His name had been Howard something. There was no one to pick him up until tomorrow morning, no one available (or willing) to call his next of kin. They would fudge his time of death. What did it matter?

"What's the point when they're already dying?" he muttered.

And Olive seemed to grasp the string of his logic in an instant. She brought it to her teeth; she promptly bit it off. "These people's lives deserve to end in comfort."

He shook his head, smooshing his brow into her sternum. "Nothing makes the end more important than any other point. I'd much rather be comfortable right now. I'd much rather say, 'Fuck my future self.'"

"Well then, there's the issue of memory. People remember endings best."

"What is there to remember when you're dead?"

"It's what other people remember."

"And when they're dead? When memory becomes another story?"

He produced the vial from his pocket. He pierced its rubber top, careful to inject a little air, before pulling back the plunger. Sucking all the beautiful, precious liquid into the clear, precisely demarcated reservoir. And pushing out the tiny, sputtering accumulation of bubbles—like insect eggs.

An amount of time passed.

"Do you want to meet Jesse?" Olive said, her voice coming from another reality. As if he were submerged in water, and she was trying to reach him from the surface. (But he could breathe just fine down here! He could see clearly and float comfortably.)

"What?" he said through a mouthful of cotton balls.

"Do you want to meet Jesse?" And this time he sensed a vague expectation, a troubling anticipation, in her voice.

"Why?"

"I don't know—just, maybe you might want to meet him."

"You want to introduce him to a drug addict?"

"You're not a straightforward addict."

"I'm trash. I'm dangerous to be around."

"No, you're not." Although she spoke with halting conviction. "Look, you're a good person."

"Don't tell me what I am."

The dead man was already beginning to exude a faint sourness. His skin was the color of greased marble.

Another body of time floated past. She was staring at him.

"Do you love me?" Her voice trembled.

"What?"

"Do you?"

"I have no way of answering that."

"Why not?" She sounded disappointed.

Because he had no shape, no interior—nothing worth sharing. And how could you love someone without being able to offer a privileged version of yourself? Besides, everything he knew about her was too tied up in drugs, too tied up in feeling good. He had no idea who she was outside the confines of an opioid high.

"I think we'd be good together," she was saying, her voice dreamy. "I think you'd be a good father to Jesse."

"I've never even met him."

"Oh, you'd love him," she said, her gaze blurry with pleasure. "He's the perfect kid. So smart." She had her hair down, the silver stripe like a beam rippling from her forehead to her shoulder, its terminal coil settling upon her heart. "I think we'd be a good family," she said.

A family. He'd wanted one of those for himself at some point. He and Milly had spoken about it.

Had they? He felt so distant from that version of himself. So exceedingly lost. Stunned that someone could love him in his current condition.

"Just think about it," she said.

But he'd already forgotten what they were talking about. He was standing up, following the animal commands of other regions in his brain. Fresh hungers awakening.

They pulled the sheets upward around the stiffening body and tied the edges together like a hammock. They lifted the sack of bones out of the bed—huffing, shaking, swaying. They nearly lost their footing, banging its limbs against the corner of the bedside table. (*Shh!* Olive giggled.) Before letting it—him—thud upon the cold, dusty floor.

She leapt onto the bed, curled her finger toward her face. "Get over here."

But he felt suddenly repulsed. "Wait."

"What?"

"Just, hold on."

"What's the matter?"

It was the thud—the inert finality of it. The sound of obliteration. He couldn't bear their sordid intrusion.

"Actually, what about the basement?" Grant asked.

Olive frowned. "Doors to the stairwell are locked at night. And the freight elevator is on the other side of B-wing, right there in front of everyone."

"How exciting," he said.

She crooked her head and smiled. "Okay, then. Come on."

* * *

Another loop. A fresh circuit of time.

"*What are you doing?*" came the voice, in Mandarin.

"*Just checking your medication.*"

"*For what?*"

Beta-blockers were still being prescribed at their usual levels. They were not nearly as potent as the other stuff, but they could take the edge off when it was absolutely necessary.

Tina Zhang stared at him as he emptied the little paper soufflé cup onto his sweaty outstretched palm. As he picked out the oblong chalky-white pill and shakily poured the rest back.

"*What are you doing?*" she asked again. He snapped back to attention.

"*Your doctor changed your prescription.*"

"*Oh.*" She frowned at him. She looked so young, hardly any wrinkles around her eyes and mouth. Only the slight, slight sag of her cheeks, which lent her a certain vividness, a depth, like an image fully rendered. "*You're sure, right?*"

"*Of course.*"

He let the pill slip into his pocket. He tested the limits of his compunction as she gazed helplessly at him. Nothing. He tested the limits of his compunction as he swooped in on a dozing Maureen Wallace, as he silently withdrew her rather small balance of liquid fentanyl and replaced it with saline solution.

He was yet to find those limits.

Not even when Olive walked in on him as he stood over Ingrid or Astrid something, who was nonverbal. He was standing over her, trying to convince himself she was fine. In spite of the tight, sharp breaths she took. The slight wormy wriggle of her shoulders and arms. The frantic eye contact. She would be fine. She didn't need all that she'd been prescribed. It was overkill, frankly. Ordered by a careless doctor who saw these people as a carousel of bodies in beds.

"Don't," Olive said.

He didn't even look up at her. He had no energy for shock. Nothing outside the tunnel of his need. "She's got a week left, max."

"I don't care if she's got a fucking minute left. It's not right."

He finally looked at her. "You are so full of shit."

"I won't let you do it," she said. "I'll blow the whistle if I have to." The ugly, pinched expression on her face.

"That's mutually assured destruction," he said.

"You're a good person, Grant."

"No."

"I swear you are."

No. She was dead wrong. Look at how he'd violated these people, how he'd intruded upon them, spat on their final moments, sucked the dignity out of their lives. Milly had been right to leave him.

"Look," Olive said quietly, with desperation. "I have some money. I think I found a way to get some more stuff. But just a little. Just so we can wean ourselves off for good. Okay? Because I don't want to waste the rest of my life being addicted to it."

"See, and the thing is, I don't care. I don't care about my worthless, fucking life. I want it."

"And what about Jesse?"

"Your kid?"

"Yes, Grant. Yes. My kid. You met him."

He scratched his neck. "No, I didn't."

"Yes. Yes, you did." Anger and recrimination like twin beams from her eyes. "Do you really not remember?"

He shook his head. "You're fucking with me."

"You came over last week, Grant. You came to my apartment and I made you dinner. Lasagna. You ate dinner with me and Jesse. You said he was beautiful, you said you could see yourself falling in love with him. And then you fucked me."

"Come on."

"For fuck's sake. How do you not remember any of this?"

And for a moment, he was confronted by genuine worry—by fear of being unaccountable for his actions. These large, bacterial gaps in his memory, in which anything might happen.

But hadn't he already done plenty of monstrous things? What were a few more? And anyway, it was not implausible that the woman who'd first introduced him to this shit might also be manipulating him now. Might be using him for her own twisted reasons.

"Where do you think our stories go?" he said.

"What?"

"When all that's left of you is buried in other people's memories—which are just stories, right? Stories that are diluted each time they're told, that hardly ever withstand a generation."

She bathed him in a look of concern and condescension. The sober person's impatience with a junkie. "Didn't we already talk about this?"

"I don't remember coming up with an answer."

"Maybe there's a great big repository in the sky for them," she said dully.

Which sounded pretty nice. As if being witnessed might palliate his despair. As if it might provide him, just for a moment, with an identity that was singular and worthwhile.

"Don't do this," she said. "Please. For me. For Jesse, even if you don't remember him."

"I'd like to remind you that this is *your* fault," he growled. "*You* were a fucking predator. You saw someone who was vulnerable and introduced him to this shit, you convinced him that life has to be a certain way for some people. And now you think you can save him."

"I don't remember convincing you about that—"

"Everything that's happened—everything I've done—is because of you."

"I told you I was sorry—"

"And I don't give a shit that you've grown a conscience now. Now that you've drawn a line somewhere that you think it's your duty to enforce."

"It's an important line."

He shook his head, like an animal doused in water. "This is your fault."

"Yes." She nodded. "Yes, it's my fault. But I wasn't thinking straight, and I loved you. I loved you. I still love you—can you believe it?"

"That we're two junkies talking about love? No, I can't."

"Beat this with me," she said, leaning into his shoulder. "Please. Don't you remember what it was like? Don't you remember all the life you had before this? All the worthwhile things?"

Yes.

He was still certain of the memories that remained, certain of their realness. But they could no longer conjure genuine feeling.

He could remember, as a teenager, staring around a classroom and falling in love with any girl who looked back at him.

He could remember the sweet, woodsy smell of his mother's shampoo in the bowl of hair ties she kept on the kitchen counter, beside the grime-slicked stove and the blue EBT card.

And walking toward Milly on a rainy afternoon, as a car overtook and splashed her with water from the curb. Feeling such distant helplessness as its spume arced over her body, the muffled desire to take her place.

He could remember the sensation of being a distinct individual, with his own private interior, assuming and navigating the weight of being alive. But he could not access it. It was like watching a ship in a bottle as it floated away.

"I don't care," he said. "I don't care about you. I don't care about Jesse. I don't. Fucking. Care."

She lifted her head. "You don't mean that."

"I absolutely do."

"Then say it again."

He stared at her. "I don't care about you or Jesse."

"Fine," she said. The calm hurt converging in her eyes. The sharpness. The clarity of feeling and conviction. "Then I don't want anything else to do with you. And I'm sorry—I'm sorry for everything. But fuck you."

* * *

He had a terrible trip one evening, in which the doors to all the rooms in B-wing burst open—light blasting into the hallway down which he stumbled.

And a troop of unfamiliar residents emerged with invisible strings connected at their joints, their jangling limbs flailing like macabre puppets. They danced before him, their mouths flapping in unison.

You're trash. You're trash. Go back to where you belong.

Oh, everything was wrong. He was a stranger inside himself; no part of him was his anymore. And how he envied these residents! (Surely he had to be somewhere near the bottom now?) He envied their straightforward nearness to a solution. To that final opportunity for escape, abandonment. Wholesale transformation. It was certain and inevitable, and it was close, and there was no guilt in waiting simply, patiently for its arrival. It arrived for everyone.

But a person could get so bored. A person could suffer so much in the meantime.

He considered a month sober. A year. He considered the unending call, the unbroken chain of need. The collecting of coins, the collecting of time. For what?

And the relapse. Because certainly, he would relapse. The month would end. The year would transpire. He would need a reward. He would need *something*. Because you were supposed to gain credit for your self-denials. You needed something to spend it on. And barring that, you needed an end.

He thought he saw Dana Yen slip disheveledly out of Bob Cowell's office one evening, passing beneath a bar of lamplight from the parking lot. Her hair was unkempt, a series of solar flares escaping from her pulled-back bun. Misery was etched in shadows beneath her eyes.

"What are you doing?" he said.

"Oh." She swallowed a hiccup. "I had a meeting."

"Just now?"

His eyes refocused: There were wet splotches on her chest and shoulder, flaky shreds of tissue emerging from her fist. She put the other hand on her stomach. "I am having—I think I might need to take some time off."

And as her voice careened, Grant was caught in a sudden, ecstatic frenzy of hope. "Were you two fucking?"

Dana straightened. "What? No. Of course not. I needed his advice."

"Look. I won't tell anyone," he said. "I promise I won't—if you can give me access to the closet at the end of B-wing."

Sadness, exhaustion pooled over her face. "You, too?"

"Please."

She shook her head and burped slightly. "I do not understand how things became this way. So out of control."

"Look, can you do it? Can you help me or not?"

Dana brought her hand from her stomach to his shoulder. The shock relieved him, for a moment, from his desperation. He noticed how the faint luminescence brought out the haggard lines around her lips and jaw. "Do you know," she said, "I cannot think of a single hunger that does not come at the expense of someone else."

And she walked away, trailed by a gleaming shaft of moonglow.

* * *

The solution, as it turned out, had always been available. It was so neat and so simple that he was shocked he'd not realized it sooner, that he'd not already availed himself of its relief.

Of course, there was the issue of being discovered. The issue of the truth, and the ugly, leaking issue of things from his body. There were the final indignities of exposure, the old considerations of privacy.

Although there was no need for privacy when you were no longer any sort of individual, was there?

"Hey—" He caught Olive leaving the dining room.

"Don't touch me."

"Just— Wait—" he said. Cornering her in the sterile hallway.

"Get away, Grant."

He could hardly stand their awkward eye contact. "Please don't hate me."

"Get the fuck away."

"Please." He grabbed her shoulders. "I just need to know that you don't."

"What is the matter with you?"

"I just—" He was realizing that Olive was the last person on Earth who might care about him. And he was wondering why this mattered so much. "I would just love if you promised not to spend the rest of your life hating me."

She looked at him now—her eyes wet, her voice plangent. "I don't hate you, okay?"

He nodded.

"But I don't want to feel guilty about you anymore. I need you to be accountable to yourself, because I have too many of my own issues—too much of my own shit."

"Okay," he said. "Honestly, that's perfect."

"Why is that perfect?"

"It just is."

She took his hands; she pressed them to her chest. "Tell me there's hope. Tell me you can change."

He closed his eyes.

"You can fix it all, I promise. And I promise I'll help. But you have to tell me you want it. Tell me you want to find yourself again, to get clean."

"You said you knew someone, right?" he said. "A source?"

"Oh God."

"You said you knew someone who could get us enough stuff."

"To taper us off, Grant. To get us better. If you can just remember what hope feels like. If you can just regain that bit of yourself."

It was ruthless, this carousel to which his life had been reduced. A line folding back into a loop. He nodded. "Okay."

"Okay? Let me hear you say it."

"To get us better."

"You promise, right? You promise?"

"Yes." He promised. Although this promise comprised words alone. Mere words.

And to work in a place like Lark's Landing, to hear the babbling of the demented, the gibberish of the insane, was to understand how little words mattered.

* * *

And then phones were blaring throughout the facility. Sharp, electric screeches were emitting from each room, crashing in destructive waves down the hallway of B-wing.

"There's been an alert." Olive was staring at him with terror, her hair down, so that the strands of white were spread like the minor currents of a swiftly moving river, curlicues of foamy turbulence formed around jutting stones.

"What?"

"An alert for, like, missiles," she said. "Nukes."

"Here?"

She nodded.

"So this place—this place is fucked."

She nodded again.

"What do we do?" he said, knowing the precise answer. Feeling his impulsive steps toward the closet at the end of the hall. Although there were still people here.

"Oh God—Jesse," she was saying. "I need to get to him. Will you come with me?"

There were still people here.

"There are still people here," he said.

"What?"

People who'd depended on him.

"People here who depend on us."

"You're joking."

He shook his head, which was bursting with clarity and will.

"Are you serious?" she said, the coldness returning to her face. "You've done some of the worst possible things a person can do to these people, and now you want to run some fool's errand to try to save them?"

Yes. This was exactly what he needed to do.

"Please, just come with me," she said, shackling his wrist. Yanking it. "Come with me. We'll go back to my place. You, me, and Jesse." She lowered her voice. "And if it's the end, I have some stuff. We can take it. If it's the end, we'll be together."

But he'd been so selfish. He'd committed such terrible crimes. And now there was a chance—a vanishingly thin one—at correction. Redress. How funny, he thought, that an ending might provide such hope for transformation.

"I can't."

And she glared at him, her hands on her hips. "I will never understand you—some of these things you've done—I will never, ever, understand."

"Probably better that way," he said.

Commotion was building in the halls, staff members caroming toward the exit.

But wasn't it better to die comfortably?

No. No, no, no.

There was the roar and screech of a car beyond the window—Dana Yen's—peeling out of the parking lot. Taking the key to the stockroom with her.

Someone said, "Bye, Grant."

He had no time to acknowledge it.

In the chaos, he saw several others darting into residents' rooms, stuffing pills into the pockets of their scrubs. People whose names he could no longer remember. He saw two of them take a fire extinguisher to the handle of the stockroom, bashing it off. The door swinging open.

"Stop! Stop!" He ran toward them.

"What the fuck is the point?" someone snarled back at him.

"Put it back. Help me get everyone to safety."

"Fuck you."

They were yanking at drawers, flipping madly through charts, taking handfuls of vials and packets and pill bottles.

"Stop it!" He lurched blindly at another orderly; a fist connected with his temple. He felt a thundering, sickening shock—followed by a wave of dull pain. Which was fine. It was fine! The warm flicker of hope kept him upright, pointed him forward.

"How much longer do you think any of them have? If there's a missile headed right the fuck here?"

"Just help me," he said. "Help me get everyone to safety."

"You are fucked. Take an Oxy and fucking chill."

Grant shook his head. He was overcome with such grief, such walloping regret, for the time he'd let pass. The falseness of every feeling he'd experienced while high. How much of his life had been frittered away. How much love.

And suddenly he remembered the private, musty basement at the other end of the hall. Accessible by freight elevator. He remembered being there with Olive, as parking lot lights smeared through grimy casement windows, as cool air swept from ground level. Sanctuary.

It was important now to keep everyone away from windows. It was important that everyone stay as low and as close to the center of the building as possible.

And here was what he could do—he could move everyone into the B-wing hallway. He could keep a steady chain of folks moving down the elevator, to the basement—"Come on! Come on!" He grabbed walkers, IV poles. He pushed the bedridden ones, in their plastic pallets, out of their rooms, lined them up in the hallway. He stabbed the down arrow with a manic finger, until there came the sweet chime of the cabin's arrival, and the doors breezed open. He ushered a group of them inside.

"When you get down there, someone send it back up, okay?"

"He's a hero!" a frail voice shouted.

The other residents joined in the chanting. "Hero! Hero! Hero!"

It would strike at any moment. He could feel it. He could sense its approach. Was he ready? He was waiting for the elevator to return. He stared out the window, into the sky. The ripped-open procession of clouds.

This bizarre, unknowable life.

ACKNOWLEDGMENTS

This book began as a thought experiment. Before I placed my characters in their petri dishes for observation, I considered my own life, and the people I'd reach out to and thank if I knew something irrevocable was about to happen. How preposterously fortunate I am to have been able to write this novel, and to have grown that list of folks in the process.

Thanks to my agent, the inimitable Chad Luibl, for his faith in me, for his advocacy and skill, and for his steady guidance and friendship. Thanks also to Roma Panganiban for her enthusiasm and insightful feedback, and to the rest of the team at Janklow & Nesbit.

Thank you to Caroline Bleeke, whose patience and support provided the perfect home for these stories, and whose keen editorial vision revealed a version of this book more complex and satisfying than I ever could have imagined. Thanks also to Mary Retta for her careful and diligent shepherding of the manuscript through its various iterations, and to both Caroline and Mary for providing me with a writerly education more robust than any MFA.

Thanks to Kelly Gatesman, Katherine Turro, Marlena Bittner, the copy editors, proofreaders, production editors, sales representatives, and the rest of the incredible team at Flatiron.

To Maria Isabel Guardado, who, over the years, has accommodated my frustrations and disappointments and bad jokes with the same steadfastness with which she has celebrated my triumphs. I only started writing seriously after I met you.

Thanks to the many colleagues and friends who provided inspiration, feedback, expertise, and encouragement throughout the writing and publishing process: Claire Oleson, Emma Peters, Claire Wallace, Aimee Lam, Carrie Polvino, Liam Chasen, Erik Fahlgren, Peter Miller, Alane Mason, Kevin Lombard, Belle Boggs, Viraj Degaonkar, Ariel Eaton, Bob Weil, Gina Iaquinta, John Glynn, Dr. Caitlin Parmer-Chow, Dr. Chris Chow-Parmer, Dr. Mahlet Assefa, Andi Zhou, Jake Viola, and Bradley Cho.

Thanks to Pam Schirmeister and the late J. D. McClatchy, professors at Yale, who read my earliest, grubbiest pieces with generosity and encouragement; to Priscilla McGeehon for her staunch and proactive support; and to the editors and staff at *Ploughshares* for their commitment to new writers.

Thanks to my mother, father, sister, and grandparents, who gave me everything I needed, and whose legacy I hope to live up to.

And thank you, finally, to the readers, for spending time with this book and bearing witness to its characters. Thank you.

ABOUT THE AUTHOR

Vincent Yu is a sales manager at W. W. Norton/Liveright and the winner of the 2021 Ashley Leigh Bourne Prize for Fiction from *Ploughshares*. *Seek Immediate Shelter* is his debut novel. His work has been published in *Prairie Schooner*, *StoryQuarterly*, *Ninth Letter*, *Able Muse*, and elsewhere. He lives in Brooklyn.